"'Tis my understandin' you have a code to live by. That true?" the sheriff asked.

Keven nodded; he'd already been through it all with himself too many times and didn't really feel like traveling that path again. The sheriff looked expectant.

"An' you tell me you're not a troublesome man?"

"I don't cause trouble."

"Ah . . . then mayhaps you be like a lodestone. You attracts it to yourself."

"I can be trouble to those who trouble me. And to those who trouble others, who are unable to defend themselves."

"Ah-h!" There seemed to be a far glint of something in the sheriff's eyes—amusement or sarcasm. "A hero, then!"

Keven felt himself blushing. Damn it! "I can't change the way I feel, Sheriff! I don't like bullies. I don't like those who take advantage of others simply because they can. Perhaps the others cannot or will not do anything about it, but I can! And I do *not* feel I am alone in my dislike for dullards and street dogs who have not the wit to control their mouths or the manners to leave someone else alone!"

"So you take it upon yourself to teach manners!"

Keven only frowned.

"Why not go out an beat on a tree fer growin' the wrong way? Or throw stones at the river fer bein' where you don't want it to be? Makes as much sense as you gettin' angry at fools."

"'Cause a man's supposed to be able to *think!*"

"That be what I hear, too, but you expect a damnish huge lot, lad!"

They glared at each other. . . .

Other  Books

The Road West

Gary Wright

Cover Art
CAROL HEYER and ROY PARKER

TSR, Inc.
PRODUCTS OF YOUR IMAGINATION™

THE ROAD WEST

Distributed to the book trade in the United States by Random House, Inc., and in Canada by Random House of Canada, Ltd.

Distributed in the United Kingdom by TSR Ltd.

Distributed to the toy and hobby trade by regional distributors.

DRAGONLANCE is a registered trademark owned by TSR, Inc.

FORGOTTEN REALMS, PRODUCTS OF YOUR IMAGINATION, TSR, and the TSR logo are trademarks owned by TSR, Inc.

First Printing: August, 1990
Printed in the United States of America
Library of Congress Catalog Card Number: 89-52095

9 8 7 6 5 4 3 2 1

ISBN: 0-88038-927-3

TSR, Inc.
P.O. Box 756
Lake Geneva, WI 53147
U.S.A.

TSR Ltd.
120 Church End, Cherry Hinton
Cambridge CB1 3LB
United Kingdom

For Polly, wife and friend,
who rendered writing advice and encouragement
so valuable it is repeated here in its entirety:
"For God's sake, luv, just do it!"

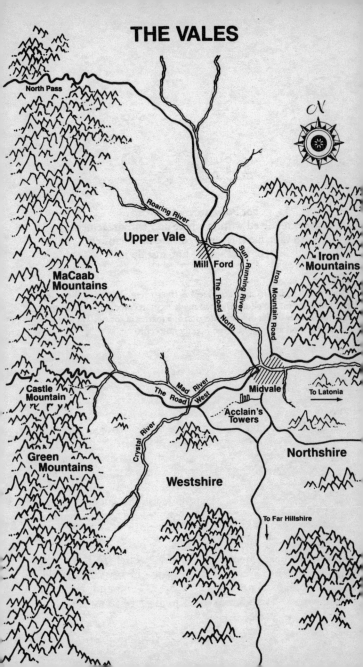

Prologue

From *Keven of Kingsend*, a manuscript by Acclain, Wizard of Vale, begun in the autumn of the 1340th year of The Age of Exploration:

"It is from Corleon, Wizard of Latonia, from Santon of the King's Arms Academy and from a number of other pertinent, trustworthy persons, that I have garnered these notes. I am not sure why I do this. It is an awkward curiosity to be so compelled, as I have not yet met the young man of whom I write. To quote The Fonda, legendary wizard of old: 'In studying my Basin of Understanding, what I see more than anything else is my own puzzled expression frowning back at me. Often there are times when the shadows shift in a meaningful way, yet scrutinize as I may, I cannot devise the underlying pattern. Something there is I cannot perceive, and it chafes at me.'

"So it is with this young man. His name is Keven.

"Born aboard his father's trading vessel, to Keven the land was but a strange, ragged edge of his water world. Their home port was a place known as Kingsend, far to the west, on the Inner Sea in the Kingdom of Coronal.

"He cared not for what he saw of the Land—rough, vulgar men in rough, vulgar ports, laughing at a callow seafaring boy. The land was crude and brutal to his innocent eyes. His father often said, 'The very worst th' land has t' offer, the evil an' the foul, it all slides down t' the shoreline an' piles in these wretched ports like charnel pits.'

"Keven had seen how his father seemed to change when he was in port, becoming a harder, coarser man, able to outshout and outcurse the vilest there, outfighting them when he must, becoming for a while one of the very same. And he remembered his early resentment of that behavior, and how his mother would stay shuttered aboard in their small cabin during those times, and he remembered the pain in her eyes.

"His world, as wide as the sea yet as small as their ship, ended in the Port of Latonia in cruel misfortune.

"He was fifteen then, a work-hardened, lean fifteen. His father called him Cargomaster, but not mockingly—he was never treated thus. The lad was given as much responsibility as he could shoulder at a time. Keven took his position seriously, and with a good-natured acceptance of the nature of things, the three-man crew took him seriously, too. They knew him well enough—they had helped rear him from a tiny crawler, underfoot or headed overside—so that they were family to him. There was old, gnarled, knotted Edgar, a small bald bear of a man, with three teeth in a wide grin and great muscled arms hanging nearly to his knees.

" 'Ya sees in me, Keven lad, wot a life o' labor do to a good man. I be once tall an' most outstandin' han'some an' among th' wisest o' men, but see now how th' work has drained me wits an' youth t' settle in me arms an' han's. An' though I still be most outstandin' han'some an' right lusty, I knows narthin' else but t' pick up an' pull an' carry. Now I nar mind the strength, yew unnerstan'—it be useful ofttimes t' keep me face pretty—but if I had me choice, I'd be taking the brains, like yer father there. He be the bestest man I ever know at thinkin'. So keep yer brains in yer head, lad. It be th' right proper spot fer 'em.'

"Keven, it is reported, has a most remarkable talent for mimicry. When speaking of Edgar, his face would twist into a grinning grimace, his shoulders hunch to a worker's stoop, his hands hang like grapnels, and his voice become low and grated, heavily accented with the tongue of the Inner Sea. He would, for the moment, become an image of that person.

"There was quiet Tuck, with the distant, dark eyes, who knew the wheeling of the stars, the curves of currents, and the sweep of tides. He knew the numberless shores and headlands, and where the rocky teeth lay hidden beneath the surface of the sea. 'Mayhaps 'tis magic,' he would say with a smile and a wink. But the lad Keven would watch him smell the wind, study the cast of the waves, point out a fleeting glimpse of low shore through shreds of fog, and then tell them within half a league of where they were. And he was always right. Tuck, who seemed to converse with the birds and knew the tales they told, who could foretell the weather by the color of the sea, the rake of the wind, and the tone of the sky, who could place an unseen river by a taste of the water; Tuck, who said very little, spoke volumes to young Keven. One suspects a touch of sea elf in Tuck, giving the boy a close contact with fay at an early age.

"There was also Young Tom of the quick, glad laughter and the slow wit, his forthright face alternating between joy and bewilderment, a little boy lost in a big man's body. He was one of those who, regardless of age, would be known always as 'Young Tom.'

"A shoreman once snickered and taunted Keven. 'Hoy, ship's boy, it looks like yer big puppy thar has altogether pissed hisself.' And in the joining laughter of the other dockside loungers, Young Tom charged the men, a savage

howl of rage wrenching from him, throwing wild, un-
trained fists. Four were down in the end, and Tom, and
Keven, too, for he had plunged into the melee to help his
friend. Keven was merely pinned, but Tom was beaten vi-
ciously to the planks, his wide eyes not fully understanding
the great pain, yet searching to see if the boy was all right.
He had thought the men were laughing at Keven.

"The small ship, the *Crester*, these men, his parents, and
the sea were Keven's home, his family, and his entire world.
I am told that when the words 'Father' or 'Mother' or
'friend' intrude unexpectedly into a conversation, he
swerves abruptly aside from the subject as a ship veers from
a sudden reef. It seems he attempts to ignore a pain that
gnaws from within, a pain that guides him more than he
suspects.

"At night, five men slipped silently aboard the ship. The
gods only know what they hoped to find. Anything, perhaps. The *Crester* was a neat and trim craft, but hardly a worthy target for robbery. Later, in recall, Keven remembered his
father being paid for certain cargo with a pair of golders. Although that coin was later spent for other goods, the glint of
the transaction may have carried into foul corners.

"Old Edgar must have been napping on watch. He was
found curled among some urns of oil, a grimace of horrid
shock frozen on his face, his throat slit from ear to ear. The
thieves then crept forward to the small crew cabin. Tuck fell
at the hatchway, an unused knife in hand, apparently attacked from the rear as he responded to some intuition.
Young Tom was slain in the same manner as old Edgar. The
bodies were robbed of a few paltry coppers. In a sense, the
villains murdered Keven's older 'brothers.'

"Something—a muffled sound, an unnatural shifting of
the hull—wakened Keven's father then, and he came on
deck from the aft family cabin. He fought them as well as
he could, but they were five veterans of the night and

armed with swords, and he was but one thundering angry
man with an old cutlass. They slashed him down. And
Keven was on deck in time to see his father fall like a crum-
bled shadow, sliding down and diminishing to a dark and
silent sprawl. The lad attacked them then with the first
thing at hand—an oak half-staff, one of the handy deck-
tool staves a bit more than a full arm in length. Two went
down with crushed skulls in his first unexpected rush. The
other three circled warily at first, then finally seeing but a
length of wood in the hands of a boy, they came snickering
to meet him.

"On their own ground, or had they more familiarity with
swords as weapons rather than badges of bullyship, it is possible they may have slain him easily. However, as I first
stated, there is a thing about this Keven like a vague
shadow cast on fog. I sense something about him that ex-
ceeds his history and appearance.

"Also, Keven was well at home on this deck; he had
known nothing else for fifteen years. He struck, evaded,
struck, and dodged away again into the dark, tangled ship-
board maze of lines, spars, and cargo. Barefoot in the night,
he slipped like a relentless demon amid his enemies. He
struck from ambush, he appeared at their rear, he sprang
from one side while a noise had them alerted to the other. He
parried their clumsy thrusts and slashes, and always the half-
staff connected with a head, an arm, a knee. He was struck,
but he knew not the cuts. There were shouts from the wharf,
calls of alarm echoing from the stones and cobbles of the
port, but no one came to his aid. He managed to fell another
thief with a savage rib-smashing attack, leaving the murderer
coughing out his life in gasps of bloody foam, but he took a
mean slash across his back in the exchange. He remembered
having difficulty holding the staff, learning only later that it
was slimy with his own blood.

"The dreadful picture he will carry forever burned in his

mind is of his mother coming on deck, poised in the light of an upraised lantern in one hand, a long carving knife in the other. She attacked one of the dark figures, and he twisted like a cat, sword winking in the light. She fell, and in the splash of lantern oil, she was instantly ablaze. Keven tried to reach her and was wounded again.

"It is told by witnesses of how he became a screaming madman then, raging at the two remaining men in the glare of the flames. It is told of how he beat down their swords and then beat down their skulls with the staff. It is told of how he then fought the fire with hands and sailcloth and drove it, too, from the decks.

"When the City Guard finally arrived, they found him burned and bleeding, carrying his mother to her cabin. In the wild threat of his eyes and his bloody staff, they stood aside. As he was lifting his father, the man roused himself for a final instant. He looked around at his ship and at this new face of his son, as if to fix forever these images for his imminent voyage. And he then died.

"Only after satisfying himself that the fire was completely out, that Edgar, Tuck, and Tom were beyond his, or any other, concern, and that he could do nothing more for his family and his home did he allow anyone to administer to his injuries. And then it was as if he were quite unaware, sitting on a stool in the aft cabin, shaking, staring at the bodies of his parents.

"I am told he will not speak of any of this beyond the picture of his mother falling, and that spilled forth only in an unguarded moment of wrath. The story has been pieced together from the guardsmen and the cowardly observers on the wharf who crept close enough to watch but kept far enough away to avoid any threat of harm.

"There was chaos for the lad then. There were officers of the guard, magistrates, healers, bargainers for ship and cargo. Advice and turmoil. Disorder and unreality. Too many people, all strangers. All shoremen.

"It was exceptional good fortune that he met a hospitable and compassionate sergeant of the guard, one Raylon of Watling. In that city of cruelty and indifference, such men are as rare as fine emeralds. In a moment when the boy needed the best, the best appeared. We and all the fine gods together know this is a singular event.

"Raylon of Watling took this beached sea lad into his home, seeing that he was not cheated in the dealings over ship and cargo, relating over and over, like a proud father, how the boy had laid five armed men to their graves with only an oaken half-staff. The story lost nothing in the retelling and led the boy eventually to the attention of the captain of the City Guard, Dannel of Lake, who saw Keven as a likely candidate for training in arms in the guard.

"His progress was astonishing, with speed, agility, and surprising strength for one that age. The story of his fight with the five bandits in the night took on a firmer reality when considered in the light of his exceptional reflexes, as fast and as sure as a cat, it was said. It seemed the sword came naturally to his hand, apparently driven now by fires no fifteen-year-old should know.

"His ability to learn, his fervent eagerness, amazed his teachers. Here was someone impatient to learn, not like the usual surly dullard, flinching cowardlike from teachings as if from threat. He emerged as a full man-at-arms, yet unfit for service in the City Guard because of his tender age. By now the tales of his talents had come to the attention of Rusker, weaponsmaster of the King's Arms Academy, and Keven was encouraged to contract with King's Arms in return for further training at the academy. Keven agreed, though probably more from logic than trust. Trust, it seems, is not one of the lad's qualities. The footings of his walls of distrust had been laid at sea; the night of the swords and the fire erected them firmly.

"His life anew in the King's Arms Academy was far from peaceful. Rusker is famed as an outstanding weaponsmaster and teacher, but he is also an arduous taskmaster and particularly demanding of those who show promise. To those very few who approach the level of his own proficiency, Rusker can appear a tyrannical master. It is a stance, however, summed up by one of his own expressions: 'The mountains be steeper at the top.'

"Many of exceptional talent wither at this unexpected treatment, sullenly supposing rewards instead of harsher criticisms of what appear to be small, petty points. It speaks well for the excellent insight of young Keven that he was apparently able to see through this facade to the true man and to understand the reason for this seemingly unreasonable behavior. As others grumbled, Keven never spoke of unjust treatment.

"He was not a model student, however. His first year was marred by rough behavior: a hostile, humorless attitude, an irritating moodiness, a rigid independence, and an unsettling tendency to solve major disagreements with fellow students by attempting to remove the source of disagreement itself. On only his third day at the academy, a second-year student, whose brains apparently bore little relationship to his overbearing size, taunted Keven.

" 'So . . . you are the fabled little orphan who kills grown swordsmen with a stick. Seeing you now, I think there must be some great mistake. I would say your mother abandoned you when she left the brothel, and—'

"An instant later, the oaf lay utterly dazed with a number of injuries, two of which forced his dismissal from the academy: His left kneecap was severely displaced, and his right wrist was eventually unable to bear the weight of anything heavier than a mug of ale. Although the general opinion was that the ass deserved being repaid for his words, the severity of the accounting cast doubts on

Keven's ability to accept academy discipline.

" 'I truly don' believe the young Keven goes about searchin' out trouble,' Rusker said, 'but he be not altogether unprepared when he meets it.'

"And Keven seemed to find trouble often enough—or it found him.

"The same witless jackass who had insulted him, upon leaving the academy a tenday later, attempted to avenge his poor fortune by attacking Keven. There are always some who seem determined to ignore a useful education. He struck from the rear, at night, with a staff. He apparently succeeded in landing one glancing blow. He was later, after some minor attendance to his new injuries, evicted from the grounds quite senseless, his remaining good wrist now badly broken, several teeth gone, his previously damaged knee now bent to a fresh, most intriguing angle.

"There was a curious incident in the city one night. Keven, alone as usual, was accosted by four young men who apparently took his academy tunic as a source of some rough humor. What their true intentions were is unclear; Keven claimed they tried to strip him and rob him, under the stated belief that all academy students must be rich.

"He marked two of them severely with his dagger, broke another's elbow and then pursued the fourth down a crowded street, overwhelmed him, and then, deliberately and quite brutally, slashed the palms of both hands.

"Again he was before Rusker and Santon, the other master teacher of the academy. Where Rusker's area of instruction is weaponry and the body, Santon's is with the marvel of the mind. Again Keven was questioned about his tendency to respond beyond the realm of reasonable self-defense.

"His only answer was an indifferent, 'They deserved it.'

"He was placed on a probationary status and restricted to academy grounds for three months. On his first evening free, still forbidden to carry a weapon in the city, he thoroughly thrashed two grown men who attempted to rob him. His weapon was an iron pot snatched from a vendor's stall. While Keven was acquitted of any wrongdoing in this event—it was a clear case of self-defense—Santon suggested that Keven was trolling the night streets of the city to attract such attacks, and any such incidents in the future would be assumed to be of his instigation.

"While Keven was never again detected, it came to Santon's attention that the number of unexplained injuries to the city's lower life forms seemed to increase in the proximity of the academy at night. The City Guard took no great interest in this. Raylon of Watling, called in his capacity as both Keven's unofficial guardian and as a sergeant of the guard, gave Santon a broad wink and told him, 'These midden rats o' the street prob'ly asked fer it. An' it gives us o' the guard less bother to attend.'

"Santon suggested that a natural athleticism, a terrible will to win, and a raging hatred of thieves and murderers in the night could all combine to produce a being bent on mayhem.

"One could say it was a matter of a lonely sea boy trying to prove himself among alien shoremen. It could be said, too, that the five murderers who crept aboard the ship that night unleashed a vengeful demon. Keven once told Santon in a conversational moment, 'My father said of the sea that a man survives by understanding it and by being better at its tricks. I think that applies to the land, too.'

" 'Would you hunt the sharks of the sea simply because they are there?' Santon asked him. 'It seems an intelligent person would accept the shark as a part of its world and see such an avenging pursuit as a childish waste of energy and direction.'

"Keven gave a peculiar frown, as if Santon were the one in need of understanding.

" 'A shark has no choice,' he said. 'It knows no better than to be a shark. A man has choices.'

"Corleon, Wizard of Latonia, was called to cast a small but deep-probing spell to detect evil intent in the boy. He found none. It was his belief that the boy was a complete innocent, bearing no guilt for his actions, feeling he had done no wrong whatsoever.

"Keven managed to stay relatively trouble-free thereafter, which, according to the prevailing academy humor, is more a matter of not being caught at something.

"There was the singular incident of Rusker's personal sword, a battle-scarred blade of such intense value to Rusker that it stays well within his reach even when abed. It was discovered one grim, thundering morning some twenty spans into the stormy sky, lashed to the very top of the gatehouse tower flagstaff. While Rusker's rage was further fueled by the public display of eight grinning workmen and a winching arrangement required for the retrieval, his later, private bearing indicated pride and respect for one who could accomplish so stealthy and physically demanding a deed under such circumstances.

" 'Whoever the culprit be, he be a right fine specimen an' a pride t' the academy,' he admitted to Santon. 'But if I ever finds him out, he best offer up what be left o' his mangled arse to the gods!'

"The embarrassed night guards had heard nothing. No one had passed through the gatehouse guardroom. It had all been accomplished from the outside—ten spans of dark, vertical, wet stone wall to the top of the tower, another ten spans of flagstaff.

"The offender was never surely identified—even, most remarkably, among the students themselves—but whispered suspicions tended to target on Keven, and he was seen to display a thin smile when Rusker once commented to the assembly about the difficulty of climbing such a mastlike staff in a storm.

"Rusker himself bore little doubt as to Keven's guilt, but barring hard proof or a confession, he would pursue no punishment. The matter was never directly faced. The closest it ever came to surfacing occurred a tenday later, when Rusker chose Keven to demonstrate to an incoming class freehand climbing of a high wall.

" 'Ya laddybucks think that be as easy as the clever Keven up there make it seem? Try it in the black, howlin' bowels of a stormy night with a sword in yer teeth! Somebody at this academy once did that!'

"He let the awed youngsters absorb that thought while he watched Keven edge up the vertical stone, then added loudly, scowling up at Keven, 'Once!'

"As expected, Keven excelled in weaponry and the more injurious forms of unarmed combat. Rusker once mentioned that it would hardly be an exaggeration to say the lad was probably more dangerous unarmed than most common swordsmen armed. He was quick to grasp that martial lore of any sort is as much mental discipline as physical. Many never understand that relationship and remain mere sword carriers of limited ability.

"He was schooled in languages, history, and philosophies, and was nearly as astute in these as in the athletic and physical disciplines. He learned the lore of the wilderness: survival, stalking and concealment, disguise, traps, and signaling codes. He learned the ways of horsemanship and the relationship between man and animal. And he learned all exceedingly well, as if he were to the land born.

"Yet all the while he remained well outside the fold of fellowship usually forged among young men engaged in such close and difficult endeavors. This indifferent reserve led to the frequent accusation of being 'a cold barstid' by some. Even when overhearing that, he seemed not to care.

"At graduation from the academy, Santon told him,

'You have learned well, Keven . . . perhaps too well. You are a serious young man, and that's good—we are engaged in a serious trade—but I wish you would also learn to laugh, learn to see the ridiculousness in the world around you, and, yes, acknowledge it in yourself as well. It's not something that can be taught, laughter, and it can be a most valuable weapon in difficult times.'

"Just short of his eighteenth year, he attained the highest rating of an academy graduate: King's Ranger-at-Arms.

"The rate of attrition at the academy is quite high. Out of a hundred entrants, the odds are that only thirty will endure to graduation; out of fifty such graduates, there may be one qualified to the proficiency of King's Ranger. In weaponry, faculty, and knowledge, there is assumed to be no better. There wasn't unanimous agreement in Keven's case, however. Although Santon voted for the classification on the basis of final examination results, he held the reservation that Keven may not have the judicial requirement to apply his craft wisely.

"Santon writes, *Although he probably would not admit it, Keven bears a great guilt over the death of his parents and his friends. In an unguarded moment, he once said to me, 'If I am so good, why couldn't I do something to save my parents?' There is a possibility, Acclain, that we may have unleashed a superbly trained demon into a world he would relish.*

"It is generally agreed that Keven is not at first glance an extraordinary young man in appearance. It was once said of him, 'He can walk into a crowd of three and disappear.'

"Perhaps, but as soon as anyone noticed his eyes alone, his attention would be ensnared, for his eyes are the deep blue-green of the sea out beyond the breakers. And he seems to be regarding the world from that offshore distance as well, not with the grim, brooding suspicion he showed before, but now with a severe and studious intent. That impression is reinforced by a slight frown, as if he were always trying to determine some far horizon. One feels he is constantly vigilant, suspecting more murderers in the night. His face often reflects a gravity too stern for one of his years—nineteen now.

"His mother often told him that his hair was the color of a frayed mooring line and just as unruly. He keeps it cut shorter than the style, and ragged, as if he cuts it himself with a knife, which he does. Although he could well afford to dress himself in finery, with the money from ship and cargo, he refuses.

"At a distance, he appears to be about two fingers over average height, with an athletic build, though nothing striking, but it is when one comes closer and observes a certain thickness of wrist, the breadth and set of the shoulders, that his true size and power become apparent. He appears to grow in the eyes of the beholder. There is often such a poised potential in his casual stance and movements, such an implied menace, that one suspects, given some sudden threat, he would react much like one of the big cats of the wilds. He appears not firmly planted, moving with that cat-like grace and alertness, as if he expects the earth to shift suddenly underfoot. With his slight frown into the distance and his alert posture of leaning into the road ahead, he appears to be a young man with a purposeful place to go and a deadly intent to get there. In Rusker's colorful words, 'He looks like he's seen a few bears come out o' the woods.'

"He is usually forthright in his beliefs—he worships Marin, the no-nonsense god of the sea—but he holds a somewhat erratic skepticism of spells and magic, a wary distance. While he tolerates small charms and cantrips, the nature of larger, abnormal mechanics and their practice is a realm he would prefer to ignore.

"With the money from the ship and cargo held for him by Raylon of Watling, he bought his contract from service to the king and pledged his allegiance and honor to the law and the cause of good. He left Latonia last spring on a venture deep into the weald of the Northeast Kingdom, Norlenor, but it is said he has now returned downriver. He often expressed a wish to return to Kingsend. It is logical to presume he will follow the Great Western Trade Road this spring when the roads become passable. Perhaps he may encounter some of the witless evil that plagues the roads lately and teaches it some better manners.

"This Keven of Kingsend is important. I sense it so strongly that it is like a portentous presence, yet I cannot define its substance.

" 'Something there is I cannot perceive, and it chafes at me.' "

Chapter One

Out rode the hero, brave and bold,
To range the dangerous western wold;
New was he to face the old;
His eyes were barely open.

Beneath a flowering fillip tree,
He spied a dragon drinking tea;
"And what is this I certainly see?"
The dragon swore, "'Tis nothing."

From "Walter Would A-venturing Go,"
folk song from the Old Age.

Two ragged men sat hunched and cold, back to back atop a steep outcrop that rose above the trees on the ridge. One frowned one way along the muddy road as it wandered up and down forested hill after hill into the misty distance, while the other watched the opposite direction. They were wet and filthy. The one named Isten was telling a joke.

"So this wagoner, he needed help with a broken wheel, so he says to this Upper Vales lad what were standin' there, he says, 'Go gits yer father, lad.'

"An' the lad, he says, 'I nar be knowin' whar he be.'

"An' the wagoner says, 'Wull, be he a-workin' now?'

"An' the lad says, 'I nar be knowin' thet.'

" 'Wull, now,' says the wagoner, 'be he to home?'

"An' the lad says, 'I nar be knowin' thet.'

" 'So,' says the wagoner, gettin' cross. 'Does yew think he be in the village, then?'

"An' the lad says, 'I nar be knowin' thet neither.'

"So the wagoner looks at him, yew know, an' he says, 'Wull, yew dullard lad, does yew know narthin' at all?'

"An' the lad says, 'Wull, I knows who be me mother.' "

He roared at his own line and slapped his thigh. The other grunted in a surly manner.

"Thet nar be funny, Isten. I nar knows me own mother, too."

"Wull, then"—Isten scratched at an armpit— "riddle me a riddle, Norly. 'I throws away th' ones I catch, but I keeps the ones what got away.' What be it?"

"It be lice. I heared it 'bout a hun'ret years ago."

"Fine. How 'bout this one, then? 'Beyond th' hedge be a field more plowed than planted, an often thar be a tillage tithe.' Hah?"

"F'truth, Isten, I be peein' in me breeches when I first heared thet. Just quit tryin' t' funny with me. I tells yew once again, I be some cranky 'bout this. We be total wastin' our time perched up here on this high point like a pair o' fool ravens."

He spat over the steep side of the rock and watched it fall to the dark branches below before continuing.

"It be too arly in th' year fer anythin' worthwhile t' be travelin' th' damn road. It be more mire than road anyhow. In two day o' waitin' now, thar be narthin' but a cart o' hides passin', and then somethin' too b'damn big, snufflin' an' gruntin' aroun' in the brush behin' us." He cast an anxious glance at the thick spruce trees along the ridge. "I tells yew true, Isten, I nar admires it out here one damnish trifle! This be deep forest, yew know, an' thar be things out here I nar e'en want t' think about."

Isten gave a grunt of disgust. "Yew want that we should go back inta town an' be pummeled an' docked agin fer tryin' t' finger a mere purse? Me had 'nough o' that!" He scowled and also spat over the edge of the cliff. "Bein' stripped an' whipped! It be a bitter insult me'll nar forget."

"Wull, yew can go on bein' spleenful 'bout thet if yew likes, but it should nar make yew some breed o' hermit highwayman what lives out here in th' far forest. Mayhaps yew nar notices, Isten, but we nar be like them true deadly bandits in th' mount'ns t' th' west, them with their awful creatures an' such. Them would eat us fer supper."

"Yew just be tryin' t' catch my cat, Norly. Methinks yew nar be happy unless yew be argumentish all the time. But me, now—" He broke off, stood, and peered into the distance.

"Thar be comin' a harse, Norly! Way out t' the east thar."

Norly stood and squinted in the direction Isten was pointing. "I don' be seein' it."

"Course yew don'! Yew got eyes like a mole! A big black, it be. Man walkin' 'longside."

"Just one?"

"Yar."

Norly scowled. "Me nar fancies it, Isten. A man alone on the road be likely t' take care o' hisself. It be best we leave 'im go on by."

"Nar!" Isten hitched up the scrap of rope that held his breeches. "We be in the trade, Norly. They be two o' us'n an' but one o' him, an' thet allus counts as odds the way I tallies it. An' if yew thinks I be planted out here just t' watch some fine bounty ride by whistlin' 'Blithe be a Bluebird an' I cares not,' then yew be as simple as the cobbler's cat."

Norly shook his head. "Me still nar fancies it. A big harse, yew says? Thet could mean a armsman, yew know. I gots nar fancy t' rub up ag'in nar armsman."

"An' mayhaps it be a runted, one-eye harse trader with a cripple leg. Thet be t' yer likin'?" Isten grinned a wide, toothless grin.

"Now . . ." He sniffed deeply and wiped his nose with the back of his hand. "It's jist as we schemed it, Norly. I goes down t' the road with me sward an' hides in them rocks." He drew a rusty, nicked blade with a handspan of the tip broken off. "An' when I jumps out at him, yew holds on him from up here with yer bow. An' be quick 'bout it, too—I nar wants t' point up here with pride an' see narthin' but bare rock! An' fer th' fear an' mercy o' five or six gods, Norly, I knows yew can nar see t' the end o' the arrow, but will yew try t' nar come close t' me if yew shoots? I has no yearnin' t' get me arse augered by yer arrow."

"Bowstring prob'ly too wet t' work, anyway," Norly muttered.

Isten glared at him. "Norly . . ."

Norly continued to frown. "Me still nar fancies it, Isten."

*   *   *   *   *

Keven had started talking to the big black horse the day he bought it.

"Ho, horse, you're a monumental thing, aren't you?"

It had lowered its huge head and regarded him with grave brown eyes that were seemingly the size of ale mugs. The trader considered Keven's dress and demeanor with an appraising eye.

"Ah, yar, sar, he be a right big'un. Just right fer the likes o' yew, I'd say. A big ugly harse like thet, he'll carry yew straight up a castle wall, he will. But yew needs ten or twelve good powerful men if yew wants to hammer shoes onto him."

Keven had liked horses ever since his introduction to mounted warfare at the academy. "By all the gods together," he said, nodding, still smiling at the horse, "you are indeed the king of horses!"

The horse had offered no disagreement, and so the one-sided conversation was begun. It was a harmless habit, Keven supposed. He had seen people in the city talking to the air, and apparently getting answers. He traveled alone, kept his own counsel, and there weren't many people he cared to converse with anyway. At least the horse didn't interrupt or talk back or babble on like a fool. It was a very good listener, in fact. It plodded along behind him, nodding agreement with every step, its massive hooves falling heavily and exploding mud in all directions. Head lowered, eyes nearly closed, it appeared in immediate danger of falling asleep in midstride or running Keven over should he pause in the road for a moment.

But it was more than just a monstrous horse: It was a war machine. It had feet like chopping blocks, a head the size of a bad dream. Its back was fully two hands higher than a man's head; most people would imagine a ladder to be a required part of its equipment.

Armored, with its armed rider astride and an enemy to the fore, it became a terrifying creature. No more sleepy, dull demeanor, no half-lidded eyes. Instead it took on the hostile mien of demons. In a demonstration with its trainer, it had demolished seven dummy figures in the time a tossed stone could strike the ground. The heads of two were found twenty paces away.

But now it was just an immense, muddy horse, clopping and splashing along a long, rutted road, its reins looped casually over the saddle. It wore only its vast breastplate; the rest of its armor and accoutrement—and most of the man's, too—hung from saddle and saddlebags, shield and plate clanking with the pace.

"Walk a league, ride a league," was the old saying, if one would save his horse on a long journey and at the same time keep his own legs limber. He glanced back at the huge animal. That beast could probably carry an ox all day and still be ready to fight a pack of wounded bears, he thought.

He walked far enough ahead to keep clear of the mud spraying from the horse's hooves, wearing what was called "casual arms and armor," that which was more easily worn than carried.

A hip-length, belted tunic of chain mail hung beneath a plain breastplate. A broadsword in an unadorned scabbard was slung over his back alongside a quiver of arrows, both within easy reach over his right shoulder. He carried an unstrung longbow and a single arrow in his left hand, although the dampness had probably rendered the bowstring useless. From the belt on his left hip hung an old curved cutlass in a battered sheath. His shield, slung from the saddle, was a peculiar diamond shape, the corners curving out into sharp points. Other than the pattern of rivets of the reinforcing bars, it bore no decoration.

Now that the sun was out again, his rough, brown traveling cloak was thrown back over his shoulders. Dark woolen leggings ran beneath high leather boots bearing riveted greaves from ankle to knee. Mud from the road marked him from foot to thigh.

Although the last sudden rain had rushed away into the hills, it seemed to make little difference. Rash little gusts of wind blew bursts of water from the trees in glistening showers. Ah, well, he thought, the traveler's complaint: cold feet and a wet arse. He'd have to do some hard polishing again tonight to keep the rust away from his arms and armor. If only he could as easily scour off the smudges he felt inside. . . .

He regarded these brash mountain storms with interest.

They were quite distinct from sea storms, most likely driven by entirely different spirits. Like the storied forest cats, they seemed to lie in wait behind the ridges to spring out on unwary travelers, pouncing unexpectedly from the steepening hills ahead with mischievous wind and rain, and then rushing away to rollick elsewhere, and a bright moment of sun would sparkle across the land. The month was Mayor— "the Flowering Moon," some called it—and early summer blossomed in the lower lands behind him. He had traveled through brilliant days with supple winds brushing the urgent new greenery, all under a sky of such tempered blue that it would surely ring like a great bell if struck just right at the horizon. But as the gentle hills rolled higher and higher and the road steepened, it seemed he was moving backward in seasons. Low, fast clouds would suddenly drag ragged sheets of rain down the dark slopes, down from the higher hills ahead where, when the surprising breaks occurred, he could glimpse bright snow still patched on the rocky peaks.

"Short spring we had, Horse. Here we are into winter again."

He gave a quick smile, remembering the wiry, grinning, toothless old armory keeper at the academy, a pensioned King's Armsman of thirty-some years service.

"No matter whar ya go, lads, thar ya be!" he would say. "Ain' no sense in goin' back. Ya already been there!"

The students had laughed and repeated it to each other until the saying had become their own, an academy cliche.

"No matter whar we go," he told the horse, "thar we be!"

And here he was, heading into mountains and storms.

He didn't really have a firm destination. There was once a place called home. West, he knew, but far. West to the sea called the Outer Reach, then probably south; he would know if he ever got there. At times he felt he was retreating from something rather than moving toward a goal. For days he had just frowned ahead at the next turn of the road, moving with a casual alertness but expecting nothing special. He had been told the road was dangerous for a man alone, and he had smiled at the warning. So far, the most danger he'd encountered had been the possibility of twisting an ankle in the ruts. It had been a long road since the academy, and the part of it he had ventured in the Northeast Kingdom he would just as soon forget—if he could. But some things became scarred into one's memory. All a person could do with those private wounds was look the other way for a while and try to ignore the ache. Still, he often found himself angry and sullen for no apparent reason. It was as if some unnamed demon rode his shoulder, and as soon as he began to feel comfortable with himself, it would whisper in his ear, "Remember . . ."

And it was doing it now.

"Silence!" he growled aloud, and his scowl deepened.

How wonderful! Here he was arguing with himself, raising his voice to himself, having a conversation with himself like the poor, foolish street wanderers of the city.

"Good day, Keven of Kingsend," he said sarcastically. "And how are you this fine day?"

"I'm well, Keven," he answered. "And thank you for asking. It is very kind of you."

"It is of no bother to me at all. But what *is* a bother is this little matter of death that seems to keep you so angry."

"Angry? Why should I be angry? Just because I lost—"

He broke off the dialogue with a wry smile. If anyone noticed this peculiar behavior, he could always tell them, "Oh, don't mind me. I have this demon on my shoulder, you see, and we talk together all the time."

He walked on with his jaw clamped.

He offered a silent prayer to any god that might be listening in this bedamned wilderness. Please . . . give me peace.

Some time ago he had thought to keep a journal. Of all the writings available in the library at the academy, the journals of various graduates were the most interesting, but he hadn't entered some of the events in the northeast, and as the leagues and days traveled past and began to mingle one into another, there seemed to be less and less to write about. His last entry read, *On this damned dull day, which I know not, in this damned desolate place, which I care not, absolutely nothing happened.*

Sometimes he felt he was plodding in place while the land drifted by, indifferent to his passage. Once, bored almost to the point of sleepwalking, he unsheathed his sword and left three deep scars on the smooth trunk of a huge beech alongside the road.

Someone will see those and wonder what they mean, he thought, and continued on his way wondering if those would be his only mark on the land.

Often he detected the lines of old roads tracing off through the forest, barely noticeable now with full-grown trees blocking their way. There were sometimes old tumbled, overgrown foundations by the side of the road, stone walls wandering out of sight, marking the boundaries of forgotten fields now reclaimed by forest. There was once another culture here, he thought, another people in another time, like an underlayment to this day. And he wondered if it had rained in their spring of the year.

The road was apparently well used in better season, but now it was more often rivulet than road and empty of travelers. Deeply scarred with old ruts, it followed the easy lay of the land, together with a large, muddy river on the left bend for bend through forested hills. Occasional squalid huts and small holdings sometimes appeared off to the sides, but he saw no one. Only one lone, gaunt dog had marked his passing with fierce barking from the far safety of a sagging log shed.

It has to be the Great Western Trade Road, he told himself. The bridges are stout log and stone. No one's going to do that just to travel from Upper Grunt to Lower Pud and back.

He examined some fresh tracks that cut into the road from a muddy side trace, then turned west in the direction he was traveling. A heavy, two-wheeled wain drawn by a single unshod horse or mule, he determined. Probably a mule. Two people, a man and a boy.

"We are not alone, Horse! Rejoice! There's apparently life in the Great Western Wilderness after all!"

He sang a song from the academy to pass the road away.

> "Spanned by the Gate of Damning Spells
> Runs the Road to the Seven Hells;
> Trod by those with souls of night,
> Warriors who ran, who wronged the right.
>
> "Bedamned be they who pledges bent,
> Whose lives were vile and greedy spent;
> Bedamned be they who therein dwell,
> Even they who chose their Hell."

"Damned grim, isn't it, Horse? Is this our chosen hell?"

The horse plodded and nodded. Keven whistled the tune and gazed ahead to where the road broke over the top of a skylined ridge.

* * * * *

Norly squinted down at the road, where Isten was angrily motioning for him to get back out of sight. He could hear the horse coming. By the pounding of the slow hoofbeats, it sounded big enough to shake the ground, and it clanked mightily. Norly frowned and moved back from the edge to where he could just see the road below.

"Me narver heared a harse clank a-fore," he muttered to himself. "An' me nar fancies a dab o' it."

Isten slipped into the tumble of large rocks that bordered the road below the cliff.

The horse came into sight, treading along with its head down. There was no one with it. Norly raised his head to see better. Isten was doing the same from his hiding place, peering down the road to where it curved out of sight. Isten turned to look up at him and shrugged. Norly shrugged back.

"Mayhaps he be makin' manure," he whispered harshly. "An' the harse just be—"

Isten waved furiously for him to be quiet and to move back from the edge again.

"Wull, could be," he muttered, moving backward out of sight of Isten. Then suddenly he froze. "Whut th'—"

"Keep backing up. Don't make a sound."

The voice was low and calm, almost conversational. Norly took a careful step backward, then another. There was little doubt that the acute point in the small of his back belonged to a sharp weapon. He ventured a glance over his shoulder and wished he hadn't; the weapon was a sword, bright and long. A young man with level, blue-green eyes was on the other end of it, studying him with a slight frown. Norly grinned to show that he bore no intent to harm anyone.

"Wull, now," he said, then again. "Wull, now . . ."

The young man placed a finger over his lips in a hushing gesture, then indicated that Norly should hold out his bow. He did so. The tip of the sword barely brushed the bowstring. It parted with a soft *tunk*. Norly grinned again and nodded to show that he understood perfectly just how sharp that sword was. The young man pointed to where the back side of the rock sloped down to the trees. The sword made a small urging motion. Norly bobbed his head agreeably and led the way. Although the weapon was no longer touching his back, he imagined he could still feel it.

He parted the last branches and stepped out onto the road. The young man motioned him toward the rocks where Isten was hiding. The big horse was cropping at the new grass beside the road. It raised its head and regarded them with what seemed like a bored expression in its big eyes. As Norly approached, Isten peeked one cautious eye around the side of a boulder. He indicated the big horse and its armor with a scowl and a toss of his head.

"We may be havin' some troubles, Norly," he whispered. "I nar knows where he be."

Norly gave him a sickly grin and jabbed a thumb back over his shoulder. "He be here," he said with a feeble laugh.

The young man beckoned to Isten with the sword. "Come out onto the road."

Isten licked his lips and offered a weak smile.

"We jest be hidin', sar," he said, sidling into the open. He didn't have his sword. "Yew c'nar be too careful, yew know. Thar be dreadful bandits about th' roads these days."

The young man nodded. "There are indeed, and if I kill you two, then there'll be two less."

"Ah-h, nar . . ." Norly turned to face the sword. "We be nar bandits, sar. Me an' Isten, we be but mere—"

"Poor travelers," Isten interrupted. "Just a-restin our weary legs here by the road."

The young man's eyes seemed to hold the hint of a hard smile.

"Then I should kill you for being liars as well." The sword made a small motion. They both flinched away.

"Yer be a parcel harsh, sar," Isten said, a husky tightness coming into his voice. "We may o' picked up a thing or two here an' there, stuff thet were a-layin' loose, yew might say, but we never actual harmed nobodies. Norly here, he couldna hit the inside o' a room with his bow. An' as fer meself, why jest last year a li'l barstid younger pointed a knife at me, an' me runs near to Lower Fishkill." He licked his lips again. "We be narthin' like them other brigands, them true bad uns to the west."

Norly bobbed his head in urgent agreement. "Yar, thet be total true, sar. As robbers, we be right harmless."

The young man leaned closer, with a hard smile. "But I'm not."

They exchanged puzzled glances. Isten shook his head. "Wull, we has narthin' to—"

"Strip. Boots and all."

"But we'll—"

"And I'll have to take your right hands."

They turned ashen. Norly's knees wobbled as he took a step backward. "Ah-h, nar . . . ah-h, nar . . ."

"Yew can nar do that, sar," Isten pleaded. "Whate'er 'twas we done t' yew, 'twere nar *that* bad. Yew can nar honest do that to us!"

"I can. It is said the king's roads are filthy with robbers and brigands, and—"

"We be leavin' the road!" Isten said, nodding vigorously. "Right now, sar! This very breath! Come, Norly . . ." He started to turn away.

"Hold!"

They held. The young man appeared to be thinking it over. "Very well," he said, frowning. "You may keep your hands, then. But your clothes and boots . . . take them off and bundle them up with stones. We'll go down to where the road banks along the river, and you will throw them in."

"But thet's—" Isten began in a rising voice.

"Jest a fine idea," Norly said, with a frown to Isten. "Thet be right fair."

"It be a wretched long, cold way down to Riversides Town," Isten remarked weakly. The young man nodded firmly.

"Then wretched and cold you'll be, and thankful you still have life to feel it. Now, bring out that pitiful sword and break it in two, and that comical bow, too. I'll not have you two dullards threatening others again. And I tell you this: I may be riding this road often and visiting the villages alongside it, and if I *ever* see you two again engaged in *any* deed I may not like, if I ever even *hear* of it, then I *will* take your right hands . . . perhaps both hands. And a foot as well. Count yourselves fortunate that you are both witless and amusing and I'm in need of any foolish diversion from this miserable road I can find. Now, move!"

They moved. It began to rain again, a cold, gray drizzle, as they shivered their naked way down to where the road bordered the river.

"Tol' yew me nar fancied it!" Norly muttered. "It be yer grand idea, this bein' road robbers. An' yew tellin' o' how bein' stripped an' whipped were a bitter insult! Whut be *this* fer yew?"

"We can sneak inta Riversides an' steal some clothes an'— "

"Sh-h-h!" Norly stopped him. They both glanced back at the young man. He was wearing a thin smile.

* * * * *

The road wandered on, hill and hollow, forest and field, following the river bend for bend. Keven recalled the words carved in stone around the parapet of the main courtyard at the academy: *Courage. Compassion. Fortitude. Self-respect. Generosity. Wisdom. Honor.*

He thought of the two would-be robbers. Well, he had satisfied two of those, perhaps three.

"Ah, it's a never-ending battle against evil," he muttered sarcastically. "And the greatest danger on the road seems to be falling asleep, toppling over, and injuring oneself."

The clouds again swirled away in wet tatters, revealing a broad cut in the steepening barrier hills ahead, as if a great notch had been chopped away by an axe of the gods. The river rolled from wall to wall through the gap, and the road, with no room at the river's edge, climbed higher on the ridge to where a narrow shoulder, like a high shelf, provided passage between rampart cliffs and river gorge. The cliffs were the end of a rumpled mountain range that ramped off higher and higher into the cloudy north. Through heavy forest, giving way to ledges and boulders long fallen from the heights, the road climbed unevenly to its final crest. Here, looming over the narrow way, a harsh outcrop of granite blocked out nearly half the sky. He stopped to rest the horse. Just as if it really needed it, he thought idly.

To the left, off the abrupt edge of the road, were the tops of a few trees clinging to the steep incline. The river murmured far below. Gazing ahead from a high point, Keven saw what appeared to be an early summer again. A gentle valley opened in the west, the river sparkling in the sudden sun, and beyond rose another abrupt mountain range, high and broken, laced with snow and shredded clouds.

The great, gray granite, ragged wall of the massive, mangled Macaab Mountains, rampant as the backs of dragons, or perhaps a fence of hell . . .

The line sprang to mind unbidden, something he had read at the academy. But considering the tone of the remembered text, the mountains didn't look that forbidding, if they were indeed the fabled Macaabs. His attention was diverted by the horse. It raised its head suddenly and snorted, eyes and ears focused above the road.

The ledges bordering the high side of the road had taken on an unusual, ordered face. Dressed stones had been fitted into the natural outcrop, rising to a grim wall overlooking the road. A row of dark openings along the top peered down like baleful eyes. Higher yet, a crumbling tower loomed over all. He frowned at the overgrown ruins. There was a silent, brooding atmosphere about the ancient place. In many spots, the walls had toppled, overthrown finally by the gnarled roots of old trees. Wild grapevines and moss covered most of the stones like a shroud, and coatings of bird droppings told of its only apparent residents now. With an easy brace and motion, he strung his bow and tested the damp string. Twice he heard a faint sound from deep in the old stones; it could have been a squirrel or a resident rockchuck. The horse, judging by its leery alertness, apparently didn't think so. He fingered the arrow in his left hand into a more ready position on the bow. Ruins were sometimes not as empty as they should be . . . he had learned that in the Northeast Kingdom. He had learned too much there.

The road curved around a projecting point of the ancient wall. A laden cart lay tilted sideways, a solid planked wheel wrenched off in one of the deep ruts. A mule stood dozing in the traces; a man and boy were piling stones near the fallen side of the cart; a freshly cut pole lay alongside. They were frozen in position, staring wide-eyed at him and the horse. He raised his right hand in greeting as he approached, bow aimed at the ground.

"A good day to you, Landsman." It was the traditional salutation. The man straightened, glanced quickly over his shoulder, and then back.

"An' to yew, sar," he replied warily.

"I am Keven of Kingsend." It was also traditional—and polite—to identify oneself. "I travel west."

"Ah . . ." The man glanced away again, nervously

searching the road behind Keven and the overwhelming dark battlements above them. "Then yew be headed arightly, I s'pose. . . . I be Pratt. This be me boy."

His gaze rose again to the ancient stonework. The boy continued staring at Keven, gaping in awe or fright; it was difficult to tell. They were dressed in dirty, worn, and patched woolens with scarred leather tunics. The man was a broad, solid figure with a brimmed leather hat pulled low over his eyes. Keven motioned to the somber walls.

"What sort of place is this?"

"It be ol'. . . ver' ol'," the man muttered. "It be ruined fer many a age, but still . . ." His voice was grim. "It nar be a place t' break a wheel. There be ol' stories . . . an' methinks I be hearin' things off in the stones."

He still regarded Keven with suspicion, licking his lips as he edged toward an axe leaning against the cart. Keven frowned at the wall and the road behind, too. The man's apprehension was catching, but he hung his bow over the saddle, followed by the quiver and sword.

"May I be of service to you, Pratt? You have a heavy load."

The man relaxed somewhat now that the weapons were not at hand.

"'Tis narthin' o' value, sar. Some hides fer the tanner in town."

Keven approached the cart, and the boy scuttled away to the far side of the mule.

"I'm more interested in its weight, Good Pratt. I have no present interest in cargo." He adjusted stones on the pile, picked up the pole, and levered it under the cart.

"Ready?"

Pratt nodded, spat on his hands, and tilted the heavy, iron-bound wheel upright beside the axle. Keven leaned his weight on the end of the pole; the axle barely lifted from the road.

"Are you sure you're not carting stones by mistake?" The words strained through clenched teeth.

"'Tis a goodly load, sar."

"Truly!" He swung the pole over one shoulder, jammed it farther under the cart, brought his back and legs under it, and lifted. The pole bent and creaked. The cart groaned high enough. Pratt gaped at him.

"Now!" Keven grated. Pratt nodded. The wheel slipped on. He hammered a newly cut wedge into the axle end.

"Thar!" He nodded in satisfaction, then turned to Keven with a stiff, quick bow. "I truly thank yew, sar."

Keven returned the thanks with a short nod. "How far is this town you spoke of?"

"Thet be Midvale, sar. It lie some two leagues yonder, at the bend o' the river."

"And the name of this river?"

A look of amazement came before the answer. "Why, thet be the Sun-Runnin' River, sar! It come from way up in Upper Vale down through Outer Vale yonder." His arm swept the whole of the route. "They say it run then all the way to the Great City an' the sea!"

"Ah, yes." Keven turned to trace the river's twisted gleam back toward the misty east. "Now I know."

The man gaped at him blankly.

"I lived in the city for a while. Latonia, it's called. I've seen where this river meets the sea. I came upon it from the north a few days ago, but I didn't know where I was. So this is the Great Western Trade Road, then."

A puzzled frown. "Nar . . . this be the Sun-Runnin' Road." The man was regarding Keven strangely again, edging away.

"A matter of different names in different places, Goodman Pratt." Then he added, "May I ask a question of you?"

"Yar . . ." It was a decidedly qualified affirmative.

"Why are you so wary of me? Do I appear that dreadful?"

The man considered Keven's frown for a moment, then deepened his own scowl as he glanced again at the wall and the road in both directions. "Thar be . . . bad things about these days."

"What sort of bad things?"

After a pause, Pratt said, "Bandits an' brigands. Them thet offers nar mercy. An' there be . . . other things. E'en this close to the town, so 'tis said."

"U-m-m . . ." Keven thought of the two would-be bandits he had met earlier. "And you thought that of *me*, Goodman Pratt? From what I've seen of the robbers on this road, I should be insulted." He knew he was glaring at the man too intently, but Pratt was not backing down. He faced Keven squarely.

"Yew be a stranger . . . sar. I meant nar insult."

"None taken." He went to the horse, took down his sword, quiver, and bow, and rearmed himself. He glanced at the load of hides with a thin smile.

"If you fear bandits, Goodman Pratt, then I shall be your escort."

Pratt considered that for moment, then with something between a shrug and a nod said, "Yer be truly a kind armsman, sar." He cast a calculating eye to the sun.

"It be near on to midday. We could move a way on down the road beyond this place, where a spring offers a drink. Would yew share bread with us? 'Tis but poor man's fare."

Keven hesitated, wondering if the offer was sincere or merely polite, then said, "If you'll share my tough travel rations, Pratt, then I'll share your bread. But I warn you, a man would have to have a taste for leather to enjoy them."

A surprising grin broke over Pratt's weathered face. He made a motion to his cart.

"Leather be a staple o' life, sar. Thar be nar *hidin'* it." He chuckled deep in his chest.

Keven shook his head but smiled, too. "I hope your

bread is better than your jokes."

"Ah, 'tis right wondrous bread, sar. Most folks just break their bread. I broke me mule with mine. Any balk an' I tunked him 'tween the ears with a loaf. He larned fast, though some numb now from it."

Keven smiled again; the man reminded him of Old Edgar when he would— He broke away from that thought.

"Ho-o!" Pratt called as he slapped the mule on the flank.

The mule leaned into the traces. Keven's horse gave a sudden, loud snort. Its head came up, ears alert. There was a snap of a branch ahead, a crash of underbrush, and a furry, upright creature half again the size of a man lurched into the road in front of them. An arrow was nocked and Keven's bow was up almost instantly.

"*Nar!*" Pratt shouted, holding an arm in front of Keven. "It be harmless!"

"Harmless?" Keven scowled at the beast, still holding aim on the juncture of throat and breastbone. He mentally paged through the academy bestiary, trying to identify the thing. It snarled at him, thin lips peeling back from yellow teeth, its tiny eyes glittering. Pratt approached it, making soft, soothing sounds, as if to a frightened child.

"Now-w-w . . . so-o-o . . . It be jest fine, Uglar. Calm yerself."

"Uglar?" Keven still kept the arrow aimed.

"Yar," Pratt nodded without turning. "Thet be what it call itself." He reached the creature and gently touched one brawny, hairy arm.

"It be jest fine, Uglar. Thar be nar trouble here. We be jest fine. But yew be a bad boy, Uglar. Yew be follerin' after us, did yew nar? An' yew be up in them ruins a-scarin' us, too. Thet be nar nice, Uglar."

The creature called Uglar made a whimpering sound as it looked down at Pratt. Keven lowered the bow.

"Now I tells yew what, Uglar." Pratt was shaking a finger at the creature as if it was a huge, naughty boy. "Yew has to go back home now."

The whimper sounded again. Pratt nodded forcefully.

"Yar, yew does! Now, yew nar haggles 'bout it no more! Yew goes right back home! If yew be follerin' any more, then the men'll get yew. Yew know thet."

The whimper was somehow different.

"Thet be right!" Pratt nodded again. "If yew foller, then the men'll get yew. Now, go!"

The creature gave Keven a dark look, curling its lips and showing its teeth again.

"Yew jest never mind 'bout thet man," Pratt admonished. "Yew go home an' stay there. We be back on the morrow."

The boy had moved up by Pratt. Now he stepped forward and hugged the beast around one massive leg. It gave Keven a final glare and a low growl, then eased back into the underbrush above the road. There was a slight rustle of movement, then silence. The horse's head lifted to follow the creature's unseen route into the ruins.

"What from several hells . . ." Keven breathed.

Pratt made a mollifying motion. "Now, I nar be knowin' what it be," he said, shaking his head, "so don' be askin'. It come to our place in the mid o' winter two year ago from out o' the forest. We'd had a hard snow for near onto a tenday—up to a man's chest, it war—then came a real quick sizzler o' a thaw, an' then a bitter freeze. The snow war so tough-crusted o'er thet yew could o' danced on it with a ox. So here this thing comes, near to starvin'. Beggin', it war. So . . ." He shrugged. "What would yew do? Gods know he could o' took anythin' he wanted, but he war beggin' . . ." He looked at Keven with a slight frown. "Yew understan'? He be much like a sort o' big dog what walks like a man an' helps us aroun' the farmstead."

"Um-m." Keven nodded. "It's just that I never saw anything like it before."

"Wull, we, too! It a-frighted us some, I be tellin' yew! The wife near lived in the root cellar thet first winter. But it be a gentle beast, though. An' I be tellin' yew somethin' more. . . ." He raised a finger to mark his point. "We actual feel some safer with him bein' aroun'. Not often somethin' from out o' the dark o' the forest be good, y'know."

They moved off down the road, talking of strange beasts and old tales and things heard of, and agreeing that there was more in the dark forests than a man knew . . . and too much of it was vicious.

* * * * *

The road wound down from the mountain shoulder, down through lower hills and forest, and from the now talkative Pratt, Keven learned about the valley ahead.

The steep, rugged mountains some four leagues on the other side of the valley, standing like a long, crumbling wall from north to south, were indeed the storied Macaab Mountains. A tall crag, towering a full half a league above the valley floor, dominating the horizon like a dark, broken tooth against the sky, was Castle Mountain, so called because of its semblance to great towers and sheer ramparts. A deep notch just north of the big mountain was Castle Pass, where the road continued west, a most dangerous place now.

"Bandits!" Pratt was assertive. "An' awful things, too! Dark beasts! Fer years now it be gettin' worser an' worser on the Castle Pass! Ain' many will even try thet way now. People been most awful kilt. Some were skint!"

He pointed to the far north, where the Macaab Mountains faded into dark clouds. "North Pass be up thar some twenty leagues or so. But last year they say the bandits an' the wicked beasts be up thar, too." He shook his head sadly and made a mystic sign in the air with one hand. "It hurt the trade somethin' terrible. Urban th' Tanner now be sittin' on hides he can nar move west." He looked at his own load wistfully.

"And is there no guard?" Keven asked.

"Ah, yar, thar be the Vale Guard, but it nar seem to do much now. A lot o' them war kilt up thar on the pass, an-'King's Armsmen, too." He frowned over his shoulder with suspicion and lowered his voice. "Folk say the mount'n rises ag'in."

"The mountain rises?"

Pratt placed a gnarled finger beside his nose, nodded, and winked. "Yew'll hear."

"And what are these 'wicked things' you mention?" The sarcasm was a bit too sharp in his voice. "Things like your pet Ulgar?"

"Thet be Uglar, nar Ulgar," Pratt said resentfully. He strode on in stubborn silence, then halted abruptly and faced Keven. "I'll nar tell yer o' things I don' know meself, sar, but thar be too much talk now t' be takin' it lightly. The Vales has a right ugly past." He wheeled and started forward again. "Yew can sort it out fer yerself if'n yew a mind to, sar. The town be full o' tales."

Their slow way continued down to the valley, and early summer showed once more in new leaves and grass. Wild flowers brightened the roadside. And Keven learned how the long, curving valley of the Vales and the course of the Sun-Running River "war bent like a elbow" coming down from the north and turning sharply east. The village of Midvale lay at the point of the bend.

"The Mad River join thar at the town, comin' in from the west. This part of the valley here be the Midvale. Upper Vale be up thar, to the north."

"I thought it would be."

Pratt glanced at him quickly but found no offense. He continued. "It be a large town, Midvale. Mayhaps a city—I don' know what decides them things. A goodly amount o' trade come through." He grunted and corrected himself. "Did!"

He pointed through a break in the trees to where the towers of a small castle rose.

"Thar be the castle o' Lord Damon. He rule the Vales. A good lord, I guess, from what 'tis said. Firm, but I nar heared narthin' cruel o' him. He truly love horses, 'tis said. Ain' thet a good sign? Fer some reason, the castle be called the keep. Don' know why." He shook his head at the mystery of it all.

"It nar sit in the town, but on a great rock whar the Mad River meet the Sun-Runnin'—an island—an' th' way to it be most curious."

He thrust his left arm straight out in front of him.

"Say thet this be the bridge o'er the Mad River to the Road North—the Keep Bridge, 'tis called—an' then this—" he brought his other hand over at a right angle to the extended arm—"this be the bridge to th' castle on the island. See? It join right in the middle o' the Keep Bridge! Now watch!"

He tilted his right hand up and away from his left arm, eyes widening at Keven.

"In such a manner thet part o' the bridge to the keep can draw right up ag'in' the wall!" He demonstrated again. "Yarsar! I seen it once! 'Tis a sight o' wonder. It put the keep all alone on its rock, with narthin' but river all aroun', yew see. An' then the archers can shoot down anybody still on the bridge itself." He scowled sideways at Keven. "Yew ever seen anythin' like thet?"

Keven frowned thoughtfully . . . and did not smile. "No . . ." he mused.

"Thought nar!" Pratt gave a firm nod. "'Tis all some

wondrous."

And he related other wonders as well . . .

Hidden in the hills to the south were littlers, the small people! Good folk and fine farmers. Their fruit and produce and sausages and preserves and such were of the very best, and much in demand. And their cloth was of the finest, some so closely woven that it was said to be waterproof! They even had their own market on South Hill at the upper edge of town! Some even served in the Town Watch!

"Tough as a keg o' spikes, they be, but true good folk. Yar, I talked to some once." He gave that assertive nod.

"An' them mount'ns thar, south o' thet Castle Mount'n?" He pointed to the Macaabs again. "They be called the Green Mount'ns from the big mount'n south. Elves be in thar! Truly! But I ne'er seen one, though. They come seldom into town, an' me, too, an' narver at the same time, it seem." The wistful head shook again.

"An' the mount'ns just behind us, layin' off to the north? The foot o' them whar yew came upon us? They be the Iron Mount'ns." He lowered his voice confidentially and leaned closer. "Dwarfs!"

Keven frowned at the pronunciation; it rhymed with *scarfs*. He tried it out. "Dwarfs?"

"Yar—dwarfs!" The same *arf* sound. "But I ne'er seen one o' them, neither, though I hear tell o' them bein' often in town." He sighed at the unfairness of it all. "I seen their metalwork once, though. It be right wondrous."

The smell of woodsmoke rode in the air. Huts of woodcutters and their charcoal kilns appeared through the trees. Cleared fields opened, with small farmsteads.

"Freeholds hereabouts," Pratt said, indicating both sides of the road. "Lord Damon's land be t'other riverside north. An' o'er thar" —he pointed to the south—"'crost the river an' east o' town, be the Ol' Castle. It be ver' ol'. I nar been to it, but 'tis said it be most huge, though most fallen an'

growed over. 'Tis said it be o' the same age as them walls on
the road whar yew met us. Times was when things was even
more bad hereabouts than now."

The road widened until two wagons could pass abreast
and broke from the trees to open fields. Pratt halted, with a
wide sweep of both arms.

"These be the campyards fer the caravans. Times war
when thar be so many wagons here yew could nar count
'em. Now look! Narthin'!"

"Early in the year, isn't it? The road is in no condition for
travel."

"It be time fer trade t' roll."

From the open ground of the campyards, Keven had his
first good look at the town.

* * * * *

The Sun-Running River flowed down from the stormy
north, wide and rolling high with spring rains and mountain snowmelt. At the town, it turned sharply and disappeared through the wide notch behind them. A sprawling
disorder of wattle huts and pole buildings filled the inside
of the bend. Across the river, the main part of the village
climbed from the water's edge. Houses seemed roofed one
from another up the steep hillside, a crowded clutter of roof
angles, chimneys, and trees. Wandering streets followed
the natural lay of the land, angling, zigzagging in apparent
random paths. Blue-gray curls of woodsmoke patterned the
air.

The small castle of Lord Damon was perched on a large
midstream outcrop, where another river joined from the
west. Keven had to admire its advantage of defense. The
green and gold banner of Latonia flew from the highest
tower, a green and silver pennant from a lower tower—-the
colors of the Lord of the Vales, he presumed.

Large piers bordered both sides of the river, and he noted with a sailor's eye the several large craft tied off across the river. One was some twenty paces in length.

"There's a large river traffic?" he asked with some surprise.

"Ah, yar! It be the trade. Not to the north, fer the river shallows, but downriver. They run, 'tis said, down to Riversides and Armleydale. Some claim e'en to the Great City. An' they come back up, too, though I nar understan' how." He shook his head. "The river only run down, yew know."

"And no bridge here?"

"Nar. 'Twas tried three or four times, accordin' to the stories. Once at the town, but 'tis said they could nar find good footin'; it be too deep thar at th' bend. Farther up the river" —he waved vaguely toward the north— "'twas tried, too, but the spirit o' the Sun-Runnin' get angry 'bout it, I guess. It tore it up as fast as they built it. The wizard come an' ev'rythin,' an' they get some mighty rocks in midstream all ready fer bridgin,' an' the river rise up an' smash it all to flinders. The Sun-Runnin' have a mighty spirit."

A broad roadway now ran straight through the crowded, wretched buildings to where a line of pole-and-plank warehouses bordered this side of the river.

"This be the hard part o' town." Pratt lowered his voice. "'Tis called Crossriver, an' nar be part o' the Watch patrol mostly. Here be the fire trades, the smiths an' the potters an' th' like. The town council figures thet this part o' town can burn without too much bother. Thar be others here o' a diff'rent business, too. 'Tis best to nar tarry," he said, and then, with a hurried glance at Keven and the following horse, "nar thet yew couldna care fer yerself."

Rickety taverns and vendor stalls of cheap wares bordered the roadway, but the population seemed sparse and of a suspicious, sullen nature.

"Crossriver don' do much in the daylight," Pratt said,

"'less a caravan come through, an' they be few now 'cause o' the mount'n troubles. It lively up some at night, though, so 'tis said. Don' know meself. Would nar stop here to piss if me boots war on fire."

The roadway ended at the river in a wide pier. Small boats and barges were tied among the larger rivercraft, and offers of transport clamored for their attention. After hard bargaining among three boatmen, they settled on a one-eyed old man who still insisted Keven's horse was worth the ferry of a full cart. They were rowed in a cart barge across what Keven estimated to be a two-hundred-pace width of roiling muddy river to the stone riverwall of Midvale.

Beyond the piers and the sturdy stone warehouses and storage sheds on this side of the river, the town market filled the narrow bench of land below town. They parted there, Pratt turning east toward the lower edge of the village.

"They put the tanners an' the fullers out o' town, yew see. They say 'tis because o' the smell." He chuckled. "But I nar *nose* the difference. May yew fare well, Keven o' Kingsend."

Keven raised a hand in parting. "And you, too, Pratt of Outer Vale."

The man hooted with laughter and led the mule away through the jumble of the market. As he started out, the boy spoke for the first time.

"An' whut be yer harse's name, sar?" he called.

Keven regarded the big beast for a moment, a small smile in the corner of his mouth.

"I tried several different names, but he gave no attention. I just call him Horse." The animal lifted its head, bored eyes fastening on Keven. "He seems to like it."

The boy's mouth still hung open. Pratt laughed, and they were lost in the marketplace.

The sun was half down the western sky as he led the horse into what seemed to be a main thoroughfare angling uphill, and the town pressed in around him. There was not the stomach-wrenching stench of Latonia, at least. Keven could never get used to that after the clean air of the sea; there were times when he thought he had gone for weeks without daring to breathe. But even here, there was still the musk of too many people and animals crowded into a space too small and doing too many things. And there was too much of a tumult of noise and motion: carts clattering on the cobbles, dogs barking, bawdy insults called in humor and in anger, vendors calling in the streets and from crowded stalls.

"Wine! Fine wine! A cup for a copper! Fine wine!"

"Small cakes, rich cakes! Copper for a sweet cake!"

"Here be yer fresh rabbits!" a hunter called, a pole of dangling skinned carcasses held over one shoulder. "Gets 'em while they still be runnin'!"

"This cider here cannar be left alone lest it harm some strong men! It be mean an' hostile! Fer two coppers yew can be learnin' if I lie."

He fixed his eyes dead ahead, ignoring the calls directed at him and the frank stares, putting up his walls against the crowding clamor of too much happening at once.

He didn't like being the center of attention, but that was the horse's doing. Not only was its great size unusual, but also its peculiar behavior in the teeming streets could not be ignored. No sleepy beast now; head up, ears back, neck arched, it paced behind him in a quartering, half-sideways maneuver like a gigantic plow. With its left shoulder almost nudging Keven's back, it accomplished two things: It definitely cleared a path before them, its hooves hammering down on the cobbles like boulders falling in a quarry, and its position prevented anyone from approaching Keven from the rear. He didn't especially like it—it had happened before in crowded streets—but there was nothing he could do about it. In conditions like this, it was a part of the animal's training to protect its dismounted rider.

Strollers, idlers, choremen, and carters eyed him and the horse and parted like a river around an island.

"Got to get you among people more often," he muttered to the horse.

And me, too, he noted, but with care this time. There had been trouble in the last two or three little hamlets he had stopped in. There always seemed to be someone in some bedamned tavern who wanted to find some dispute. The last two times he'd had just enough drink to match their foul temper. He had felt righteous at the time, but later . . .

He shook his head and observed this new town.

Shops and stalls lined the street, their wooden shutters raised over open counters like awnings. Timber-framed, overhanging second stories narrowed the sky. Stone buildings fronted with heavily paned and leaded windows, their wide doors swung open to noisy interiors. Wandering streets and alleys interwound, as if uncertain of their direction. Frequent stone stairs led straight up the hillside through narrow canyons of buildings. Unexpected squares broadened suddenly at intersections, with low fountains spilling into stone basins. Streets and byways curved, split, rejoined, branched, dead-ended into courts, looped, turned abruptly into stairs, slanted downhill, climbed uphill, and twisted apparently to nowhere. The whole town seemed to have been laid out by drunken geese. Several times he had to backtrack to regain what seemed to be a main street. He asked directions to the King's Arms Hall and received a blank stare.

"King's Arms Hall, yew say? Thar be narn thet I know of. The Watch barrack be uphill." There was a vague wave in that direction.

"And how would I find it?"

There was a thoughtful frown, a scratching of an ear.

"Wull . . . yew could take Gullet Passage to the Goat Steps. . . ." He broke off, scowling at the horse. "No . . . thet wouldna work."

A bystander offered help. "Yew take Charter Way to the chandler's shop, then up the Bear Gulch Cut till yew see—"

"Nar, nar!" another cut in. "Thet'll only confuse 'im. He should foller Baker Road from the Old Gate Fountain as far as Big Stairs, then—"

"He should try t' take thet great monster o' a harse up Big Stairs? The rain's gettin' inta yer attic, man! He should be takin' Barkin's Alley up to Wall Way, an' then at Cow Crossin' he—"

"Yew be thoroughgoin' dazed! He'd nar get thet thing through Wiggin's Passage!"

"Wull, he takes that turn off Cherry Court, then, don' he!"

"The Cherry Court Cut lead back to Barn Lane."

"Damn it do! Barn Lane be clear up to . . ."

Keven left them arguing; they seemed to be enjoying themselves. A young man in the next square was more helpful.

"Take thet left," he said, pointing. "At the first crossin, yew'll bear right into Purly Lane. 'Bout eight or nine doors up, yew'll see Cow Court take off to the right. The Watch barrack be at the rear o' it, in the Old East Gatehouse."

He stared over Keven's shoulder for a moment.

"Be thet all one horse?"

"Only part of him. The boatman couldn't bring him all over in one trip."

"Ah . . . good one."

"I thank you for your guidance."

"I thank yew fer the sight."

* * * * *

In a small, smoky tavern in Upper Vale, two men faced each other across a table. The big man took a deep swallow of his ale, wiped his beard, and peered uneasily around the room. Although fires roared in the two fireplaces against the chill of the soggy day, the few men within sat hunched and silent. The big man leaned closer to the smaller man across the table, voice low.

"Thar be too many dire things afoot, Jeth. Ah likes it nar."

"Yar," that one muttered. "Ol' Lame Tom war drivin' in a drift o' pigs from Charcreek way when they all took foolish an' bolted. Now thet nar be altogether queer fer pigs, but he say it were too peculiar in the way it happened. He nar rounded up but 'arf o' 'em, an' he swears he heared th' others squealin' off in the woods, like they was bein' butchered. An' they jist quit o' a sudden. He went a-lookin' an' found narthin' but blood ever'wheres, some splattered up inta the trees, an' he took outta thar faster'n a burnt cat. Said he warn't shamed to run. An' I nar blame 'im. I ask yew now, what be it thet can catch 'arf wild pigs on the loose like thet, butcher 'em, an' carry 'em off?"

"Ah does nar know, Jeth."

"Yar . . . an' thet's gettin' t' be a common answer lately. Too many awful things t' chill a man, an' no good answers."

* * * * *

From *The Vales*, by Acclain, Wizard of Vale.

"Some hundred miles upriver from the City of Latonia, the western border of the Kingdom of Latonia is marked by the abrupt rise of the Macaab Mountains. They range north and south for over three hundred leagues in a steep, narrow, jagged rampart, marking the bounds of Latonia and

The Palan as surely as a monstrous, broken wall. On the sunrise side of the Macaabs, at the headwaters of the Sun-Running River, lies the long valley now known locally as The Vales. Originally this was Westershire, settled by runaway slaves, outcasts, escaped criminals, banished dissidents, and others considered renegades. But no one cares about the conversations of old bones; the valley is now The Vales and will remain so until we, too, are old bones.

"The upper part of the valley is known as Upper Vale; the lower part of the valley, Midvale; the valley east through the gorge is Outer Vale. No one knows why this illogic came to be, but at least the names are commonly accepted, so everyone knows what general area is under discussion. This is of great value when inquiring as to directions.

"At this point, for those of narrow experience, I must explain that the proper word for 'dwarfs' is *warfen*. *Warfen* is plural, and *warf* is singular. The word *d'warf* means 'of a certain warf,' while the word *d'warfen* means 'of the people as a whole.' The *a* is sounded, as in *arm*. The warfen refer to themselves in this manner; one assumes they know what they are talking about.

"The Vales are one of those unusual and fascinating places in the land where man, littler, warf, and elf all live within reach of each other without allowing the bane of ancient prejudices to govern their otherwise good sense. It is most curious and most rare. Many offer rationales as to why this accord is unnatural, yet few tender reasons as to how this harmony happens; that, too, is most curious.

"In the gentle hills south of Midvale, which reasonably should be Lower Vale, are the Three Shires of the littlers; they are quick to point out that they live *not* in the Vales but in the Three Shires—Northshire, Westshire, and Far Hillshire—and who is to argue with that distinction? They have been there longer than we have.

"Similarly, the Macaab Mountains south of the sharp

peak now known as Castle Mountain suddenly become the Green Mountains. This is the home of the Green Mountain Elves, and damned little anyone can do or say about that; they predate the littlers.

"Predating all residents of the area are the warfen of Iron Mountains, a tumbled range on the eastern side of The Vales stretching north from the Sun-Running River. They do not care what names we use. It is an interesting view of the warfen that they are much less concerned about us than we are about them.

"The Vales hold two major settlements: Mill Ford in Upper Vale, and Midvale in Midvale. Of these two, Midvale is the larger and more important by far, although this is a point of view not held by the residents of Mill Ford. The prime reason for Midvale's importance is apparent: It is in the right place to be important.

"The Sun-Running River, as if suddenly maturing from a brash and reckless youth in Upper Vale, suddenly calms, deepens, and turns abruptly east at its confluence with the Mad River. Midvale sits at this bend, astride the Great Western Trade Road. Trade eastward bound may transship to boats and barges and ride the gentle river down to Latonia and the sea. As a disgruntled trader once said, feeling he had been severely cheated by local merchants, 'It's a fine place for a town—somebody should build one there someday.'

"Barring the inevitable criticisms, Midvale offers all the services a weary traveler could want. Everything from the essential to the semi-superb is available for the correct coin.

"The Vales have endured much. In surviving writings from the Ancient Age, there are references to 'The Darke and Bloodie ground of the Upper West River (the Sun-Running), fearsome in the Grim and Dreadful shadow of the Fanged Mountains (the Macaabs).'

"While I, in my humble scribblings, cannot hope to rise

to such dizzying heights of descriptive literature, I have compiled some commentaries on history.

"They should be useful to those seeking facts and knowledge instead of wit and pretense."

Chapter Two

The sheriff of the Midvale Town Watch was a compact and competent man, somewhere in his early fifties, weathered and wiry, with an almost permanent scowl of suspicious scrutiny. He appeared to be framed entirely of used weapons and old corded rawhide. With pale blue, deep-set eyes glaring out from under heavy eyebrows, he radiated a raw, hostile energy that usually brought forth the very best manners in others.

At the moment, he was moderately displeased, not generally considered to be an unusual condition. The eyes held a hard glint of steel under that hedge of gray eyebrows, and his square beard bristled like wire. Hands on hips in his wide-shouldered green tunic of office, boots planted wide, he seemed to be occupying an area much larger than himself.

The young watchman frozen before him in the barrack courtyard was in a posture of wide-eyed, rigid attention.

"An' whose caravan be it?" The sheriff had a voice like a dull saw gnawing its way through stone.

"I knows not, sir," the young man replied. "A new name in th' trade, it is, not the slave traders that we know—that *I* know of."

A dangerous smoothness slipped into the sheriff's voice. "An' you knows them all, o' course, bein' one o' such age an' experience. Does the guard know o' this caravan?"

"Yar. They be sendin' out a escort fer it."

"Good for them. Now I tell you what you do, Stanus. You take six men, an' you meet this caravan at the Keep Bridge. Make it right clear to this trader what the law be in Midvale—no slave tradin', no buyin' or sellin' o' slaves, no stoppin' in the town at all. They go straightaway through town to Crossriver without so much as a pet-the-puppy, an' they camp by the Iron Mountain Road. Any violation o' law an' the caravan be broke up an' all property seized, by order o' Damon, Lord o' Vale. Does you think you can remember all that?"

"Yarsar, but I imagine the guard be tellin' 'em all thet, too. I imagine thet the—"

"Now, don' you go strainin' somethin' you've little of, laddy. You just tells 'em again! You imagine *that?*"

"Yarsar. Th' only thing bein', they say th' leader o' this caravan claim he got nar slaves, but instead they be prisoners. He say they—"

The sheriff seemed to grow suddenly. "I'll be not wound, wrapped, an' tangled in *that* argument!" he growled. "If they *looks* like slaves, *smells* like slaves, an' is *treated* like slaves, then they *be* slaves as far as the law here be concerned! An' if he don' like that, then *he* c'n be the prisoner! Be that clear enough?"

"Yarsar."

"Then you make it clear to him. I don' care to chew on this bone again!"

The young man licked his lips. "Yarsar. But they'll nar like it, I wager."

"*They'll* not like it?" The blue eyes blazed as the sheriff leaned forward and appeared to shout directly into the young man's open mouth.

"*They?* If you be not a-horse an' out that bedamned gate in five breaths, *I'll* not like it! An' which o' them two choices d' you think'll be th' best fer your future?"

"Yarsar!" And the young man sprinted for the stables.

"Bracken!" The sheriff bellowed, the echoes bouncing from the walls and flagstones of the courtyard. A sword-armed watchman strode briskly from a doorway. He wore the markings on his tunic and the head-up, smug expression of some minor rank.

"Sire?"

"Forget the 'sire.' I be bedamned if I fathered you."

"Yessir."

The sheriff nodded. "Guild councilman's son or not, that little piss-ant, Stanus, hasn't the spine for the work! Another tenday is all he's got to prove his head's on top an' his arse is behind him. He—" He broke off, scowling in the direction of the east gate.

"Gods a-loose an' livin'!" he breathed. "Look at the size o' that horse!"

A young man-in-arms entered the courtyard leading the biggest horse the sheriff had ever seen. With its peculiar quartering gait, it seemed almost to be pushing the frowning youth ahead of him. The young man dropped the reins, and the huge horse halted as if suddenly staked to the spot. The sheriff gave a grudging grunt of approval.

"Are you the sheriff of Midvale?" The voice was low and unassertive. Despite the frown, he didn't sound like trouble. Yet.

"I be." The sheriff nodded curtly.

"I am Keven of Kingsend. I would like lodging for myself and my horse."

"I don' know if you noticed, laddy, but this be not an inn."

The young man halted in front of him. Although the

sheriff came hardly to the fellow's chin, he seemed not to be looking up.

"And how are you called again?"

"Keven of Kingsend."

"Never heard of it."

"It's a coastal town far to the west, at the end of Kings Road, in the Kingdom of Coronal." A thin smile flickered briefly in the corner of his mouth. "As it is said, 'It's not the end of the world, but you can see it from there.' "

"Um-m. And what is your—" he glanced significantly at the young man's weapons, armor, and horse—"trade? As if I truly had to ask."

"I am a freeranger."

"Ah-h . . ." The sheriff let his eyebrows slide up. He turned to the other watchman, who wore a sly smirk. "Not a mere freefighter here, Bracken, or only a freewarrior, or not even a king's champion, but a free*ranger!*"

He made a small show of inspecting this Keven of Kingsend from head to foot. "I don' think I ever seen one o' them afore," he mused. "They bein' so truly rare . . . but somehow I thought they'd be much bigger." He stepped back and motioned abruptly to the grinning watchman.

"Bracken, arrest him!"

Bracken threw the sheriff the briefest of questioning looks, then stepped lazily forward, drawing his sword.

"Come, lad. We—"

The horse snorted, yanked up its head, and took a hard step forward. The young man called to it, "Back!" and made a blurred, fluid motion over his shoulder. There was a bright, lightning flicker of steel and a hard clang, and Bracken's sword was a sparkling arc in the sun as it spun away and clattered across the flagstones. The young man was facing them with a small frown and a large sword steady on middle guard, making no move to follow up. The sheriff noted the sword hand was relaxed, almost casual, the voice was calm yet edged.

"In the name of justice, I am forced to ask what is the charge against me, Good Sheriff?"

The sheriff allowed a small crusty smile to tilt one side of his face; it didn't seem to fit well.

"No charge. 'Twas a measure o' your words. If you be not what you say, then Bracken would o' arrested you, an' I would then 'ave booted your foolish arse down the road for bein' yet another lyin', copperpiece swaggart with a tin sword and somethin' to prove. We get 'nough o' them up on the mountain now."

The sword didn't waver; the eyes remained hard. "And what if I had strayed because of this little measure of yours? What if I had killed or cut him?"

A frown quickly replaced the sheriff's bleak smile. It was a more comfortable expression for him.

"Do you see 'fool' embroidered on me anywhere?" he growled. "Your sense o' duty would o' resisted the injustice o' it. If you be *not* a freeranger, as you claim, you couldn't o' touched him; if you be truly, you *wouldn't* o' touched him!" He glared at the young fighter for a moment. "Be there another way o' sayin' that?"

The young man scowled and nodded. " 'Let the defenseless stand innocent unless proven otherwise,' " he quoted. The sword lowered.

"Defenseless!" The watchman Bracken spun from a grim examination of his sword.

The sheriff ignored him. "It may be that we never seen a freeranger here before, but I know the rules, Keven o' Kingsend. And as for harmin' our fine Bracken here . . ." Bracken was glowering now at the sheriff and rubbing his wrist. The sheriff offered another small smile. "How could you take offense to such a kindly face like that?"

The broadsword tilted to the sky, swept over the right shoulder, and slid home to its scabbard. The young man was still scowling. "I think you gamble freely with someone else's well-being, Sheriff."

"How I gamble be none o' your concern."

"I don't like being played with." The frown swung to the sullen watchman. "And you're too slow. You thought before you acted. Another place or time, and you'd be meat on the ground."

Bracken curled his lip in a grimace. "Yew want t'try it again? I'll see if I can be a little more to your likin'."

"Put your fire out, Bracken," the sheriff said, holding up a gnarled hand. " 'Defenseless' be about the right word in this case. I know you just didn't wander in here yesterday with sheep dung on your boots, but this be a case o' the arm not bein' equal to the task. I count this fellow to be a true freeranger. Ride yourself up to the West Gate an' keep an eye on young Stanus. See if he can get the word to them slavers without pissin' in his boots."

The flushed watchman threw the ranger a final challenging glare and strode stiffly across the courtyard.

"Now . . ." the sheriff mused, turning back. "What be I to do about you?"

"Sheriff, I don't know what you're going to do about me! I came here seeking lodging, and instead I'm offered some damned game!"

"Told you why! The reason be valid an' it stands! I believe it true that you be a ranger, but that don' altogether put my mind at ease! Where be you from of late?"

"From the east and north."

"An' to where do you journey?"

"West."

"Um-m . . . west be not a wise idea in these times. Might take more than a ranger. There be things up on the pass road that'd test a pack o' rangers. There also be more inns in Midvale than good sense. Why should you want lodgin' in the Watch barrack?"

"Because I dislike carrying saddle, trappings, and barding to my chamber to keep them safe. And even then there's no warrant for their safety. Do you have a bed for me and stable for my horse or not?"

"How long do you plan to stay?"

"Of what do you suspicion me, Sheriff? I am a King's Ranger, trained at the King's Arms Academy under Rusker and Santon, Academy Masters, sponsored by Captain Dannel of Lake and Raylon of Watling of the Latonia City Guard, all of whom function, I'm certain, by the hand of King Laton. I've not come to reduce the population of your town by stacking heads in the marketplace! I've not come here to be a problem to anyone!"

The sheriff gave no reaction; his voice was the same level tone. "This be a time when all strangers are suspicioned. The road be near closed by beasts and brigands. You might be a armsman gone bad, for all I know, on your way to join with them outlaws."

"And I might be the king's nephew on a mission to investigate sheriffs, too."

The sheriff shook his head. "No, you be too bright." He seemed to be pondering something for a moment. "Are you without a copper?"

"I told you why I disliked inns. It seems our suspicions of strangers are similar."

"Um-m . . . well, I'd hate to have to haul around the gear for that great beast myself." With a wave that indicated a stairway to a second-story gallery, he said, "There be beds up there for wandering mercenaries under the Charter o' the Vales. That is, if you be truly in the service o' the king."

"I bear no warrant to that. I am under no contract, but I have sworn myself to the king's service if needed."

"Um-m . . . Someone'll show you the stable an' the bath. 'Tis but lodging, you know. The Sign o' the Blue

Boar gives fine vittles an' drink. It be on Top Street, at the brow o' the hill. You can take the Sixty-Six Steps through that rear gate." He turned and shouted. "Burkes!"

An old, raw slab of a man, who seemed to have some lapse between thought and action, came to an archway and peered out. "Yarsar?"

"Take care o' this young man."

Burkes bobbed his head and limped toward them. The sheriff turned back to scowl at the horse.

"You ever fight that mammoth great thing?"

"Once."

"Weren't he hard to control?"

"No . . . I found that if you get his head pointed in the right direction, the rest of him manages to follow."

The sheriff nodded. "Like a rock rollin' downhill, I imagine. I be Lukus Gaskin, Lord's Sheriff of Midvale."

Keven returned the nod, smiling to himself. For all the brash and bark, there was a likeable quality in the man. He was much like Rusker at the academy.

"How long have you been sheriff?"

The normal scowl deepened. "Is that some information you can't live without?"

"Just curious. You . . . aren't quite what I've seen of higher-level law officials."

"Not noble enough, hah?"

"I didn't say that."

"But that's what the question was; I heared it afore." He faced Keven squarely. "I be named Sheriff o' Midvale Town by Lord Damon th' Eighth some eighteen year ago—that be our present Lord Damon's father. He wanted somebody to uphold his law in his town, an' bein' o' the proper birth had nothin' t' do with it. I was the Commander o' th' Watch then. The sheriff at th' time . . . well, he sort o' done things his own way."

"What happened to him?"

"He was called to th' castle . . . an' ne'er came out." He nodded firmly. "What the Lord Damon say the law to be, thet be the law! It be fair law an' just, an' it be true applied."

"Then you'd been in the Watch a long time to be commander."

"Some twenty year. Afore that, I was conscripted for the King's Arms to fight in that mess with the Southeasters at Kalendai. Came out a sergeant."

Keven studied the sheriff anew; his estimation of the man had raised several levels. That "mess" with the Southeasters at Kalendai was a major study at the academy.

"Anythin' else I can help you with?" There was an edge of sarcasm in the sheriff's voice.

"That's more than enough," Keven said, nodding.

"I know!" With a grunt punctuating the end of that statement, the sheriff wheeled and strode away, back straight, boot heels pounding on the flagstones, hands hooked and seemingly ready for weapons. "Bestian!" he roared.

A voice called from somewhere. "Who?"

"Bestian! I want him in my room! Now! I want t' know 'bout them three swaggart fools that him an' Wicket arrested a few days ago!"

* * * * *

The Sign of the Blue Boar was a large, rambling old inn, shouldering over its neighbors on the hillcrest. Under steep slate roofs, the upper stories were cracked plaster and dark, hewn beams overhanging a stone-block first floor. Small multipaned windows of wrinkled glass were ranked along the sides, and a heavy, oil-dark oak door stood open to the street.

The big commonroom was already filling with celebrants

of the day's end, raucous with good cheer. The room was warm with the glow of many hanging lanterns and four screened fireplaces, and redolent with flowing ale and the gathering of bodies.

"Ah'll tell yew lads sumthin', the day'll nar come mornin' when John Falen kin put *me* down! Ah'll forge 'im a new nose, I will!"

"Thet damn wagon ain' been right since th' day Li'l Jack put 'er astride th' lower wall."

"Thet be the same Li'l Jack whut fathered Enid Parn's boy an' then pumped up Arly Barr's two girls?"

"Be the same!"

"Venturesome, ain' he?"

". . . so this tinker says to the maid . . ."

". . . tell yew true, if th' trade don' roll soon, thar'll be a great abundance o' folk with narthin' t' do but listen to their bellies growl."

". . . bandits and beasties, that's all we hear 'bout!"

Keven took an empty table in a corner far to the rear, where windows overlooked the gabled roofs of the town below. He was beginning to relax, at least as much as he ever was able to relax. Horse was stabled, grained, and curried; his room at the Watch barrack was clean and secure; he was bathed for the first time in much too long, and in clean clothes and his spare, dry boots; his travel clothes were washed and hanging to dry; it was as close to comfort as a man could want. And—the realization was still a shock whenever he thought of it—there was over twenty thousand goldworth in gems sewn into his cloak and clothing. But it had been goldworth bloody earned. . . .

He spun away from *that* memory; the demon nearly got him that time.

The twenty thousand, though—that was worth some thought. He had never heard of that amount before, much less called it his own. His father had always transacted the business of cargo, and he had seen little of the actual sale of the . . . *Crester.* It still hurt to even think of the name. Sergeant Raylon had handled the disposal of ship and cargo and then had seen to the security of the gold. For himself, he had felt a strange antipathy for that money; it seemed to represent his life and his parents, all reduced to a sum. He had used it to buy his contract from the academy, and he had armed himself well. He had left presents for Rusker and Santon, Captain Dannel and Raylon, and, after too much pondering, had finally rid himself of the balance by giving it to a holy man of the god Marin who ran a home and kitchen for beached, crippled, and aged seamen. He had left Latonia riding in a freight cart with but two silvers in his purse.

In the Northeast Kingdom, Keven was well reminded that the image of the god of Fate and Fortune was two-faced. His joining with a venturesome party had resulted in more gold than they could carry away, but it had also resulted in . . .

And he could not stop it—the memory overwhelmed him again. He had relived it so much that it was like a play.

The pitch-black corridors were like tunnels through the night. He remembered the dank walls and the fetid reek of the place. He remembered how he had been sipping steadily at his wineskin, confident in his abilities to cope with anything, ignoring the suggestions of the others to stay alert. He was fresh from the Arms Academy and a freeranger; he didn't need to be told how to behave. This was what he had been trained for, and he was good. Everyone said so.

Beside him, Gohn the Silent, the Blue Hill dwarf, stalked like some deadly dwarfen bear, shield and axe at the ready. Their shadows loomed before them, cast by the single flickering lantern held aloft by Pola, the quiet woman slipping along behind. As they approached an intersection, a black archway carved in the stone to their left, Gohn halted and motioned questioningly with his axe toward the dark opening. Keven nodded. He meant to indicate for Gohn to stand clear, intending to slash blindly around the corner with his sword in case someone, or something, was hiding in wait there—it had been that kind of place—but there was no time. He was too slow with his sword, too benumbed by wine.

There was an enraged roar, a huge shape rushed from the opening, and there was a flicker of a huge sword falling toward him. He tried to wheel away, shield rising to the blow, knowing it was too late. But the impact never came. There was a savage clash of arms, a grunt of surprise and pain. He was thrown backward to the floor, and there were footfalls as something large fled away into the dark.

And Gohn the Silent, his friend, lay dying, sprawled across Keven's legs. Keven had lurched against him as the dwarf leaped to intercept the weapon, throwing him off balance, and the great sword had cleaved him from shoulder to brisket. Even then he said not a word, only looking at Keven with sadness and a wry smile and a final small shake of his head.

Keven carried that scene with him like the drag of an anchor chain around his heart. And lest that weight were not enough to drag him down, there were the words of Pola, who asked quietly after Gohn was dead, "More wine, Keven?"

* * * * *

He wrenched himself back to the present with a savage grinding of teeth. So now he had a giant horse and riches to carry him west. What more could he ask?

Some peace?

The thick lamb stew came steaming hot in a glazed bowl. There was a generous cut of fresh dark bread, a bowl of butter, sharp cheese, and a pewter tankard foaming over with good ale, all served neatly, without spilling, by a pretty girl in a clean blue dirndl. She even wore shoes, he noted.

"Thank you," he said, smiling, and was rewarded with a quick grin and a pert curtsy.

Saucy wench, he thought, and then he had to stifle a sudden laugh. That was one of old Rusker's sayings: "I don' know why I waste my days tryin' to teach the finer points of fightin' to a litter of stable pups like the lot o' you! All you'll ever do is sword-swagger 'round an' get your lance bent by some saucy wench with no more weapons than a sidelong eye an' a hidden treasure."

He took his spoon from an inner pocket, another memory of the academy. It was hard silver, with the handle shaped like a tall torch. It was sort of a graduation award, paid for, it was rumored, by Rusker himself.

"Now every time you boys load your faces, consider what you are—or at least what you're *supposed* to be, what we *tried* to make o' you. Don' lose it!"

He ate. And let his memory wander through the academy.

So many had failed, sliding away to some meaningless duty in some meaningless post on the far, ragged edge of nowhere. Some were superb swordsmen but failed because of an abysmal lack of anything suggesting thought. Of those who stayed—"survived" was a better word—there were none he'd felt close to. Many were nobility with a born understanding and acceptance of upholding tradition, knowing it was their right and obligation. Others were sons of merchants. "Bought-ins," they were called, striving under a drive of their own, or of their father's, working in a quiet rage and a fear of failing. They were all aliens to him. Landsmen. Or, more likely, he was the alien.

"The Terrible Talent," they called him. The "Half-staff Executioner." "Keven the Killer." They had called him a lot of things he should as well forget. But somehow he still missed the academy. At least there, even without friends, he hadn't been so . . .

Alone?

He tore himself away from that thought, too. To the hells with it! At least he had been fortunate enough to be able to buy his contract; those unable to were most likely on the eastern border now, trading arrows and blades in the troubles blazing there. And why hadn't he ventured to that combat, too? The king paid mercenaries very well to fight on that far frontier. It was what he was trained for.

Too independent?

The academy. Rusker: *"Ya be too damn much a loner, lad! This were supposed to be a group exercise! Did ya miss that part? Did ya notice that there was others with ya when ya started out? It were about goin' in a group against that other group so's to learn group cooperation! That don' mean ya go prancin' off by yerself to play at bein' King's Hero!"*

Keven, embarrassed: *"We won the exercise."*

Rusker, shouting from barely a finger's width away: *"I don' care a pinch o' shit worth if ya took the king's castle an' captured the queen's scantlin's! When I by-the-gods tell ya it be a by-the-gods group exercise, then I by-the-gods expect it to be! Ya be just sharper'n a Beldian blade alone, Keven, but in a group ya be not worth a smithy's fart!"*

Even in the burn of recall, he had to admit it was partly true. He did not like being led, he did not want to lead, and he did not want anyone in his way. "Trust," he had once heard someone say, "is a currency better acquired than spent." He was not exactly sure what that meant, but it had a solemn, meaningful sound. He was a small craft in a big sea, and his voyage was entirely up to him; maybe that's what it meant.

So here he was at a mooring. The academy intruded so

much into his thoughts because it was one of the few good moorings he had in the past—no, not the academy itself, especially. It was Rusker and Santon; he missed them.

"Ah, well," he mused to himself, remembering the academy saying again: "No matter whar ya go, thar ya be."

He lounged back against the wall in the corner with his ale and watched the sun leave the valley. It was murky to the north, with almost constant lightning flickers in dark clouds, playing wavering tricks through the uneven glass. The sunrise had been a bloody red that morning; "Red in the morning—forewarning," he remembered thinking. Well, he was under a roof now; let it rain. A peculiar shadow crept across the town below, as if cast by a great spear of the gods. He leaned close to the window and peered westward; it was the high peak called Castle Mountain, silhouetted against the sky like a broken black fang. Thunderheads bulked dark behind the whole range of the Macaab Mountains, storm gods rising to stalk the coming night. He settled back and glanced around the room. It was warm here and, considering the coming night, comfortable and secure. He listened to the laughter at a nearby table.

". . . so Billins says t' the cobbler, 'Can yew mend me boot while I waits?' An' the cobbler says t' him, 'Thet be the onliest damn way I *can* do it, yew fool!' "

The inn was filling up. He relaxed against his corner and called for more ale.

* * * * *

He frowned at the wiry, sour little man who leaned across the table opposite him; he had made the mistake earlier of saying there did not appear to be much excitement in Midvale. For the last hour, the fellow had been emptying Keven's pitchers and filling him with words, pointing out the error of that observation.

"Ex*cite*ment!" the scowling little crab snorted for the twentieth or fortieth time. He took a hasty gulp of Keven's ale, belched, and wiped the foam from his face with the palm of his hand.

"Ex*cite*ment, is it!"

Keven sighed. He glanced at the other two men at his table, and waved for another refill. That preface could only signal further tales of high adventure in the realms of Midvale. . . .

How Rob th' tanner's dog chased Hud th' butcher's cow right inta the upper pool of Mill River, whar she drownded like a stone.

How Jame th' cooper pulled out the caulkin' of Blinky Taggart's boat fer not payin' fer four barrels, an' the whole damn thing sunked halfway acrost the Sun-Runnin', an' Blinky rode one of them barrels down clear inta Outer Vale, an' how righteous mad he were when he got home the next day an' Jame tol' him that if it weren't fer that barrel, he'd be down there with his boat, an' Blinky threatened to tie a rock to him so's he could go down lookin' fer the boat.

How Pursy Biggins, called "Pursy Big-uns," ran sheer naked from Top Street all the way down to Pig Passage afore the Watch caught her, an' the sher'ff locked her up overnight fer peddlin' after curfew an' then gave the Watch pure hell 'cause they'd been runnin' an grinnin' along behind her since Baker Lane. Keven admitted that one caught his attention, but right after that came the story of how Will Lerkin would ofttimes pull his lower lip up over his nose an' lift the patch off his bad eye an' scare the piddlin' squats out of Jack Miller's dog.

Ah, there was excitement aplenty in Midvale!

Keven stifled a yawn and tried to keep his eyes focused on the little man. It wasn't easy; the warmth and the ale were beginning to work a sort of spell in him. The man aimed a crooked finger across the table. With one eye closed, he seemed to be sighting along it.

"Why, jest this last tenday," he continued, measuring out each word carefully, "they war a *be-serker* in town! Now, whut does yew think of *thet?*"

Keven considered him for a moment, wondering if he had dozed off and missed something.

"Well . . ." Keven shrugged. "Unusual, maybe, but not necessarily exciting."

"Hah! Shows whut *yew* know!" The man helped himself to another ale from Keven's pitcher.

"How do you know it was a berserker?" Keven asked. "I never saw one carrying a sign." In truth, he had never seen one at all, only heard the old warrior tales in the city. "Most people say there's no shus—*such* thing as 'serkers—*ber*serkers."

He shook his head and frowned. He was losing control of his tongue. That hadn't happened since . . . well, never mind when. He could remember if he really wanted to. Let's see, how many pitchers had there been now? Four of us here at the table, and most drinking from my pitcher, and—

"'Cause e'erybody say so!" The little man nodded, with a triumphant curl to his mouth. The other two men at the table nodded in agreement.

"'Cause everybody says what?" Keven asked, momentarily puzzled.

"Thet the be-serker were a be-serker! Pay attention!" The little man leaned across the table again and began measuring out the story with that bent finger as if he were counting words.

"This be-serker, he come up the Sun-Runnin' Road, same as yew. He come 'crost th' river in Limpy Lang's boat an' ne'er paid 'im a bent copper fer the ferry! Right up through town he come, as smug as a new rooster. Right up Sixty-Six Steps out here, stridin' along like he owned the

whole damn kingdom, an' the town in partic'lar. An'
Limpy doin' his best to keep up an' a-yellin' thet the man
war a thief, an' a few other things, too, an' him nar e'en takin' note of Limpy an' half the town follerin' along. True
arr'gant, he war, an' ugly. Yew could see it in his eye. An'
big! He war bigger'n us four here stacked together. Woulda
dressed out at close to twenty stone!"

"Was he armed?" Keven asked. He had to admit his interest was momentarily caught by the tale of an armsman.

"Armed!" The little man's eyebrows shot nearly to his
hairline. "I'd say *some!* Full plate, he wore! Had a shield
slang o'er his shoulder the size of a shed door. Had a sword
big 'nough to kill beeves with. All beat up 'twas, too, his
armor. Seen some fightin', he had." He nodded wisely.
"He certain carried hisself like he knowed which end of the
sword did the struttin' an' which end did the guttin'."

A great yawn overtook Keven. Not wanting to insult the
little bore, he asked, "So what happened?"

"Stop fallin' asleep an' I tell yew! So he gets up here to
where Top Street crosses, an' he turn west. Thar war a
goodly throng of folks gatherin', whut with Limpy a-yellin'
alongside an' a-wavin' his arms, an' a bunch of folks
laughin' an' urgin' him on. So then, of a sudden, this here
be-serker, he wheels aroun' to Limpy an' he says, 'Begone,
ye scummy piglet!' an' he reach out with one hand an'
snatch ol' Limpy right off the cobbles by his neck! One
hand! Gods be me witness! Picked ol' Limpy right up! Folks
thet war facin' the brute say his eyes war gettin' all wide an'
red, an' he war grinnin' in a most monstrous way! An' then
he take Limpy in thet hand, wheels hisself 'round an' jest
pitched him right inta the middle of the crowd thet war follerin' up Sixty-Six Steps. Wull, 'twar like a clean swipe in a
game of bowls. Folks went tumblin' down them steps arse-
o'er-tophair in all directions."

Keven nodded to show some minor interest, but his

thoughts were adrift. He would welcome an opportunity to meet an overbearing ass like that. Now *that* would be rousing. Let's see, what would be an interesting way to open conversation? He could slap the dolt across the helmet with the flat of a blade and say, "Now that I have your full attention, you bitch whelp, how about facing someone you can't throw."

That would probably get the match off to a stirring start.

The little man was still narrating. ". . . so this be-serker meets ol' Kelt th' Scribe on Top Street."

At this, the other two men, and three more who had wandered up to listen, chuckled and nudged each other; apparently this was their favorite part. The storyteller was pure melodrama now.

"Now, it be no twist o' the truth to say thet ol' Kelt be one of the most self-stuck, sharp-mouthed, miserable ol' wolf baits thet e'er come out in the daylight. Meaner'n a bungshot bear an' uglier'n a mud witch, so cross-eyed he can nar count sheep, an' so nasty thet he has to know ev'rybody's workin's. Just as cranky as a new rope."

Keven nodded again. Yes, new ropes were hard to handle. He could remember that. On the *Crester*, they would soak a rope until . . .

"So ol' Kelt gets aimed in on this be-serker with his eyes glarin' off both directions at once, an' he says, 'Wull!' truly loud an' nasty. 'Whut be *yer* business in Midvale?' "

His voice lowered dramatically.

"Thet be-serker, he ne'er e'en broke stride. He hardly e'en leant o'er. He just scooped ol' Kelt right up in passin' like he war narthin' more'n a ugly pup, an' then he spun 'round an' flang him clean up onta Edden th'Tinker's second-story roof! Slicker'n a trout, he did thet! No more effort'n pissin' out a window!" He bobbed his head for emphasis.

"Wull, now, it jest happened thet they war a trio of

dwarfs standin' thar at th' tinker's counter, an' they jest
kind of leant out from under the shutter an' watched ol'
Kelt pass o'er like he war some kind of strange bird they nar
seen afore. Thet be-serker saw ol' Kelt clingin' to thet roof
like a spider, an' he begun to laugh."

Keven found himself nodding once again, agreeing with
himself that the so-called berserker was in burning need of
an education. Now if he had been there, he could have . . .
well, something.

"Them dwarfs war scowlin' at thet be-serker like they
would enjoy seein' jest how far they'd have to mine his
head afore they hit brain, when ol' Kelt finally come off the
roof. He'd been a-clawin' an' a-pawin' up thar, an' he
brung off a few big slates with him. He hit thet shop shutter, broke the prop, an' it come down on this one dwarf's
head like he war slammed in a door. A slate near took a ear
off'n 'nother dwarf—one Otter Oaktree—an' t' other—
big fer a dwarf, one Barley Granitledge—he took a big slate
right flat 'cross the top of his head, an' it drove him right to
his knees. Sort of like watchin' a post hammered inta the
ground with a griddle!

"Thet be-serker, he war laughin' now like a sick wolf.
Now, I don' know if'n yew know 'bout dwarfs or nar, but
hurtin' one be absolute bad fortune, an' laughin' at one be
some worser, an' when the two happen together . . . wull, a
normal man would think of packin' up ev'rythin' he might
need in the deepest hell."

Keven looked deep inside for a quick moment. Yes, he
knew about dwarfs. . . .

"Thet Otter Oaktree, he took his hand off'n his ear, an'
he marveled at it like he could nar believe all thet blood war
his'n, an' then he reach behind him, up under that big
leather yoke thing they wear, an' he drag out the ugliest
damn double-bitted axe yew e'er seen! The one with his
head slammed in the shutter—one Helm of Hawk Ridge—

he come flailin' out of thar like he war makin' kindlin', an' he sheer tore the edge plank right off thet shutter! Gods' oath! With his bare hands! A good span-an'-a-half of solid oak three fingers thick!

"Thet Barley Granitledge, he come up off'n the street with a cobble in each hand, an' them be big cobbles 'long Top Street! Bigger'n a man's head! An' he jest simple tore 'em right out of the street by they tops! An' he had a most dreadful look on his face.

"Thet crowd come unstuck then, an' they war some hard jammin' to give room 'round all this, an' them three dwarfs, they come at thet be-serker!

"Wull, he nar seen 'em a'tail. He had his head back, still bayin' at the sky like some fool dog, when Barley Granitledge flang one of them cobbles right at his head. It took thet be-serker true under the jaw, like from a catapult. His teeth cracked together like two rocks slammin', his head war whanged back, an' I swear, his helmet war the first part of him to hit the street! Dust flew outta his armor like a high wind through a mill!

"After the echoes died off, it war so quiet yew could of heared a gnat fart. Them dwarfs walked o'er—an' thet be-serker be layin' thar stiffer'n a dead carp, an' ol' Garth—he talks some Dwarfish—said they war discussin' choppin' off the head an' usin' it t' scare bears."

The little man finally stopped, gazing at the scarred tabletop and shaking his head in a vague, bemused way. Keven was still thinking about dwarfs . . . thinking of Gohn the Silent, silent now forever. Silent because—

"Well? . . ." Keven frowned, tearing himself away from that thought. "Wha' happened?"

"Oh, the Watch come 'bout then an' hauled th' beserker off. They war some grumpy 'bout it all at first, sayin' thet fightin' in the street war 'nough to get ev'rybody jailed, but thet Barley Granitledge war still scowlin' an' tossin' thet spare cobble up an' down in one hand like it war narthin' but a walnut. An' them dwarfs, they jest fit them cobbles right back inta the street so slick yew can nar tell which they war now. An' they fixed up the tinker's shutter better'n e'er war afore. Ev'rybody agreed they done jest fine an' bought 'em beer, an' ev'rybody war happy. 'Cept ol' Kelt, o' course. He war some outstandin' vicious fer a while."

He cackled, sighed, and looked pointedly at the empty pitcher. Keven signaled for another refill; the tale was probably worth that much. Several men were lounging at the table now. One, a big, weedy man with gangling arms, who had seated himself and began pouring down Keven's ale like a man filling a barrel, spoke in a morbid tone.

"That berserker were on his way t' join up with them bandits on the pass."

The storyteller snorted. "Now, how do yew know thet, Arnold? He pass the day with yew?"

"Watchman Luker say so."

"Luker don' know his arse from a hole in the snow! His mind be wanderin' like a lost puppy ever since he survived thet awful attack on the pass."

"Well, bandits is bandits, ain' they? An' they still be on the mountain! Vale Guard could nar open the pass this spring. They war a fearful fight."

Keven was turning from one to another, trying to follow the conversation about the bandits and the pass, but the words and the faces seemed all the same. Another man spoke, pulling the new pitcher over and helping himself.

"They've had a sword on the throat of this town for too long. It nar be worth a chicken's ear to get over Castle Pass, an' last year it war North Pass, too."

Another hand reached for Keven's pitcher and lowered it by half. Keven refilled his own tankard and caught the serving maid's attention again. There was something he wanted to ask . . . what was it?

"How . . . far's it to this Castle Pass?" he asked.

"It be 'bout nine mile to the top," one said. "Three league, if yew wants to call it thet way."

"So . . . how d'ya get to this Cashle—*Castle* Pass?" Keven asked. His tongue was failing again.

A face like a broken axe squinted one pale eye over another one of those aimed fingers.

"Now . . . the Road West . . ." he said slowly and importantly, "heads west from here." The little man nodded wisely, leaned back, and folded his arms.

Keven waited, then finally raised a mock toast. "There's a right-damn healthy chance I could've figured that out by myself."

The man scowled at him. "I war just tellin' ye thet the road go—"

Another broke in. "Lewy here couldna explain how t' find his left boot. Thar be two way to the west. Yew can head out the Road West an' over Castle Pass, or yew can go by way o' North Pass. Thet be a long hard way 'round t' get to the Palan, an' it be nar too safe lately neither."

"Yar," one said, nodding. "Thar be bandits an' what-all up on the North Pass, too. Thar be nar road safe nar more."

"Caravan of slavers come over North Pass without nar troubles."

"Well, I 'magine yew could take a load of cow dung o'er, too. Thet don' mean narthin'!"

"An' the ground been shakin' lately, too," another added in a low, moody voice. "'Tis the dragon stirrin' under the mount'n."

"Wull . . ." Another rubbed his face with a grizzled hand. "I be nar sayin' if 'tis a dragon, but when the ground shakes, 'tis nar for good, I know that. Me mother always said 'twas a portent, and that's what I think, too. 'Tis a bad sign."

"Well, mark yew my words," another offered, "there be somethin' more afoot in them mountains than a few fool bandits."

Heads nodded solemnly.

"Yar, they be too many things now told t' be narthin' but ugly tales fer t' scare childers."

Keven poured himself another ale and tried to pay attention. This talk of dragons and the shaking of the earth was something worth consideration. He searched for the words and found them. "Such's what?" he asked.

The men glanced at each other.

"Wull . . ." one muttered, "some things be better nar mentioned."

"Oh, fer Great Pandra's pud an' paps, Ed'ard!" another growled. "Yew be numb as a newt! Talkin' 'bout things are nar goin' to make 'em crawl through the door!"

Edward scowled into his ale. "Jest the same . . ."

"Ed be right! It be a danger t' call a thing by its name!"

"Them things got nar name! They be from the mount'n."

"Thet's right! 'Member whut them folk said last fall? Thet caravan thet got hit on North Pass? They could nar tell whut them beast things war!"

"Wull, they truly tried, di'n't they? They war namin' off all sorts of things of the dark side of fay."

"Dark side of fay be gone in the Chaos. Thar be nar left." The speaker glared at the gloomy one who had mentioned a dragon. "An' thar be nar dragons, neither! Be nar such thing!"

A big man snorted. "Wull, I nar seen a one-legged elf, but thet don' mean they nar be any! Thar be plenty of dark things in the Macaabs besides bandits, an' there be 'nough o' them!"

There was heavy silence at the table, and it seemed no one wanted to meet another's eyes. Keven frowned into his ale for a moment, then said, "Ev'rywhere I've been there're tales of things from dark shide—dark *side* of fay."

After an expectant waiting, one spoke. "So?"

"Well . . ." Kevin couldn't seem to get his thoughts in order to say what he wanted to say . . . and what was it he was going to say, anyway?

"Just seems t' me . . . that some of those things . . . are prob'ly true."

History, that was it! Histories of the wars; he had never liked that study. But there was a point to be made here somewhere, if he could only find it. He spoke slowly and carefully, choosing the words painstakingly to avoid the slurring that was getting in the way of the point he was trying to make.

"If there were creatures an' beasts an' things of the dark side back then, it's . . . reasonable to think there still are." There! That's what he wanted to say. Close, anyway.

"They war all kilt off in the Chaos," said one.

"Th' hell they war!" said another.

"Wait . . ." Keven said.

"The dark side o' fay be allus thar!" affirmed another. "It cannar be kilt off; it just *be*."

"Ol' granny tales!"

"Granny tales, me arse!"

"Wait!" Keven said again. "There's more . . ."

"Dob be right! Th'dark side be—"

"No dark side of fay," Keven asserted, finally getting a grip on the elusive thought. "No good side, either. Only fay. S'neither good or bad. Jusht is. Learned that in the academy."

"But the dark side—"

"The dark side—"

It all seemed to dissolve into a rain of sound, like the rain on the windows now, running together in streamlets. There was something more he wanted to say, but it was another drop in the rain lost in the flow. His pitcher was empty again. He frowned at it; how did that happen so fast? Didn't anyone else buy ale in this tavern? The heavy man's pitcher was empty, too. They contemplated each other, their pitchers, then signaled the serving maid together. She brought three pitchers; someone else was buying, too? Good!

He became lost in the swirl of words, when a familiar, sarcastic voice seemed to target him. Something about ". . . and just look at him, the great ranger, fighting sobriety and losing."

He focused his eyes on the three men who were standing at the end of the table, and the sneering image of Bracken, the under-officer of the Watch, blurred into view. Keven was aware of the sudden silence in the room.

"Want to match me now, Ranger?" Bracken said, smiling. Keven regarded the arrogant man for a moment. He could feel his attention coming into focus, his mind and body coming alert. This was something he understood. Again he chose his words and his enunciation as carefully as he could.

"Last time . . . you lost your sword, Bracken. This time you might lose somethin' you can really use. Feel like it?"

Bracken grinned at him, then laughed. He motioned to the two others with him and moved away. The men at the table snickered. Two slapped Keven on the back. Someone signaled the serving maid for more ale.

Keven leaned back in his chair and let a sour, sullen mood overcome him. Ever since the Northeast Kingdom, there seemed to be swaggart asses who wanted trouble. What was curious is that this always seemed to happen when he was drinking, just when he was in a temper to provide the contention they apparently were seeking.

And the serving maid brought a few more ales.

* * * * *

He reeled from the tavern into the night and directly into the path of a slight, shadowy figure. The small man opened the shutter of a shielded lantern and raised it to examine him.

"Keven of Kingsend?"

The voice was an abrupt baritone. Shielding his eyes, Keven could see that it was a littler in the uniform of the Town Watch. If another small figure hadn't moved from the shadows, he probably would have overlooked it.

"Am I . . . that famey . . . famous already?" Keven asked in an insolent manner. "Really some . . . some kinda . . ." He couldn't find the word he wanted. It probably didn't make any difference anyway.

"The sheriff has noted you as an outstanding stranger."

The voice was surprisingly deep for such a diminutive body; he came hardly above Keven's waist.

"I am Bestian Stonewall Tasker," he continued, "of the Tasker Hill Taskers of Northshire. I am a subcommander of the Watch."

"'Bout th'right size for a subcommander, I'd say."

The other littler approached. "And I am Wicket," he said, grinning up at Keven and then at Bestian. "We meet some big ones on patrol, don't we?"

Keven frowned from one to the other; they had the well-set bodies of full-grown adults but in six-year-old proportions, and with faces that had somehow matured to those of young men in their mid-twenties. They wore efficient-looking shortswords on their left hips.

"That's right, sir," Wicket said, nodding. "No need to look back and forth. There are really two of us."

Keven laughed. The one called Bestian seemed to stiffen and his voice sharpened.

"You have something against the small people?"

"No, not a'tall." Keven shook his head and learned that was a bad idea; the whole street started whirling. He leaned back against the wall of the inn to keep from reeling.

"There's . . . good friend of my father," he said. "Tanner Applehill. He's . . . small."

"And is he still?"

"Guess so . . ."

"Then he must be a littler. You think we can't fight?"

"O' course y' can." He was beginning to feel silly. The idea of having trouble with two littlers was ridiculous.

"Y' can fight all y' want to."

Bestian studied him for a long moment, intent brown eyes steady, yet with a sparkle of something unsaid; it appeared to be a touch of humor. Dark brown hair curled from beneath his Watch helmet.

"Take a care, Keven of Kingsend. We must continue our patrol. Don't come to harm."

They turned and strolled away.

"Harm comes lookin' f' me," Keven muttered. He scowled one way, then the other, trying to remember the direction of the barrack. It was lost. Or he was lost. Well . . . any direction was better than standing here. He turned a corner and collided with a figure.

"Watch yer path, yew sodden stonewit!" it bellowed and flung a wild fist that grazed the side of Keven's head. Keven roared, reached out, and lifted the man completely off the ground. The surge of rage brought out his words clearly: "I'm in just a mood for some dung lump like you!"

He hurled the man against the wall of the inn, and was in the act of picking him up for another throw when he lost his balance and staggered. He was dimly aware of motion behind him. Another man. Something struck him hard across the shoulder. He tried to turn but lurched instead. He had a glimpse of a dark figure swinging a cudgel. There was a bright crash of light in his head, and he was surprised to find he was on his hands and knees. He was certain he was trying to rise, but nothing seemed to be happening. There was a scurry of movement around him, the sounds of blows and voices, and someone calling gleefully. It was the littler called Wicket.

"I got this one, Best. You need some help with yours?"

There was an answering laugh. "Well, mine was bigger. How's that ranger?"

Keven felt hands exploring him.

"He's alive."

* * * * *

The sheriff contemplated Keven across a cluttered table. With brittle blue, humorless eyes under a deeply etched frown, he offered the impression that he had spent entirely too much of his life looking upon displeasing things. Keven sprawled in a chair, arms crossed, regarding the sheriff with his own frown in place. In the hard light of dawn, he was in no mood for conversation. His shoulder hurt from the blow, his head ached from both the attack and from the surly dregs of last night's ale, and there was some unfinished dispute in his stomach. The sheriff's voice was an irksome, bitter drone.

". . . and so this mighty ranger—one o' the king's best, so we are told—starts a fight an' gets hisself cudgeled down on the street by a pair o' night crawlers, then lugged home by two o' my Watch littlers who just happened to be on patrol at the right place an' time. I calls that luck overcomin' foolishment."

Keven made no response.

"Whether you say yar-nar, ranger," the sheriff went on, "I get the itch that you be trouble just waitin' to happen. We got 'nough trouble in this valley already."

Keven was eager to change the path of conversation.

"Oh, yes," he said. "Trouble is all I've heard about here. Evil events! Dark doings! Cursed mountains and monsters! Bandits this and bandits that! Bandits here and and bandits there! I'm filled to the gullet with talk of beasts and bandits! How is it that a few brigands in the mountains have the whole trade road closed and half the valley afraid to venture beyond their gates?"

Weather wrinkles tightened around the sheriff's eyes. Again they traded frowns.

"I don't understand the problem," Keven went on. "Bandits are everywhere in the land. Every road has its bandits, just like it has fallen limbs, rocks, and muddy spots. What's a few more in the mountains? When they get too bothersome, then people get together and do something about it. But not here! No! Here, everybody just talks. I've never heard of brigands falling under an attack of talk."

The sheriff leaned back in his chair and regarded Keven for a long time. He finally took a deep breath and rose abruptly.

"We'll go get somethin' to eat, an' I'll tell you 'bout our bandits. If you're not int'rested, I'll eat an' tell you anyhow."

*   *   *   *   *

The sheriff told him.

It was nothing uncommon to have bandits ranging through the Vales and along the trade road—it was a rich road for those disposed to reap the harvest of other men's labors—and traders traveled armed for just such attempts. Bandits were indeed a routine hazard of travel, but about three years ago there had been an abrupt increase in the number of robberies on the road over Castle Pass. Lone travelers at first, then larger parties and pack trains, the attackers always outnumbering their victims. A company of

Vale Guard combed the pass; they found nothing.

The problem grew. Large, well-armed parties and small caravans were raided, often in the middle of sudden storms. The attacks were savage and, where earlier the bandits had been satisfied with what valuables they could loot, lives were now taken needlessly. As if for sport, defenseless people were struck down, men tied to wagons for bow practice, women raped and carried off, children taken, some to be found later in slave caravans with their tongues cut out.

Enraged, Lord Damon and Lord Jeth of the Palan East sent companies of Guard over Castle Pass from both sides. At first, as before, they found nothing—but then, as the patrols continued to search, an entire company of ten mounted Palan Guard was attacked and slain. The next caravan headed west, escorted by fifteen mounted Vale Guard, was ambushed. A single survivor, hidden under a wrecked wagon, told of a sudden mountain storm and the animals, including the guard mounts, going mad with fear and creating chaos before the attack even came.

Castle Pass was eventually abandoned, and trade and travel shifted north, taking the much longer and rougher road over North Pass. But last year the same had begun there as well.

* * * * *

Keven mopped the bowl of his venison pie with a piece of dark bread. "It still strikes me more than moderately strange, Sheriff, that a band of brigands holds the whole trade road hostage. Have you no soldiers?"

"*I* have no soldiers. My responsibility is with the town and the Town Watch, and where the village ends, so does the reach o' the Watch. The responsibility o' the Vales overall lies with Lord Damon, and his arm is the Vale Guard. It numbers some . . . oh, sixty or sixty-five men-at-arms now."

Keven frowned. "And sixty men cannot protect—"

"Ride escort for every caravan, packtrain, an' traveler between here an' the Palan? Get your boots on the ground, lad! That's a big country out there! Besides, it's been tried. Both from this end and from the Palan. There just not be 'nough men. I don' think you realize the amount o' trade that goes through here."

"Not much lately."

"An' does that have some special meaning?" the sheriff growled.

Keven ignored the question. "Is everything attacked? Big and small?"

The sheriff shook his head. "No, an' that's the halter on it. 'Bout a third o' the travel is hit, maybe more now, an' that's why some trade braves it. The odds be fair, an' the profits be better than fair. An' there be no regular drift to the raids, no pattern. Grain, hides, slaves—they hit anythin'. An' they that gets hit are—" he shook his head— "they're just gone! Hardly ever does anybody get out of it breathin', an' then it be by good fate if they do. The attackers are well armed an' seem to be well led. An' now there's talk of dark creatures an' . . . *magic* at work!" He spat out the word.

"Well . . ." Keven finished off the last of the bread, chewing thoughtfully. "I believe little in that—magic, I mean. I think it's an overrated art."

"Well, believe what you like, it nonetheless exist here an' there. What I *don'* believe is thet some itinerant mage be passin' his time raidin' trade in the mountains."

"Dark creatures, though . . ." Keven frowned thoughtfully into his ale for a moment. "That's another matter. There are such things. What happens in the winter? The passes are blocked. How do these bandits winter over?"

"Gods only know," the sheriff answered. "I suspect they slip down into the towns. Some to here an' to Mill Ford an' downriver, some over to the Palan. They true have the damned riches to go where they like! There were a few swaggarts in town last winter with too much to spend an' not 'nough to do. I wanted to talk heavily with 'em, but Lord Damon said no. He's a man whose fairness sometime get in the way o' justice."

"How about more Guard?" Keven made a vague gesture that seemed to take in the whole surroundings. "It seems to me this valley could raise more than sixty men."

"Time to train 'em, lad. Captain Mikel o' the Guard be an ol' soldier, an' he be not sendin' out lads that don' know their spears from their spit. There be prob'ly a hundred at drill now, an' they'll stay at drill till he be certain they be ready." He glared at his ale mug as if the last swallow had been sour. "Any year now, prob'ly," he added. The sheriff seemed to be fighting some small inner battle. "Captain Mikel be a true spike up the bung!"

"Are there no King's Arms available?"

The sheriff gave a disparaging snort. "A company o' forty-some King's Arms come laughin' an' scratchin' up the Sun-Runnin' Road two year ago in answer to Lord Damon's call. By Pandra's pud, they were a scrubby lot! Spent two days in town swillin' ale, then went staggerin' an' singin' up the pass an' got the sour piss pounded right out o' them. Some King's Arms! I could o' rounded up a better pack o' fools an' childers in Crossriver. Four or five o' the girls at Berkie's be more dangerous than that whole rabble."

"The best soldiers are in the east," Keven said.

"So we hear! We was told that 'the eastern troubles prevent the sending o' any more armsmen at this time.' " The sheriff spoke as if mimicking someone. "But I hear talk that the traders an' merchants o' Latonia are gettin' heated some. The loss o' a few golders here on the edge o' the kingdom don' mean spit down in Latonia, but the loss o' a copper there because o' it—now, that gets to be urgent. Traders say the merchants to the west are gettin' cranky, too. Someday the kingdoms of Latonia an' the Palan will do somethin' 'bout this—money moves the crown, you know—an' they'll prob'ly send armies in here to kill everythin' in the Macaab Mountains right down to the ground squirrels, but till then, it be our problem."

Keven drummed his fingers absently for a moment. "I heard a tale about a so-called berserker in town."

"Well," the sheriff snorted, "I don' know if he were a berserker or not. There weren't a lot o' berserkin' in him when I seen him. Big man. Brute mean. Had eyes like a pair o' little blueberries. 'Bout as much life to 'em, too. Locked him in overnight. Found he could get them eyes focused in the morn an' get one foot down in front o' the other, an' we escorted him out o' town. He wanted the Road West, up the pass. Prob'ly a mistake to let him go that way, but he'd find it sooner or later. Told him if I found him in town again actin' in a manner I didn't like, I was goin' to pound on him till I recognized somethin' I did like. He just blinked like a toad. Not a lot o' brain in there."

Keven couldn't help smiling. "I've heard berserkers don't respond well to that kind of talk."

The sheriff grunted. "I believe he were more stupid than berserker. The condition he were in that mornin', he couldn't 'a' hit the ground with his helmet. An' I'll tell you somethin' honest true—I didn't get appointed Lord's Sheriff o' Midvale by bein' shy o' trouble! No matter how angry it gets!" He leaned back and regarded Keven with a flinty stare. "So . . . what d'you think o' our li'l bandit problem now?"

Keven shrugged.

"I think I'm going to continue west as soon as the road is dry," he said.

"It be dangerous," the sheriff said, scowling.

"Danger and I are old companions," Keven replied. It was a statement he had heard Rusker use once, and it had impressed him. The sheriff blinked at him in momentary astonishment.

"I'll be a double-damned ring-tailed dung dog," he breathed. "If you don' top the pile! You be bare old enough t' piss over the toes o' your own boots, an' here you be makin' noises like some old warrior with more scars than brains." He glared across the table. "An' t' hell with the bandits, hah? 'King's service' don' count a dollop o' dung to you."

Something clenched inside Keven, but he spoke quietly. "I journey west, Sheriff. In spite of all the tales, I'm going over Castle Pass. If anything happens up there, it's up to those bandits I hear so much about. You can't use me here. What do you want me to do—charge up there alone and challenge them all? Raise a regiment? I'm not a soldier; I'm a sword."

"An' prob'ly better out o' town before you find more trouble and use that sword to butcher out some o' our citizens!"

"What business is it of yours if I want to travel west?"

"*Damn none!*"

* * * * *

The thing lurched through the dark night forest with peculiar, ponderous movements, as if there was simply too much massive muscle for its brain to control, yet it moved quietly. The soft brush of a branch pushed aside. The hushed rustle of old leaves, like a breeze in passing. Night sounds.

It could have been a man—it walked upright, with two arms, two legs, a trunk, a head—but the dark bulk was twice too large. The head was set directly on hunched shoulders, almost inset, it seemed. It wore no clothes.

It crouched in the hedgerow at the edge of the field and breathed the damp night air, nostrils quivering. It couldn't see the sheep yet, but it knew they were there—a rich, warm smell of life. And it knew they were nervous, rising to their feet and beginning to mill about, making low murmuring sounds. They could smell him, too. That wasn't good. The dogs would be alerted. The thing studied the object that hung around its neck on a small chain. The memory was clear; there were certain sounds to be made, the object held just so. There had been much practice, over and over, many times over. And the sheep would be calm then and unafraid, and the dogs would sleep. That was good. It had never been able to catch a sheep before without running it down, and sometimes the dogs had to be killed first.

It held the object just right, and after three attempts made the sounds just right, and the sheep were silent. They were lying down again. It moved from the hedgerow then, too quickly in its eagerness. A stick snapped underfoot, and it froze in midstride, but nothing gave alarm, not even a nasty, always suspicious goose. There wasn't a sound from the farmstead. The thing stalked into the small field and to the stone-walled paddock. The smell of the sheep was strong now and exciting, but it kept itself under control. There had been much practice with that, too.

Careful not to dislodge a stone, it clambered over the wall and let itself down into the paddock, pausing for a moment to remember.

Yes, it was to bring back as many sheep as it could carry.

That was puzzling—one sheep was all it needed—but the practice had been well learned. It picked up a sheep, the animal hanging limp, as if sound asleep. Another, and another. Grasping a hind leg of each, it slung them across its back. Three more in the other hand. It paused to peer around at the others. It wouldn't hurt to taste. And it would be another sheep, wouldn't it? Bring as many as it could? Yes, it remembered—bring as many as it could. It bent down and picked up another in its mouth. The taste of hot blood was nearly overwhelming, taking control, calling to old memories. Good blood! But another, newer memory came.

It was not to eat now. Later. Now it must bring back the sheep.

It swallowed the blood in its mouth, made a soft, muffled whimper at the taste, and crept away into the night.

Chapter Three

arly the next morning, Keven had the big horse saddled and laden before the murky red sun showed a finger's width above the eastern hills. The sheriff watched from a doorway across the barrack courtyard. Finishing the final adjustments, Keven slung his sword over his back and led the horse clopping across the flagstones toward the gate. Just inside the old, massive doors facing Cow Court, a man was doubled over with head, hands, and feet clamped in a pillory. The hands had been dyed red—a thief. Keven halted and turned to the sheriff.

"You've been busy this morning."

"Busy every morning," the sheriff grunted.

"I am in your debt, Good Sheriff, for the lodging and stabling."

"It come under the charter."

They considered each other for a moment. The sheriff scowled up at the sky.

"You headed for the pass?"

There seemed to be something in the sheriff's voice—more sarcasm?

"I think I'm capable of it."

"You think?" The sheriff gave a thin smile. "My Aunt Perky might think she's capable o' racin' a fast horse too, but she wins no wagers. 'Member what you said yourself: You be but a sword. There prob'ly be more than that up there."

Keven wryly grinned. "Why the concern, Sheriff?"

"Concern?" He made a gruff sound, something between a cough and a grunt. "'Tis no concern o' mine *what* you do!"

"Fare you well, Sheriff." He turned away to the gate.

"An' you, too, Freeranger Keven o' Kingsend!"

Sarcasm again? Damn sheriff, he thought. He's something like Rusker—cuts like a new sword. But one always knew what was behind Rusker's frowning front; the sheriff kept himself shadowed. Well, to hell with it! It was none of his concern, either!

He left the barrack and bought waybread and traveler's sausage that was hard enough to fell an ox. The old joke was that the sausage always made a passably good cudgel on a venturesome journey. He mounted and turned west. At the old west gate, an old man reached for the bridle.

"Rowan twigs for the warding of spells!" he cried. "Alder and amber."

Keven reined aside and passed him by; whatever was before him on the road, he doubted that alder, amber, and rowan twigs would be of much use.

The Road West traveled the shallow Mad River Valley. Horse had been well fed and over-rested; he stamped his huge hooves with each step and tossed his head impatiently, snorting when Keven reined tighter.

"Calm yourself, Horse! Don't be so fretful. You're going to need something left to climb that."

He was gazing ahead at the soaring, ragged peak of Castle Mountain. Rising fully a half-league into the sky, it dominated the Vales like some incredible castle of giants.

He could see some vague lines of the road scratched along the rocky lower slopes leading to where the sharp notch on the north side marked the pass. Cloud remnants tore from the upper ramparts and swept swiftly out over the Vales.

On a low rise of open land, he passed a small roadside shrine. It had been debased and desecrated, the intricately carved symbols chipped and sundered by what must have been hammer blows. Filth was smeared and splattered across its face, as if someone had stood in the road and hurled handfuls of manure. He felt an unreasoning rage welling up within him. While but passingly religious himself, this sort of mindless behavior was the conduct of animals. He reined back and dismounted. Using bunches of grass dampened in a roadside pool, he cleaned the filth away as best as he could. He didn't know which god's shrine it was; he couldn't read the odd symbols.

A rickety farm wain drawn by an ancient, angular ox creaked and wobbled past, accompanied by a hunched man who threw him furtive, frightened looks and tried to switch the old beast into a faster pace. Keven nodded to him.

"A good day to you, Landsman."

There was no reply, only a harder laying on of the switch and a final fearful glance over the shoulder.

The valley narrowed. A gusty breeze was beginning to bend the treetops along the ridges, and gloomy cloud shadows scudded swiftly, like hard-riding scouts of darkness. Clearings and fields were becoming infrequent and smaller, given over to weeds and brambles, the huts of cotters more wretched than those closer to town. Many were abandoned to the slow advance of forest. There was evidence of old woodcutters' work—an old, deserted cabin and charcoal kiln—then nothing but heavy forest on the rising hills.

Over a gentle hillcrest, the road broke into a sudden and surprisingly well-kept field sloping down to a sparkling river. For a moment, he thought it was the Mad River again, but it was smaller and brighter. Parallel lines of birches, like uniformed guards, marked the roadway to where a large stone bridge arched above the river. Beyond the bridge, the land rose again to fields. A sprawling log and half-timbered building stood there beside the road. Outbuildings, fences, two cows, a horse, goats, and hens were scattered behind. It appeared to be a small wayside inn, but the yard was grassed over and showed little recent use.

"Must be the Crystal River and the First Bridge," he commented to the horse. "Remember the directions?"

The horse snorted as they started down.

"That's right. I forgot—you weren't there."

He studied the inn as he approached. A slim figure came to the door as he passed. At first he thought it was a girl dressed as a boy.

"A good day to you," Keven called.

"And to you." It seemed the voice of a young man. "Do you journey the road to the pass?"

"I do."

A slight frown marked the sharp, young face. "I have heard nothing untoward lately this side of the Second Bridge, but beyond—" there was a small shrug—"it has been unwholesome at times."

"Yes." Keven nodded. "I've heard it all in town."

Again the slight shrug. "May you fare well, then. That's a magnificent horse."

"Thank you." He lifted a hand in salute. "And may you fare well, too."

The road climbed gently through deep forested hills, each winding bringing a closer view through the trees of the steep mountain wall ahead. The morning was quiet now but for a soft thrumming of winds from the high peaks above. He was half a league away from the inn before a nagging thought finally came clear: considering all the tales he'd heard about the Road West and what he'd seen of the dejected dwellings along the way, that inn had a well-warded appearance.

In patchy midmorning sun and cloud shadow, he rode over a low ridge and into sight and rumble of rushing water. Plunging bank to bank, as if to justify its name, the Mad River wasn't the wide murmur here that it was in the valley. Though much smaller, it made up for its lack of size in sheer rage. It surged and cascaded along the foot of the mountain's sharp rise. Another high-arched stone bridge barely spanned the river. Spray stormed into the air as the torrent crashed against the abutments. On the other side of the bridge, the slope of Castle Mountain rose abruptly, pitching upward in dark forested folds. A curious spire of gray rock reached high above the trees just across the river.

An excellent watchtower, Keven thought . . . if anyone or anything wanted to keep watch. With a slight frown wrinkling his face, he dismounted and began arranging the horse's barding. The huge animal's stance became fully alert now with the buckling on of plate and mail—nostrils flared, neck arched, eyes glinting from beneath its visor.

"So, Horse, you think you're going to work, do you?"

He donned thigh- and kneeplates for himself, breast-, back-, and shoulderplate over a chainmail tunic, helmet, and a scale gauntlet for his right hand. The old cutlass was strapped to his left hip. Pulling himself to saddle, he unslung his peculiar diamond-shaped shield from the pommel and loosened the sword in its scabbard across his back.

"Slow." It was a working command; the war-horse set out in a purposeful stride, the fall of its big hooves pounding on the stones of the bridge above the river's roar.

He had always felt somewhat foolish in armor, imagining himself through the eyes of others: an awkward, clanking construct, half blind, barely able to make its ungainly way. But he had been early and well taught the primary benefit of armor . . . over his original objections, as Rusker hurled stones at him during training duels.

"How 'bout that one, laddy?" as a fist-size stone slammed him between the shoulderblades. "Were that a arrow, ya'd be coughin' out yer last bloody breaths right now!"

"It slows me down, damn it!"

"Slows ya down, do it?" Another stone glanced off his shoulder. "I wager a unexpected blade'll slow ya down a lot worser! Want t' see just how much I can slow ya down with a few more rocks?"

He felt an inner wince at remembering the limp he had tried to hide for days, the consequence of Rusker pounding an oak training blade across his unarmored thigh in a fierce three-on-one skirmish.

"Could be ya might go without needin' yer armor fer a long time, Keven laddy. But I'll tell ya somethin' so true ya can hang yer helmet on it: When ya needs it, yer gonna needs it in a gods' gruesome hurry!"

But he still felt like a cumbersome ass.

* * * * *

The road climbed higher, a sidehill slash cutting across the steepening slope. It was washed and rutted from the rain, with brooklets still chuckling down from the mountain above. Outcrops of jagged ledge showed through the struggling trees. He rounded a sharp curve and halted. There were wolves in the road ahead. He counted ten.

Wolves were certainly no strangers in the land—he had heard stories enough to last his lifetime, and once in the Northeast Kingdom he had been trailed by a wolf pack—but he had never heard of wolves languishing casually in mid-droad in full daylight like a group of village loafers awaiting the next interesting event. Those that had been sitting or lying rose smoothly to their feet. They all faced him.

"Slow," he said quietly. The horse paced forward at a slow walk, neck arched, head pulled in to protect its throat. Keven could feel the massive muscles tensing beneath him. The wolves were not giving way. Their yellow eyes watched him, heads low; two edged toward the downhill side of the road. He gave the toe signal that prepared the horse. It snorted, and its forefeet slammed down with each step in deliberate, hard poundings. About twenty paces from the waiting wolves, Keven signaled full charge and drew his sword.

As if planned, the wolves divided to each side and sprang, some at the horse's legs, some leaping high to snap at him. The sword arced right then left, finding targets; he felt the horse kick out in midstride. There were yelps of pain. Two wolves dashed in from the rear, aiming for the horse's hind tendons. The horse kicked again, and there was a satisfying crunch.

With toe signal and rein, he spun the great horse on its heels. It struck out with forefeet, and a wolf died in mid-leap without time for a yelp. The sword slashed another's head nearly off as it leaped for him, the twisting carcass flailing into him, spraying blood. He gave the foot signal that left the horse to its own masterful defenses while he cut away at any attackers within reach. The wolves, but three now, withdrew from the gory blade and massive hooves and circled to gain the uphill road again. He signaled another charge. One more fell bleeding out its life; the horse kicked another completely off the road into the downhill trees. The remaining wolf stared at them for a moment with blank yellow eyes, then slid over the edge of the road like a shadow.

He frowned at the spot where it had disappeared, trying to clear an afterimage. Had he seen a collar half hidden in its ruff?

It couldn't be!

He dismounted and examined Horse. There were several slashes low on its rear legs, but they were barely seeping blood; he applied a salve. He cleaned his sword of blood and fur and stood for a moment, scowling at the dead wolves in the road. He had never heard of this sort of wolf behavior before, no matter how wild the stories. Perhaps in the cold, hungry heart of winter—in Janning, the Wolf Moon—wolves might act in such a manner, but not at this time of year. It had seemed as if they were waiting, confident and unafraid. And it had been a deliberate attack.

Damned strange.

He considered another thought for a moment—wolf pelts made fine winter furs—but then turned away; he was not in the mood to skin wolves.

"Welcome to the hell of your choice," he muttered. It was an academy jibe when one scored on another. Let them lie dead and bedamned.

Remounting, he resumed guiding the horse up the steepening road. The thought of the wolves attacking as they did was still gnawing at him, but he felt good—and it *was* good to feel the pulse of battle blood again, even though some of his swings had not been precisely accurate. And he could feel the added surge in the step of the big horse.

"Alive again, aren't we?" He leaned forward and patted the firm neck. "Damn true!"

He began to sing.

>   "The Hero faced the foulish four,
>   Their weapons grim with gouts of gore.
>   'Only you? Send me more!'
>   And he leaped among them swing-ing.
>
>   "The bells of battle rang the air;
>   A head went here, a thigh went there.

He chopped them up with flailing flair,
And looked around a' grin-ning."

Who was it that said: "Nothin' like a little death to put
the spice in life"? Of course, the old armory keeper at the
academy again.

He flexed his right arm; the muscles felt the exertion of
even that little workout. He had not been as effective as he
would like in the skirmish with the wolves. He tried to remember when he had last practiced with his sword. He
couldn't really remember. In any case, it had been a long
time since he'd swung a weapon. He drew the sword and
worked through a few mounted drills. A limb overhung the
road, and he flicked the sword point at a leaf. He missed,
and swung again with a backhand. The leaf trembled at the
passage, but it was another miss.

"Scared it, though," he told the horse. "You see it
shiver?"

He had never seen country like this. It was a world of
sheer heights and plunging depths, a land careened on end
as if to climb to the very sky, a land too vast and terrible for
men and other puny beings, built instead as thrones for
gods or on a scale for giants.

Green leaves gave way to darker fir trees, and then the
low, stunted evergreens lost their domain to ledge and
stone, with gnarled and twisted shrubs fighting for life
among the mountainside boulders. The road began switch-
ing back upon itself, carved from the steep slope like a
winding ledge. The sun dimmed. Glancing aloft, he saw
clouds scudding overhead, seemingly torn into shabby tatters by the towering peaks themselves. He could see the entire Vales now, patched with the dark gathering cloud
shadows.

"Just what we need, Horse . . . rain."

As if in reply, thunder bumped hollowly from above,

grumbled, and echoed away. As the road climbed, switch-back after switchback, the clouds thickened to a dark ceiling and the day dimmed to dusk. The first spatters of rain began to fall. He drew his hooded traveling cloak from a saddlebag and fastened it about his shoulders. As the wind rose, he began to sing again.

> *"Oh, Walter would a-venturing go,*
> *Away in the wold of ice and snow.*
> *No bother if the wind did blow,*
> *He limped along a-sing-ing.*

"How about that, Horse? More, you say? My pleasure, sir . . .

> *"The rain came down from angry skies,*
> *And filled his armor to his eyes;*
> *It chilled his ballocks 'tween his thighs,*
> *And ran out through his toes-es.*

"That's an academy verse, you understand, not—"

A crack of lightning blazed overhead, so close he actually ducked; thunder crashed behind it. Horse flinched and pranced a few steps sideways. Keven stroked its neck.

"Calmly, old friend. What do you suppose we've done to anger the gods so?"

The rain came then in a roaring wall of water. He reined the horse to a slightly overhanging ledge and dismounted. It was nearly as dark as early night, slashed by ragged lightning. The big horse tossed its head, yanking him off the ground.

"Ho-o!" he yelled over the uproar of rain and thunder. He peeled off his cloak, the sudden, savage wind tearing at it as he bundled it over the huge head. With his face buried in the cloak, his arms wrapped around the horse's head to hold it tight, he waited. There was a thought trying to make its way through to the fore, something nagging, something about storms. . . . Of course! He reached into the neck of his tunic and grasped his mother's gold wind charm. With it, she had called breezes when they were becalmed, averted the fiercest winds in a storm. It had truly worked . . . hadn't it? Or maybe all mothers had magic. But how was it supposed to work? He didn't know any words to go with it. He turned his face away from the cloak.

"Sheer off!" he shouted. "Abate!" If anything, it rained harder.

"Cease thy storming!" Lightning and thunder answered him.

"I command thee, by Marin's might, to subside!"

Wrong god for this setting. And there was probably a formal liturgy required.

"Be damned entirely to the hells, then!"

It seemed there was a plaintive cry in the storm, and that something swirled nearby in the chaotic dark, but the rain continued. Had he seen a hulkling shape?

"Say something, Horse," he muttered into the sodden cloak. "You'll do as well as I."

It didn't last long. The squall wasted away to smaller gusts of rain and buffets of wind, then spats of sprinkles, and finally nothing but the gray shreds of clouds racing eastward across the valley.

"Mountain storm spirits!" he grumbled, flinging the dripping cloak over the saddlebags and leading the horse from their crude shelter. "I should've asked how people handle them around here. Probably don't. Haven't the brainworks to do it. That's why there's so many damned storms!"

The road climbed relentlessly. A warm midday sun broke through and soon heated him to an itching, soaking sweat inside his armor. Steam rose from the huge horse beneath him, and the higher they climbed, the more restive the horse seemed to become.

"*Now* what!" He slapped the reins against its neck. It was alien to its training to behave in this manner, but here it was, shying at shadows like a colt and snorting its displeasure.

"What in four hells is into you?"

The horse balked and shook its head against the reins. He urged it on, but the strange behavior increased. He dismounted and seized the lower bit bar.

"It will be unseeming, you big brute bastard, for me to drag you over this damned pass, but I shall if I must!"

The horse followed, but reluctantly.

The road was on a long southern reach when it bent around a sharp ridge, and the sheer bulk of Castle Mountain towered full against the sky. Snow clung to its high battlements like ragged white banners draped from immense walls. A low, vertically walled shoulder jutted toward the valley, a blunt pinnacle atop it like a tower on a corner wall. Broken tops and cracks completed the illusion of crenellations and archer slits. The road climbed directly to that sharp spur, where there appeared to be some sort of wooden structure built against the face of the cliff. The horse stopped, both forefeet planted. Keven hauled on the bit.

"What in all the hells together—" He stopped suddenly. Horse's big eyes were glassy, wide, and rolling from side to side. The huge animal was actually trembling. Keven reached for his sword as he spun into a slight crouch, then froze, blade but halfway unsheathed.

"I wouldna thought it possible," a voice laughed. "A man pullin' a beast o' thet size uphill!"

A lanky man dressed in dirty leathers was standing atop a projecting rock above the road, leaning casually on a strung longbow.

Another voice called, "Ah wouldna want t' fight 'im

meself. A man thet strong would be a fearsome 'un."

"He could throw yew clear to th' Palan from here," another added.

"Yar," chuckled still another. "But he be true turrible numb. Yer doesn' pull a great harse like thet; yer pushes 'im."

Others joined in the raucous laughter. There must be thirty or so of them perched above the road, Keven thought, some sliding down the rocky slopes to cut him off ahead and behind. They were all smiling.

"Is *this* whut sent Willy a-runnin' back all a-shiver an' full o' whimpers?" One of the men in the road ahead made an expression of mock astonishment.

"It musta been the harse thet did it," another laughed. "Willy prob'ly thought 'twas 'is mother a-comin' fer 'im."

They all grinned at Keven for a moment. He let the sword slide back into the sheath and straightened. He did not reply. It was their small, private game for the moment; they were having a good time in their assurance, and they would laugh at anything. They were a ragged lot in filthy odds and ends of clothing, some rusty pieces and bits of armor here and there. They carried a variety of battered arms, but mostly bows and dirty swords. These were the dreaded bandits? He kept his gaze on the first to speak, the tall man on the rock.

"What leads yer wanderin' way up here, young fighter?" that one asked, smiling. "Did yer nar hear thet this road be nar safe for travelers?"

There was another round of guffaws and winks.

"I travel west," Keven answered. He gazed calmly around at the surrounding men, marking their positions, their arms, and their attitudes.

"Now thet be a right poorly direction t' travel. Yew may have to pay a toll."

Keven nodded vaguely. "I see it takes . . . what, twenty-five or thirty to collect it?" He regarded the four men in front of him, meeting their eyes directly. "Is it a lack of training or a lack of courage that so many are required to tax but one?"

Some of the smiles disappeared. The man who appeared to be the leader laughed. "Ah, 'tis possible yew could break through. Yer geared fer it, seems. But yer horse holds 'nother idea. Thet be true strange, don' it?"

Keven glanced at his bow, slung from the saddle pommel. It was strung, but he knew the bowstring was wet and could cast an arrow hardly twenty paces. But there was the chance they didn't know that.

"Perhaps an arrow spitted through your chest would change matters for the better," he said.

"Yar, there be thet possibility," the tall man said, nodding. He looked up the road and made a wide arm signal. "But yer prime problem lays yander."

A big, full-armored figure came into view from behind an outcrop, striding purposefully down the road.

"Ah, yes . . ." Keven muttered. He turned calmly to the horse; it still stood trembling, eyes wide, nostrils flared. He took down the shield with its strange pointed corners, hung on the saddle since the storm. It slipped onto his left arm as comfortably as an old sleeve. He reached over his shoulder, and the sword made a soft slithering ring as it cleared the scabbard. He scanned the men grinning at him from various surrounding perches.

"Think you have enough arms to handle this?" he asked.

The leader laughed. "Oh, we be just the bystanders."

"And the reserve force when this bullock of yours gets butchered out?"

"Oh, no," the man chuckled. "Yew get through him an' yer be clear t' continue. Howsomever—" he smirked around at the others, and they dutifully snickered—"I must tell yew thet the odds nar be in yer favor."

"Don't lay your whole purse on it," Keven muttered softly. He could feel the tart thrust of anger beginning to pulse through him, yet he put his mind in a dead, cold place. It was a practiced state.

He could hear Rusker's words echoing in his mind: *"Ya be the sword; the sword be yaself. Ya be the center o' yer world, an' it all be bound by the realm o' yer cuttin' edge. Anger be banned elsewhere. It be a distraction. If ya uses it, use it to unsettle yer opponent an' not as fuel fer yaself."*

Once learned and mastered, it was a simple exercise, and immediate. A icy calm took over; he was the sword and all the sword could reach, the center of a circle of steel.

He watched the big man's deliberate approach. It was more machine than man, he thought.

Metal clinking, long sword swinging. Very big. Berserker? Heavy, double-handed sword. Large, rectangular shield with a strange emblem, dented. Oddly flared, whole-head helmet with a nose guard sweeping down like a poised snake. Eastern . . . sculpted to effect a demon face. Unblinking eyes glittering in the shadow of visor. Heavy beard framing a hard clamp of mouth. No sound but metal pacing. Death in tarnished armor.

Keven slipped into middle guard.

It came on with a standard military, front-line attack, full-stride momentum, shield rammed suddenly forward, sword swinging a great overhead arc intended to cleave him from crown to buttocks. Keven let it begin, and instead of shielding as expected, he sidestepped quickly to the left and parried with his blade, barely diverting the hard downswing past his right shoulder. The rush of that heavy sword rang on the road beside his foot. At the same instant, he flicked his wrist and slammed the other a resounding blow across the side of the helmet with the flat of the blade. It wasn't intended for damage but for bafflement. It set the tone of the fight. It also unfocused an opponent's eyes for a moment and left a bright song in his ears. Immediately, as if by rebound, he repeated the blow.

"Unnerve 'em!" Rusker shouted from somewhere in the past. *"Make 'em fight yer fight, not theirs!"*

The effect was as intended; the big man charged again. Keven easily ducked under the attack, spun, and swung a backhand up under the trailing edge of the other's mail tunic, using the blade. Few fighters were armored there. It was virtually the ultimate in insult blows.

"Make 'em angry! Make 'em make their own mistakes! Make 'em break their training!"

The other wheeled, eyes blazing, more a raging thing, it seemed, than a man.

"You fight with your arse," Keven told it. "Mayhaps you should back into battle."

It roared forward. Keven stood to the attack, parrying and shielding, hooking off glancing blows with the points of his shield. It was, as he'd heard it termed before, "beef-line fighting," standard tactics of beating through by strength and ferocity. He let the other establish the pacing, then broke it with a combination of fast parry replies that left blood trickling from the man's lower sword arm, point of chin, and shield arm armpit. How did the bystanders like that!

"I suggest you stay your arm, fighter," he said. "There'll not be enough left of you to hold your armor together."

The attacks became more fierce, punctuated by deep, guttural grunts. There was little talent to the technique, just brute strength behind the big crashing sword. Keven kept that sword away with parries, hard armor, and shield. The mountainside echoed with the clash of arms, and the impact of that big sword taken full shield was enough to rock his stance. While he was able to ward against telling blows, he wasn't damaging the other much, beyond a few nicks and bent armor. And he was tiring! That wasn't right! He should be able to hold this pace till the dogs fell down, but he could feel the fatigue pulling on his arms. It was time for something skillful while he still had the speed.

He feinted high to the left, with a slight lean in that direction as if fully committed, drawing the other with him, then threw himself into a deliberate tumble to the right as the other's responding blow fell on his shield. Rusker had called it a true idiot's trick because it depended too much on fate; Keven maintained it was a matter of agility and timing. The feint was to raise the other's shield, while the fall had to appear real, as if a result of the shielded blow. The instant the fall took him below his foe's big shield, he lashed out at the armor joint where greave joined kneeplate—there was always an opening there—as the other bent to follow him down.

It worked. He could tell by the satisfying *chunk* of his sword and the man's clenched grunt of pain. He continued rolling back onto his feet, drawing the sword with him lengthwise from the joint and coming erect two paces away in middle guard stance.

The other wasn't even looking at his knee. His breath hissed between clamped teeth, and his glistening eyes were locked on Keven. He thrust his left leg forward and locked the knee joint. Bright blood was leaking freely from the junction of armor and running down the tarnished greave. Keven was aware of a rising mutter from the other men around them.

"Will you stay your arm?" he asked, a little out of breath. The man was making almost squealing sounds of rage with every breath. He lurched forward, swinging the crippled leg out and locking the knee to be able to stand on it. Keven backed away.

"It is not my desire to kill you, fighter!"

The man still advanced. Grotesque, limping armor, big

sword raised.

Keven dropped his stance, backed away a few steps and scowled up at the cliff above the road.

"Can you stop him?" he shouted. "I don't want to kill him if I don't have to."

"Seems yer goin' t' have to," the man in leathers replied with a frown. "I don' think he have a whoa to him, an' I don' think I like yew much, young fighter. Yew hurt him, an' we're gonna be doin' somethin' 'bout thet! We—"

An arrow bounced off Keven's backplate, coming from the rear.

"Nar!" the leader shouted. "I don' want 'im dead, yew fool turd!"

"You haven't got me at all!" Keven yelled. He turned to put his back to the road edge, where the mountainside fell steeply away. The enraged armored thing was still coming. Keven pointed his sword directly at the twisted face.

"You're first, you spawn whose mother knew not your father's specie!"

Everything went wrong at once. He heard the horse scream in terror or rage, and a great commotion broke out just beyond his line of vision. He swung slightly to meet the oncoming attack of lurching armor, intending to press his advantage there to a quick victory, when a rock slammed off the side of his helmet. His timing disrupted, he shielded an arcing forehand blow badly. His shield pivoted on his arm and crashed back into his face. Using the force of the blow, he threw himself sideways in a clumsy roll to his feet again. Something hit his leg. There was a quick glimpse of confused images: struggling figures surrounding the horse, the maddened animal striking out in all directions in fighting leaps, men rolling away. Someone appeared to be trying to trip the huge oncoming armored brute from the rear with a staff; apparently even the leader couldn't command him to stop. There were shouts and clamor all around.

Keven sensed movement behind his right shoulder and
slashed a backhand to the rear. He hit something, and there
was a howl of pain. Then a blinding blow to his head from
the side. Dimly he saw the big armored man tripped from
the rear, toppling toward him, the long sword falling in one
last roaring overhead swing. He couldn't get his shield up
in time. It hit his left shoulder, and he felt the bite of steel
as it carved through the pauldron plate. Something hit him
again from the side. He struck once more behind him.
Something connected with a ring of steel. He wheeled. A
bearded man was staring stupidly at a sword broken off at
the hilt. Another man, teeth gritted, had a sling blurring
around his head. Keven tried to dodge, but the hand
flicked out and his head seemed to explode. He could feel
his sword arm swinging, keeping clear his immediate space.
Through a chaotic fog, he seemed to see an enormous,
screaming shape approaching, men tumbling out of its
path.

"Horse!" he choked and made a staggering reach. It was
the wrong motion. A massive black shoulder struck him
like a solid, warm wall, and he was falling . . . and there was
no road beneath him.

Remembered later, it was a long, thundering, battering
churn of boulders and brush and gravel and wet snow, tumbling, sliding, armor crashing, every part of him pummeled and pounded, and it kept going on and on. But no
pain. Not then.

In the sudden stillness, he focused his eyes on wet gravel.
He lifted his head; the road was only about twenty paces
away. But why was it tilted up sideways like that? That was
very strange indeed. Oh . . . it seemed he was looking down
at it, but how could that be? He pushed himself up, and
the falling started all over again.

This time it was sky he saw, and a high mountainside filling up one whole side of it. He lay there, examining the

mountain. Men were standing on it a long way above him. Something tried to explain to him that he had fallen, slid, rolled, and tumbled down some three hundred paces of rocky slope to a switchback below. It didn't seem likely. Why should he want to do something as stupid as that?

"Fighter!" The call was far away, echoing, barely understood over the roaring in his head. "Can you hear me?"

He lay a moment longer, waiting for his wits to come wandering back from whatever whimsical place they had journeyed. A cautious inventory seemed to indicate that most everything should work. He rolled to his left—a mistake! Pain ignited his shoulder and the arm buckled. He rolled the other way, paused, and then pushed carefully to his knees. He wriggled his toes, and they seemed to work; that was supposed to be a good sign for something. He took a deep breath and swayed to his feet. His shield still hung from its arm strap, the weight pulling his left arm painfully. He eased the shield off and let it drop to the road. His sword was gone.

Hooves hammered on the road, and the big horse came into view in a pounding, ponderous gallop. Several arrows had found their marks in its flanks, low under the skirt of mail. It slowed and stopped, favoring its left rear leg. It nudged Keven with its nose, nearly pushing him over. He grabbed the bridle to steady himself; the whole world had suddenly tilted.

"Fighter!" came the far call again.

Keven squinted upslope and shouted as loud as he could. "Does it please you dung worms to hurt animals?"

"It please me t' do whut I please!" the voice answered. "Here! Carry this message back with yew. In yer condition, it should be clear!"

Keven watched as the tall man bent a bow. He made a staggering attempt to pick up his shield, but the arrow was wide. It struck the road a few paces away and splintered.

There was something rolled and laced behind the head.

"Take thet to yer Lard Damon! Tell him yer a example o' whut happens to armed men on the pass!"

He picked up the broken shaft, got a firm grip on the bridle, and started downhill; at least his legs seemed to be working—well, the right one was.

"Limp home, lad, an' be thankful I've allowed yew that!"

The first returning sensation through the numbness and the daze was a familiar burning rush to his neck and face.

"I'll meet you again, you whoreson whelp!" he called.

It was a small response but the best he could do at the time.

Chapter Four

High on the western side of North Pass, where the rutted road north wound down through a lush mountain meadow, aimed for the wide plains of the Palan, the morning birds sang their morning songs and gathered at a place where the travelers and caravans always camped by a small stream.

The bright mountain jays chattered and argued among the burned and broken wagons and tore at the soft parts of the dead draft animals, while the crows fought over a few sprawled bodies, and the ravens stalked with dark dignity wherever they liked.

There was a clatter of wings and squalls of anger as one of three approaching wolves dashed to a small body and began dragging it away. The other two wolves moved in to tug in another direction, but the argument was settled by a few snarls, and the two charged among the birds for trophies of their own. The birds scattered and shrieked but settled on other feeding sites. There was enough to go around.

It was a busy morning for the birds.

* * * * *

The sheriff stood over Keven, fists on hips, scowling down at the figure on the pallet.

"Some freeranger!" he muttered to himself, then louder, "Mather!"

A bent figure hurried from another room. "Yes?"

"He be not a-stirrin' yet."

"It be but a short time since you last told me, Lukus. Give him time. He been beat upon severely."

The sheriff leaned closer, snorting to clear his nose. Sweet woodruff had been strewn on the floors, but the scent of sickness hung heavy in the room.

"Have you got a room that isn't filled with this stench, Mather? I can't smell if he's got the rot in his wound or not! If he's not got a sickness now, he'll have it by the time he be out o' here!"

"There's a small room upstairs, but—"

"Then move him up there!"

"But the cost, Lukus! It's—"

"Mather—" the sheriff dropped a strong hand on the other's shoulder—"you be a good healer. The best in the Vales, I say. But you got a problem. You be argumentish. Now, put this lad in your good room, an' don' make me chew it over again."

The little man scrubbed his hands together nervously. "It be a Watch matter, then—the council pays."

"It be *my* matter!"

Mather bobbed his head. He paused and seemed about to say something more, but instead he frowned the thought away. He turned and scurried out, calling to someone, "Rob, we be movin' the new one upstairs!"

The sheriff swung back to the cot. "Ranger?" He leaned closer. "Keven!"

The eyes opened, a glazed blue-green, and stared at the ceiling planks for a moment, then shifted, focused, and frowned at the sheriff.

"Horse?" The voice was raspy and dry.

"Taken care of."

His teeth clamped, Keven began to push himself up on his elbows. "My gear . . ."

"Everythin's safe, 'cept your sword. It be apparent lost."

Keven released a long, clenched breath and lay back.

"What in all the seven festive hells happened up there?" the sheriff growled. "How many did it take t' do this, and how many bodies did you leave behind?"

Keven scowled at the ceiling. "What's this place?"

"Healer's. You be in town."

"I . . . don't remember . . ."

"Kenth o' the First Bridge Inn found you. He knew you was gonna get misfortuned when you went by, an' he trailed you up the road. Said you weren't gettin' one foot in front o' the other too good when he found you. Said 'twas hard to tell if you was holdin' up the horse, or if the horse were draggin' you. 'Bout an equal pair. He gave you a drink that knocked you colder'n a stone post. He be a halflin' elf, you know. He fixed you up some, then brought you in to me. He'd heard 'bout you—elfs have a way o' knowin' things—an' thought 'twas more my concern than his."

"Horse was hurt."

"Kenth did good work on your horse—elfs be better with animals than people anyhow—but the chances be thet it were not enough. One o' them arrows got a bad spot on a hind leg. Kenth couldn't fix it right. It nicked a tendon, an' it were poisoned."

Keven tried to rise again, but he fell back once more. "Bastards!" he muttered. The sheriff shook a finger at him.

"What you gotta do is rest. Kenth healed up your shoulder right fair, an' you'd better thank a few gods o' your acquaintance that he were around. Elfs can do things like that, you know. All you're goin' to have is a scar and a foul memory. What happened up there?"

"How long've I been asleep?"

"Well, you left here five day ago, if that gives you any answer."

"Good Marin! Five days!" He frowned suddenly at the sheriff again. "There was a message. . . ."

"We got it. Kenth said you had it clamped in a fist tighter'n iffen it were lodged in oak. Some arrogant babblin' 'bout chargin' toll over the passes west. Drunken, mindless amounts. Threats o' all sorts o' dire things happenin' if th' toll be not paid. In advance." He let a moment pass. "How many be there?"

"I saw about thirty."

The sheriff's hedge of eyebrows arched up. "An' you took 'em all on, I suppose."

"They took me on."

"How'd you get out o' it?"

"Horse shoved me off the road." He rubbed his eyes again. "I think that's what happened."

The sheriff snorted. "Damn horse be smarter'n you!"

Keven rubbed the back of his head. "I got hit from behind."

"Ah-h-h . . . they didn't play fair? You mean them nasty brigands didn't line up an' give you a whack at 'em one at a time? Now, weren't that just spiteful o' them!"

Keven's eyes blazed. "Well, I'll tell you one thing, Sheriff—your damned so-called berserker is caught halfway between sitting down and standing on one foot! He's got a left leg now that'll be strange for some time to come, and another crack in his arse!"

"You don' know what a grand relief that'll be to the whole o' the Vales."

"Go to hell!"

"It be not nice to swear at the sheriff."

Keven turned away. The sheriff's scowl seemed more concerned than angry.

"Were he a true berserker, d' you think?"

Keven uttered a hard grunt of irritation. "You tell *me* the difference between a berserker and a big, angry man with the brain of a red squirrel!"

"How was they armed, these bandits?"

"Snowballs and nasty names! How in four hells do you think they were armed?"

"I be back to talk to you when you feel better."

"That's not damned likely! Where's a good armorer?"

"Artur, in Crossriver."

"Where's my horse?"

"At the barrack. Your gear, too. You plannin' to head back up the mountain right now? Or will tomorrow morn be soon 'nough."

"How much do I owe this healer?"

"Ask *him!*" The sheriff spun toward the door, then halted and turned back, a hard finger pointing.

"Now you listen, you mighty freeranger! Some things be afoot, an' you're not to tangle it all up by chargin' back up there with an eye on blood an' a burr up your arse! You understan' that? Do that make a cut in your oaken head?"

They glared at each other. The sheriff's voice rose until heads turned in other rooms.

"If I even *think* you be headed up that pass, if I even see you glance in that direction, I'll lock you up so tight you'll be breathin' through a pipe! Just 'cause you got the earwax pounded out o' you be no cause to be numb as a brick, less they pounded out some brains, too! Now, you rest up an' stay *out* o' it!"

He started to wheel away, then turned back.

"An' I tell you somethin' else! At the same time you was playin' sword up on Castle Pass, a caravan were hit on North Pass an' total slaughtered! Now, how's that catch your cat?"

He slammed out of the room to bump into Mather, wringing his hands, almost jumping up and down in his anxiety.

"Lukus! Sheriff! Please, this be a sick house."

"Damn *true* it be! Give that simpleton somethin' to knock him colder'n an iron wheel! If I see him out on the streets in the next tenday, I'll send him back t'you with some new problems!"

* * * * *

Keven lived in a bitter, antic whirl of memory, some distorted, some as clear and sharp as icicles. Over and over the fight raged, each step recalled, each blow reswung, each image frozen, to be examined as part of a pattern, and then the whole reexamined as a flow of movement and countermovement in one continuous recollection.

And there were comments from the past, as if Rusker and Santon were watching too. . . .

Rusker:

"Ya have a flaw that'll kill ya someday, Keven! Ya can't perceive the true lay of things! Ya color all ya see an' all ya do by the set o' yer mind! Til ya see the truth, ya can't be a part of it!"

He tossed on the narrow cot, frowning, feeling the heat, even now, rise to the back of his neck.

"As far as yer behavior be concerned, lad, ya tread a true fine edge between assurance and arrogance. One is knowin' what ya can do, the other is thinkin' ya can do it better than anybody else! The truth is seein' the difference! An' ya best know that difference before ya end up as dog feedin's facedown in the road!"

And then a peculiar lesson—Rusker had suddenly cracked him across the side of the head with his staff. As he reeled back, amazed, Rusker nodded.

"Come back at midwatch an' tell me exactly what just happened."

He returned and said, "You hit me."

"A fine start. An' how did that happen?"

"You were angry and—" He flinched away from the launch of another swing.

"Wrong!"

He pondered a quick review. "You held your staff in your right hand about two-thirds up its length. By swinging your arm sharply forward, you caused the bottom part to spin toward my head."

"And?"

He shrugged. Rusker scowled at him.

"The truth, lad! Ya didn't see it comin'. Ya didn't duck! Accept the responsibility of that! Ya didn't do a damn thing! Ya stood there like yesterday's dog turd an' let me hit ya in the head! Yer mind just skipped right past that little image, didn't it! The knock ya got was yer fault! See it! The staff came right at ya, an' ya didn't have the wit nor the reaction to move!"

Rusker started away but turned back. "I'll allow ya the lack of reaction—that's my fault, a fault o' trainin' that'll be repaired—but the misleadin' o' your own mind in reviewin' it, that's your fault!"

And then it was Santon's turn:

"Problem-solving is a simple matter, once one has mastered the first step. The problem is that few people ever bother to learn the first step.

"The first step is to define the problem. Determine the true shape of the beast, and recognize it. Do not delude yourself as to its true nature.

"You cannot deal with any problem that is ill-defined, misrepresented, hidden, avoided, or otherwise excused. You cannot attack an enemy by thrusting at his shadow. You cannot solve a problem by explaining away its facade."

And the problem here . . .

The problem here . . . was so large, so obvious, so close that he could not at first see it. It was a problem difficult to recognize as a problem, until it began to assume its true, ugly form . . . and he had to accept its reality because there it was.

He had never been beaten before.

And now, not only had he been bested in arms, it seemed he was being bested by everything. His world was out of his control; he hadn't lived up to the standards expected of a ranger.

The demon on his shoulder, the one who always called upon him to remember, remember, now had a new burden to chuckle about.

* * * * *

The brash stream fell white and shouting from the last rocky wall of the mountain to a swirling, foam-flecked pool. In the dark, dense, dripping foliage alongside the pool, hidden as well as two more glistening leaves, a pair of large, deep green, almond eyes watched the farther bank. Two men stood there, frowning downstream as dusk darkened the deep forest. Two slain deer lay in the leaves at their feet. The men were dressed in dirty leathers and armed with bows and swords. One wore a helmet, the other a hard leather conical cap. They appeared to be arguing, turning frequently to glare around them. One glanced directly in the direction of the watching green eyes and then swung away.

With scowls and angry gestures of impatience, they turned toward the mountain, to a large tumble of broken slabs and boulders, and, dragging their game, they moved carefully into the rockfall and disappeared.

About an arm's span in front of the green eyes, a long,

thin arrowhead lowered. Across the pool, deeper into the
evening trees, a thrush called and was answered by another
from close downstream. A dark green, mottled shadow,
difficult to follow, glided to the rockfall where the men had
disappeared. It seemed to vanish for a moment, then reap-
peared and paused. It seemed to nod across the pool. The
eyes disappeared from the leaves, yet there was no sound of
movement. A thrush called nearby, a liquid melody
through the halls of trees, and three soft forest shadows
slipped silently away.

The rain, which had been sporadic all morning, seemed
to settle in with purpose.

*   *   *   *   *

Keven awoke to the fifth cold, dark, dismal day in a row
with the relentless rain falling straight down like streams of
wet lead. His bed and blankets were clammy; his clothes
were clammy; his brain was clammy; he was getting mildew
of the mind. He was feeling overall as bleak and morbid
and as useless as the weather. His muscles were sore to the
bone. There was a sour, surly churning in his stomach; his
head ached and was surely set awry, and he had a lurking
suspicion he had somehow made a fool of himself at the inn
last night. He was healed in body, but it seemed his mind
was still wounded. The days of inaction and the constant
rain were making him gloomy and restive at the same time.

He got his cold, damp boots pulled on, shivering and
pausing once to let the room settle down. He needed
warmth and something to eat, but the sudden thought of
food . . . well, that could wait for a while until his stomach
ebbed its troubled tide. Warmth first; he seemed to be losing his ability to stay warm without a fire lately. It was this
damned, perverse mountain rain! The storm spirits here
were of a frigid, more spiteful nature than those of the sea.

He hadn't seen anyone paying homage to them. No wonder the weather here ran wild and wicked. It was a backward area, this mountain country.

There would be a roaring fire in the barrack hall, but he didn't feel comfortable there. The mood among the watchmen was tense when he was present. Conversation faded when he entered the hall, eyes shifted toward him and slid away. Bracken was the center of little bursts of laughter behind his back.

Well, at least the Blue Boar was warm and friendly. He had found a roundabout path through twisting alleyways and narrow stairs where overhanging second stories provided some protection from the downpour. They kept the fires hot at the inn and the ale cool, and the glow of the ale and the good companionship was genial and welcome. And the more pitchers he bought, the better the company at his table. But still there was Bracken! That self-important ass!

He was going to have to rap that sullen little dog turd firmly between the ears; the man didn't have the mettle to face him directly with that sneering, malicious mouth. He was a little wolf in a big pack. Bold barks from a safe circle. Distant daring! Well, he'd see how brave the mouth was when it was face-to-face with its target.

He finished dressing, slung his soggy traveling cloak over his shoulder, and stalked down to the barrack hall. It was crowded with the morning watch preparing for their day. As usual, a joke was underway.

". . . an' so the man's wife was some terrible sickly, an' she expressed her heart's desire to be buried up on Tibbet's Hill, overlookin' the river, an' he jumps right up an' cries out, 'Get yer sister t' help yer dress while I hitches up the mare!' "

There was a ripple of laughter, which dwindled away as Keven entered.

"Bracken here?" he asked into the sudden silence.

Bracken scowled up from a helmet he was polishing. "You want somethin'. . . *ranger?*" He sneered the last word, the usual surly smirk curling one corner of his mouth.

Keven nodded, composing his face in an expressionless mask. "Yes . . . I want to tell you that I wish you no great misfortune, Bracken, but when you go home tonight, I hope your mother breaks out of the sty and bites your ass."

He grinned then and waited. The room, for a moment, was much like a painting he'd seen in the city, figures locked in breathless silence, broken here only by the snapping of the fire. Bracken's face turned an ugly dark red, and he appeared to be leaving his fingerprints embossed on the helmet. There was no reply; he stared slit-eyed at the helmet.

"If you have anything to say about me, brave Bracken," Keven continued, "mayhaps you can lever up your courage to whisper it to me in the dark. If you can write, you could put it down in a message and have it delivered. If you can't write, here's a copper to get it done for you."

He flipped a coin in a high arc to rattle on the stone floor at Bracken's feet. He waited.

The fire popped sparks from the hearth, and not a person in the room blinked. Eyes shifted from Bracken to him like birds unable to settle. Bracken continued to stare at his helmet. Keven turned and left. "Never leave a coward behind you" was the old saying. Fine. Just let him try something! Rusker had once described a person like that as having a dangerous intelligence—just high enough to believe himself a great intellect, but too low to understand that he was an obvious impostor.

The rain smeared the world to a narrow gray view of distorted buildings, watercourse streets, and an occasional scurrying, huddled figure splashing from one cold shelter to another. He pulled up the hood of his cloak and ducked and dodged his way uphill to the inn.

The crumpled little man hunched over his ale mug, as if protecting it from predators, and frowned at the streaked window. "All this rain be a true evil omen," he grunted.

The chubby man at the end of the table shook his head. "Ah, Parcy, if there war but one horse turd in town, yew'd be sure t' step in it an' then complain. The reason yew be so skinny be that the goodness somehow got soured right out o' yew."

"Laugh at whatever foolishness suits yew," Parcy said, scowling, "but five day o' rain be nar natural. It rank o' dark forces. Thet wizard up thar on the hill be workin' at evil things." He tapped the side of his nose. "Yew mark me."

Another man spoke up. "The wizard Acclain be nar o' the dark side, yew true fool." He turned to the rest of the table and grinned.

"Yew know thet Parcy here be so skinny he war standin' once by the Road West fer too long an' Piter Newly hung a fence rail on him."

The chuckles rippled around the table; another man lifted a finger. "Thar war this landsman hereabouts who hired this Upper Valesman to build him a pole fence. Well, first day the man built two hundret paces o' good fence, an' the landsman say, 'Thet be true good! I don' know why ev'rybody say such bad things 'bout yew Upper Valesmen.' Then on the second day, the man built but eighty paces, an' the landsman say, 'Well, thet be all right, I s'pose.' But on the third day, he only got ten paces done, an' the landsman ask him how come he did so poorly, considerin' the last two days. An' the Upper Valesman say, 'Wul, 'tis nar me fault, sar. Ev'ry day I gits farther an' farther from th' axe!' "

There was a burst of appreciative laughter.

"Yar, thet be a Upper Valesman fer yer!" More laughter. Nudges and nods.

Another man spoke up. "Ol' foolish Lencer, he went out

to the rock quarry, yew know, an' after lookin' an' watchin'
fer a real long while, he finally shook his head an' he says to
one o' the haulers, he says, 'Call me fool, they does, an'
here yew gots all them statues standin' all over the place.'
An' the skidder says, 'Statues! They be the Upper Vale
quarriers!' "

Keven leaned back, smiling. He caught the serving
maid's eye for another round. It was a good feeling to be a
part of this, this raucous exchange of bawdy banter—it was
new to him—and although he often felt sluggish lately and
nervous at the same time, the company here was comfortable. Because of the rain, he was unable to continue west if
he wanted to, and in this group, with the drink and laughter, he didn't have to think. The ale and the wine took the
place of thinking. The voice of the demon on his shoulder
was dulled and distant.

Keven bought more pitchers for the table, and the dusky
day wandered on, with ale and food and laughter and dark
rain on the windows. Someone pressed a mug into his hand
and insisted he drink. Deeply. He missed seeing the winks
and grins around the table as he took a healthy gulp, then
stared at the mug in wide-eyed, breathless shock. His immediate thought was that he could have gained much the
same sensation by swallowing a mouthful of molten lead.
The gathering collapsed in laughter. The man who had offered the mug drained it down and then beamed at Keven
with tears streaming down both cheeks.

"It be a true dreadful drink," he gasped, "but it test a
man's measure to survive pure pain."

"Then I'll probably recover?" Keven breathed. They
laughed and pounded him on the back.

A minstrel with a sly grin and twinkling eyes sang a song.
Keven remembered singing along with the chorus.

There was more, much more, and more ale and wine and
more talk, and it got late early.

It was still raining.

*   *   *   *   *

Water cascaded down Sixty-Six Steps and the other stairs in town like wonderfully fashioned waterfalls. Courtyards became pools, streets became brooks, then rushing streams. Rapids rolled from door to door. Wavelets, instead of people, danced in the plazas, and the music was the rash fall of the rain. Shops closed and people retreated to their second stories. The Sun-Running River raged a frothing brown through the Lower Market as high as Crosshill Street. Wooden storage sheds in the lower town folded and rode away. A great pine tree, plunging on the flood, caved in the end of a stone warehouse like a bizarre battering ram. The long Keep Bridge to the Road North, with the rampaging Mad River beginning to tear away its planks, finally buckled and was gone in a great groan of splintered timbers. The part of the town known as Crossriver was a wide swirling lake, with surviving buildings like shaky, unstable islands, the residents hand long ago fled to the slopes of Iron Mountain.

And the Blue Boar, high above the flood, stayed open.

*   *   *   *   *

Another day rained away, a dull, funeral drizzle now, slow and cold, as if the storm gods were bored with it all and could think of nothing more exciting. The talk in the Blue Boar was more quiet, less cheerful.

"The lands from Oak Downin's as far as Upper Grubbin's be flooded. Folks been raftin' out on their roof timbers."

"Somebody say th' river be up th' highest ever."

"I tell yew, the whole of the Macaabs be extendin' their evil shadow."

"Well . . . tis true I be nar sure o' the dark side o' fay, but somethin' be wrong. Rivers ain' never done narthin' like this afore."

"Barr th' Miller lost his wheel an' flume. Tore right away an' complete gone."

"Thet be narthin'. John Dobs lost his whole damn mill! River digged right under it, an' she be utter gone, stones an' all!"

"Can't get any closer to Mill River than the old Pawly place now. It overflowed the upper swards, come down Three Sheep Lane, and cut a new channel right through the Sign o' the Pig's Pizzle."

"Well, thet be a boon, at least. Their ale taste like piss anyhow."

"How come yew be so familiar with the taste?"

One of them waved a careless hand, as if brushing away a cloud of gnats.

"Well, we nar had a bad fire in town lately."

"By th' gods, that be true!" another agreed.

Keven leaned back against the wall in his customary corner seat. He listened, but gave little reaction.

What th' hell difference does it make? he thought. It rains, the rivers rise—so what of it? It happens. Is this supposed to be of importance to me?

* * * * *

The rain lingered, but unsteadily, in final fitful squalls and gusts, as if the storm was struggling against its death. The showers diminished to an occasional dull drizzle, then finally to a clammy mist. But the sky remained dark, a low, brooding overcast just above the trees and chimneys. From the rear windows of the Blue Boar, Midvale seemed a village sloping up from the edge of an angry, muddy, rolling sea. A few stone walls and buildings stood like reefs on the shoals of Lower Market. The keep was an improbable island at the merging of the two flooded rivers, its walls rising from the roiling water with no sign of its rocky base, like a mythic floating castle anchored offshore. Crossriver was a shallow, swirling chaos of flotsam and crumpled stone and a few tilted buildings. A few surviving boats were tied to trees above the campyards where the Sun-Running Road dropped down from Iron Mountain. One stayed there for years, a small punt, a prideful curiosity, hanging from the top of a tall pine.

The former degree of cheer at the inn was difficult to regain. No matter how much wine Keven poured down for fuel, he remained in the same somber, sulky dullness that chilled the world.

"Seems strange," Keven said with a frown. "People'd rather . . . sit around and grump 'bout things they can't help than . . ." He forgot where the thought was going, but it didn't matter anyway. Some stern faces turned his way.

"Whut d' yew care 'bout all this?" one growled. "It nar be yer home."

"'Least my home knows how t' handle a little water."

"Then why don' yew jest swim back thar an' handle it!"

Keven glared at the man, who pushed away from the table and got up.

"Yer ale be good, lad, but yer company be goin' sour."

"You've had enough of the first," Keven replied, scowling.

"An' I've had 'nough o' the last!"

It was not a good day at the inn. And the days were becoming more like that, and blurred together, awash in wine. He remembered only pieces of conversations now, an argument here and there. Some lout of a man, drunk, disheveled, and dangerous, wanted to fight him, and he wanted it to happen, but it was broken up, and he couldn't remember what it was all about in the first place. He remembered singing a bawdy song of the sea and hearing some appreciative, hollow laughter and thinking at the time it was the first time he'd sung that ditty since he and Young Tom and Tuck . . .

And then, veering quickly away from that thought, he tried to urge a fight with someone. He thought it was successful.

He sank lower in his chair by the wall. The edges of his world were becoming too frayed, and all he could ponder now was losing, losing the fight on the pass, losing a friend in the caverns of the Northest, losing his parents. . . .

If he was swamped in the moody impatience of idleness before, he was thoroughly morose now, huddled in his corner with his cloak wrapped around him. Few others sat with him now. That suited him fine; he had his own dismal thoughts and his own personal demon for company.

A minstral sang.

"Tis a tale of a maiden most grievously used,
An innocent flower, betrayed and abused;
She walks now in madness in the mid o' the night,
Leaving bodies behind her, cold dead at the sight.

"The first one to hurt her was a traveler alone,
Who caught her and showed her where the dog hid the
    bone.
He chased her and charmed her and well took his ease,
And went whistling his way as blithe as you please.

"She waited and wondered, for his promise she yearned,
But he was far down the road, and he never returned;
And deep in her heart, a hard fire began,
For she'd seen him as a warm, kind, caring man.

"A dull neighbor lad was the next to the maid;
She was thrown in a hayrick and violently laid.
She fought him and marked him but was forced to a yield,
Then he left her and ran like a beast of the field.

"Her heart turned to stone and she told not a one,
And a fortnight later, the lad was undone;
He was found in the pool where the two rivers meet,
Deep down and drowned, where the big fishes eat.

"An old friend of the family, long she had known,
Said, 'Come kiss me, lass. Oh, my, how you've grown!'
They tickled and laughed and rolled on the floor,
And he finished a game that was childish no more.

"It took her not long to put things aright,
Just the rest of the day and half of the night,
And the old fool was dead, as cold as could be;
His ease-cup was wolfsbane and peony tea.

"She decided then on, if this was men's want,
She'd see that they got it with a flirt and a flaunt;
And help them along to their goal with the grave,
Be they young men or old, craven or brave.

"So beware of a maid who smiles in the night
And promises things of desire and delight;
You may find some magic, you may find some fun—
And your cold, dead eyes may ne'er see the sun. . . ."

The song broke off as a boisterous dandy by one of the
fireplaces grabbed a passing serving maid around the hips
and wrestled her onto his lap.

"And here's one that needs some of the same!" he
laughed. His surrounding group grinned and snickered.

One or two subdued chuckles sounded from the rest of the room, then a loud burst of laughter as she finally twisted far enough around to backhand him across the cheek. With a sudden, savage curl to his mouth, he hit her full in the face with his fist, and she sprawled to the floor. In the following hush, Keven's voice was clear.

"Swaggart ass!"

The man's haughty face tightened again, and hard eyes searched the far, dim corner.

"Drunken lout lowlies shouldn't so speak to their betters," he sneered to the silent room.

There was a scrape of chairs and a rustle of movement as Keven stood and others nearby shoved out of his way. He strode slowly as men and a couple of suddenly waking dogs opened a path; someone even hurriedly pulled a table aside. The girl scurried out of sight, unnoticed. He halted before the man and calmly studied the arrogant face, the half-lidded eyes, the too-carefully trimmed beard in presumed city style.

Keven felt completely sober, cold, and deadly. In the short distance across the room, he had dropped once again into that familiar fighter condition. He knew his hands would not tremble, his feet would not fail. He knew his words would be clear and concise. Sometimes the demon on his shoulder was also on his side.

"I don't have any betters," he said quietly.

The man considered him with a slow, cold smile. "We shall have to determine that. Allow me to introduce myself. I am Lester of Mill Ford, and—"

"Is it true what they say about Upper Valesmen?" Keven interrupted calmly. "That they are so dull they can't find their own dally in the dark without help?"

A growling mutter from the man's table was the only sound in the room. The man raised a hand to his companions, his indulgent smile beginning to show signs of tension.

"I believe you have insulted and maligned us, young man. I feel—"

"It took you long enough to think that out, Lester. All the tales about Upper Vale must be true."

Lester of Mill Ford rose to his feet. He was dressed in fine linen, with fancy cloak and polished boots contrasting greatly with the drab wear of others in the room. A lightweight sword hung from a decorated girdle.

"Am I *challenged?*" The smile was more of a grimace. Keven smiled also.

"Why don't you puzzle that out, too, if it isn't too much trouble? Or" —he casually indicated the man's scowling friends with a wave of a hand—"if you need these to help feed and clothe you, you probably need them to fight for you, too."

Rusker spoke to him from out of the past: *"Isolate your opponent! Get him to stand alone!"*

Lester straightened. The smug smile was gone now. "I need no help to match such as you!"

Keven looked almost happy. "Am I challenged?" he asked softly.

"It is quite ignoble to duel so far beneath my station, but I can certainly give you a sound drubbing in repayment for your squalid insolence!" He turned brusquely to one of his followers. "That staff! By the fireplace!"

"Bring two," Keven called after him. The man by the fireplace looked questioningly at Lester, who was frowning at Keven in a puzzled manner. "*You* will fight *me?*"

"If you think I plan to stand still and receive your blows, then you're as dull as everyone says you are."

Lester inspected Keven for a moment. A slight trace of reconsideration may have glimmered in his eyes, but it was lost in the reddening of his cheeks. "Very well," he said, nodding. "I shall accommodate you, although staffs are the weapon of the lowly."

"That must be why you chose them." Keven slipped off his cloak and cast it over a nearby table; he was looking forward to this, but—

The academy. Rusker:

"There always has t' be men who know how t' fight an' do it well! But don' ya get t' like it, lads, lest ya become the same that ya fight against.

"Ya has a firm an' formidable obligation, lads, to yaself an' to ya fellow men. Ya don' hurt somebody just because ya can! T' harm a man who can't defend hisself, who is much less at arms than yaself, is a insult to yaself an to the academy. 'Tis a lowly and dishonorable thing t' do!"

Very well, Rusker . . . but I can teach the pompous, arrogant son of a street bitch a lesson.

"Your . . . 'weapon,' *sir.*" Lester scornfully offered him a staff. Keven examined it: oak, stout—excellent. He gave Lester a smiling mock bow.

"I should inform you, lofty Lester of Mill Ford, that the oncoming contest may leave you walking strangely for the rest of your life."

Lester sneered and swung quickly, a hard sideways arc aimed at removing Keven's head, but he ducked and it whirred harmlessly past, twisting Lester far out of position. Keven responded by tapping him firmly between the shoulder blades with the tip of his staff.

"One mark," he said.

Lester spun and swung again. Keven easily parried it away and touched him on the chest.

"Two marks."

Another attack, delivered savagely, was met directly with a loud crack of staffs. Keven pivoted his staff around the other, rapping Lester alongside the head.

"Three marks."

A muffled cheer sounded from the awed room. Lester paused, breathing heavily. He braced himself in a more at-

tentive stance and began a better-thought-out fight. Staffs
met in a flurry of blows from Lester and parries by Keven.

"Four marks.

"Five marks.

"Six. Is this getting beyond your ability to count?"

There was cheering aloud now and calls for Keven to attack.

"Whack 'im, lad!"

"Yar! Cross 'is eyes fer 'im!"

"Send 'im home with somethin' missin'!"

The other Upper Valesmen at Lester's table had gathered
together, their expressions ranging from concern to hatred.
Lester was grunting with effort, his breath rasping in his
throat. Keven's breath was beginning to come short, even
though he was putting less than half the effort into the
scuffle that Lester was. As yet, he had not offered a single
aggressive blow.

"Seven marks.

"Eight."

Lester made a desperate, almost whimpering sound and
drove straight at Keven's stomach, staff thrusting like a
spear. Keven slapped it aside. Dropping his own staff, he
seized the other, wheeled it over his head, and twisted it
away. He thumped Lester in the groin with it.

"Nine! Enough!"

There was a thunderous cheer from the room, followed
by taunts and insults to the now surrounded Upper Valesmen. Lester stood half crouched, teeth bared, squinting at
Keven with rage.

"You base bitch spawn!" he spat. With a convulsive motion, he drew his sword and attacked.

Keven dropped instantly into a slight crouch, staff
poised in both hands, an intent frown fixed on the other at
midbreast. The sword thrust and met wood; it slashed and
met wood; it flickered and rang, and wood chips flew away.

Lester was gasping with every breath, and each effort was accompanied by a grunting cry. The blows were coming slower, in wide, reckless swings of desperation.

In the instant when Lester was starting another wild two-handed swing, Keven twisted like a cat and met the sword halfway along the blade with a blurred counterblow of his own. The sword rang like a bell as the broken piece bounced from the stone fireplace. Keven punched Lester hard in midchest with the tip of the scarred staff.

"Ten marks, you feebleminded little bastard dung beetle! You get no more!"

And then, as if Lester suddenly represented all his frustrations, all his past angers and disappointments, he slammed the man across the side of the head with the staff. It felt so good that he did it again from the other side. Lester dropped like a rag doll. Keven looked down at him and fought back the rage to hit the man again, and again, and again, to beat him into the floor and then kick the pulp. Before that fury could consume him, he hurled the staff against the wall and pushed through the cheering crowd out to the street.

* * * * *

Keven prowled the late, damp streets, wrapped tightly in his thoughts, not wanting any part of the high celebration going on at the Blue Boar. They insisted he was a hero— Lester had been a noisome pest at the Blue Boar for too long—but Keven didn't know what to think of himself. Whatever it was, he was sure he didn't like it. He wished he could talk to Santon and Rusker now, instead of hearing them lecture in his memory. He would try to search out answers inside, and Santon and Rusker were a whirl of words and lessons reeling in his head, and he was trying to ask questions, and the three of them were interrupting each other, and it wasn't until two dark figures in the night leaped warily out of his way that he realized he was arguing out loud.

What in several hells was wrong with him?

He wasn't sure who he was, or what he was. He wasn't sure of anything. He was being overwhelmed by adversaries he couldn't name.

The academy. Santon:

"No matter what the contest, be it battle or bout, you are always outnumbered. There is always one of two opponents in addition to the one you face. They are the phantasms of Defeat and Overconfidence.

"The specter of Defeat causes your opponent to appear something more than what he really is; the more you may fear him, the larger he becomes. If you dread Defeat as a possibility, he will watch your every move, grinning, waiting, and your own self-consciousness will eventually aid him, and you will make a mistake because you fear it so.

"The specter of Overconfidence blinds you by making your opponent appear to be something less than what he really is. Overconfidence is a marvelous magician. He can make the obvious disappear and then reappear as obviously something else. Overconfidence is so good at deceit that he often goes by another name: I-Know-All-the-Answers."

"No, Santon," he said to the night. "I have no more answers. They're all lost somewhere."

Santon: *"You fight with a savage, teeth-bared intensity that often seems excessive, Keven. Why is that?"*

He blinked, then shrugged: "To win."

"Then winning is the whole point?"

A pause. A frown. "Isn't it?"

"I wish you could break out of the hard structure of your thinking that there must be a 'winner' and a 'loser' in every encounter. You now approach all armed encounters with the conviction that they are a living or dying matter."

He gave a short, cynical laugh at Santon's sincerity.
"Aren't they? Swords kill. Arrows kill. Spears, pikes,
maces, battle-axes—these aren't tools of carpentry!"

"Swords also disarm; arrows warn; spears, pikes, maces,
and axes threaten. Weaponry wisely used can preserve the
life of a deserving opponent as well as your own." He leaned
forward and stared intently into Keven's eyes. "If a child
braved you with a stick, would you kill him?"

"Of course not!"

"If a robber threatened you at swordpoint, would you
kill him?"

"I . . . don't know. It depends. . . ."

"Then you must think more about the difference be-
tween winning and remaining undefeated. For if you killed
the robber, you would not have won. Indeed, you may have
suffered an appalling loss of honor by killing a poor, un-
trained man in the last fevers of desperation simply because
you could. Swords have flats as well as edges."

"But if he were breaking the law—"

"Then a mere disarmament, a fright, and a warning
would be sufficient for the moment. In order to mete out
justice and punishment, one must know the true nature of
the crime and disassociate oneself from the judgment. You
are in the profession of dealing out death or disablement
simply because it is within your capabilities; if you apply
that to all opposition, then you are little better than those
you contest. You must learn self-control, Keven. Consider
that you have a battle within yourself you must win before
you venture to evaluate others."

"I defeat myself," he told a passerby, then gave a cynical
laugh. "I've no defense against myself."

He remembered an academy exercise in disguise in which
the students had to travel through the city dressed as fools.

Santon: *"I followed you at a distance, Keven; it was ex-*
cellent work. You are a superb mummer, who could become

an outstanding player should you ever favor to change your profession. The walk was perfect, the posture, the speech, the sudden shifts from bewilderment to purpose. When those three young men began taunting you, you were stable in character. Even when they became abusive, you held yourself true." He nodded thoughtfully.

"Indeed, you were exceptional—right up to the point when you laid two of them senseless in the street and sent the other away with a hurried limp. Now . . . it is my considered opinion that a broken jaw, a broken wrist, a leg that doesn't swing right, and various other smaller injuries are hardly the work of a fool—even one in the savage throes of fear and panic, as you now attempt to justify.

"You fail. You will do it again, several times, until you can don the disguise, the character, and the purpose of the exercise, and leave your childish pride behind you.

"You seem to feel that winning is the whole point of existence, that losing must be your fault. If you shoulder that much guilt, Keven, then you will *lose, and continue losing until you have entirely lost yourself.*"

"An' you're right, Santon," he muttered. He could feel his head dropping. "'S'lutely right. Again. An' I'm tired of bein' wrong."

He yanked himself back to consider his surroundings. He was in another tavern. He ordered wine.

* * * * *

Storms of nightmare scenes and phantom images raged, bizarre tempests lanced through memories of death and guilt. Old voices sniggered with taunts and jeers. There were again armed shadow figures stalking the night—he could see them. He could see his father falling . . . his mother. And Gohn the Silent, silent now forever because of him. His fault! His fault! And no matter how he turned and twisted from the torments, they veered to face him still; they grabbed his shoulder and shook him. . . .

He was in a hell . . . there was no other answer.

He raised his head. No . . . he was in another small, dim alley tavern. And the tavern keeper was shaking him and asking if he would mind t' please head on home.

Yes . . . that was a fine idea. A true gem of an idea. Of all ideas he had examined lately, that one was superb: He would head on home. West. West to the sea called the Outer Reach. Then south . . . he would know when he got there. But his first problem, once he gained the dark, wet street, was that he had no idea where the barrack was. Again. The damned place kept disappearing. He set out in search. It was still in the town somewhere; he'd found it before. He stumbled over a crooked curbstone and sprawled into the gutter.

Wonderful! This is just what he needed now—filth all over his clothing. Perhaps it would match the sludge he found smeared all over his mind.

Dear God Marin, he thought, why have you led me to this hell? And he heard Santon in his mind:

"*Assume as much guilt as you like, Keven. Your capacity is entirely up to you.*"

"Santon!" he shouted. "Go away!"

He shook his head violently and pushed himself up to a sitting position. Slowly he became aware of two littlers standing in front of him.

"Well, here we are again, sir," one of them said with a grin. "Wicket and Bestian, the two watchmen, utterly void of bosh and smuggery . . . which accounts for our condensed size. I am Wicket the Unexpected; this is Bestian the Best. How chance your ventures this night?"

Keven considered them for a moment, then decided to be truthful. Sitting in a gutter, weaving, it would be foolish to attempt otherwise.

"I've overwined m' brain . . . and it's wandered off somewhere in shearch of better 'panionship." He examined his legs. "And it's 'parently taken m' balance with it."

Wicket grinned again. "Well, you know the old saying, sir: 'Maintain thy balance upon wending home from the tavern, else the road shall rise and smite thee.' "

"It would be a fine idea if we could accompany you to the barrack," Bestian said. "Not that you would have any trouble, of course, but to see that no one attempts to victimize you and then has to pay the cost of his folly."

They stood casually, smiling, but there was something in their stances that indicated an alert preparedness. The thought occured to Keven, considering his condition, that they could probably take him back to his quarters whether he agreed or not. And he had to smile at the small man's tact.

"Tha's well said, Watchman Bestan. Bestian? I agree. It'd be a shame if shome—" he waved a hand, as if trying to sort the air for the right word—"bandit! Yes . . . bandit should attempt to . . . um, relieve me of m' purse." He lowered his voice. "They're everwhere, y'know. Ask anyone."

He offered his arms, and they helped him to his feet. Bestian in front, Wicket behind, they started slowly down a narrow, twisting alley. The only light was the wavering flicker from Bestian's lantern.

"This is a short way to the barrack," Wicket explained. "Short people take short ways, you know."

Keven laughed, but it was cut off when he veered into a wall. Wicket reached up and took his arm.

"I saw it, sir! 'Twas not your fault! The alley dodged right off to the left without a single warning."

Bestian halted suddenly ahead of them and raised the lantern. "Who's that?" he called.

Something sparked a distant warning in Keven's erratic thoughts, but he couldn't locate its source. He nearly stumbled into Bestian. A darker shape detached itself from the shadows ahead. There was the glint of a weapon.

"So," the figure said, "here be the mighty little rock-chucks theyselves."

"I know you," Bestian said. "You're one of the drunken dullards we arrested last tenday."

"Yar, thet be true, but we nar be drunken now, yew runty li'l squirrel."

There was a scrape of boots to the rear as two more figures emerged from the dark. Wicket turned to face them.

"I've two of them trapped back here, Best," he said calmly, his shortsword sliding free.

"You're lucky," Bestian said without turning. He lowered the lantern to the cobbles and drew his sword. "I've only got one."

"Need someone their own size," Keven declared as he wheeled and pushed past Wicket. At that moment, the two attacked. One shouldered Keven out of the way, and he collapsed against a wall. There was the bright sound of steel and the scurry of shapes scuffling in the dark. Keven tried to rise, but his hands skidded out from under him. He could do nothing but lean against the stone wall and listen to the baffling fight. He was in the center of it . . . and helpless.

"Killum, Wicket," he muttered. "Bashtards!"

There was a low groan of pain, and it seemed someone was down. A sword rang against the stone over his head. A new voice called out in the confusion. It sounded like a woman.

"I'm behind you, Bestian! I have the two back here."

There was another flurry of action, and a body fell across Keven's legs. Two more swirls of sounds and motions, curses and swords mingled, and it suddenly became very quiet in the alley. The lantern was raised from the cobbles, and Bestian's voice asked, "Who is that?"

"It's Slyt," answered the woman. "I think Wicket is badly hurt."

The lantern moved and swung to reveal a small shape crumpled against a wall. There were two larger shapes on the ground, one sprawled across Keven's legs. He tried to roll it off. The woman's sword was instantly aimed at his throat. Bestian pushed it away.

"He's all right."

She peered at Keven in the unsure light. "Doesn't look like it."

" 'M fine," Keven asserted, still pushing at the body. He frowned at her and then changed his mind about frowning; she was rather pretty. And then he frowned again; there was the possibility she had just saved his life. That was not funny. It was not right. It was, as a matter of fact, damned embarrassing. Even insulting. If he hadn't been drunk, he'd have—

"Wicket's dead," Bestian said quietly. By the wavering glow of the lantern, Bestian's face seemed carved of stone. Only the flicker of his clamped jaw muscles showed. Slyt glared at Wicket's small body, seemingly in anger, and then aimed that scowl at Keven, as if it were somehow all his fault.

Keven tried to rise and failed. Wicket? The sparkling littler? Dead? No. That wasn't right.

Keven let out a long breath. He was a fighter . . . he was a ranger . . . and a brave little man had died right in front of him. And he couldn't do anything about it. A woman had stepped in to save Bestian. And he couldn't do anything about it. He couldn't do anything about anything, it seemed. The world kept killing good people all around him, and there was not one damned thing he could do. In fact, he seemed to be at fault most of the time.

The demon on his shoulder snickered and summoned up his memory. "More wine, Keven?"

* * * * *

The sheriff called Keven to his room early in the morning to see if he could add anything about the circumstances of Wicket's death. Keven could offer little.

"Yes," the sheriff mused. "I can see even now, by those beady little red eyes, that your brain had other things to do last night. I imagine trying to focus them poor things was a major task."

Keven made no response. What could he say? He was still numb with blame. He could well be a statue, he thought, physically and mentally numb, emotionally dead.

The sheriff continued. "A fine little man an' a good friend be dead." The voice was low and cold. "An' there be a ranger drunk on his arse."

Keven had to clamp down on an urge to react in rage, perhaps hit the sheriff. He took a deep breath. "You can't hurt me any more than I can hurt myself," he said evenly, "so just keep your damned mouth shut about it."

The sheriff nodded, seemingly unaffected by the words. He shifted his gaze to an overhead beam and spoke as if to himself.

"There be a popular local story," he said. "It seems this Upper Vale smithy was truly pourin' it right down one night. His friends kept tellin' him, 'Barnold, you be quaffin' it too rapid, an' you be gettin' pure drunken.' But he nar listened, an' he just kept it up, tankard after tankard, like he was puttin' out a blaze. Well, it come closin' time, an' they set off for home 'bout a mile out o' Mill Ford, an' on the path, they came upon this huge centaur. An' he commands 'em to give way—you know how centaurs supposed to be, just pure disagreeable—but this smithy, he just walks right over an' throws that centaur arse-end-up! An' it jumps up, madder'n a drenched cat, an' the smithy throws it down again. An' every time the centaur tries to do somethin' 'bout it, the smithy yanks him all over the place an' throws him a-rollin'. Finally he flung him too far, an' the centaur got his feet firm under him an' he was gone like an elf arrow.

"The smithy, he just set down in the path an' holds his head an' he says, 'Ah-h, lads, I must be true dreadful drunk. I could nar e'en drag thet big bastard off'n his horse.' "

Keven gave a small nod of acknowledgment; he wasn't in a mood to be amused.

The sheriff considered him a moment. "Methinks you be havin' some problems tellin' centaurs from horsemen, too."

"My problems are my own, Sheriff."

The sheriff's voice was a raspy growl. "No . . . it seems your problems are becomin' everybody's. An' 'specially mine. An' you made a true fine enemy o' Lester o' Mill Ford. Once he heals up, he'll be right sulky."

"Try to imagine how much I don't care. He's the same as something scraped off the bottom of my boot."

The sheriff's abrupt, fleeting grin, quickly come and gone, was surprising. "Well, that be mainly true. He be a cocky li'l fart. Son o' one o' the small lords o' Upper Vale. Too overbearin' to have any sense, and not enough courage to truly get him into hard trouble with the law. But be wary o' him. He be a mean one."

"I'll count that among my lesser problems," Keven said.

"Well, watch your back. I suspicion he not be above that sort o' thing if the conditions be right for him. But what I want to know is, how come you got yourself into that thing? 'Tis my understandin' you have a code to live by. That true?"

Keven nodded; he'd already been through it all with himself too many times and didn't really feel like traveling that path again. The sheriff looked expectant.

"An' you tell me you're not a troublesome man?"

"I don't cause trouble."

"Ah . . . then mayhaps you be like a lodestone. You attracts it to yourself."

"I can be trouble to those who trouble me. And to those who trouble others, who are unable to defend themselves."

"Ah-h!" There seemed to be a far glint of something in the sheriff's eyes—amusement or sarcasm. "A hero, then!"

Keven felt himself blushing. Damn it! "I can't change the way I feel, Sheriff! I don't like bullies. I don't like those who take advantage of others simply because they can. Perhaps the others cannot or will not do anything about it, but I can! And I do *not* feel I am alone in my dislike for dullards and street dogs who have not the wit to control their mouth or the manners to leave someone else alone!"

"So you take it upon yourself to teach manners!"

Keven only frowned.

"Why not go out an' beat on a tree fer growin' the wrong way? Or throw stones at the river fer bein' where you don' want it to be? Makes as much sense as you gettin' angry at fools."

"'Cause a man's supposed to able to *think!*"

"That be what I hear, too, but you expect a damnish huge lot, lad!"

They glared at each other. The sheriff continued.

"You be a *ranger*, too! How 'bout doin' some thinkin' for yourself? What in all the hells you doin' venturin' aroun' in the bottom o' a ale barrel?"

"Is that part of your sheriff's concern?"

"It be my personal concern for so-called skilled people!" He glared at Keven. "An' seems to me if you goin' t' drink, you should be doin' it when you're in a good mood."

"No matter whar ya go, thar ya be," Keven drawled.

"Well, you be just funnier'n th' drover's left nut."

Keven didn't reply.

"I hear all the stories in town, you know. I don' have to be everywhere. An' the stories I hear 'bout you are true remarkable. I hear tell that you once made a proclamation at the Blue Boar—how did it go? 'A fighter must fight like a miller must mill, or he be nothin' but a pimple on the arse of mankind?' Somethin' like that. The story got to me in several dif'rent versions."

Keven just frowned at him; the sheriff continued.

"I were also told that you volunteered to pound heavily upon one o' our more noted ale-souses. On two different occasions, I believe."

"He's a drunken troublemaker who bothers cripples and serving maids."

"A part of his true nature," the sheriff said, nodding. "An' accordin' to the tale told, you suggested his lusty life might be better suited to the sows of the sty . . . if he could possibly find enough friends willing to catch an' hold one for him."

"I . . . don't remember saying exactly that."

"M-m-m . . . an' that's the one thing all the tales agree upon, too. A most quotable story." The hard blue eyes dropped to Keven.

"An' these be not all the tales I hear. Ah, no. Seems you an' Bracken be somethin' less than lovers, just 'bout ready to jump at each other like a couple o' rams in rut. Can't blame either o' you, though—you both be true talented in bein' dislikable. An' last night you taunt one o' our leading bull-bungs into flailin' his sword in a public tavern, an' I'm supposed to believe you're not a troublesome man."

He was waiting for an answer this time. Keven shrugged. "Surely a matter of some harsh words and a few blows in an inn is not uncommon around here."

"Oh, no. 'Tis probably an evenin's best entertainment. But—" the eyes and the frown hardened—"we like our troubles in familiar forms. Then when somethin' happens, we know who to look fer. We sit here on a busy road, an' too many strangers pass through, lately with great suspicion attached to 'em. So when one appears, directionless, armed, an' obviously well trained, who starts gettin' to be the center of a few cracked heads an' a lot o' stories, then I get int'rested in 'em an' wonder just how much trouble they goin' to be!"

Keven was beginning to feel a strong thud of pulse, anger trying to take control again. "The rain is over, and I'm going over that pass on my way west, Sheriff."

"On the road to hell, you will!" The sheriff gave a bark of a laugh. "I told you before, you not be goin' that way! There be a job to do!" He gave a grunt of disgust. "You be one fine freeranger, you be!"

"You just said it! I'm *one!* I'm a damned good ranger, and that also means I'm not foolish! This problem requires a company of rangers! *Two* companies! There's not that many!"

"An' we be prob'ly better fer it! Any more rangers in town an' th' Blue Boar'd have t' cart in ale by th' caravan!"

"Just because I spent a damned week of rain with some friends in—"

"You got a pack o' drinkin' cohorts, but you got no friends!"

"They enjoy my company!"

"As long as your silver an' th' drink hold out! I doubt you'd know a friend from th' cobbler's cat!"

They glared at each other. The sheriff leveled a finger.

"I be tellin' you one thing you best remember, Keven o' Kingsend: You be treadin' the edge o' trouble."

"I'm really worried."

"If you have a breath o' sense, there will be a day when that statement come true."

* * * * *

A misty yellow sunrise, like steaming gold in the sky, heralded the next day's dawning, and people came out into the streets smiling and squinting against the uncommon light. Bedding and clothes appeared on railings, windowsills, and balconies. Laden clotheslines were everywhere in the town, arcing from house to house like flag streamers at a fair. Brooklets still tumbled through the streets, and the river yet rumbled and roiled through Lower Market, but a few mud-caked carts pulled into Upper Market from the Shire Hills, driven by smiling littlers, loaded with their preserved foods. The word spread rapidly, and people crowded Shires Road to the market. The town was coming to life again.

Keven sat on the high parapet of the barrack upper court, legs dangling over a three-story drop to the street below. It was part of the old town wall, overlooking the valley and the river. He was quietly playing a small flute. It was one of the few things he had kept from the ship. Tuck had given it to him when he was a small lad and had taught him strange, haunting tunes of the sea.

He played and watched the mist rise from the town and valley as the sun warmed the sodden land. The mist gathered like low fog at ground level until the valley disappeared and streets and houses dimmed beneath him, and it seemed he was isolated on a tower wall on a cloud. . . . It would be nice if he could be, he thought. This world was not working right. Somewhere in the tapestry of this life that he had begun weaving for himself, he had made a mistake, and he couldn't devise where the threads went wrong.

Later in the day he walked to the old west gate at the edge of town and the crossroads where the Road West split away. Wagonloads of long pine logs blocked the muddy road north down to the naked stone abutments of the keep bridge. Lines had already been strung to the great stone pier in the middle of the Mad River, and the scene was a swarm of workers preparing tripod cranes and timbers to bridge the still raging waters. Figures watched and waved from the walls of the keep, and he could hear an occasional call across the rumble of the river.

He walked the Road West for half a league; it was drying in the warm sun, still mud and mire in the low swales, but passable. It wound and wandered through sloping field and forest to where the abrupt rise of the Macaab Mountains and the sheer, looming peak of Castle Mountain seemed to float above a layer of mist like mountains of another land.

He remembered Santon speaking to the assembly at the academy one morning:

"*It is called 'Seeing the Demon.' It means facing the true, brutal reality of events. Here you practice with weapons and techniques, you flail away at each other in all seriousness and fervor, you attack and defend, and when it's all over, you laugh and review the mistakes and prepare for another match. But there will come a time when truth will wield a sword more sharp that any living opponent. If you have the insight, that sudden realization of truth can be a shock. You will See the Demon. You will see yourself. And you may not like what is revealed.*"

Yes . . . he had seen the demon in the Northeast Kingdom, he saw it when Gohn the Silent was killed, and he did not like the things he saw when he looked within himself then. And now Wicket was dead, falling nearly into his hands, and the demon was there, too. If he was truly such a fine fighter as people supposed, then why couldn't he prevent friends from dying? How come he was beaten so badly on the pass? If only he hadn't been drinking when Gohn fell. And Wicket. If only he had been more alert the night the thieves crept aboard the ship. If only . . .

And all the festering thoughts gibbered and jeered in the murky caverns of his mind. His memory was killing him.

No . . . find the truth, he told himself.

It wasn't his memory that was killing him. It was his memory inviting in the wine for comfort, and the wine convincing him it was doing a good job. And then, in the swirl and falter of his days, more mean memories were added to the pyre. And they required more wine. It was the wine that was killing him.

And it was his hand that was raising the cup.

And it was his mind commanding the hand, telling itself, "You can't resist these demons. Here, this will help."

He had been trained to fight everything but himself; in that, he was a failure. He was an insult to the academy . . . and to himself. The demons were winning.

"I can't fight them," he said softly.

And as if from over his shoulder, so clearly he nearly turned, Rusker's voice echoed from the academy:

"*Think ya can, think ya cannot—either way, ya be right!*"

Chapter Five

hildren's song and game, from the legendary exploits of Charl, Hero of Novus Old.

This is the way you make your Party;
This is the way if you would be hearty:
First a Fighter, brave and strong,
Then a Dwarf who knows no wrong;
Bring a Thief, the locks to know;
And a littler with a bow;
A Mage must come, with magic spells;
A Cleric too, from holy cells;
Find an Elf to pierce the dark;
The number's right! Clasp hands—embark!

Keven signaled for another sour ale and scowled into that one for a while. No matter how many times he refought the skirmish on the pass, blow by blow, it still churned and gnarled inside. And it kept coming out the same. He relived his failures over and over, it seemed, all of them, and they were always the same. He couldn't induce a single change. Santon:

"You have eyes like an eagle, Keven. I wish you could

direct them inward to hunt down the rodents that nibble at your soul."

"Easy to say, Santon!" he snapped aloud, then quickly took a tilt of ale when heads turned. He was in a dim, grimy tavern in Crossriver, a foul place barely shoveled out from the flood. It reeked of fetid things he did not care to dwell on. There was a putrid stench to all of Crossriver. It was a bog of muck and debris and misshapen buildings left stinking in the sun after the retreat of the river.

"Yew'd o' thought th' river would o' warshed it clean o'er thar in Crossriver," someone had commented, "but it made it worser. How can thet be?"

Artur, the armorer, after days of cursing the lack of dry charcoal, was finally finishing a sword for him across the muddy street. It was going to cost him twelve golders, bargained down from seventeen, but it was good steel—at least that was what everyone claimed of Artur. There had been an outburst of braying laughter in the Blue Boar when he had mentioned a desire to obtain a dwarfen sword.

"As me ol' grammy says, 'Wish in one hand, pee in the t'other, an' see which yer gets the most of.' "

"Yew be fully daft, lad! The odds on gettin' a dwarf t' sell yew a sword be 'bout the same as fer me t' fly from here t' Upper Flattens."

"Next thing he be wantin' a elf bow!"

"An a wizard's cloak!"

He had quit the Blue Boar after that and taken his meals and leisure in a number of different places. It wasn't just the snickering about the sword that bothered him; it was everything about the place now. It was the knowing grins that greeted him, the winks and nudges passed along, the eyes that shifted in his direction, then smiled away. And there were often scowls and low mutterings and sometimes an overheard word: "Wicket . . ."

"To hell with them! They can all—"

He realized he was growling aloud again. A surly one-eyed man turned from his companions at a nearby table and scowled. He spat on the floor and spoke in a sneering voice: "Yew got some loud troubles there, buffoon?"

Keven swung all the way around on his bench to face them. At least this was something he could understand. "The last time I saw something that looked like a lost eye, it was a pig facing away from me," he said evenly. "Just about the same as I see now."

The man came roaring to his feet, snatching at a scarred cudgel in his belt, but he was instantly enfolded and restrained by two of his comrades.

"Nar, Huber! Hold yerself!"

"Rein in, man! He be thet fighter!"

"Nar much o' one, by what I hear!" Huber grated.

Another man jumped up to help contain the furious man. Keven watched the struggle with an expression of mild irritation.

"Let him go," he said. "I'm in just the right mood to take a troublesome little pismire like that and pinch his bedamned dungwit little head right off."

Huber unleashed an enraged howl and nearly broke free. A fourth man at the table rose to his feet, sighed, picked up a stool, and in a rather nonchalant manner, rapped Huber solidly over the head with it. He slid down through the arms of the other three, and they left him sprawled facedown on the muddy floor.

"Don' mind Huber," one said, grinning at Keven. "He get sheer ugly ofttimes. It be a right queer day if he don' try t' jump at somebody. He be but a hollow little turd."

"Yar," another said, nodding. "We saves his life reg'lar."

Keven turned back to the bad ale, scowling, his anger aimed now at himself more than anything else. Gods alive, he had wanted that to happen! The small demon voice he knew so well chuckled, telling him if he had played that correctly, he could have gotten them all involved.

And wouldn't that have been fun? Maybe . . .

But it might have burned off some of this rage, he thought, like fire through the fields of fall, destroying the old, useless growth. Like that clamorous ass three nights ago at the Sign of the Lost Dog. *That* one wouldn't be challenging anyone for a while.

The scene replayed. . . .

"Ho! Yew there, so-called fighter! If yew wants to leave, yew has t' pretend this door be the pass an' I be a bandit." He snickered for the benefit of his friends.

"Good idea," Keven had replied, nodding. "We'll see if I can get it right this time."

An awed bystander commented a short time later, studying the man stretched out on the floor, "Seems the pass be open now."

Yes, I know, Rusker, Keven told one of the nagging inner voices. I know! It makes me no better than they. I know, Santon. It's not enough to do the right thing but to be the right person. I know the lessons. I know . . . I know . . .

But knowing doesn't make anything better. And what in all the hells together was he doing swilling down more horse piss ale in a stable tavern like this?

"Be yew really th' fighter whut fought th' bandits up on th' pass?"

The quiet question yanked him back; it was the young serving maid, a grimy child-woman of perhaps fifteen.

"Nar," he growled. "If I be thet handsome buck, then whut be I a-doin' in a place like this?"

She tilted her head and frowned at him. "Yew nar talked like thet a bit ago."

"Ah, yar . . . then it must be yer ale whut does it. I tells yew true, y' near pretty bit, it be a ale whut can alter most anythin' fer the worst."

He rose from the table and tossed down some coppers.

"I gots t' get back t' me pigs now, lass. They misses me so if'n I be gone too long."

It was darkening into late dusk when he slogged across the street to the armorer's shop. Thunder was grumbling again in the north. He rubbed his face with both hands, shaking his head as if to cast off the evening. How many mugs of that bilge did he have?

And he answered himself, It really doesn't make any difference. Apparently I can reach a condition approaching borderline stupidity all by myself. He shook his head again, violently, wishing he could throw up right here in the middle of the street, and in so doing cast out everything that was wrong. He was in trouble—there was no doubt about that—and whatever he was doing about it, it wasn't the proper solution.

So?

"One at a time," he muttered, recalling one of Santon's slogans. "You defy your demons one at a time. First the ale and the wine, then . . ."

He wasn't sure what would be next. He would know when he got there.

* * * * *

The sword felt good in his hand. He had specified its length, about half a hand shorter than normal for a fighting sword, but still with the balance well forward and with a long, wire-wrapped grip for two-handed use. Point on the ground, the pommel came to just below his belt. He carved a few glittering arcs out of the air and nodded.

"Do you have any sharkskin to wrap the grip?"

"*Sharkskin?*" The leathery little man regarded him suspiciously. "Whut be a shark?"

"Give it no mind. It's a . . . very rough skin that's good for wrapping something you don't want to slip."

"Ah-h . . ." The man nodded. "But whut be a shark?"

"It's a . . . very big fish."

"Ah-h . . . an' it be very rough, be it?" One side of his mouth was lifting in a beginning smile.

Keven dismissed the shark with a curt wave. "How about the helmet and the shield?"

There had been a well-placed sword dent in the back of the helmet, matching exactly a long, painful lump on the back of his head.

"Helmet be fine, though a bit marked. I fixed it easy. But this here shield . . ." He shook his head as he propped it up on his bench. A long, deep dent angled across the upper half, and the shield was actually bent at that point.

"Whut in two or three hells sart o' blade did thet? An' how b'damn big war he whut swang it?"

"Big."

"Huh! Seems so!"

"And he wasn't in a good mood," Keven added. "How about the shoulderplate?"

"Ah'll make yer a new one. Don' ne'er trust plate whut's been sliced once. How much d' yew want yer shield fixed?"

"Just straighten out the bend and most of the dent."

"Yew wants to leave the mark in it?" The man frowned at the shield and shook his head. "Looks like it been folded once—an' yew wants it thet way?"

A flood of inner heat rose in Keven. It was not the blaze of anger or the burn of embarrassment; it was the kindling of conviction.

"I want it exactly like that," he said. "I want to remember just how it got that way."

* * * * *

To the north of Midvale, a woman frowned into the dark rain from an open doorway. She could see the glow of a lantern in the stock shed.

"Norm?" she called, then louder.

"No-orm? Yew been gone awhile."

There was nothing but the rush of the rain.

"Yew childers stay here in the warm," she said to the two small ones behind her. She pulled a shawl over her head and plunged out into the murky night.

There were fresh tracks in the mud outside the shed. They were almost manlike, but huge. Too terribly huge.

"What war botherin' the stock, Norm?" she asked as she ducked into the shed. "Yew been gone on to—"

In a whisper, "Norm? . . ."

The lantern was on the lid of the grain bin.

There was an arm beside it.

And a leg on the dirt floor.

And the rest of Norm was hanging head down from the slaughterhook.

* * * * *

The muscles of Keven's arms and shoulders burned like molten lead, and there was a sharp, solid cramp beginning to spear under his left shoulder blade. Damn! He was going to have to drop!

He hung for a moment longer, measuring the distance down to the flagstones of the barrack courtyard a full story below. Some of the upturned, watching faces smiled, some frowned, some shook their heads.

He dropped. As he landed, a lance of pain flashed through his bruised left knee. He gritted his teeth and knew a grimace flickered across his face. The sheriff, hands on hips, gave him a wry frown.

"Well . . . I s'pose every fool has the right to kill hisself in whatever brainless way he desires, but for you to do it right here in the barrack courtyard be more than casual embarrassin' an' prob'ly not altogether right. What in all o' the seven hells be you tryin' to do?''

Keven scowled up at the crenellated second-story parapet circling the courtyard. The area here was smaller than the training court at the academy. That had been fifty paces to a side; this was closer to forty. Still, he hadn't been able to make it all the way around.

He explained.

It was called "The Parapet Journey" at the academy. Every morning after running the outer wall walkway, trainees were required to travel around the outside of the training court parapet hanging from their hands, pulling up to the merlons, swinging down to the crenels, a drop of nearly two stories beneath them to the flagstones. The first month, one side; the second month, two sides; then so on until reaching a complete circuit. Those who fell or dropped had to begin again immediately, if they were able; those who pulled themselves to the guardwalk before completion also had to begin again. Five consecutive failures resulted in probation from the academy; a flat refusal to attempt the journey resulted in immediate dismissal. In what little free time they had, there was much practice on the parapet. Once, he had completed two continuous turns at night, alone, just to prove to himself that he could do it.

"I've neglected my training," he told the sheriff. "With your permission, I'd like to train here."

"M-m-m . . ." The sheriff seemed to be regarding the surrounding walls with some suspicion. "And what other odd and injurious things do you have in mind?"

Keven scanned the parapet again. "Ropes strung from merlon to merlon across the court. The exercise is to travel hand over hand along the ropes, then swing to another rope when you're close enough." He pointed out part of the ancient town walls. "Climbing those walls without aids. Both up and down."

The sheriff put on his best scowl as he leaned back to squint up at the ancient East Tower. "You part squirrel mayhaps?"

Keven glanced at the grinning watchmen. "Some of your men could use such training."

"M-m-m. I can just see the bodies splattered all over the court here. I got more for the Watch to do than make pavin' stones out o' them."

"It's for strengthening. Some of your Watch couldn't run the length of this court without crumpling as if they'd been axed!"

The sheriff nodded slowly as he frowned at the men. "M-m-m . . . you got any things that won't kill 'em off quite so easy?"

Keven smiled. "I can think of a few, but I'm not going to oversee it. I'm going to be busy on my own."

The sheriff regarded the lounging, laughing watchmen with a thoughtful gaze. "Let's go eat," he mused. "I'll buy your meal. You tell me 'bout your academy trainin'."

*   *   *   *   *

Keven told him.

There was staff fighting every day, one on one. The victor could leave the circle; the loser had to stand to another, and another if he lost, and yet another, until injuries or exhaustion forced a surrender. Five consecutive surrenders resulted in probation.

One student stood in the center of the training court with a shield while another tried to hit him with sling stones. If he couldn't do it with five stones, it was his turn with the shield.

Armed with chalk-coated staffs, they would stalk each other through the night corridors and courts of the academy. They had to mark ten certain points on the circuit with their particular sign to assure that none hid from being marked. The three showing the most body hits had to do an immediate Parapet Journey.

There was daily proficiency training with Rusker or one of the advanced students in all weapons.

There was bow practice at targets swinging behind an archway, but only a certain color target must be hit.

Dressed in armor, they would have to shield against incoming stunning arrows.

Another drill involved catching sling stones in flight in a small leather basket.

And there was running. They were to run everywhere they went during a training day, and their training day was measured from the moment the morning sun touched the top of the gatehouse flagstaff until the sunset left the same point. When it rained or was overcast, the day began when Rusker said it began, and it ended when he said it ended. The rest of the time they studied.

And they would stand together in the training court after the morning run and before The Parapet Journey, raise their right hands as if grasping a sword and shout as loudly as they could: "Courage! Compassion! Generosity! Wisdom! Honor! Self-respect!"

And then brace themselves as if shielding against attack and murmur: "Jealousy! Hypocrisy! Self-deception! Self-involvement! Greed! Evil!"

Keven didn't mention it, but he remembered how Santon would sometimes glance at him with a hint of a smile at the word "self-deception."

* * * * *

The old, unused training area at the barrack, actually the roof of the downhill wing, was refurbished with new bow targets, staff trees, pivoting swordplay arms, and mock-armed dummy opponents. And the men of the Town

Watch came to regard Keven with fervent resentment; he was a brash outsider tampering with their well-ordered lives. They knew where the sheriff was getting his fancy ideas. And the wiry old bastard seemed to enjoy watching them gasping around the courtyard in a ponderous trot or struggling to clamber up a rope to the parapet. And all the while that bedamned ranger went swinging hand over hand along ropes and parapet like some bedamned creature from the dark side.

"I din't join the Watch t' be treated like some damn slave!"

"Yar. I be gonna let me dally hang out. If I gonna work like a harse, I just as be look like one."

"Bracken, how d'yer cock this here crossbow?"

"Alden! Git that thing away from him! I don' want any crossbows on this roof! Somebody gonna get killed!"

"We got nar more crossbow bolts anyhow, Bracken. Somebody shoot 'em all away tryin' t' hit the river from here."

"Thet's just fine! We gonna have irate an' wounded citizens all over town! Things be bad 'nough without folks thinkin' they be under attack by the Watch! Damn ranger!"

"Yew hear what thet ranger done now? He swammed the river clear o'er to Crossriver an' back! Yew e'er heared anythin' like thet? An' thet river still be rollin' high an' hard."

"He do that every day. Half the women in town be down thar at Lower Market to watch his bare arse hit the water."

"He nar be quite common, yew know. E'ery morn he be up afore the sun an' runnin' near on to five mile!"

"An' he run Long Stairs e'ry day, too. Bottom to top! Try *that* an' see how yer fruit falls!"

"Hell, he don' walk narmore narwhar!"

"Good gods alivin', Clyde! Watch yer damn arrows! Thet one went clear o'er to Steep Street!"

"Hell o' a shot, warn't it?"

* * * * *

The day was sliding away, outlining the Macaab Mountains against a bloody western sky like some black, jagged lower jaw. There were again storm clouds in the north. Keven and the sheriff were eating in a small tavern, the Sign of the Dancing Pig on Purly Lane. The sheriff spoke without looking up from his plate.

"You be goin' back up there, true? That's what all this tough trainin' be about? You gettin' yourself all polished up to pay back them bad boys that pounded on you?"

Keven didn't look up either. "I'm going up there and bring that damned mountain down around their knees, Sheriff!"

"U-m-m . . . an' you consider that all your healin' an' trainin' this past half-moon be 'nough fer you to just stroll up there and carve arse in all directions?"

Keven marked out his words with his knife.

"If I had two men that graduated with me as archers, we'd leave nothing up there but the ravens!"

"Yes, yes . . ." The sheriff frowned at his slice of roast as if it had committed some minor crime. "How you do change your song, Freeranger Keven o' Kingsend."

Keven could feel a flush beginning to climb his neck. "That never should have happened the way it did. I . . . let the academy down."

"Ah-h, so this now be somethin' t' do with your pride."

"Call it whatever you want. I don't care a foul flux one way or another. The result's going to be the same!"

"Um-m. Let me see if I got this true. You wouldn't fight this out when 'twas the right thing t' do, but you'll fight it out 'cause you got pounded. That 'bout it?"

Keven attacked his roast in silence. The sheriff nodded.

"Yes, yes . . . it true take some private things to get your bowels a-boil. You new to gettin' embarrassed?"

"It's not something I care to get used to! And what concern is it of yours?"

The sheriff slammed down his knife. "You be the most irksome an' tempery damn dagger I know! What in the seven hells be wrong with you? You be not afraid o' a mountainside o' killers, but somebody ask you a personal question an' you be ready to kick their head off!"

"I don't like sarcasm!"

"An' I don' like mouths that run off afore the brains be hitched up!"

There was no reply. Keven scowled at his platter. The sheriff recovered his knife, and they ate in silence for a while. The sheriff signaled for another wine; Keven shook his head no when the serving boy looked inquiringly at him. The sheriff leaned back, chewed and studied him across the table.

"So you think a couple o' good people would help."

"It would make it so I could get in closer to watch their faces. Right now, that's important."

The sheriff churned a swallow of wine around in his mouth, stared thoughtfully over Keven's head at the ceiling beams, and said, "Um-m."

Keven dipped a finger into his tea and traced letters on the table. "You know what this is?"

The sheriff peered at the letters: *B-e-S-T.* "Says 'best.' Do I win somethin'?"

"I found them scratched five stones below the top of the East Tower at the barrack. On the outside. Freshly done. Someone had to climb the outside, probably down from the top, and then hang from one hand to do that."

"Be b'damned." The sheriff shook his head.

"Found them again about midway up the north wall to the upper court from the alley." He frowned at the four letters. "And it's a strange way to spell 'best.' Three capitals."

"You must find a lot o' int'restin' things in your climbin'."

"Anyone in the watch climbing those walls?"

The sheriff shrugged. "Could be. There be a few that take your trainin' as a challenge. There be some with dangerously little sense."

"Whoever he is, he's good."

"Um-m." The sheriff finished his wine. "Or outstandin' foolish."

Keven considered the older man's face. There seemed to be something there . . . a hint of humor? He was about to ask what was amusing when the tavern began trembling. There was a deep, seemingly distant rumble, overlaid with the clatter of loose objects. Keven grasped the table, staring at the sheriff. The sheriff leaned back in his chair, calmly chewing a bite of roast.

"It be just th' earth shakin'. It happen sometimes."

Keven relaxed his grip. "I've never felt it before. What causes it?"

The sheriff shrugged. "Omens, mayhaps. The old folks say 'tis a dragon under the mountains, but that be just old folk talk."

"I don't like it," Keven admitted.

"Can't say I enjoy it meself," the sheriff replied with a nod.

* * * * *

Captain Mikel of Lord Damon's Vale Guard was a bearded, graying man, slightly taller than Keven and stiff as an oak plank. He was dressed in a colorful uniform of green and silver, with ornate strappings, highly polished boots, and shining helmet. The engraved hilt of a curved sword topped a decorated scabbard on his left hip. The man refused to sit; perhaps he couldn't bend, Keven thought.

He stood beside the table in the sheriff's barrack room, sourly considering Keven's seated slouch and tugging at the point of his beard. The sheriff was seated behind the table with hands locked behind his head, gazing at an upper corner of his office room. He seemed to be mildly bemused by what he found there.

"You say you saw the Waystation," the captain asserted. Somehow it came out as an accusation. "It is a building of timber and wattle construction, two-story, attached directly to the cliff face of the—"

"Yes, I saw it." Keven said curtly. He had begun to take a vicious pleasure in interrupting the pompous officer.

The captain pulled at his beard and frowned; he appeared to tug down his eyebrows when he did that. "So you were able to see the Waystation . . . so this would put you on the—"

"On the road switchback ascending directly to the Waystation, yes."

"And they—"

"Surprised me by hiding in the rocks above the road, yes."

"And you say there were—"

"About twenty of them, yes."

"But you—"

"Did not count them, no."

"And they—"

"Wore a variety of arms in great number but poorly maintained. They scratched in all the right places for people that filthy, and they also laughed a lot. Not well, but a lot."

The sheriff made a sound suspiciously like a chuckle, then turned it into a cough.

"Yes . . ." the captain said with a nod. "Now, this leader . . . this . . . this—"

"Sander, he signs hisself," the sheriff offered, still examining the corner.

"Yes . . . Sander. You say he—"

"Was a tall, short, thin, fat man with a large emerald up his arse, who stood on his hands and sang poorly!" Keven slapped the table. "I realize you may not have a lot of room under that helmet, but how many times do you have to hear something before it batters its way inside?"

The captain huffed and drew himself even straighter. He leveled a rigid finger at Keven. "Now, you listen, young man—"

"I would like to listen! I would enjoy hearing some sound reasoning! But all that happens here is that you ask the same damned questions over and over, and I give you the same answers! How were they disciplined! What was their attitude! Could any of them whistle and jump on one foot at the same time? It seems to me you'd be able to get the track of it after a while!"

The two glared at each other. Captain Mikel seemed to be having a problem gaining his breath. "Now, you listen, you young—"

The sheriff gave an explosive sigh and brought his attention back to the captain. "You do march the same ground over, Mikel, an' it be as tiresome as a cat in heat. It be time to get on with it." He looked at Keven. "As I said afore, there be a plan now—"

"Oh, merciful gods!" Keven breathed in a little girl's voice. "Does it entail someone actually *doing* something? I don't think I could *stand* it if anyone was going to *do* something."

The sheriff stared him into silence. "Be you through now? You got any more o' these little urges you must get out?"

Keven reddened, slouched, and waited. The sheriff scowled at him and continued.

"Now, since you be o' such a fierce an' righteous nature

to run back up there an' kill everybody in sight, there be a good place in this plan for you! D'you want it?"

"I haven't heard what it is."

"An' I'll tell you a pretty part of it—you *won't* hear what it is till you agree! Ain' that a fine feature? An' if you don' agree, I'll lock you up till it be all over! It get interestin' all along, don' it?"

Keven blinked at him. "But—"

"A 'but' be somethin' a bull hauls around behind 'im, ranger. The point is, I'll not have you chargin' 'round on your own an' blunder-footin' this whole thing into a clutter! Told you that afore! This be a plan that'll only work once, an' if we shoot our bolt wild on it, we'll not get 'nother chance. Now, you be goin' with it, or you be not goin' anywhere at all! Which be it?"

They traded scowl for scowl.

"You don't give me much choice," Keven muttered.

"Sounds like daylight beginnin' to make its way inside there. That be some improvement."

Keven frowned away, then at the rigid captain, then at the wall, then out at the sunlit courtyard. "Agreed," he muttered. "Done and done."

"Good!" The sheriff settled back into his chair and unrolled a parchment map. After a moment of scowling and squinting, rearing his head back like a balky horse, he finally stabbed a finger at what Keven could see was clearly labeled "The Pass by Castle Mountain."

"There! That be Castle Pass right here. The Waystation you seen be just this side o' the top by 'bout . . . oh, four hundred paces, I'd say."

"It is five hundred and fifty paces from the courtyard of the Waystation to the top of the pass itself," Captain Mikel asserted. "From there . . ." He stopped and cleared his throat as the sheriff glared at him.

"Now," the sheriff continued, "from what we heared

an' seen, we think them bandits be usin' the old Waystation for their quarters—hell, it be the onliest sensible thing up there they could use."

Captain Mikel cleared his throat again. "Except for the possibility of the old dwarfenhalls of the Macaab Mountain—"

"We be *not* gettin' into some endless yammerin' 'bout the Macaab Mountain dwarfenhalls an' how they might be used! It be only necessary to say that this band have some fast way to get back an' forth from Castle Pass to North Pass. It be close onto twenty-some mile by bird's flight through some true raggedy mountains 'tween them two places. Now—"

"About seven leagues," Keven interrupted.

"Call it what you like! Now, I don' care if they be usin' the old dwarfenhalls, hangin' onto some eagle's tailfeathers, or runnin' the mountain trails like a pack o' goats with their arses on fire. They be somehow *doin'* it!"

"You don't think it's two different bands?" Keven asked.

"No." The sheriff shook his head firmly. "This buck in leathers you told 'bout, this Sander, he be seen in both places too many times. Folks describe him from way back. Now, somehow he knows when anythin' worth raidin' be goin' over them passes, which be not difficult, considerin' the number o' people wanderin' 'round in town here. An' he got a good way to get from one pass to t'other. We figured one time he made that trip in a little more than a day! Now, goin' lengthwise down the Macaabs in that time be fever-footin' right along."

Keven nodded. "Horses?"

"Doubt it. A horse would bust all four legs up there quicker'n you'd say 'Steven-in-a-swivet.' An' the warfen claim they be not a road nor good track. Now, I admit, when they told that, they used our words, not their own.

An' they sometimes put different meanin's to things when they speak in Tradish."

"So there could be a road," Keven affirmed, "but not a road as we mean it."

"Somethin' like that."

Keven spread his hands. "Then what is it?"

The sheriff shrugged. "I not be sayin' that there be a warfen road through the mountains! I not be saying there *not* be a warfen road through the mountains! I don' say one damnish thing 'bout things we don' know!"

"But things are possible," Keven said, remembering academy speculations about dwarfs and dwarfenhalls. It was generally considered that humans knew as much about dwarfs as they knew about the bottom of the sea.

"Ah, yes," the sheriff went on, nodding. "Things be possible. As 'tis said, there be more things we never heard 'bout than things we think we know. Now . . ."

He stared Keven directly in the eyes.

" . . . here be what we got afoot. . . ."

* * * * *

Essen the Elder, gem merchant, was a crumpled little man. It seemed as if some essential inner supports had given way in the far past, and his body had slowly settled in upon itself. Yet a fervent fire burned within, evinced in narrow, cynical eyes that glittered like jewels. It was said he was old enough to know the majority of the gems in Western Latonia by their given names. He turned the purple sapphire in delicate fingers, close to his eyes, catching the sunlight that angled through the shop's single window.

"Three hundred," he said in a tired, rusty voice. Keven gave a short laugh of amusement. For once, he was enjoying himself; this verbal fencing over trade was something he understood.

"I would have thought better of you, merchant. That's a Belanese five-hundred-golder trade sapphire, a standard anywhere in coastal trade."

"Tutor me not, young man. Though Belanese cut, 'tis of poor clarity. And as you may have grasped, this is not an area of coastal trade. Three hundred."

"Teach me not, merchant," Keven sighed, reaching for the stone. "'Tis not the first such Belanese I've had or seen. I fear the remoteness here from the major centers of trade has created some artificial values. The goldworth of this particular item tends to increase in relation to its distance from coastal trade. The rarity factor, you know. I shall keep it until I return to areas of its genuine exchange."

"Um-m . . ." The slitted, sparkling eyes studied Keven for a moment. "If you have another such Belanese, I will give you eight hundred for the pair."

"I do indeed have another, and if you sincerely desire them, you will give me a thousand for the pair. That is their fair trade value. I should be asking twelve hundred, considering their curiosity value here, but I'm tired today, and I don't feel like playing the game. If that is not to your liking, then I shall deal with Chester's son in Box Court. He has treated me fairly in the past."

Essen snorted. "Chester's son deals in waterstones and flawed baubles and—"

"Then he should appreciate true Belanese trade gems," Keven said with a shrug. "I thank you, kind sir, but—"

"Nine hundred, the pair."

Keven smiled and shook his head. "You're not listening, gentle merchant. In the first place, for me to offer two Belan-fivers here at the edge of the world for a mere thousand is utter foolishness on my part! You know it. I know it. And we both know the profit you will turn. You should treat your customers with the same respect you accord your merchandise, good Essen."

"Tell me not my trade, young man!"

"Insult not my knowledge, good merchant!"

The old man's face seemingly never changed expression, but the eyes crinkled with what could have been anger, or assessment. Or even humor.

"Let me see the companion to that stone."

Keven was prepared; he brought out the other from an inner pocket in his cloak. The old man peered at it closely in the sunlight. He examined it through a glass. He balanced it against his weights.

"Um-m-m . . . now the first one again."

After the same diligent inspection, he nodded. "The second one is somewhat better," he grunted. "A thousand golders for the pair."

Keven stifled a smile. The two sapphires were absolutely identical; it was the consistent quality of Belanese stones that made them legitimate trade gems.

"I have no need for a thousand gold at this time and no desire to haul around that much weight," he said. "Choose one of them for five hundred. It is the figure I came in with, and it is the figure I will go out with, or I shall go out with nothing but my gems, and you will be the loser for it."

"I will give you my note for that amount you care not to carry."

It was Keven's turn to look doubtful and make an *Um-m-m* sound. He knew the note would be good; the sheriff had recommended this man highly as being the most trust-worthy among the town's several gem merchants, perhaps the most honest along the Trade Road. Essen's notes were "as good as the gold he harbors," it was said, acceptable among local merchants and far along the road. The old man scowled at him.

"You are either an utter stranger to Midvale or too se-verely suspicious for your own progress if you hesitate too long, young man. My notes are honest exchange."

Keven nodded. "Done—the pair for a thousand. I will take your note for eight hundred and the remaining two hundred in Palan platins."

Palan coins had milled edges, reducing the likelihood of being shaved. Essen gave him a sharp look.

"I deal not in crippled coins, young man! Keven of Kingsend, is it? I shall weigh them out if you wish."

"If you would, please. I have my own weight." He produced a bright Latonian golder wrapped in soft leather. The old man examined it, carefully balanced it against his own ounceweight, nodded, and handed it back. A thin smile broke new wrinkles around his mouth.

"I took you not for a trader, Keven of Kingsend."

"Everyone must be a trader, Elder Essen, if they would survive the merchants of the world." He smiled. "One is either the arrow or the target."

The old man nodded at the old saying. He weighed out the coins, then wrote the note in a firm hand:

I, Essen the Elder, Gem Merchant, who do abide in Ash Court in the Town of Midvale upon the Great Western Trade Road, do Promise and Affirm to pay to one Keven of Kingsend the full amount of Eight Hundred Goldworth at his demand.

If he so desires, he may sign this note to Another, who may sign to Another, but only to a limit of Three such shall I honor.

"See me again, Keven of Kingsend, when your purse needs rearranging."

Keven grinned. "I'll not let you benefit so easily next time, Elder Essen."

The slight, brittle smile showed again. "I will look forward to that time."

* * * * *

He was striding back to the Barrack, head down, as if enraged at the cobblestones, the resultant bright mood from dealing with Essen entirely gone; he was angry at the damned overbearing sheriff, angry at this damned noisy, crowded town, and most of all, he was furious with himself! In buoyant good humor—as they said at the academy, "Just for the merry tickle-arse of it"—he had stopped to consult an old witchy soothsayer on the way back from the gem merchant, and he pondered now what it was that made a man go completely witless every once in a while and do that sort of thing. After the usual rich gravy of how fortunate he was despite his travail and many hardships, how long was the arduous road he traveled, and how cruelly evasive was the thing he sought, she suddenly broke off, eyes widening. She gasped, clutched her bosom, and spoke then in an ominous, high-pitched voice:

"Death surrounds you! You carry it with you! It awaits you on the road! Death is your companion!"

That's even better than the line that made the sheriff so angry, he thought. Danger and Death are my companions. It had a certain ring.

"Is that all?" he had asked sarcastically.

"You are aimed into dreadful darkness as surely as an arrow into night. There is great evil." She put on a good face of being shaken by this horrible insight, huddled in her dark cloak and trembling, her watery old eyes wide and staring into some terrible void. "Please go. I cannot continue."

He had paid her price, a whole damn silver, and stalked out. Blithering old crone!

Well, it was his own feeble-minded fault! No band of robbers had overwhelmed him and dragged him in there.

But he *had* been dragged into something by the sheriff! And that was like the pestering of nettles in the back of his mind. And, too, there was that statement the sheriff had made after the meeting with Captain Mikel: "You be like a new coin o' a far land, lad—bright an' crisp, but o' an unknown value. You be yet unspent."

What in several hells did *he* know about it? The pompous, overbearing, irksome old bastard!

He knew he shouldn't be irritated; he knew such little angers pulled at his spirit, shoved him off center. *I know, Santon! I know! I know!* But be damned, how he hated being told what to do! There seemed to be a whole world of self-important, pretentious fools who were somehow appointed to tell others how to conduct their own business.

He remembered an instance last year, somewhere in the far Northeast Kingdom, when a man with nothing better to do had been watching him load a mule, a sullen scowl pulling at his sour face, and finally he sneered, "That's not how yew load a mule, lad!"

He hadn't even bothered glancing up. "You aren't giving it enough attention, old man. This is exactly how I load a mule."

After an indignant moment: "Yew young pups know ev'rythin', don' yew?"

"Know enough to keep out of other people's business."

And the man had given a derisive snort and swung away in anger.

Old pud! Keven thought. Sometimes it seemed the people with the least experience were the ones with the most advice. . . .

The connection was curious, but he suddenly remembered Santon once telling him some long pointed story about a man who had a horse called Pride. It was an admirable horse, magnificent in its beauty. Everyone warned the man not to try to ride the horse, but he wouldn't listen to others. Once a-saddle, however, he found he couldn't dismount, and the horse trampled the man's family and friends and finally bore him away to some damn terrible place forever and ever. And he had seethed inside that Santon would sit him down to tell him some childer's tale. It was embarrassing. . . .

"Ranger!"

The call snapped him around. The sheriff was motioning him over to his office room.

Keven blew out a deep breath. What now?

* * * * *

The sheriff was more formal than Keven had seen him before, not so conspicuously abrasive.

"This here be Balak Flinthill, Axemaster, Clan Granite o' the Iron Mountain Warfenmass," the sheriff said. "He be goin' with you."

At first, fast glance, standing beside the sheriff, the figure could have passed in late dusk as some short, stocky, compact, reddish, dressed-up bear. His skin, what could be seen through the beard, was a ruddy tan like that inflicted by constant sun. The beard was heavy, curly, dark reddish-brown and his long hair was the same under a leather skull-cap, pulled low to a scowl of bushy eyebrows. He was dressed in a bark-brown woolen shirt under a dark leather jerkin, leather breeches, heavy leather leggings laced with thongs, and short, flared boots. A black and dark-blue cloak in a complex weaving of the two colors was thrown back over his square, muscular shoulders. With blazing blue eyes glinting out at Keven, he appeared to harbor suspicions that whatever he saw, he would probably dislike. His head, seemingly a size too large, was planted directly on his shoulders without apparent benefit of a neck, and he stood with a rigid head-back posture, fists on hips, straight as an oak stump chopped off about half a span tall.

A pile of equipment was behind him against the wall: a small round shield with an embossed pick-and-hammer emblem, a conical helmet, a heavy compound crossbow and a quiver of bolts, a tunic of chain and scale, a wineskin. Bulges under his cloak suggested other weapons.

"There may be a bit o' a language problem," the sheriff said.

Keven shook his head. "I speak Dwarfish." He offered a slight, stiff bow. *"Gartaggen, Balak Fruntalish. Shatta daelsta Keven d'Breeskerkrunstad. Ta mournik s'om postarnatteparg."*

The dwarf frowned at him for a moment, the blue eyes blinked, and then he returned the bow abruptly and swung that frown on the sheriff. *"Fruntalish?"* His voice was a guttural rumble but vibrant, like stones rolling underwater.

"Ah-h . . ." The sheriff squinted at the wall over the dwarf's head. *"Farn d'karshen.* Flinthill."

Balak gave a deep grunt and glared at Keven again. He uttered a short, rough sentence. Keven looked questioningly at the sheriff.

"I didn't understand that."

"Well . . ." The sheriff coughed and absently scratched his square beard. "I think he said that you talk Dwarfish like he—Well, it be not important. You see, this here be Iron Mountain Dwarfish. The Iron Mountain Clan don' even understand each other that good."

Balak grunted again; there may have been a far glint of humor in the glance he gave the sheriff.

"Th' lowlan' creeturs allus haf much dif'cult t' unnerstan Warfish," he rumbled. "'Tis oldspeak. Ver' old. More gooder language." His scowl ranged Keven from head to foot. "Ya good at fight, Kiven o' whate'er 'twas ya say?"

Keven nodded. "Yes . . ."

Again the deep grunt. "Nar wut heared. Got beat, ya did."

Keven stiffened. "You'd better understand the whole story, Axemaster Balak!"

The sheriff stopped him with raised hands.

"Don't even begin! First, you be not in here more'n two snaps o' a finger, an' you be aimed straight into a squabble! Second, you might as well go out an' yell at a rock as argue with a dwarf. All you need to know is that this dwarf can fight like five demons an' still be there when the last dog crawl for home! Now, there be somebody else, too. . . ."

He motioned to the far, dim corner of the room, and Keven was aware for the first time that someone was standing there. It was the woman who had come to Bestian's defense the night Wicket was killed. She gave him a bold smile.

"Hello again, Keven of Kingsend. You are in better condition than when I saw you last."

She was dressed in a dark, rough-spun linen shirt and breeches. A hooded, dark brown cloak was thrown carelessly over one shoulder. It was the sort of clothing—and the thought came suddenly to him—that one would wear to slip into a shadow and disappear. Amused, pale green eyes watched him from under a wing of dark hair. She was a slim, pretty young woman, but her smoky good looks were a bit daring, Keven thought, impertinent . . . challenging?

"I am called Slyt," she said quietly, stepping forward, a small smile curling in the corners of her mouth. She moved like a shadow, too. Keven regarded her, feeling a heat build in him.

"You're a thief." It was flat statement.

Slyt's smile remained the same. "There are some who suggest that." The green eyes laughed at him.

The sheriff continued. "I be total convinced that this fine female blade here has talents o' great use to our venture." He leaned closer. "She be called the Cat. Be that not just the most cunnin' thing you ever heared?"

"Good Sheriff "—Slyt made a low but mocking bow—"you do me too much honor. I am sincerely flattered, but I feel, being the peaceful and retiring woman that I am, that a venture of any violent nature would be—"

"Indeed," the sheriff cut her off, still speaking to Keven. "Her talents be *so* useful that I *insist* they be required. They be required so much that if she don' decide to go, she'll have the chance to practice them talents in one o' my best cells. Let's see . . . you e'er been down to level three, Slyt?"

"Ah, Sheriff Gaskin, how good of you to invite me." She turned the bright smile on Keven. "In the light of such reason, how can I refuse? Even though weapons are alien to me, I—"

"Don' let her get it piled too far o'er your head, ranger. She be slick as a trout. There be some right curious tales 'bout her little fast sword."

"Stories of the street, Sheriff. I spread them myself." She grinned at Keven. "A sharp reputation often cuts more than the actual blade, don't you agree?"

Keven had not taken his eyes off the slender woman with the sly green eyes. A pulse began to pound in his head, and his voice was cold and precise. "I have reason to dislike thieves. They are animals who prey on others, and I will not have them near me."

"Mm-m . . ." The sheriff rubbed his forehead, eyes squinted shut for a moment. He sighed. "I truly hate to repeat things. It bother me muchly. But I'll do it just this one more time." He tapped a hard finger against Keven's chest and spoke slowly, emphasizing each word.

"*I* be the sheriff—I think that be clear to all involved here. *You* be the young man what agreed to this venture—I think we can understan' that without a lot o' discussion. *These*—" he made a wide motion to include the others— "they be some ones what be goin' with you. Now!" He waved that finger under Keven's nose. "There be no need for you to court this Cat. You don' have to dance with her. You don' have to like her. There be no need fer you to e'en look at her pretty face. She be entirely dependable, in that you'll always know when she be lyin'—she be talkin' at the same time. But she *be* goin' with you! An' *you* be goin' to accept that! An *she*—" he spun to face the smiling Slyt— "*She* will do her very true best! She *will* take orders! She will *not* disappear when the clamp gets tight! An' when called upon to fight, she will fight like her true precious life depend on it. For it *do!*"

"Ah, Sheriff!" Slyt spread her hands in a helpless gesture. "Once again your magic tongue has woven its spell. I would, of course, be delighted to accompany this fine fighter if it should please you in any way."

"Ah, Slyt the Cat." The sheriff returned the smile with a chill grimace. "I knew I'd find brain in there if I just hammered hard 'nough. But you *do* know—" he placed a hand on the cloaked shoulder in a confidential manner—"if you displease me in this, in any way I might possible find to be displeased, if I become unhappy with *any* of your actions in this matter, there won't be a single corner o' any hell dark 'nough to hide you."

He turned back to Keven with what may have been a twinkle in his eyes. "You got any more problems I can help you with?"

Keven shook his head.

The sheriff nodded, sarcasm in his voice like vinegar in honey. "Now, that be just fine. We be all good fellows here. Almost o' a family."

"Ya! T'ief!" grunted Balak, stabbing a gnarled finger at Slyt. "B' mindful y' narver walk b'hind me! Narver!"

Slyt made a florid bow. "Good Warf, I shall be at your very side."

Keven gave the sheriff a look that could have crumpled a weaker man. The sheriff smiled.

*   *   *   *   *

The two huge beasts lurched through the night with peculiar, ponderous movements, yet quietly, as if to the forest born. Abruptly they both halted, heads turned alike, noses wrinkling. One touched the other, and they grunted softly together for a moment. They moved off in different directions then, with no more sound than the night wind.

The man drove the cow down the dark path, cowbell clanking unevenly. His lantern cast bizarre, weaving shadow shapes around him. He switched the animal ahead of him and cursed it with every harsh blow.

"Ya bedamned ugly errant beast! Ya wanders off inta the dark wilds! Ya niver mind if'n the wolves git ya! Ah'll eat ya meself one o' these days, ya bedamned stringy bitch!"

The switch sang and fell.

"Ah hasta search the whole Vale fer ya! Should o' left ya out here fer the wolves! They prob'ly would o' larfed at ya worthless carcass!"

He threw quick, fearful glances to the rear and both sides, squinting into the darkness.

"Ya nar know whut awaits ya out here, does ya!"

He laid on with the switch as hard as he could. *"Thet's* whut awaits ya, damn ya!"

He threw another hasty, frightened look over his shoulder and never saw the massive shape looming in the path ahead. The cow balked, jumped sideways, and crashed away into the night.

"Whut now, ya—" He froze, lantern upraised.

"Ah, holy mother of all gods!" he breathed, making several quick signs with the switch hand. "Whut be ya?"

There was no response from the dark figure. It stood unmoving, monstrous. The lantern light reflected from tiny eyes.

"Ah carries iron and silver!" the man warned, but in a wavering voice. "An' wolfsbane . . ."

Nothing. Off in the forest, the sound of the cow ceased abruptly.

"Ah, gods," the man groaned, seeming then to wilt in upon himself. "Ya be one o' them things o' the dark side, don' ya?"

The figure moved forward, one great limb raised to strike. The man turned to flee, then gave a tiny shriek and dropped to his knees. Another figure stood directly behind him, but this one was much smaller and slim. If it hadn't been so close he would never have seen it, for it seemed to blend with the night. It held up a hand to the advancing beast and spoke in a low, lilting voice. The words were in a strange tongue.

The creature stopped. It whined. The slender figure spoke again. The creature whimpered and slowly sidled away into the dark.

"Ah, gods," the man moaned. "Ya be a elf, don' ya? I were allus good to the fay bein's. We allus left out milk an' bread."

"Be unafraid of me," the elf said, "but go directly home and venture not into the night again. It is very unsafe these times. Your cow is no longer yours—another beast has taken it—but you have your life."

The elf moved silently into the night and was gone. The man broke into a stumbling run for home, errant cow forgotten, gasping over and over, "I seen a elf! Ah, gods all, I seen a elf and a dark beast, too!"

Chapter Six

They rode south out of town in the early morning sun, Keven and the sheriff, up Shires Road into gentle hills of fields and farms and woodlots. The sheriff was mounted on a handsome chestnut mare, Keven on a older roan borrowed from the sheriff's cousin; his big black still limped badly. Keven was running through some simple sword drills. As they passed under trees, he would say, "One leaf," or "Two leaves," or "Half a leaf." The sword would flicker and the stated amount would flutter to the ground. Once, with two flashing swings, he nipped off a piece of small branch and kept it bouncing in the air with the flat of the blade. He tossed it higher and slapped it away.

"I still don't like the idea of that thief," he said. "I think you're just shoving her into this thing because you want her out of town." He rode a moment in silence. "And you're probably hoping she'll be killed."

"Well, gettin' her out o' town be a thought o' some merit," the sheriff mused. "She be a irksome citizen. An' if half the tales be true 'bout her talents an' weaponry, she prob'ly should o' been hanged long ago. But . . ." He re-

leased a long sigh. "She have a fine talent for always bein'
just one li'l leap ahead or a quick dodge to one side. I *know*
the little lizard be guilty o' a lot o' things, but I can't prove
it." He shook his head sadly.

"But still, she be havin' her uses. She be buyin' her way
out o' more than a few troubles with information more
valuable than her bother. An' more than one true culprit
got their time on the gibbet or the pillory 'cause o' Slyt.
An', too, there be a few times when some true outlaw sort
greeted the mornin' as a cold corpse, an' more than a couple things pointed to Slyt as bein' the instrument o' his passin'. But, o' course, she were clean on t'other side of town
when it all happened, with twenty-seven witnesses swearin'
their eyes out for her." He sighed again.

"So don' overlook her value while you're judgin' what
she be. An', too, I be sendin' her 'cause she can do things
you prob'ly can't."

"Don't lay your whole purse on that point."

"You think a woman be not up to the task?"

Keven didn't answer for a moment. "I just don't like it."

The sheriff turned in the saddle to scowl directly at
Keven. "I cares not a small puppy piddle if you likes it or
not! I be truly an' altogether damned if I allow this thing to
swing on your young likes an' dislikes!"

They rode in taut silence for a while, their attentions
fixed on opposite sides of the road, their expressions suggesting they were hardly two hearty comrades out for a
pleasant morning ride. Keven flicked a single leaf from a
tree and then sliced it in two with a backhand.

"An' I s'pose you got some feelin's 'bout Balak Flinthill,
too," the sheriff grumbled.

"He seems capable." Keven's voice was flat.

"*Capable!*" The sheriff said it so violently it sounded like
a sneeze. His horse danced sideways a step. "Capable? He be
some hellish number o' leagues up the road from capable!"

Another long silence followed, the sheriff muttering to himself and the roadside trees.

"Capable! Tell a dwarf that he be mere 'capable,' an' he probable show some capability by spikin' you straight into the ground like a post!"

About a league from town, at the brow of a hill, the sheriff led the way into a narrow cart track that wound west into deep woods of beech and birch. Keven hadn't even noticed the path until the sheriff turned into what first appeared to be a heavy growth of roadside brambles. He blamed his lack of observation on too much involvement in his practice, but still, he should have seen that turning. He glanced back toward the road. The brambles seemed to have filled in behind them.

"You still haven't said where we're going," he said.

The sheriff did not turn. "To see a man."

"Some old fighter lives up here?"

"Might be you could say that."

The academy. Santon:

"*Be wary of old warriors and the tales they tell. They often tend to diminish the fear and the horror of their past, their friends falling and the pain of staying on. Only humor and heroics remain. It is an imbalanced remembrance.*"

Another half a league brought them over a low hill and into the clearings of an orderly farmstead. Trim stone walls blocked the fields into neat portions and lined the track ahead. Cattle, sheep, and goats grazed in lush pastures. Pigs and poultry were penned near several low stone buildings, and a pond served as a gossip center for ducks and geese. But dominating all was a huge, bizarre stone structure sprawled across the opposite hillside.

It was walled, castlelike, but with battlements often too low to be well defended, and the walls bent and wandered at wild, irrational angles, as if laid out at different times by different crews of drunken workmen. Odd towers rose at unreasonable intervals, some peaked, some crenellated; some massive and obviously roomed, some too thin to be functional; some connected by frail bridges, some standing alone. They crested above a rambling, haphazard jumble of seemingly unrelated buildings and erratic roof angles, as if everything had somehow been collected there over a thousand years by thousands of independent builders, all bent on their own whimsical designs.

"What in all of the seven hells is it?" Keven said in amazement.

"It be called The Towers."

"Gods alive! It's nearly the size of the king's castle in Latonia!"

The sheriff shrugged. "Mayhaps. I wouldna know."

The track ran straight between its own bordering stone walls, aimed for a large, double-hung oak gate flanked by two towers more decorative in appearance than functional. Brown-robed figures straightened and waved from their tilling and planting in the fields. The sheriff raised a casual hand in return.

Keven studied the insane structure ahead with suspicion. "This another of your little 'surprises,' Sheriff?"

"No."

They halted before the gates. The sheriff leaned in his saddle and swung the polished bronze knocker against the striker plate. Surprisingly, it rung like a great bell. Keven studied the lichen-covered walls and flaking stone.

"This place is ancient!"

"And so would you be if you'd been here this long!"

It was a small, sharp voice. The sheriff looked extremely bored as he glanced down at a toad that had hopped from the grass at the foot of one of the towers.

"We be expected," he said evenly, a grim curl in the corners of his mouth.

"Expected? Expected?" the toad peeped. "Who says?"

"If this gate don' swing open by the time I take four breaths," he said, "I'll see if your master can come down here an' open it hisself."

"Ah, the magic password!" The toad blinked, shot straight into the air, and shouted, "*Open!*"

Keven's horse snorted and backed abruptly.

"Ho!" He tightened the reins and rose in the stirrups to stare at where the toad had fallen back into the grass. "What in the whole hells of—"

"Give it no mind." The sheriff waved a hand in a gesture of abrupt dismissal. "It pleases the silly little pup to startle folks. He be bothered by a small burden o' virtues."

There was a sliding rasp of bolts, and the gates swung inward to a small flagstoned courtyard. Directly across from them, a tall, gray-robed, cowled figure stood just inside an arched doorway. The sheriff led the way across the courtyard and reined in before the figure.

"Welcome," it said. "I am Eugon."

The voice was deep and deliberate, the tone carefully correct, as if speaking to someone of lesser understanding. Framed within the dark archway, the figure presented a spectral effect. The face had been hidden at first, but as they neared, Keven could make out the features within the shadow of the cowl. They were composed to reflect little expression, yet there was a slight, scoffing tilt to the mouth and eyes. It was a young man, possibly no older than himself, he thought. A thin hand appeared from the folds of the robe, motioned, and a young lad in a brown smock came running from a larger archway to the right.

"Piglet here will care for your horses," the figure droned. They dismounted, and the sheriff surprised Keven by offering a sweeping bow. The effect was belied, however, by a stony expression and a curt whiplash of sarcasm in his voice.

"Your kind manners know no bounds, glorious Eugon. Now quit actin' like the almighty king o' wizards afore I kick your pompous, overbearing little arse."

Eugon bowed his head slightly and turned. Keven saw a faint smile before the cowl cut it off. The young lad took their horses. They followed Eugon along a long, stone-walled corridor lighted by torches in elaborate iron sconces.

"Midvale lad," the sheriff said, making no attempt to lower his voice. "Always were a self-satisfied little snot." Eugon led them through a heavy, iron-bound door into another long, echoing corridor. Keven was beginning to move in an almost stalking manner, glancing over his shoulder.

"What is this place?"

"Acclain's Towers," the sheriff grunted.

Keven halted in midstride, staring at the sheriff and then at the robed figure moving off ahead of them. "*Acclain?*" he said in a harsh whisper. The sheriff stopped, turned back, and nodded. Keven shook his head.

"But . . . he's a myth!"

"And he enjoys it, too."

"But . . . *here?*"

The sheriff made a sound vaguely like a chuckle. "It ever occur to you that everybody's got to be someplace? How did you say it? No matter where you be, there you be?"

"But . . ."

"A 'but' is somethin' a bull hauls aroun'. Ain' I tol' you that? Let's move." He jerked his head in the direction of the robed figure, now waiting in the distance. "Yon Eugon is enjoyin' your reaction too much."

After many corridors, doors, stairs up and stairs down, odd-angled courtyards, and strange, dark chambers, and the sheriff saying patiently, "We don' need the full mystic tour, Eugon," they were ushered finally into a spacious chamber without windows. Massive braziers of turned bronze, taller than a man's head, stood in each corner, burning a bright, pale yellow that seemed too intense for ordinary flame, lighting the room even to the dark, heavy beams of the high, peaked ceiling. Tapestries draped the walls between tall cabinets, depicting heroic scenes of old wars and conflicts, some so ancient as to be faded nearly to monotone. In the center, dominating the room, stood a massive oak table, fully a span in width, three spans long. It was littered with books and scrolls, instruments and paraphernalia of unimaginable nature.

The whole chamber was an erratic mix of method and clutter. Neatly stacked leatherbound books on a side table rose from an untidy sprawl of folios and manuscripts; an orderly rack of scrolls supported a pile of old, flaking parchments; a polished mechanical apparatus stood amid a disarray of parts and pieces; labeled pottery containers filled neat shelves along one whole wall, yet the floor beneath them was a scatter of dried plants and things Keven really did not want to identify. He found his attention held by a huge, overdecorated map tapestry.

"A highly imaginative interpretation of the Twelve Ancient Kingdoms," a sharp voice said impatiently. "It keeps the cold draft from that wall."

Seated at the far end of the center table, nearly hidden in a huge, intricately carved chair, was an old man in a worn and discolored white cloak, drawn tightly around him. His hair fell over thin shoulders, a streaked silver-gray, and his skin was like weathered parchment shaped over the bare bones of his skull. Dark, deep-set eyes glared out from under scowling white eyebrows. A hard clamp of mouth showed through a tangled white beard. The voice, however, had conveyed no such impression of age.

"The good and gracious Sheriff of Midvale," Eugon announced, with the faintest of mocking lilts in his voice. "And . . . a young fighter."

Keven gave him a sharp look. Eugon made a bow.

"Goodmen, may I present Acclain, Wizard of Vale."

The sheriff and the old man made almost identical, irritated waves of displeasure. Eugon bowed again, smiled, and stepped backward through the archway, pulling the heavy door closed.

"Well, Lukus . . ." Acclain said, although examining Keven with probing eyes.

"This be Keven of Kingsend," the sheriff said. "The one what had the . . . incident on the pass."

"Yes . . . well, tell me about it, boy." He waved an imperious hand.

Keven felt a rise of heat—boy indeed! "I've told this story over and over, sire, and—"

"Then you should be well practiced and able to relate it without the usual problems young people encounter when attempting to speak their native language. And 'sire' me not; I am fairly certain we bear no related blood. Be seated." He motioned to chairs on either side of the huge table close to his end.

Keven glanced at the sheriff as they seated themselves. He started to say something, but the sheriff raised a hand and spoke quietly.

"Tell the story."

Keven let out a long breath, fixed his eyes on the old man, and told the story once again.

With thin, bony hands folded under his chin, his eyes squinted nearly shut, the old man interrupted only for further details about the particular behavior of the wolves, the sudden storm, and the balky actions of the horse. His only comment at the end was a muffled grunt. He turned to the sheriff.

"Well, Lukus, what is it you expect from me?"

"Whate'er you can offer. With Lord Damon's approval, Captain Mikel an' I devised a plan. 'Tis—"

"I know all about it." He glared at them both for an extended moment, then concentrated on Keven. "Keven of Kingsend, is it?" he mused. "How came you to the Vales,

Keven of Kingsend?"

"By the Sun-Running Road." Keven accompanied this with a self-satisfied smile. The old man nodded patiently.

"The hollow, defensive little soul often employs cute and cutting words as weapons, operating under the callow belief that this equates with some mystic cleverness. It is, however, a childish behavior and a flimsy facade; it is a precautionary maneuver to divert attention from an underdeveloped personality. If you wish to duel here in such a manner, you should come better armed, more experienced, and know at the outset that you play a small game. I am under no courteous obligation to tolerate pretensions to wit or allow it free, kittenish play in my presence. At my age, what little patience I ever had is entirely outworn. Now, allowing you that single, unknowing misstep, let us begin again. How came you to the Vales, Keven of Kingsend?"

Keven's jaw clamped and he straightened in his chair.

The academy. He couldn't remember now exactly what it was he had said, but it had been a quick and witty reply to Rusker. At least it had seemed quick and witty at the time.

Rusker, the cold blue eyes hard and blazing, the voice like a rusty blade:

"*Ya've a damn mouth damn sharper than damn needs be, laddybuck!*"

"*You've taught us to cut while parrying.*"

"*Thet be true . . . but it total depends on whether it's yer life or yer jackass wit that be in danger! One o' them ya can do without!*"

"How much do you wish to know?" Keven asked levelly. "And to what end do you need to know?"

Legendary wizard or not, this sour old burr was damned irritating, but nonetheless a commanding presence.

"Well put," Acclain said, nodding. A wave of his thin hand brought a brown-smocked young man with a tray of cheese, fresh bread, and wine.

"Help yourself. Relax." But the eyes did not soften or relax. "I wish to know about you in relation to this problem in the mountains. You have an integral part, it seems, and I wish to know how well qualified you are to fulfill it. Tell me about yourself."

Keven told him, and in the telling, he found he didn't enjoy recounting his own story. He brushed quickly over the circumstances of how he came to the attention of the King's Arms Academy, concentrating instead on his training and weaponry, and he briefly mentioned exploring some old ruins in the Northeast Kingdom. He didn't tell all; there were some things others could do without. The old man's frequent nods and humorless smiles seemed to indicate to Keven that he knew more than the words. At one point he pressed Keven for details.

"Well, it was a peculiar room," Keven said. "It was walled all about with shelves of glass containers, hundreds of them. They held—I don't know—foul things! Organs, it seemed . . . body parts . . . moldy plants . . . the gods only know what! The place stank like a fetid butchery! It made my skin crawl. I wanted to burn it!"

"You *what?*" It was a rasp of astonishment. The eyes snapped wide open. The wizard seemed ready to pounce. "And *did* you?"

"No . . . the others prevailed against me."

"Bless them for being equipped with rudimentary brains! And did anyone exercise his reasoning to the point of bringing back any of these containers?"

Keven looked puzzled. "No . . ."

"Good gods all-knowing," Acclain breathed, falling back in his chair. He gazed in seeming bewilderment at the high ceiling for a while, shaking his head slowly. Keven frowned over a quick swallow of wine. Acclain lowered his eyes and regarded Keven again. Keven decided the scowl was an unalterable feature of the old man's face.

"Why should anyone be interested in bottled refuse?" Keven asked.

Acclain stared at him for a moment. "Let us say that 'bottled refuse,' as you put it, would be to me what a tree is to a carpenter, what iron ore is to a smithy."

"We came out with much gold," Keven said uneasily. "There was more than we could carry."

"Yes . . . of course . . . gold. The ultimate rationale! Humankind begins by wanting gold, progresses quickly to needing gold, and thrives finally in the conviction that they deserve gold. Of the four Deadly Dishonors—Power, Greed, Self-involvement, and Hate—gold figures highly in two. It seems a suspicious association."

"It was not all we gained." Keven shifted in his chair; why was he feeling so defensive here? "I came out with three old scrolls."

"How very good for you. I suppose you used them to start a fire at some time."

Keven fought the heat that was starting up his neck. "No, they're in my belongings."

"I should like very much to see them."

Keven shrugged; it made little difference to him.

Acclain continued looking at him expectantly. "Now . . . if it is not too much trouble for you," he said.

"They're at the barrack—in a safe place."

The old man gazed at him, nodding. "Good. Would you be so kind as to go for them."

Keven glanced a frown at the sheriff, who gave a small nod over his wine goblet. Acclain clapped his hands. The door opened.

"Eugon, conduct this young man directly to his horse without your usual tiresome, morose journey. Await his return and conduct him directly back here." He turned to Keven. "Lukus and I have matters to discuss, but please do not tarry."

"I don't understand why—"

"My young man, if you have any power of observation at all, you will notice an increasing number of things in the world that do not instantly reveal themselves to your youthful understanding. This is one of them. Please."

Somehow that final, quiet word soothed Keven's flare of anger, but the coals of tension and resentment remained. Following behind the silent, cowled figure of Eugon, he examined the thought that at least the young man *looked* somewhat like a mage, but Acclain . . .

Acclain!

He had just met a man that some claimed never existed, or had been dead for hundreds of years, or had pursued Evil into the far Dark and never returned, and here he was living in the hills above a little mountain town in a huge, mad castle—and he turned out to be a bed of nettles! An irascible, self-righteous, contentious old pest, with all the geniality of a bear with an arrow up its arse! And as for himself, he had been nineteen riding up here with the sheriff. Now he was off on a chore as if he were five years old!

"Is he always like that?" he asked the robed figure ahead of him.

"And how is that?" Eugon didn't turn, but Keven knew he was smiling.

"Don't be dull, because it's easy for you!" He didn't mind challenging this young bore at all. "What do you think I mean?"

There was a moment before Eugon answered. He never turned. "The master is being especially pleasant and hospitable today."

Keven stalked behind Eugon in silence, contemplating all the possible consequences of leaving the surly little bastard crumpled in one of the dark doorways.

*   *   *   *   *

Keven tossed the three scrolls carelessly on the table; the ride had calmed him somewhat, but he still couldn't say he was having an enjoyable day.

"Is there anything else I can do for you?" he asked, making little attempt to hide the sarcasm.

The old wizard breathed a small sigh. "Yes. If you have the education and the discipline, you can make some feeble attempt to be mannered. May I? . . ." He indicated the scrolls.

"After being sent for them like a page, do I have a choice?" He pushed them within reach. They were of brittle, brown parchment, wrapped loosely in oiled leather. Acclain carefully unwrapped them.

His examination of the scrolls was lengthy, composed of a variety of frowns, grunts, and small hums. He gently re-rolled the scrolls eventually and placed them on the table. He made a small, belittling gesture.

"These are of little use to you. You know what they are, of course."

Keven shifted uncomfortably. "Magic."

The wizard nodded. "That seems to make you somewhat uncomfortable."

Keven shrugged. "Perhaps."

"Um-m. Many people feel that way. However, magic is what one makes of it." He made a brief series of coughing sounds that came suspiciously close to a hoarse chuckle. "To you, these are nothing but worthless rolls of parchment. I will give you . . . oh . . . a hundred golders for them."

Keven reached for the scrolls, smiling. "Well, I think they may be worth a little more than that."

"And how would you know of their worth?"

He shrugged. "As my father once told me, a thing is worth just exactly what someone will give and what you will accept. A mage offered me five hundred apiece . . . but he's far in the east. And that's all he had at the time. I remember a wizard who spoke to us at the academy about the value of old magic scrolls. He said—"

"Seven hundred." Acclain snapped.

"Apiece?"

The frown darkened. "Yes . . . apiece."

Keven shook his head. "No . . . I think not."

"You gravely overrate your merchandise, young man."

"Oh, that's possible, I suppose." He was on familiar, firmer ground here. He had been a good listener and a quick learner while standing beside his father in hard bargaining sessions with tough traders. He leaned back and regarded some vague spot on the wall with a searching frown.

"There was a wizard in Latonia," he mused. "He told us about magic at the academy, and the cost involved in the creation of spells . . . so much time and effort and money to gather the proper ingredients, and then there's the process. It was surprising."

The old wizard was tapping the fingers of one hand on the arm of the chair in a galloping rhythm. There was a far glint of something in his dark eyes.

"A thousand then, and I'm done."

Keven gazed thoughtfully at the scrolls for a moment, then shook his head. "No."

"Gods' blood!" Acclain slapped the arm of the chair, turning to the sheriff. "You seek my aid in the conquest of bandits, and you bring me one of the same to ply his trade within my very walls!"

Keven regarded the scrolls with a speculative frown, but he was smiling to himself. "If you were to duplicate these spells or charms or whatever they are, and there's no doubt you could, I imagine it would cost you . . . oh . . . somewhere around thirty thousand goldworth."

Acclain's eyes widened in astonishment, then nearly disappeared in a dark scowl. A talonlike finger stabbed at Keven. "You are quite irrational, you know. Thirty thousand indeed! A preposterous figure!"

"True," Keven mused. "Probably closer to a hundred thousand."

"His sickness grows more acute," Acclain said to the sheriff, then added to Keven, "How can *you* judge? You have no idea what these are! Why, these are—"

He stopped abruptly, with the sudden frown of someone who had narrowly avoided stepping into a hole. He sank back in his chair, considering Keven with what may have been a hint of humor.

"I don't understand why you must be so—" Keven waved a hand vaguely—"miserly. Can you not create all the riches you need?"

Acclain glared at him for a long, cold moment. "I will forgive your ignorance; it is, after all, in an esoteric area. To answer your question in terms you may understand: In the words of the legendary drover who attempted to drive both pigs and geese together, it just don't work that way! When something is 'created,' as you suggest, it does not simply manifest itself in the world out of nothing. There is a cost of both energy and material. The cost and the material are dependent upon the thing being 'created.' Gold and gems, being rare, valuable, and held in high esteem, are costly however they appear. The outlay alone to create gold is so excessive that it becomes more expensive than—Why am I bothering to explain this to you? Would you burden yourself to explain the finer points of swordsmanship to a babe? Unless you have the capacity to understand the inner workings of magic, which I doubt, then I suggest we confine ourselves to a subject more fitting to your life. Have some more wine."

The young man appeared again at his summons, bringing more refreshments. Acclain raised his goblet.

"Miserly indeed!" he grumbled. "But to the matter at hand—I will give you five thousand for the three. Nothing more!"

Keven leaned forward, inwardly excited but showing reluctant concern; this was the end game. "Twenty," he replied.

"You dream. Seven."

"Fifteen."

"Impossible!"

"Then I will take ten and be cheated."

"You will take eight and begone!"

Keven rolled the scrolls idly with a fingertip. "Ninety-five hundred. In gems."

"Oh, of course!" Acclaim cast a look at the ceiling. "Gems!"

The sheriff was glancing from one to the other. There was a small but definite grin on his face. Acclaim sighed.

"I'll give you eighty-five hundred."

"Nine thousand."

"Eighty-seven!"

"Eighty-nine."

Acclaim slapped the table. "Eighty-eight and be done!"

"So be it, and done," Keven said quickly, nodding. "Eighty-eight hundred. My hand."

They touched hands briefly.

"I should now count my fingers," the wizard muttered. He reached to the base of his chair and touched a complex combination of carved flowers. A small wooden chest slid out. He lifted it onto his lap, opened the lid, and scowled at its hidden contents.

"Here! Four large, perfectly matched Southeastern blue sapphires of extraordinary cut, clarity, and color! Five thousandworth if a bent copper!"

Keven rolled them in his hand, his stomach tightening as he watched the bright sparkle, like sun on a choppy sea; he had never imagined such gems. If anything, he thought the wizard's evaluation was a bit low.

Acclaim reached toward him again. "Two matched emeralds. Somolese cut! Twenty-five hundred!"

Keven examined them; well, perhaps twenty-five hundred. Acclain shook the chest and made another selection. "Here, warfen turquoise from the Copper Mountains of Old Augernor. Believe me, young man, it is worth thirteen hundred."

Keven took the stone and tried not to show a reaction; it looked like a large, shiny, speckled bird egg.

"Done!" he said.

"Are you unafraid?" Acclain said, voice lowering and eyebrows rising. "These may carry some sort of . . . spell."

Keven rolled the turquoise in his hand, smiling. "Oh, this one carries a spell, I'm certain of that. A magnificent spell—its color is gold!"

"Of course!" Acclain snorted, waving a reckless hand. "Gold again! What is a gem but a more easily transportable form of gold? Be wary of what I mentioned earlier, young Keven. It is the gold that carries the spell."

His eyes seemed to flicker with a spark of humor as he glanced at Keven and returned the chest to its hiding place. "As it is said in some of the craftier parts of town, be wary of your jewels, young man."

And then his manner changed instantly. The sparse good humor disappeared, and the hard scowl fell back into place. He turned to the sheriff; the game was over.

"There appears to be some minor magic at work with these bandits," he snapped. "Some kitchen witchery of animals, some small weather spell poorly handled." He made careless gestures of deprecation, as if brushing away insects, before continuing.

"The horse balking, the storm, whatever—they are but trivial workings. It was all feeble enough to escape my attention. Simple tampering. We can provide some aid in that area."

"There be the tremblin' o' the ground a number o'

times," the sheriff pointed out.

Acclain shook his head. "There have always been movements of the earth, Lukus. I cannot reasonably attribute them to the uneasy shifting of great buried dragons, or evil spirits beneath our feet, or the angry footfalls of approaching gods."

"What, then?" Keven asked.

Acclain pursed his lips. "I do not know."

Keven indicated surprise and glanced at the sheriff.

Acclain lifted his eyebrows. "Does that surprise you?"

Keven nodded. "A little."

"Well, I happen to think it shows some wisdom on my part. The major conquest of knowledge is recognizing what one does not know." He turned to the sheriff again. "How is this raiding party of yours to be formed?"

The sheriff told him. Keven shifted in his seat, frowning first at the sheriff, then at the wizard.

"Is there some mystic rule I never learned?" Keven asked with an edge of sarcasm. "Is there some unwritten doctrine that says a venturing party must be composed in a certain manner? Always a fighter! Always a dwarf! Always a thief and a littler and an elf and . . ." He shrugged. "Whatever!"

Acclain studied him for a moment. "Do you speak from some vast experience on the questing road? It was my understanding that you are relatively new to the work."

"Well, I'm not stupid! The library at the academy is full of such accounts. And it always struck me as peculiar that they should speak so frequently of such a mix of people, as if it was absolutely necessary to have it that way."

"Um-m . . . Tell me, are you as clever with locks and traps and hidden devices as you might be?"

"Well . . ." He shifted uncomfortably. "We studied them and worked with them some. . . ."

"How very nice for you. So now you know what happens when you carelessly trip one of the old standards. How

about practical experience where your well-being, if not
survival, depended on your talents to locate and disarm
these sly devices?"

Keven didn't answer. He frowned as Acclain continued.

"Are you as light and as quick of foot as a littler? Do you
question their extraordinary fighting abilities? Quite seriously, do you know what it is like to be forced to fight a determined, unrelenting opponent from a low crouch while
defending your kneecaps? Do not smile; many accomplished fighters have found that to be a concluding event to
an otherwise successful career. Did you know that warfen
and elves can see in the dark to a certain extent? Are you
armed with defensive or offensive spells? Do you have some
mystic foresight allowing you to prepare for eventualities
that these others may be able to handle?"

"No." He felt like squirming in his chair but managed to
sit still.

Acclain nodded. "Good," he snorted. "I was beginning
to think you were magic. As for your question, venturing
parties are mixed because it is logical to combine varied talents into a single weapon. I am surprised you failed to learn
that at the academy."

Keven was burning; how quick the shift from the peak of
bargaining to this pit of being belittled. And why was the
old bastard doing this?

"And another thing," Acclain continued, apparently
unwilling to allow his victim time to recover. "This callow
and narrow reluctance of yours to accept magic as a valid
tool in the world is again a reflection of ignorance and lack
of experience. It is as absurd as a stoneworker refusing to
believe in carpentry. Why should it make you so uncomfortable?"

"I . . . don't know. It's just . . . difficult . . . to . . ." He
ran out of words and closed with a helpless shrug.

Acclain nodded again. "Yes, magic is difficult for some

to conceive. It is like a blind man trying to understand a bear: He may hear it, he may smell it, he may sense its presence by mystical means; if he reaches out a hand into the dreadful dark, he may touch it . . . and that would be frightening indeed."

"It's just that I've never seen—"

"Exactly! You have not seen! You have eyes and a mind and they operate selectively. Magic is not all thunderous walls of flame, you know. There is minor magic; there is major magic. There are kitchen witchery, cantrips, so-called white and dark, wild and vast! What is this?"

He made a quick, blurred gesture, a snap of fingers, and a pink rose appeared in his hand. He offered it to Keven. It appeared real; it felt real; it smelled real. Keven tried regaining control of his embarrassment.

"It's a . . . magic rose."

"Wrong! It is a real rose. Its appearance was sleight-of-hand. It has been up my sleeve since you entered the room. But this—" And he pointed to a spot on the table next to Keven's elbow. There was a clear, bell-like tone, and an identical rose appeared there.

"*That* is magic, young man. Minor. So-called white magic. The bell is optional."

Keven stared at the rose and at the one he held in his hand. "Why do you say 'so-called' white magic?"

"Because there is no such thing as 'white' or 'black' magic. Magic itself has no more morality than a hammer. It is a tool—no better, no worse than its user."

Keven frowned. "But what about the flood and the—"

"Do not confuse magic with natural forces. Magic is created from energy; natural forces are simply there, although they may be triggered magically, sometimes aimed magically."

"I . . . don't understand. . . ."

"And it is likely you will remain in that state of mind."

The old wizard turned abruptly to the sheriff. "I will send the young fool Eugon with your party when the time comes. He needs a humbling experience."

The sheriff snorted. "I were hopin' for somethin' considerable less childish."

"He is at the journeyman phase; he has talents. Perhaps he can turn your brigands into toads for you; I understand he is very good with toads. I will arrange for some other help as well. Pass the word to your Lord Damon that there will be no charge for my services, but I must examine whatever artifacts and items are recovered, if any, and reserve the right to choose among them."

The sheriff nodded. "Sounds agreeable to me."

"Good. And to you, young Keven of Kingsend, I wish a successful venture. You have possibilities. I pray for a time when your mind becomes as well presented as your apparent physical condition. You seemingly have the capacity to think, but that is nothing more than a similarity to having an exceptional horse—useless unless one has the ability to exercise its full potential. Should questions arise in you that appear baffling, consider me a likely source of information. I have been known to provide such from time to time. But try not to be too idiotic in your questions. If I weigh them lacking in intelligence, I shall address you to a project to discover your own answers."

Chapter Seven

They rode back to town in silence. The sheriff seemed particularly absorbed in studying the trees, the sky, the fields and woodlots, and the hills around them. Keven was in a bewildered state, his eyes fixed on his horse's ears. He felt as if he had turned an unforeseen corner and blundered into an entirely different world. It looked the same, it smelled the same; those were the same stone walls and cottages they had passed on the way out, but . . .

He *knew* he hadn't had that much wine—he'd been very prudent about *that* lately—yet there was a murky whirlwind racing through his mind, as if through autumn leaves. And the spinning thoughts were all clamoring for attention, all trying to find some proper niche at once and none even recognizing a familiar link when it flew past.

Wizardry! Magic! Acclain, of all people!

Acclain!

Acclain, who, according to the legends, once created a towering fortress of fire around a beleaguered company of King's Arms during the Chaos; who became a great white eagle hurling lightning bolts among the dark forces; who once appeared as a thousand ghost warriors, shining in a foggy dawn, and turned an enemy attack into a rout; who reversed the flow of the Blood River to flood an enemy encampment; who caused roads to travel in circles; who, with an angry snap of his fingers, turned a hundred—four hundred!—eight hundred!—a *thousand* dark warriors to statues of clay and then produced a storm to wash them away; who . . .

Yes . . . believe all that, as they said at the academy, and I want to show you this sack of river pebbles that are actually Coral Island pearls in disguise.

Acclaim . . .

Who had been as insulting as an alley witch.

Yet, in spite of being humiliated, Keven was having a difficult time maintaining his anger. He would try to fuel it by recalling the scathing words, but it kept sliding away under the overwhelming aspect of the man. Damn it, he was in *awe* of him!

Well, why not?

How many legends had he met lately?

And he was carrying more riches in gems now. Why, those four matched blue sapphires alone . . . Had he truly outbargained the old man? All barter was a game—everyone knew that—but had this been a game in which the outcome was fixed before the start? And he still had the two damn roses, and they were still identical as far as he could perceive.

Toys! Acclaim had handed them over like playthings to a child.

And he had been a toy, too, as well as the child.

There were children playing in the rutted road as they entered the village, chanting, circling, and acting out the old rhyme:

> "*Four fingers on a man;*
> *One, two, three, and four.*
> *Four fingers make a hand;*
> *One, two, three, and four.*

"*Both arms out on a man;*
One, two. One and two.
Both arms out make a span.
One, two. One and two.

"*Four fingers make a hand;*
Eighteen hands make a span;
Two arms or paces in a span;
Thus is the measure of a man.

"*Pace an hour in the sun;*
Pace, pace—do not stop.
That's a league you have done.
Pace, pace—down you flop.

"*If that's too much and you fatigue;*
Oh, yes—we'll need a crutch;
Then three miles will make the league.
Oh, well—that's not so much."

And that's what he felt like at the moment—a child, trying to learn the measure of the world and often finding it all too confusing. Perhaps he should begin over. Dismount and join them. The fumbling outsider again. He couldn't feel any more confounded and ridiculous.

"*Copper, copper, ten for a silver;*
Two, four, six-eight-ten.
Silver, silver, twenty for a golder;
Five, ten, fifteen, twenty.

"*Golder, golder, five for a platin;*
One, two, three-four-five.
Platin, golder, silver, copper;
That's what to have when you go a-shopper."

It had been a long time since he had learned those rhymes. Or had it truly been that long? The voices fell behind, fading away into the town sounds, but he continued to chant silently to himself:

> *"A single golder is an ounce;*
> > *Drop it on a cobble—does it bounce?*
> *Sixteen ounces and a pound is known;*
> > *Fourteen pounds will weigh a stone."*

"You say somethin'?" The sheriff's quiet question startled him back to the present.

"No . . . I was just thinking." He didn't glance over at the sheriff. "Acclain has all the peeve and pester of a wounded wolf, doesn't he?"

"M-m . . ." The sheriff frowned thoughtfully. "Let's us just say that he tends to be impatient with anybody younger'n him."

Keven gave a short, derisive bark of laughter. "That's everyone, then!"

"Could be."

"How old is he?"

"I don' think nobody knows." He looked blankly at Keven. "I don' think nobody true *wants* to know."

* * * * *

From *The Ancient Age*, by Acclain, Wizard of Vale:

"The impatient reader will forgive me if I point out that understanding the past is an absolute prerequisite to understanding the present. It does not alter the fact if I am forgiven or thought to be simplistic; if it were not for the past, there would be no present.

"With the exception of a few peculiar experimental forerunners, created for unimaginable godly amusements, so we are told, man and other sapient beings start with the Ancient Age.

"I will not be drawn into an evaluation of any of the various Creation Myths, other than to point out the curious agreement in many that man was an experiment gone awry. It is interesting to ponder the notion that we are an accident still happening.

"The Ancient Age lasted eight thousand thousands of years, or it lasted for eight thousand; it depends on whom is telling the story. It began with the Creation, a historical point with which nearly everyone agrees. It ended much later. I await challenges to this point of view.

"It takes time for beings to sort themselves out, to take serious note of their differences, to determine who is intelligent and who is not, and by whose measure that attribute shall be ascertained. It takes time to discover who can communicate and who cannot, time to learn who will bear the spear and who will flee from it. And for those beings to whom it is supremely important, it takes time to become organized. Villages must be built, walls erected, and boundaries established, trade developed, roads carved, governments conspired, intoxicants concocted so that humans, in particular, could confound themselves while engaged in confounding others. In what must have been an utter burst of misguided genius, someone initiated nobility, the conceited concept that claims the common act of reproduction actually produces an exclusive line of individuals endowed with superior rights to tell others what to do. Mankind has always had an astonishing propensity to listen believingly to anyone speaking from the altitude of a horse.

"It would not exceed the normal application of logic, then, to presume the horse partially responsible for many of mankind's ills.

"Nobility and the horse promptly divided the world into

neat portions. Some claim there were ten kingdoms of the Ancient Age, some say twelve. However, since twelve kings named the Twelve Moons after themselves and portioned the year into months, we can be comfortable with that number.

"Most extraordinarily, we have no tales of great strife during the Age of Ancient Kings, no fully fledged wars to rise and rage throughout the world. Perhaps the concept of war was too irrational for the time, too monstrous. We hear, of course, of a few cranky border brawls, and there have always been magnificent heroes charging off to fight whatever they could find to ignite their displeasure. These were little battles, practice for greater things to come. Man's imagination was evidently sadly underdeveloped at the time. But his future, according to enduring lore, had already been blazed.

"In many religions it is stated how the gods told their beings: *The Wheel of Life is complete; all that is vital is here.* But then a minor god, going by different names in different religions but most commonly called Larn, turned over the Wheel of Life and revealed its underside.

"This act is known as Larn's Revelation: Power, Greed, Self-involvement, and Hate. This provided man with the required ingredients to begin the Ancient Wars.

"Bartog was a great wizard of the early Ancient Age, devoted entirely to the study of magic. He is now considered as being thoroughly evil, but no such proposal is suggested in what little trustworthy information survives; at that time, good and evil had not yet worked out their alignments. It was a time still in the murky beginning of things, and Larn's Revelation was but a bud about to blossom. It is sufficient to say that Bartog, in the beginning, was a resolute student of that mental machinery quite beyond the lift of levers.

"It is said he wandered the world for many years in pursuit of his study and settled finally here in the Vales, which was then called Mountainvale, in the Kingdom of Novus. In what is now Upper Vale, he caused a great castle to be built of the hard black rock from the eastern face of the Macaab Mountains. The quarries can still be discerned today, vast boxlike canyons on the lower slopes, in the area of the upper Roaring River. The work was performed by the Macaab Mountain warfen, excellent engineers and rocksmiths. Like many of the warfen, unfortunately, their foible lay in a passion for gold. The bud of Larn's Revelation was showing color. Bartog supposedly paid well, and the work continued for many years until the Black Castle was a dazzlement of exquisite carvings and wonderful warfen engineering.

"Then, having captured their imaginations with gold, and being the wizard he was, Bartog charmed the Macaab Mountain Warfen into his service.

"How this enslavement was accomplished is not easy to say. The warfen, though no strangers to magic themselves, have a deep distrust of it outside their own secrets and are ever alert to its workings. The Iron Mountain Warfen think the gold payments were charmed, the surreptitious magic cumulative over a long period of time. Others feel the Black Castle itself projected a captivating power. Some allude to the ancient warfen legend of the Warfenstone, a powerful object dating from their own version of the Creation, embodying the dark side of warfen lore. Whatever the means, Bartog had warfen slaves.

"Slavery is held to be the vilest of evils among the warfen. In this case, it was even more foul, for not only were their labors held in bondage but also their souls and minds as well. What followed, then, can best be described as a holy war, for it was fought with the total conviction of right and wrong, good and evil. Bartog, by his enslavement of the Macaab Mountain Warfen, aided in the creation of evil; the banding together of the free warfen to oppose him was midwife to the birth of good.

"The Iron Mountain Warfen of the eastern Vales, the White Mountain Warfen of the north, and the Palan Warfen of the west all banded together in alliance to war against Bartog and his enslavement of their brotherkind.

"Until information emerges to the contrary, we can say this was the first large conflict the land had ever seen. There had been arms raised in anger and in combat before, as mentioned, a few skirmishes here and there—Larn's Revelation assured that—but this was a matter of thousands of beings hurling themselves against each other with total victory as the sole acceptable goal.

"The world had a new entertainment to occupy its idle time.

"War had been invented.

"It is said the Warfen War of Mountainvale lasted thirty-three years in the Upper Vale alone. The toll was devastating. Bartog threw his charmed forces against their brothers with vicious abandon, and the free warfen fought with tears of grief and then of rage. The stories are too many to relate, and they have a sad and somber sameness: the assault at what is is now Upper Ford, where it was said that for a short while the armored bodies formed a dam across the Sun-Running River; the fight at what was later known as Bloody Brook—it was in a drought of the Augern Moon, yet the brookbed flowed bright red; the story of the Iron Mountain Fifty who, when surrounded on what is now the Hill of Fifty, outnumbered ten-to-one and offered the opportunity to surrender to Bartog, declared as one that the ground upon which they stood was free warfen ground and would be so dedicated with their lives.

"The unrelenting pressure upon Bartog was eventually too demanding, the death toll upon his enslaved fighters too great, and he was forced to abandon the Black Castle. With the remnants of his forces, he retreated to their warfenhalls in the Macaab Mountains. The castle itself was then torn down, black stone by stone, and the pieces scattered and buried. It is said that each piece of the Black Castle is bound in its entombment by warfen magic, so that it may never again see the light of day. A great burial barrow was made for the fallen Macaab Mountain Warfen in Upper Vale, since it was impossible to return the bodies to their own caverns for the required ceremonial cremation, and because of later circumstances, the barrow was never opened by the warfen to complete the transfer of the fallen to their Macaab Mountain home and thereby lay their spirits to rest.

"With the exception of but one special spot, to this day no warfen will travel at ease through Upper Vale. They still fear the charm, and it is their belief an unrested enemy is an enemy yet, that unrested warfen become impatient and dangerous. The one spot they will visit, and there feel at ease and pay homage, is the Hill of Fifty. For over two thousand years, it has been free warfen ground.

"Bartog and his charmed forces held the Macaab Mountain warfenhalls, and The Great Mass of the Three Warfen Armies, as the free warfen called themselves, were unable to penetrate. Although the construction of each mountain warfenhall is similar, each *mass*, or collection of clans into a single homesite, has particular and peculiar methods of protection. Thousands of Macaab Mountain Warfen had fallen in defense of the Black Castle, yet there were still enough to hold the advantage in defense of their home caverns. The toll had also been too great on the three armies; they fell back to hold the Macaab Mountains in what amounted to a state of siege. In an unprecedented act of co-operation, the Green Mountain Elves held the south firm.

"It was an entirely different warring style the elves preferred. While the warfen favored fighting shoulder to shield, with axe or sword or hammer or whatever lay at hand, the elves were seldom seen. The bow was their weapon of preference, and their arrows found targets in single flights, or as a devastating rush like the fall of hail. Bartog's forces exploring to the south simply disappeared, or they were found neatly aligned along a road with arrows sunk precisely through the right eye of each, or they returned bewildered to the north, believing they still traveled south. Although the warfen dislike displaying their magic, it became evident the elves had no such reservations.

"In the following years, Bartog strengthened his hold in the mountains and entered into a vast construction feat—to turn what we now call Castle Mountain into a stronghold, through the talents and labors of the charmed warfen.

"The Ancient Age closed with what we call the Ancient Wars. We cannot say with any assurance that they lasted from some definite date to some definite date; they were ongoing conflicts for hundreds of years, mayhaps thousands, king against king against king, culminating finally in the end of the Ancient Kings, their age, and a large portion of the population.

"However, 'Ancient Wars' is a misleading term; it would have us visualize the whole land flaming at once against itself, all choosing sides, all entirely devoted to their cause. It was instead a vast scattering of many wars and engagements, like stubborn forest fires, in many mountains, springing alight after each lightning storm. Bartog's forces against the three warfen armies was but one of these fires. But eventually the flames burned throughout the land. Beings of all cultures were caught up and found themselves choosing sides. Man, who enjoys his ideals served in simple fare (and who also does the majority of history writing) has expressed the Ancient Wars as being between good and evil. Nothing is ever that cleanly cut, but we can use the concepts as a general framework upon which to hang this particular era. I shall not enter into a discussion at this time as to the natures of good and evil. Accept them as you will; as has been, as is now, as will always be. It is an individual matter.

"The Ancient Wars brought beings to light that had lived mostly isolated until then. It has been suggested that these grim creatures of mean demeanor and menacing shape were the early toys of the gods. Called forth by the most part to serve the leaders of evil, they were simple creatures of brutish strength, more muscular than mental, with no concept of good or evil, right or wrong. When moved by magic evilly used or fired by Larn's Revelation, they raged horridly in the world. Whole armies of grotesque things marched against the forces aligning with good, and fear and enmity arose then against anything misshapen and bestial. The notion of the dark side of fay was born with these.

"Larn's Revelation seduced many of the higher sapients as well, particularly man; its alluring promises of Power, Greed, Self-involvement, and Hate were too attractive for the weak to resist—a fascination, deplorably, still at work today.

"Outnumbered by those choosing the side of good, evil enlarged upon powers that were then little understood. The term 'dark magic' came into usage to describe outside energies directed to harm. Although magicians, sorcerers, and wizards arose also on the side of good to counteract these forces, it is interesting to note that the first uses of major magic were for evil ends. Destruction has always been an easier endeavor than construction.

"A moral choice is the most difficult of choices. And, unfortunately, morality is not highly considered among survival skills. Humans are pulled in two directions at once, inward and outward, toward self and toward others. Those whose prime, pretentious interest is engrossed with themselves are trapped within their own acquisitive walls. This overbearing concentration on self, when carried to the detriment of others, becomes evil. It is distressing when people value faulty personalities more highly than character. It is further sad that most are not even aware of the imbalance and will react as savage, great cats if so charged.

"The Ancient Wars were a time of little neutrality. The working assumption at the time was simple: 'If thou be not of Mine, then thou be of Theirs.' It reduced the effort of thinking and saved valuable time—there was, after all, a war to be fought.

"The men of the Vales forged arms and ventured to serve their king, while the warfen and the elves kept their firm siege of the Macaab Mountains. King Novus ruled the Vales at the time and had raised a castle east of the village and a keep on the narrow roadway above the Sun-Running River. These two points controlled all movement east and west through the Vales. Although Bartog had been reluctant to engage in battle with the king up to this time, such conflict was unavoidable. The first large engagement in the Vales to involve men was the Battle of the Rivers.

"By some vile design, either called by Bartog or sent by another of his ilk, a large army of foul creatures slouched up the Sun-Running River valley from the east and attempted to fight their way to Castle Mountain. They were hulking, upright brutes, things from what we choose to call the dark side of fay, creatures with no names until it had become necessary to identify them. Call them goblins, bogles, ludorcs, ogres, trolls, bugans; call them whatever dark names come to mind; no two bestiaries agree on what names go with what shapes. They were met in vicious battle by the elves, the warfen, and the men of the Vales. It was not a time to stand disunited by culture. Of the thousands come to bolster Bartog's forces, but a wounded few gained the mountain.

"The warfen tell of terrible slaughter—how the rivers ran pink with blood, and bodies of friend and foe littered the banks and shoals like flotsam after a flood. Not given to overstatement, their legends tell of how a being could have walked from Outer Vale to the foot of the mountains on the bodies of men, elf, and warfen, beasts and creatures. There were floes of dead lodged in the Sun-Running and what we now call the Mad River as if jammed with ice in the spring. King Novus fell at the castle and, according to legend, was buried on the spot of his last breath. For centuries now, stories persist that the spirits of these dead prowl the Middle Vale, and to this day, it is a brave or foolhardy or an unknowing few who will venture the river roads at night, and certainly not when the dank river fogs lie low along the banks.

"As war raged elsewhere in the land, bringing terrible tales to the Vales, Bartog played a most monstrous joke. In tampering with the very elements of life itself, by horrid spells and unimaginable methods, he caused the creation of a ghastly, perverted race to spring from warfen and dark fay creature, a grotesque combination so foul it held none of the good qualities of warfenkind. It was called *gulgen*, a Warfish word best translated as 'abomination' or 'foul miscarriage.' To fully understand the feeling behind that word, one must understand the fervent hatred the warfen hold for dark creatures; it borders on fanaticism. To have such crossed with warfen blood is an appalling insult beyond our human comprehension.

"It is said these *gulgen* were so filled with self-loathing they were consumed with a hatred of all living things. In the following years, Bartog sent them against warfen, man, and elf in fierce battle. It has been suggested their only food was what they could kill in battle. The warfen and the elves drove against them in near madness as these things forayed from the mountain. We are told the waters of the Stad River ran so foul with the mountain's evil effluent and the blood of slain *gulgen* that its very touch was madness. Hence, the Mad River.

"The elves say the *gulgen* eventually turned on their creator; the warfen say the spell upon the Macaab Mountain Warfen was somehow broken, and they fell upon *gulgen* and evil creatures all.

"Whatever happened—and we are unlikely to know—there was a horrible war within the mountains. And in the end, there was silence. Warfen of the three armies explored the known entries to the mountain, and many were killed by traps both mechanical and magical. In their probes, they found remnant bands of foul creatures and met them in combat. They found survivors of the Macaab Mountain Warfen and led them to their own halls, but they feared delving too far into the mountain. The miasma of evil and dread of dark magic was so great that the warfen, to whom stone is no barrier, declined to venture into the grim depths. They sealed the old warfenhalls, keeping only certain passages and hidden entries open for patrol purposes.

"The warfen are a practical people, little given to fanciful fears, yet a whispered belief perseveres that Bartog sleeps beneath the mountain.

"The Ancient Wars ended with an uneasy balance in the world. Good held sway over the most of the land; evil had been driven to dark holes and to the wastelands. For a thousand years, no great armies marched to face each other. Arms clashed and death prowled the night and along dark roads, of course; it seems that swords are crafted too cunningly to not fit the hand and nature of man.

"And beastly things, too, prowled the nights.

"We call this time of precarious peace the Old Age, often the Age of The Twelve Kingdoms, for now there were definitely twelve; we date our years from its beginning.

"Kings again ruled, bards sang of heroic deeds in old wars, trade resumed as roads became safer little by little, and the Land prospered. Evil still waited in furtive shadows and in the mysteries of the night and lurked in distrust of different races, but good was largely triumphant. Law and order was the rule; chaos and confusion were shunned by all righteous beings.

"Everyone did his best to live as happily as his limitations allowed, perhaps doing better in the Vales than elsewhere in the land; the cooperation of cultures against a common enemy had formed an uncommon bond in the Vales.

"It was a bond that was to be of great value in the future; what we generally think of as 'peaceful times' appear to be but preparatory lulls between wars.

"The Macaab Mountains remained a curious, steep island of dread along the west side of the Vales. The Palan Warfen warded from the west, the White Mountain Warfen from the north, the Iron Mountain Warfen from the east, the Green Mountain Elves from the south. No one traveled those grim mountains, not even hunters. Only warrior patrols walked passages known only to them.

"Men, however, eager for trade in this new, exciting age, were worried less about old tales of evil and warfen spirits than they were about loss of gold. The tales of old wars were growing stale and dull; the gold of trade was new and shiny. The occasional trader's wagons rattling over poor roads were fast becoming whole caravans of wagons; the roads were feeling the roll of iron-shod wheels. At first, it was trains of mules daring to carry trade goods over the mountains. Then, when nothing more hapless than a broken leg or two occurred, the old Bartog Road to the castlelike mountain was extended over the pass and into the vast western plains of the Palan. Section by section, from trail and wagon track, The Great Western Trade Road was coming into existence. The pass, of course, became Castle Pass; it saved thinking.

"Just below the top of the pass, where the road makes its first switchback descending to the Vales, a minor ridge juts from the mountain. It is called East Bastion. A truncated rock formation atop it, called East Tower, completes the bulwark effect. The interior of this ridge is tunneled with rooms and corridors, entered from a naturally flat area at the curve of the road. There is apparently no connection

with the mountain interior; one suggestion is that this was a
guard station for Bartog's forces. A two-story timber building was erected against the face of this rock. It was called the
Waystation and operated as such for many years. It is said to
be haunted. It is my opinion that if any location deserved to
be haunted, it is there."

* * * * *

Keven was uncomfortable, sweating through his daily
sword practice on the upper court of the barrack. He was
still uneasy from the previous day with Acclain, his concentration wandering like an errant puppy. A few moments
earlier, he had noticed Slyt lounging in the shade of the
northwest tower. The woman would appear and disappear,
as if showing off some special talent. Leaning there now,
watching, smiling, she seemed to embody Santon's ghostly
specter of defeat, just waiting for a mistake.

"I'd give that third post another smack," she called, the
sly smile appearing even in her voice. "I think I saw it beginning to recover."

Keven clamped his teeth on the spiteful remark that
rushed to the fore, and he continued with a series of parry
replies.

"Do you always practice with such passion?" she saked
with a grin.

"Do you ever practice at all?" he replied. "Or do you
just lurk in the shadows and act smug?"

An eyebrow lifted. "Oh, I practice all the time."

"Yes, I imagine you do."

"Keven of Kingsend?" The voice was an abrupt baritone, not Slyt's soft purr. Keven turned, wiping sweat from
his eyes. If the small figure hadn't moved from the shadow
of the far stairhead, he probably would have overlooked it.
It was Bestian, the littler watchman. He approached

briskly, almost marching.

"We have met before," he stated. "Sheriff Gaskin has asked me to join your company."

Keven suddenly remembered his question of the day before about the varied makeup of venturing companies; his reaction must have shown in his face. The littler stiffened, and his voice sharpened.

"Again you show a reaction. I am sure you hold some resentment against the small people."

"I assure you, Bestian Tasker, that is not the case at all. I am confounded that the sheriff continues to fulfill this plan without consulting anyone but himself."

"He usually does."

"I was being sarcastic."

"So was I." Bestian regarded Keven for a moment with a hint of humor in his small face.

Keven hesitated. "I never had the chance to tell you . . . I'm sorry about Wicket."

Bestian nodded. "He was a good and brave companion. I have to go on watch now. We'll talk again." He turned away, back straight as a plank, striding to the stairhead.

"Hello, Slyt," he said, nodding. "You coming in to jail or just getting out?"

"Just waiting here to save you a trip, Best."

"Considerate."

"I try, Best."

Keven stared after him; this company was becoming a strange mix.

Slyt laughed softly. "Don't look so bewildered. That little bear cub could tear the toenails off a dragon with a dull rock. He arrested me twice. The second time was much easier. I beat him here by twenty paces and was ready to lock myself up. I don't clearly remember the first time." She smiled in the direction of the stairs. "I feel much safer now about this venture. He's an intense little rifter."

Keven didn't respond, but instead attacked one of the dummies savagely. Steel rang on hard oak. He suddenly stopped and turned to Slyt.

"Bestian . . ." He frowned. "And you called him Best?"

"Most everyone does."

The strange letters B-e-S-T he had found scratched on the outside of the tower came to mind . . . Bestian Stonewall Tasker?

* * * * *

The four of them were eating supper in the Sign of the Dancing Pig: Keven, Balak, Slyt, and Bestian. Slyt was telling a story. In spite of his feelings about her, Keven had to smile at her ability to mimic the nuances of the local speech.

"There were this Upper Valesman what traded for some chicks, an' a few days later, he were back for some more, an' then he were back for some more the next tenday.

" 'Whut be yew doin' with all these chicks?' his neighbor asks.

" 'Wull, they just dies, they does,' says the Upper Valesman.

" 'How can thet be?' says the neighbor. 'They be perfect healthy, the ones I keeps here.'

"The Upper Valesman frowns. 'Wull,' he says, scratchin' his head, 'mayhaps I be plantin' 'em too deep.' "

Balak only glowered at Slyt as the others laughed. To Keven's surprise, Bestian and Balak were getting along like old friends, conversing often in the guttural Dwarfish that Keven could hardly understand; one word in ten was about all he could follow. Slyt would glance at them and then wink at Keven, eyes twinkling. The woman had a sly sense of humor and an almost childish urge to encourage it in others. Balak or Bestian would say something in the rough language, and Slyt would make deep, grating sounds in her throat and then pretend it was a cough.

"Ah, yes, this stew is best when gargled," she said once, then concentrated her whole attention on her bowl in the following, frowning silence from Balak. Together the four of them talked of the town, the valley, the flood, the weather, everything but the coming venture. The sheriff had threatened dire consequences in the wake of any public discussion about that. Little by little, Keven was beginning to relax somewhat in the presence of Slyt, at least to the point where he could tolerate her without wanting to cut her down. Female or not, she was still a thief. But still he didn't want the woman behind him, and it was bothersome having her in sight one moment and gone the next. She was unpredictable in her actions and reactions; Keven didn't feel that was a trustworthy trait and had questioned the sheriff about Slyt's ability to keep their plan secret.

"It seems to me this will be as much of a secret as the mountain itself," he grumbled.

"Slyt'll do what's best for Slyt to do," the sheriff had said. "An' believe me, she be knowin' right now that it be clear best for her to keep her mouth clamped."

"I still don't like it, and I don't trust her. If something goes wrong up there, as they used to say at the academy, I'll be looking for a handy peg to hang some blame."

"'Nother reason that Bestian be goin'. He knows Slyt true good. 'Less you got some doubts 'bout *his* nature, too."

"No . . ."

"You don' sound too awful convinced. Well, let me tell you. Best be a hunter afore he come to the Watch. An' one true damn good one, too! He can thread a needle with a crossbow, an prob'ly wouldn't pause at takin' on a bear with a bent nail. But he be doin' things his way. Don' expect him to stand there toe to toe an' blade it out with a man in a fight. He can disappear quicker than Slyt when that sort o' thing rise up, but you'll true see some quick an' sturdy action 'round the corners an' in the shadows. There were two sharp blades here two year ago what thought it were high funny that a littler be in the Watch, an' they were goin' to throw him into the river. They limped out o' town with a lot more information than they come with."

Keven watched Bestian and Balak chuckling over some dwarfen joke and wished he could follow the language; he quickly corrected himself: *warfen.* A man seated about a table behind them rose and began complaining to his companions about a lost purse. His friends laughed.

"Ah, we know, Ewen. Yer lost yer coin ag'in. 'Tis a tale to wrench the true heart right out o' a man."

"Yar, Ewen, I be knowin' yew fer many year now, an' yer purse be like a lazy dog: When there be work fer it, it be off hid somewhere."

"But I *had* m' purse, I tell ya! Right on m' belt, 'twas!" He peered once again under his table, then scowled suspiciously at Slyt and Bestian, whose backs were to him.

"Thar be thieves o' all sizes e'erywhar," he said, just a little too loudly.

Bestian turned and regarded the man with a slight frown. "I'm of the Watch. Look for your thief elsewhere."

"I look whar I please!" He searched under their table. "I *know* I had it."

Slyt leaned back and peered under the table, too. She scuffed with her feet. "Is this it?" She reached down and brought up a worn leather purse. It gave a feeble jingle.

"Yar! Thet be it!"

Slyt tossed it to him, smiling. "Must have slipped into the shadow there."

As she returned her attention to her ale mug, she flickered a wink at Keven and gave the barest suggestion of a shrug.

Balak glared at her, then turned to Keven, his voice a hard grating. "We goes lookin' fer t'iefs an' we gots one wid us."

Keven raised a hand and made a slight motion of caution. Balak lowered his voice to a dull rumble.

"Dis bandit lidder—dis Santer, ya calls 'im."

"Sander," Keven said softly.

"Yar, Santer, he too be called Pauduk. Name o' ver' ol' warfen sp'rit. Means 'He wut make mount'n fall.' "

"Where did you hear that?"

Balak grunted. "Know."

Bestian spoke to him in Dwarfish and received a short reply. "He says it's 'a warfen thing.' "

Slyt laughed softly. "It's a warfen thing to be secretive, you know. Any time they don't want to answer a question, it's a warfen thing."

Balak raised a finger like a carved piece of red oak and aimed it at Slyt. "Ah gif ya warfen t'ing, t'ief!"

Slyt leaned back, palms out, smiling. "Becalm yourself, Good Balak. I am but a—" Her eyes widened suddenly at something over Keven's shoulder. Her startled expression was such that Keven spun, almost flinching defensively. Behind him, the entire room had frozen—a serving maid was caught in midstride, mouth open; a wide-eyed man, mug raised to his mouth, poured ale down his chin; another man stared over a goose leg clamped in his teeth. A woman and a dog were standing just inside the door.

"Holy mother of all the gods together!" someone breathed.

The two were white. Shining white. An elegant, dazzling white that seemed to glimmer in the dull, smoky room.

The woman stood wide-stanced in tall, white leather boots. A white linen tunic fell to midthigh beneath a belted coat of shimmering mail; a heavy white cloak, bordered in red and black, was thrown back over both shoulders. A brilliantly polished round shield with the embossment of a bull's head hung casually from her left arm; a mace with a bleached white handle and a gleaming head of what appeared to be a huge lump of raw silver dangled from a thong on her right wrist. Her hair framed her face like a white cowl, spilling low over her shoulders. A triangular pendant of onyx surrounding a huge blood red ruby hung from her neck. She was beautiful, but showed as much expression as a marble statue; tall, about a hand under a span, but she seemed towering. An eerie glint showed in eyes so dark there was no distinguishing a pupil, and they seemed not to focus on anything.

The dog's eyes, unfortunately for those in the room, were in piercing focus. They were an unworldly white, slanted, and seemed to lance directly to the soul. It was a huge dog, snow white, and stood with its head low like a wolf.

"I seek Keven of Kingsend," she called into the deathly silence. It was a curiously uninflected voice, but clear as a trumpet.

No one stirred.

Her distant gaze searched the room slowly, fastening finally on Keven. He felt himself chilled and was conscious that his twisted position in the chair put the old cutlass in an awkward spot should he need it quickly.

"Thou art he," she stated. All eyes in the room shifted to Keven. He blinked and turned to the others.

"Is there some distinguishing sign on me?" Turning back to the ominous woman, he answered calmly, "I am."

She approached the table, her cold eyes never leaving his face. The dog stalked with her.

"I am Albina." She placed the emphasis on the first syllable. "Bishopess of Baalab the Avenger. I will join thy mission against the evil ones."

Balak snorted and scowled. "Some sicret, dis."

"I am under a compelling oath," the ringing voice went on. "With thee, beside thee, behind thee, before thee, I will combat this evil, for Baalab has touched me and filled me with terrible resolve. Baalab has said in truth, 'Thou shalt live in goodness, or thou shalt die in evil!' I am but a poor instrument of His awful will."

There was a soft stir in the room, as if everyone breathed at once. Keven held up a hand to stop her. "Can we talk about this later? At the Watch barrack tomorrow morning?"

It was as if she never heard. "I have many powers to aid you. I can detect evil and traps in their most insidious forms. I can cure wounds and disease, remove curses; I can as well inflict them. I can bless a person; I can damn him. I can fight in the tracks of any man. And"—she raised her unblinking stare to the ceiling—"with Baalab's mighty assistance, I can cast a spell to raise the dead."

There wasn't a sound in the room for a moment. Then, as if the last spell she mentioned had worked instantly, the silent patrons of the tavern rose. First a brave few, scraping back chairs and furtively starting for the door, then quickly more, then in a gathering rush of bodies jamming for exit. The front door to the street and a side door to an alley were suddenly much too narrow. Chairs and benches overturned, tables raked across the floor and were shoved aside, mugs and trenchers and utensils clattered underfoot. The only voices were grunts and curses of effort.

Only Keven, Balak, Bestian, Slyt, and two wide-eyed men trapped in a far corner remained. Keven was conscious of his mouth hanging open. He closed it. From the rear room, the taverner appeared, his face a dangerous red. He was a large man, nearly as wide as he was tall, wiping his big hands on a grimy apron.

"Yuv jest cost me a tidy sum, yer ladyship!" he began, but he seemed to be losing momentum and ire with every pace. She regarded him unemotionally. The dog rumbled

deep in its throat. The man lumbered to a halt and licked
his lips. He glanced at the four as if to enlist some aid.

"I come on Baalab's business," the woman avowed. "If
that has disturbed thy patrons to thy cost, that cost is then
mine."

She took a small purse of white leather from her belt and
selected several coins, holding them out to the man. "Five
gold is all I have. Is that adequate?"

The big man started to reach for them.

Bestian spoke sharply. "One is quite enough. Isn't it,
Roland?"

"Wull, e'erbody be gone." The big man motioned
around the room to support his point.

"They'll be back." Bestian nodded. "After this, you'll
sell every barrel you have right down to the dregs tonight.
Truly, probably a silver is enough."

The man quickly selected a golder, smiling. "One be
right fine, yer ladyship."

"Baalab has said, 'To be fair is to be good.' Thou art a
good man. I endow upon thee the blessing of Baalab."
Then, to Keven, "When thou leave on thy mission, I shalt
be with thee."

She turned abruptly and left, the dog pacing beside her.
There was a scramble of feet from the dark street as the way
was cleared for them. The big man stared at the gold in his
hand as if it might suddenly turn to something else, then at
the door, then at the four at the table, then at the white
faces that filled the alley doorway.

"Wull, she be gone," he told the frightened faces. "I
stands the drink fer the first five to take a table!"

The returning rush was nearly as feverish as the outgoing.

"From what damned depths did she—" Keven began,
swinging back to the others.

Slyt stopped him with a raised hand and a crooked grin.
"Beware. Baalabites have long ears and no sense of humor

at all. If you question them too closely, or if they suspect you of making fun of them, then you are in danger of being—" she leaned forward, widened her eyes, and spoke in a ghostly tone—"e-vil."

Balak grunted, eyes a blazing blue from under lowered brows. "Evil, 'tis it! Evil her'll get wid m' axe!"

Slyt whistled tunelessly. "Not altogether a good idea, my good warf. The Baalabites have a very direct—"

"Ya!" Balak leveled a blunt finger at Slyt again. "Ya nar narver, *narver* say wut me t' do! Ya unnerstan'?"

Slyt leaned back, her hands held up in surrender. "Unnerstan' perfectly, Balak. Narver it is."

"I never heard of Baalab," Keven broke in, hoping to divert the conversation.

"It's far southeastern," Bestian offered. "A hard religion. Cruel. Intolerant. They concede no divergence from the word of Baalab, and truth as they see it. The clerics are officers of law and magistrates as well. They seek out evil, judge it, and punish it. Very quickly!" He gave a short laugh. "It's a religion based on the premise that if you hammer on someone hard enough with the proper tool, you can eventually convert them. That is, if they survive."

"This whole thing is becoming bizarre." Keven shook his head. "That's all we need now—some religious fanatic raging along!"

"Fanatic or not, did you notice the breadth of her shoulders?" Bestian said. "That mace of hers is bound to have some power behind it! The only thing . . ." He shook his head. "There doesn't seem to be anybody alive behind those eyes. Did you see? There wasn't a touch of emotion or anything in her face. She could as well have been some kind of magic statue or something."

"Mayhaps she's not mortal," Slyt said, her usual smile unchanged. "Maybe she's of a dark nature, a demon mayhaps, and the dog is actually black, a night hound."

"I don't believe in much of that," Keven said, frowning. "The question is, how did she know about this venture?"

"Some sicret!" Balak grumbled.

"True!" Keven agreed. "There must be *someone* in town who doesn't know of it!"

Chapter Eight

Starting at the river wall, wearing casual arms and armor, Keven began to run. Ignoring the stares, the caustic calls, and the insults, he sprinted up the steepest streets, the most strenuous stairways.

A littler sprang from an alley and tried to trip him with a thrown snare. Keven slashed the cord in two, gave the small man a quick grin, and raced on. He had arranged with Bestian to fashion surprises along the arduous uphill path.

A beggar suddenly spun and swung at him with a staff; he parried with his sword, ducked, and dodged past. Two loungers swerved to trap him between them; he halted abruptly, and when they stumbled into each other, he shouldered them aside.

As he approached parts of the old walled town, a call came from above. "Ranger!"

A man was whirling a sling from atop the wall. As Keven slipped his bow from his shoulder, the man dropped out of sight and raised a wooden plank. Keven's arrow struck dead center.

Up the lower part of Sixty-Six Steps, he dashed into the barrack courtyard. Sheathing his sword and looping his bow over a shoulder, he seized a rope hanging from the parapet. He climbed, swung to another rope, and traveled hand over hand to the opposite wall. He pulled himself over the parapet and stood poised in the training area.

His breathing was fast but under control; his leg and arm muscles burned slightly but were still limber. There were no cramps. A motion off to one side caught his eye. He spun, dropped to a crouch, and caught the apple that was aimed at his back. There was a blur, and he caught another one. Bestian stepped from the shadow of the old East Tower and caught one of the apples as Keven threw it back. They raised the fruit to each other, as if in toast, and grinned as they each took a bite. Inside, Keven felt like laughing out loud or cheering; it felt good to be proud of his body again, to be able to trust his talents. His weeks of intensive training had paid handsome rewards.

"It's been a long way to run just to get an apple," Bestian commented, smiling.

Keven nodded. "But well worth it."

* * * * *

The plan was under way, and Keven was eager to get on with it. He had never been patient, and this was a long, tense time for him. There were low-voiced conferences with the sheriff, and slipping around town pretending to do one thing while accomplishing another.

"We got to be misleadin'," the sheriff said, scowling at each of them in turn: Keven, Slyt, and Balak. "Seems by now that half the Vale knows somethin' be afoot, an' the other half holds strong suspicions o' it. We can't hide it, but we *can* point it in 'nother direction. So this's how we do it. . . ."

They worked it out. Keven admitted it was a plan that could work. It was simple. He remembered Rusker's words: "*Avoid complicated plans. Most o' the time ya be dealin' with people who'll not remember step one!"*

There had been serious talk in town for a couple of ten-days about forming a large caravan to push west by way of North Pass. Trade traffic was moving up the Sun-Running Road, and goods were piling up in the warehouses. Bandits or not, it was time for trade to move. Riders carried the word down the Trade Road that the Traders and Merchants Guilds sought mercenaries for this journey, and a variety of arms and men appeared. The caravan was formed. It was big. And it was no secret that a company of Vale Guard would be in escort, led by Captain Mikel himself; it was, in fact, a matter of open, freely encouraged discussion.

"It'll take some hardy bandits to rob *this* caravan!"

"Or some foolish ones t' try."

"Yar! Trade be a-rollin' ag'in!"

And so the caravan set out in the morning, rattling over the new Keep Bridge onto the rutted Road North and bound for the far North Pass, eighty wagons and twelve pikemen of the Vale Guard, grinning mercenaries, some citizen archers and a few more adventurous swordsmen swinging up onto the wagons as they rolled out of town. It was a rousing town occasion, with pipes and horns and drums, with cheering and waving and running alongside the wagons and singing the caravaners' song whether anyone knew all the words or not:

> "*I got a maid in Rot-ten River.*
> *Roll the wagons 'cross the wide Pal-an.*
> *She'll take all what I got to give her.*
> *An' we all know how the wagons roll.*
>
> "*Tol' my love I was gone til winter.*
> *Roll the wagons 'cross the wide Pal-an.*
> *What she don' know, it won't dint her.*
> *It's a lo-ng road that the wagons roll . . . ."*

The song rang out of hearing somewhere around verse twenty-seven, with many more to go. It was said there were as many verses to the song as miles on the Great Western Trade Road, and no one really knew how long the road was.

> "*Trade Road runs from here to yonder.*
> *Roll the wagons 'cross the wide Pal-an.*
> *Go far as y' can but the end be beyonder.*
> *Bedamn if we know where the wagons roll.*"

At midday, a cry was mounted through town of some undefined trouble in the far foothills of the Iron Mountains. It was all very confusing and apparently dreadful. Thirty mounted Vale Guardsmen and twenty armed volunteers clattered through the twisted streets. They were ferried over to Crossriver as quickly as possible and pounded up the narrow Iron Mountain Road in a long charging line.

In the midst of all this clamor and confusion, Keven, Balak, and Slyt slipped by different, discreet routes into the hills on the Shires Road edge of town. They met in a wooded glen where they had previously stored their gear and made camp.

"I like it," Slyt laughed. "It's all a great game o' Hide-the-Rabbit. The Mounted Guard runs up the Iron Mountain Road and then cuts down the old Red Creek Trail, across the Sun-Running at Upper Ford, and joins the caravan tonight at Sugar Tree Fork. It makes the caravan guard twice as strong as when it left town."

"It may work as a good blind," Keven agreed, nodding. "Especially since we've spread it around town that we simply aren't ready for any action yet."

Slyt laughed. "And then we assault the Waystation while the bandits are gone up to North Pass to jump the caravan. I like it. It's just sneaky enough to appeal to my sense of justice."

Balak glared at her.

"Ya got nar justice," he muttered. "An' ah nar like sneakin' 'round. It nar warfen way."

Keven leaned back against a tree and closed his eyes. He was uneasy about the strange mix of beings in the party and skeptical of their ability to all work together. He was confident now in himself, in his own abilities—the only thing left to prove was that he could win against a real live enemy—but with this strange mix of people along, there was a lurking worry in his mind.

* * * * *

The three of them slipped through the forest in the mist and murk of early morning, climbing a sheep trail that paralleled Shires Road into the low hills beyond. They were afoot with arms and packs. Keven again wore casual arms and armor: greaved boots, breast and back plate over a mail tunic, shield and helmet, broadsword over his back, longbow in his left hand, cutlass at his side. Balak wore his suit of mail and scale, with axe and hammer at his belt, an embossed, conical helmet over his leather cap. He carried his round shield and heavy crossbow. Slyt appeared to be carrying nothing but a bedroll slung over one shoulder, but the hang of her dark cloak suggested a belted sword underneath.

As the last of the outlying farms fell behind, they gained the road. At the cresting of a wooded hill, Albina and the dog appeared from the edge of the dark trees like two apparitions; it was the first they had seen of her since the night at the Dancing Pig. Balak gave a deep grunt, and Keven noticed that Slyt edged in a little closer. The two ghostly white figures slipped to the road ahead of them and moved off in the lead without a sound. Balak bent low, scowling at the road in the darkness, as if to assure himself they were actually leaving tracks.

"Do you think she and the dog are spirits?" Keven whispered, trying to keep a smile out of his voice.

"Ya t'ink she nar be sp'rit?" The dwarf's harsh whisper could carry half a league, Keven thought.

"I think she's just as real as we are."

"Mebbe that worser," Balak grunted and loosened the axe at his belt. Slyt dropped back to the rear. Her cloak was thrown back now over her left arm, revealing the glint of a sword hilt.

Bestian met them where the road branched off toward Acclain's Towers. He seemed overloaded, shouldering a pack too large for him but without apparent effort. He wore a suit of fine mail under a woods-hued, brown and green cloak, and he carried a small shield and a light crossbow. A short sword in a finely tooled, silver decorated scabbard hung from his belt. Without expression, he watched Albina and the dog pass, then fell in beside Balak, signaling Keven that the two of them would watch the rear.

They turned toward the towers, Albina again leading the way, finding the hidden path entrance without a word of direction. Slyt moved up beside Keven. She scanned the sky, then turned to look back to where a gray paling marked the eastern horizon and the coming of the sun.

"Looking for Baalab," she murmured, indicating Albina. "She must be getting her guidance from somewhere."

Keven made an irritated, chopping gesture of silence. Slyt grinned at him.

The brown-smocked workers were already tending to the stock as they passed between the stone walls of Acclain's neat farmhold. The strange, rambling castle was dark but for a single light high in a distant tower. Keven wondered if it was Acclain at some arcane study. Eugon was waiting outside the walls, a spectral, hooded figure in gray. With a carved staff, he pointed to a path leading around the walls of the castle and led the way. Albina and the dog fell in behind him, followed by the others. Keven couldn't see Eugon's shadowed face, but he was certain there would be a sardonic smile there.

So now our group is nearly complete, he told himself mockingly. We now have everyone but an elf. . . . *This is the way you make your Party. This is the way*—He shook his head. Some hearty company this! A cocky littler lawman, an irascible dwarf, a female thief who insisted on sarcasm as a prime means of communication, a fanatic cleric whose eyes seemed to focus elsewhere no matter where she happened to be looking, what appeared to be a white wolf, a pretentious, arrogant mage . . .

Aren't we off for a fine venture! he asked himself. How jolly! How well met! He started humming quietly to himself, hearing in his mind the old words to "Walter Would a'Venturing Go":

> "*He met some men upon the road;*
> '*An' we be fierce!' their leader crowed.*
> *Two were lame, one hardly growed,*
>
> "*And another nearly ninety.*
> "*Oh, Walter, Walter,' he said aside,*
> '*What we have here is bloated pride.'*
> '*Jump 'im, boys!' the leader cried.*
> *And they thumped upon him thoroughly.*"

They traveled the dim trail through the morning forest. A dull overcast held the sun to little more than a vague glow in the sky and seemed to stifle sound as well. They spoke little—there didn't seem to be anything to say—and even the normal forest creatures were quiet. The sudden, soft whir of a sling startled them once, followed instantly by another. Poised for trouble and frowning to the rear, Keven saw Bestian move into the underbrush and return with a brace of plump rabbits.

"Supper," he explained.

Albina bore her forbidding gaze on him. "Thou hast slain innocent creatures," she tolled ominously. "Not for proper sacrifice, but for thine own pleasure hast this been done. It is an evil act!"

"Well, mayhaps creatures not *too* innocent," Slyt said, a thin smile curling in the corners of her mouth. "You know how rabbits are. . . ."

Albina swung her strange eyes on Slyt until the thief turned away.

"Well . . ." she mused, "mayhaps not."

"In these forests, it is not evil to take animals for food," Bestian explained with a frown.

"Only Baalab partakes of flesh," Albina intoned. "His disciples do not."

Bestian's frown darkened. "It would be a good time for me to point out that I am not a disciple of Baalab," he said evenly.

Keven could tell that Slyt was going to say something more by the tilt of her head and the sparkle in her eyes.

"Slyt, slip farther ahead with Eugon," he said. "Keep your eyes sharp."

"For what? I'm no woodswoman! My idea of open country is resting in the shade in Walnut Court!" She glanced quickly to the right and left. "My eyes *are* sharp, and all I see is trees and leaves and bushes. It comes not as much of a surprise to me, but that's what I'd expect to see out here."

"Then fall back and bother Bestian!" He turned to the cleric. "Albina, you will have to allow us tolerance. We are together to fight enemies, not each other."

"That is true, but Baalab has said—"

"Please." He held up a hand. "We have things to do. We are not disciples of Baalab, and I don't think this is a proper time for conversions or discussions of faith."

She studied him for a moment, no expression showing on her beautiful face, then turned again to follow Eugon, who was waiting ahead with a sardonic smile. Keven glanced back at Slyt, who crossed her eyes and gave him a broad idiot's grin, tongue lolling out the corner of her mouth. Fine! Next time Albina could pound that smile off Slyt's face with her silver mace, and bedamned if he'd do anything to stop it!

The trail led onto a narrow, leaf-covered road, which ran like a winding, dim tunnel through huge overhanging trees.

"The Westshire Road," Bestian explained, pointing southeast toward the Shires. "It branches off about three miles down there to Northshire. Runs all the way down to Far Hillshire and beyond."

"And if we follow it west from here?" Keven asked. "Which is, I believe, the direction of our travel."

"It's the Crystal River Road."

"Strangers have been lost for weeks in the Shires." Eugon spoke for the first time, his aloof, all-knowing smile fixed on Bestian. "There's a vast spiderweb tangle of roads and lanes in there, all named for the direction in which one travels. Cherryhill Lane goes south; going north, it's Boggy Hollow Road. Pigfoot Path goes one way; turn around and you're on Brandybrook Trace. And not a signpost anywhere."

Bestian considered Eugon with a slight frown. "If a stranger cannot find his way in the Shires, young mage, it is his own problem. All anyone has to do is ask. I've never been lost. I was considerably puzzled once in Far Hillshire for two or three days, but I've never been lost."

He winked at Keven as they moved on.

The road bored through the forest, following the easy lay of the land. Up and down and around, it eventually dropped down a gentle hillside to the shallow valley of the Crystal River. They joined the Road West in the cleared fields at the First Bridge. Their first good view of the mountains opened, but the sullen overcast held the upper ramparts hidden. The image was that of a dark rock wall across the world. They stopped to eat on the hillside. Keven felt it to be near midday.

"What will the weather be?" he asked of no one in particular; he was still having trouble predicting mountain weather. Bestian and Balak both squinted at the sky.

"It'll hold," Bestian said. "Rain tomorrow, probably. About evening, mayhaps later. Not heavy."

Balak grunted and nodded.

"Baalab will smile on our venture," Albina said flatly. "He who reigns overall, reigns overall."

Slyt said something about rain, then coughed and scanned the sky innocently. Albina gave her a cold, considering look.

The dog growled and rose to its feet. Two riders appeared from the far tree line at the edge of the Road West. They were followed by five men on foot, carrying stout cudgels.

Bestian gave a grunt of surprise. "Bracken and Lester of Mill Ford," he said.

Keven squinted at the approaching group. "Are you sure? They're still quite far away."

"I'm sure." He glanced at Keven. "I don't imagine they're up here to discuss flood damage."

"I don't care what their motive is. If they seek me, I'm easy to find."

The two riders halted, seemed to discuss something, then urged their horses forward. The men followed. As they neared, Bestian raised himself from the grass. Bracken halted his horse abruptly.

"Bestian!" he said. "What are you doing here?" His scowl swung to the others. "And these other people."

A slight frown shadowed the littler's face. "I might ask you the same, Bracken."

"Well, you need not interrogate me, little man," Lester said in an arrogant voice. "I come to teach some manners to the deserving boor who feels he can humiliate me publicly."

Keven gave a sharp laugh. "I see you again require others to prop up your courage, Lester. As for yourself, does your memory fail, or are you simply too dull to learn?"

Lester started to reply, but Bestian interupted.

"I asked you a question, Bracken."

"I outrank you, Bestian. You'd best be careful. But I'll answer anyway." He smiled at Keven with almost the same sneer worn by Lester. "I'm here to see that it's a fair fight."

Keven made a show of counting the men behind Bracken and Lester. "Well, including you two you might need about four more to make it fair."

Albina's voice rang like a bell. "You would hamper our mission? This would find disfavor in Baalab's eye."

The dog rumbled deep in its chest. The horses shuffled nervously. Bracken licked his lips.

"Where did all these people come from?" he asked Bestian. "And what *are* you doing here?"

"Told you the sheriff kept a tight counsel." Bestian grinned at Keven, then said to Bracken, "Who did you expect to find?"

"We heard that the fighter and Slyt were going up the pass."

"That's true," Slyt called. "The ranger and I are just having a nice hike. You know how it is. Boy and girl. Come to think of it, maybe you don't know about that."

Keven noticed that Slyt had strolled off to one side of the five men and was calmly polishing her blade with a handful of dry grass. He noted, too, how the others in the party had edged to the best fighting stations without being obvious, fanning out almost casually to the sides.

Lester frowned from side to side, scanning them all. "Now, this is just between us and the insolent fighter," he said.

Keven's sword cleared its scabbard with a soft slide of steel. "I am full to the gullet with you two," he said evenly. "You may come singly or together, with your crew or not. It matters not to me."

He fell into middle guard position. Two of the men with cudgels began to edge sideways. There was a whir of a sling, and a stone missed one by a finger's width.

"Pretend you are statues," Bestian said to the men. The white dog trotted to the other side from Slyt, head low, eyes and ears fully focused on the opposing group.

"Wait!" Bracken called, but it was unclear to whom he was speaking; head down, snorting, his horse was backing away. Eugon was muttering and fondling something in his hand. One of the men glanced nervously at Bracken as the horse retreated past them.

"Yew nar said a thing 'bout magic, Bracken, nor these other people here. This be a armed party."

The men were eying Keven's sword as they accompanied Bracken's horse backward.

"The horse demonstrates a remarkable intelligence," Keven said as he advanced toward them. "It would be best if all of you would follow its example."

Lester and his horse seemed frozen in place, the horse eyeing the crouched dog. As the others, party and opponents, moved slowly across the field, Lester suddenly drew his sword and spurred his horse. The dog leaped at its head. The horse reared, and Lester was unceremoniously unloaded, flat on his back, legs in the air. There was a burst of laughter from Bestian and Slyt. Balak was making those guttural grunts that passed for laughter. Keven waved his sword at the others.

"Go home!" he called. "You are a ridiculous band of fools."

Bracken had dismounted and was trying to control his horse. Eugon made a small motion. The horse reared, broke free from Bracken, wheeled away, and raced for the road. Two of the men exchanged glances and followed. The others kept backing away, leaving Bracken alone. Keven gave a rough laugh.

"I imagine this is a situation you and Lester fear most, Bracken, this being alone."

Bracken shook his fist, his face reddening. Keven laughed again.

"Well, that certainly frightens *me*."

Behind Keven and to one side, Lester rolled suddenly to his feet, his sword reaching for Keven. Slyt shouted a warning. As Keven dodged and whirled, he felt a light slash across the back of his left leg, just above his boot. It just missed the tendons.

"Hah!" Lester laughed.

Keven examined his leg and then Lester with a scowl of astonishment. "Why, you little whore's son!" he exclaimed and spun into a backhand blow aiming at Lester's head. At the last instant, he flattened the blade, but the blow slammed Lester to the ground, senseless.

"Bracken!" Keven called. "Come get your infant cohort, here! He needs his nappy changed!"

Blood seeped from the dark mark across Lester's cheek where the flat of the sword had slapped him. Albina knelt and touched him briefly.

"He will live," she said. "Do you wish that?"

Keven glared at the prone body.

"Yes. There's always the possibility he may be more intelligent when he recovers." He turned to where Bracken was still standing.

"Never attempt this sort of thing again, Bracken. Never! You and your turdwit friend here are alive only because you are too stupid to meet your gods!"

"And, Bracken," Bestian called, "when you return to town, it would be thoughtful of you to continue east. I think the sheriff will be interested to hear of this great blunder of yours."

The party gathered their dropped belongings and moved off down the hill. Slyt, Bestian, and Balak chuckled about the encounter, but Keven stalked in a quiet rage. His cut was minor—with some salve, the bleeding had already stopped—but what infuriated him was the curiosity that the land seemed overcrowded with fools. And wherever he went he seemed to attract them.

* * * * *

They crossed the stone arch of the First Bridge over the Crystal River, and Keven turned into the overgrown yard by the inn. At his approach, the same boyish figure he had seen before came to the door. The features, he could see now, reflected elf. The face was a bit too narrow, the nose a little too long and thin, the large eyes were a dark green and slightly slanted, the ears were large and bore the characteristic points.

"Are you Kenth?" Keven asked.

"I am." The voice again like that of a young lad.

"I am Keven of Kingsend. You cared for me and my horse when I came from the pass."

Kenth nodded slightly. "I remember."

Keven continued. "I owe you a debt. I wish to repay it."

A hesitant shadow of a frown showed briefly in the young face and was gone. "You cannot. It was aid freely given and carries no obligation of repayment."

"But—"

The frown came again, stronger. "You do not understand. You must know that, among my people, aid tendered is not a loan to be repaid. It is a gift." The frown faded. "Just to see that animal was my great pleasure. He is a splendid horse. My only regret is that I was unable to cure him completely. A contaminated arrow nicked a tendon, and I cannot fix that. I am afraid he will limp."

Keven didn't know what to say. "I wish I could do something for you."

Again the sudden frown. "You can do something by withdrawing your offer to repay what you feel is a debt."

Keven nodded. "Very well," he said stiffly. "I withdraw my offer."

Kenth smiled openly at him for the first time and gave a brief nod. Bestian called cheerfully from the road.

"Hello, Kenth."

"Hello, Best. Are you lost?"

"Must be. I'm over here in elfland."

There was a quick flash of a smile in Kenth's face. "Just on the edge of it."

"Near enough for towner folk." The two of them laughed, as if about some secret shared. But Keven thought there was a flicker of something other than humor in Kenth's dark eyes as they passed over Balak.

"May I ask you a question?" Keven said. Kenth nodded, warily it seemed. Keven indicated the neat buildings and fields.

"In the midst of all the trouble along this road, how do you keep this spot so trouble free?"

The quick smile came and went again. "If I told everything I knew, I would not have any friends left."

Keven didn't know quite how to put his next question. "Then this is a 'protected' spot?"

The halfling elf gave a slight shrug. "It is the edge of elf domain." He turned to indicate the mountains. "However, when you cross the Second Bridge, the one over the Mad River, it is a different matter."

"That's what I've been told," Keven said, nodding. "I

would guess you probably know our plans. Everyone else in the valley seems to."

"If I told everything I know . . ."

"The sheriff told me you were to be trusted. Outside of yourself, do you think our presence is known up here?"

There was a pause as Kenth seemed to be listening to something. "Your presence is known, but not to those whom you seek."

"And if we camp this night at the Second Bridge?"

"You should be safe from discovery if you stay this side of the river. But"—the small shrug again and a tilted eyebrow— "nothing is certain in these times."

Keven nodded. "Thank you, Kenth."

"Baalab awaits," Albina called, her strange eyes cast upward to the mountains. "There is work for righteous hands."

Keven was certain that Kenth's slightly pointed ears cupped forward for an instant. A blank expression fell over his face as he watched Albina with those wide, dark green eyes. He arched an eyebrow at Keven. Keven shook his head. "Ask me not. It's mostly out of my control."

Keven and his companions took their leave and continued toward the mountains. Bestian swung into step beside Keven. He glanced around to see if anyone was within hearing.

"Back there with Kenth," he said quietly, "you may not be aware of it, but he was insulted by your offer to repay what you thought of as a debt."

Keven looked at him with a frown. "I don't know why he should be insulted."

"Elves are like that. And Kenth is a halfling elf. Didn't you know that?"

"Yes, but I still don't understand. Why the insult? My offer was sincere."

"Um-m . . ." Bestian strode on for a few paces, gazing

ahead with a faint frown. "I'm afraid, Keven of Kingsend, that if you have to ask, I would have a difficult time explaining it. It can best be summed up by saying it's an elven thing."

"That doesn't explain anything."

"Actually it explains a lot. It all depends on whether one cares to understand fay or not."

It was Keven's turn to walk in silence for a while. "I don't think this is the time to discuss cultural philosophies, Bestian."

The littler glanced up at him with a measuring look. "Strange," he said. "You have an apparent knowledge of many things, yet it seems no deeper than knowing the proper words."

Keven felt the sudden heat rising. "Drop back with Balak and watch the rear!" he snapped.

Bestian tossed him a mock salute. "Ah, yar, sar!" he said, slipping into the local tongue, eyes twinkling. "I be doin' thet, sar! Donna whop me, sar!"

Keven stalked on, burning, while Bestian waited in the road for Balak. In a short while, he could hear them laughing.

I should be on this venture alone, he thought. There's too much discord here. We defeat ourselves.

He gave an internal shrug. But it's too late to call it off now.

Once again he remembered one of Rusker's sayings: "*The best way through a difficulty most often be straight ahead.*"

* * * * *

They camped far enough below the Second Bridge to be away from the rushing rumble of the river. The road curved around an outcrop of large, broken boulders and heavy spruce, forming what seemed like a small natural fortress. There was even a space within the protection of rocks and trees to build a fire that couldn't be seen from the mountain above or from ten paces away.

"Good *lartaget*," Balak grunted as he examined the shelter. "Ver ol'. Warfen." His big axe was in his hand seemingly without reaching, and with a casual, almost leisurely backhand he lopped off a handspan-thick spruce flush with the ground and threw the tree aside with the other hand. "Clear out li'l stuff."

Three more effortless swings took down three more small trees. Keven watched thoughtfully as Balak reduced these to logs and bough beds with a minimum of time and effort; any lingering doubts he may have harbored about the dwarf's ability to handle his weapon vanished.

"Looks good to me," Keven said. "We may not be able to hide our presence, but at least we can select our ground in case of attack."

Balak gave him a frown that seemed to hold a glint of humor.

"He already said it was *lartaget*," Bestian muttered. " 'Defensive place.' And warfen, too. Probably goes back to the Warfen Wars when they fought Bartog."

Keven broke away and prowled their site, examining it for the best defensive positions. Albina insisted on taking post atop the tall rock spire across the river—Watchtower Rock, Eugon called it.

"'Tis nothing for me to be wakeful," she told them. "I must meditate in isolation. I have my own food. I shalt not partake of thy cooked animal flesh."

No one argued with her as she and the eerie dog slipped away.

"I'm not sure I like her being across the river," Keven said, frowning.

Slyt laughed. "You want to try sneaking up on her in the

dark? Hah! I wouldn't try it for a thousand golders! And I'm good at it! I am *very* good at it!"

"It's not dark yet, and she and that dog stand out like two icebergs in a pond."

The others exchanged looks; it was Slyt who asked. "What's an iceberg?"

"It's . . . give it no mind." He lapsed into a frowning silence.

Slyt and Bestian continued talking, joking about the "iceberg" woman and the "iceberg" dog.

"Sounds right," Slyt chuckled. "Even if we don't know what an iceberg is."

Bestian grinned and agreed. "But it makes sense. *Birg* in Warfish is a dark spirit, so it translates, 'Ice-spirit of the Dark Side.' It's perfect!"

Slyt nodded. "Or icy dark spirit."

"That's good, too," Bestian admitted. "How about spirit of the dark ice?"

Slyt pulled a mock frown. "What catches my curiosity is, if there was a hot spirit, would it be a 'fireberg?' "

"That's possible," Bestian said, nodding. "Now take yourself, Slyt. You might be a 'nightberg.' "

"Could be. And you would be a 'gnatberg.' "

Despite their joking and laughter, at his expense and at each other, Keven again noted how these people seemed to be taking the right positions, seemed to be doing the right thing. Slyt and Eugon faded into the rocks and disappeared. Bestian and Balak told him they had made a circuit of the area and found nothing suspicious, and he hadn't even seen them leave or return. That bothered him; he was supposed to notice such things.

He picked his way through the rocks and heavy brush to where he could scowl up at the forbidding mountain, its peak hidden in the dark, lowering clouds. He wished very much to be alone on this venture. There were too many things out of his control here, too many unknown and un-predictable people involved. It wasn't good. He could probably depend on Bestian in a fight . . . and Balak. But the others . . . He shook his head. This wasn't a company. It was a . . . what? There didn't seem to be a word for it. Perhaps he could create a word. . . .

"We're a *blustatterflunt*," he muttered to himself, "a collection of unrelated persons of mostly disagreeable natures thrown together to succeed at a supposed common purpose, but it doesn't seem hellish likely, because someone is going to kill a companion sooner or later!"

It didn't seem to be a word that would catch on soon.

Bestian had produced a cooking pot from his bulky pack and was preparing rabbit stew over a small, smokeless fire. The sun was long fallen behind the high black wall of the mountains, and the deeper halls of the forest around them were darkening into night. The fire was a warm glow within their Grand Hall, as Slyt insisted on calling their hidden room among the rocks. They were discussing one of the sheriff's final speeches.

". . . Acclaim an' Lord Damon be examinin' *all* items other than loose coin," he had told them. "E'erythin'! I don' want nothin' misunderstood 'bout this! E'erythin' that not be a coin'll be produced for examination!"

He had paused to glare home that point, especially dwelling on Slyt, then continued.

"Two reasons! First be tradition. There be a lot o' stolen jewelry an' valuable items that be o' more value to the true owners than to you. If they be among your recovery, you'll be paid fair. Second be danger! There be missin' magic items, so I be told, goin' back a long time. A lot o' this be dangerous. You all heared the stories afore! There be things that can curse you, things that can burn a hand right off, things that can turn your mind aroun' without your e'en knowin' it. Acclaim affirms this, an' he ought to know. An' although I be just a specky bit o' a disbeliever meself—as be a couple o' you, I'm sure—I be not a bedamn fool neither! Only a idiot smiles to mess with somethin' he knows nothin' 'bout. An' I hope there be no bedamn fools in your families either! The true danger o' these things be for the wizard Acclain to determine, not you!

"Now, there be 'nother thing. As always, under King's Rule o' Lawful Recovery, you keep what you gain. 'Tis your reward, to be divided as you see fit. But I warn you, I seen good companies torn to pieces o'er this problem o' fair division. I suggest you get it decided firm afore you e'en get up there. Squabblin' o'er the gain after the fight be no way to discuss fairness. . . ."

"Even shares," Bestian said. He selected some small packets from his array of cooking items with a frown of concentration and added a pinch or two from them to the stew. "It's the only fair way. We all take the same risks."

"Speak for yourself," Slyt said with a grin. "I'm here because of my special talents, which do not include taking any overwhelming risks."

"Ya be at risk e'ery time ya opes ya mout'," Balak grumbled, scowling up from stoning the gleaming edge of his axe. Slyt gazed thoughtfully at the overhanging branches roofing their shelter and whistled a low note.

"I would say, 'It's impossible to discover a sense of humor anywhere in the vicinity of a warf,' " she mused. "But there exists a possibility it may not be a good idea to say that, so I won't."

Balak pulled up his left sleeve, exposing an arm that was as thick, as hairy, and as muscled as a man's leg. He poised the edge of the axe and neatly shaved a wide swath with a single stroke. He cocked an eyebrow at Slyt significantly.

"Yes . . . good edge. Nicely done." Slyt nodded and quickly turned her attention to Eugon.

"And you, our quiet, resident mage, what are your views

on this division of gain?"

"Even shares is the traditional division," Eugon said painstakingly, as if speaking to a child. "The problem lies, obviously, in determining what is even, for many things recovered are of indeterminable and sometimes arbitrary value. We will not know until the wizard Acclain and Lord Damon of Vale have finished their examination and given estimations of value on such objects. It is not such a simple matter as sharing out a few coppers from a purloined purse." He looked significantly at Keven. "Or cheating an old man out of fine turquoise."

"Oh . . ." Slyt nodded. "I see. Thank you. I'll try to remember that." She blinked away. "Why did I ask?"

Keven made a suggestive gesture to Eugon of slapping the base of a fist with the other hand; it had an obscene meaning in the streets of Latonia. Eugon glanced away with a flicker of a frown. Slyt grinned; apparently it had a similar meaning here. Keven glared at them both.

"We can agree on even shares, then," Keven said. "*If* there is anything to share. We may gain nothing. We may not even be striking at their true quarters. They may have their gain cached elsewhere. They may have spent it all. Like the old man says, 'Don't get drunk until the wine arrives.' "

Eugon gave a short, humorless laugh. "Ah, I love those cotter-yard expressions. They are so picturesque."

Bestian echoed the laugh. "You've been so long in clean clothes, Eugon, you've forgotten what you were when you first saw a cobbled street. Talk about a cotter-yard product—you wore sheep shit clear to your knees and thought everybody did."

Eugon's condescending smile became a trifle glazed, and he returned his attention to the large dice he frequently toyed with.

The stew was delicious and disappeared as fast as they could wolf it down.

"How did you do that?" Keven asked, wiping the bottom of his bowl with a piece of dark bread.

Bestian shrugged. "A little of this, a little of that. I didn't think it was all that good. I had some last year's root crop with me, but they get a little limp about now. And a little pickled cabbage. Some seasonings." He shrugged again.

"Good!" Balak unleashed an earthshaking belch and patted his stomach. "Nar 'nough. But'll do." He rose to his feet, axe in hand, and frowned in the direction of the bridge and the dark mountains.

"Go up der." He pointed with the axe. "Watch rud."

"Albina's already watching the upper road from the rock," Keven said.

"Mebbe," he grunted. "Mebbe her fly 'way lak big 'bino bat, too." He strode purposefully from the snug shelter and into the night.

Eugon stared after him. "I cannot understand Acclain's fascination with the warfen," he said. The other three frowned at him.

"What I can't understand," Bestian said evenly, "is your fascination with yourself. There just isn't enough there to be interesting."

"We can get along without cutting at each other all the time," Keven sighed. He reached for his sword scabbard and slung it over his shoulder without rising. "I'm going to take first watch over the road back toward town. It seems the other direction is well covered. I'll be just at the edge of the rocks where that first clump of spruce thickens."

"I'll spell you," Bestian said. "Then Slyt. She operates well at night. Then—" He stopped, staring wide-eyed over Keven's head. Keven instantly rolled to his left, sword rasping from its scabbard, coming to his feet in middle guard.

An elf was standing just inside the ring of light from the low fire. He wore a dusty green tunic with high, soft leather leggings. Over all was a hooded cloak that was difficult to look at directly. It seemed to ripple softly and shift from light to shadow. A quiver of long arrows was slung across his back. A slim sword was sheathed at his waist. He held a longbow behind him in his left hand, while his right hand was extended palm upward.

Keven recognized the salutation from culture classes. Its rough meaning was *I can greet you or I can trick you; it is all the same to me, but it depends entirely on you.*

He switched his sword to his left hand, held it behind him, and opened his right palm in the same gesture.

"May your journey be gentle, interesting, and profitable," he said in Elfish. It was supposed to be a formal greeting, and he hoped he had the pronunciation correct.

The elf nodded slightly with a suggestion of a smile, his large green eyes shining in the light of the fire. He had the full fledged, acute elfen aspect that had only been suggested in Kenth; the sharp features—"like an axe," as someone once said—implied a wily cunning, a quick-witted, almost alien cleverness, as if the face were but a half-human mask to ease the distrust of the world.

"As may yours," he replied in lilting Tradish. "You are Keven of Kingsend." It was a statement.

"I am." Was there *someone* in the Vales who didn't know him?

"You and your company venture upon the mountain to what you call the Waystation to destroy it." Another statement.

"We do." As Balak would say, "Some sicret, this!"

The elf's eyes flickered to the others. "If none bear me ill here, I will join you."

Keven glanced at the other three; they seemed to be frozen in expressions of surprise. Bestian recovered first. He looked at Keven, then indicated the other side of the river with a slight nod of his head and shrugged. Keven nodded.

"We four cannot answer for all," he said. "There are others."

"The two watching in the night will eventually answer for themselves," the elf said with a smile.

Keven sheathed his sword, frowning thoughtfully. "How came you to us?"

The elf glanced at Eugon. "There was a request. I have observed certain things about the mountain and those you seek. I answered the call."

Keven turned to Eugon. The mage smiled and offered a casual shrug.

"I did not know, but I suspected—Acclain."

"I see . . ." Keven scowled at him. "Any other 'suspected' things you've failed to mention?"

Eugon shrugged again in an easy, offhanded manner. It was the smug pose of knowing more, whether he actually knew or not. Keven turned back to the elf.

"I'll not speak for all, but for myself, I say welcome."

What else? he added silently. Another factor run in from outside. Additional help . . . isn't that what Acclain had said? But an *elf?* He remembered an academy joke: "What do you do with an elf?" Answer: "As little as possible!"

The elf introduced himself as Claybrook Leaf. He was as slender and as graceful as a woman, an impression reinforced by a soft, lilting voice. His eyes were seemingly too large, too close together, and of such a dark green as to hardly show a pupil. And the large, pointed ears, Keven noted with interest, could shift forward or flatten independently. As reactive to sound as a cat's ears, he thought, watching him in conversation. The ears flicked one way and another, listening to them as well as to the night around them. He recalled another comment about elves he had once heard. . . .

"Just 'cause they has the ears o' a jackass, don' be makin' the mistake that they be that dull. The ears just be there t' fool you!"

To Keven's surprise, both Bestian and Eugon spoke to the elf in excellent Elfish. Eugon's normal sardonic smile changed to an expression of near respect. Claybrook told them of a hidden trail to the top of the pass.

"It is an ancient elfen path, unknown to others. It will add a small measure of time to the climb compared to using the road, and it will be less tiring but it will not be guarded. We can climb directly to the Waystation without being seen. I recommend we take it, for nothing moves on the road from here without being known to those above."

Keven glanced at the others; Eugon and Bestian gave prompt nods of approval.

"It sounds like a good idea, Claybrook. And now" —he rose to his feet—"I was on my way to stand watch over the road below."

"There is no need to watch," Claybrook said. Like Eugon, he wore a constant suggestion of a smile, but it implied inner secrets rather than patronizing arrogance. "No one approaches from that direction."

Keven considered for a moment. "But from the other way? From the mountain?"

"Perhaps. But not close enough to be a worry. And should they try . . . Well, they won't."

"And how do you know this?"

A broader smile. "It is an elfen thing. You can relax for the night."

"Well," Keven mused, "I still think we should keep a watch, if only here in the shelter. I'll take first."

"Second," Bestian said with a yawn. "Then Slyt."

"You are fast to your feet, Keven of Kingsend." The elf smiled at him. "I have never faced a sword point quite so suddenly."

Keven shrugged. "King's Arms Academy."

"I know."

Keven stared at him. "Then why ask?"

"I did not ask. I was offering you a compliment."

"Oh." Keven poked and frowned at the fire to cover his embarrassment. "Uh . . . thank you."

"One should never thank an elf." Claybrook smiled. "It is an embarrassment."

Bestian glanced at Keven with a meaningful tilt of eyebrow. Keven nodded; it certainly had been an embarrassment so far.

* * * * *

It was in the midnight watch when Albina brought them bolting from robes and blankets.

"A storm breaks in the mountains to the north!" she announced in a voice like a trumpet of doom. "Its fetid evil can be felt even to here! The forces of evil have fallen upon the caravan with foul magic at their command, and our path is clear! Praise Baalab!"

They were instantly wide awake, arms in hand. Albina and the dog seemed to shine like spirits in the soft light of the coals from the fire. Slyt stood crouched on the other side of the fire pit, a slim sword pointed directly at Albina, its tip trembling slightly

"If you *ever* sneak up on me again," she grated, her voice barely under control, "I'll . . . I'll . . . kill your damned dog!" She spun away and slashed off an overhanging branch with a savage arc.

Albina gazed at her, eyes burning. "Thy anger unbecomes thee, Slyt the Cat. Sheath it as well as thy weapon, or face the wrath of Baalab."

Her silver mace swung up. The dog lowered its head and uttered a growl deep in its chest, its cold eyes fixed on Slyt.

Keven shed the rest of his blanket and thrust his sword between them. "Build up the fire, Best," he said. "Slyt, sheath your sword!"

"She scared the gods-bedamned sizzling flux out of me! Sneaking in here like a gods-bedamned ghost and then yelling like a demon!"

"You were probably asleep," Bestian grumbled, feeding twigs to the coals. "Dreaming of some cache of coins in town. Some thief! I thought night was your favorite time."

"Not out here in this gods-forsaken wilderness!" Slyt fumbled with sheathing her sword, still glaring at Albina. "You try that to me in town, woman, and you can look up from street level at your own headless body! Damn dog, too!"

"Thief?" Albina said softly. "Thou art a thief? Such a pursuit is evil in the eyes of—"

"*Enough!*" Keven shouted. "You people can kill each other some other time! Tomorrow evening will be fine with me!"

Enough, echoed the black mountainside.

"Well," Bestian sighed, "if they didn't know of our presence before . . ."

"I am stuffed full with you two!" Keven went on. He stabbed a finger at Albina. "You said you wanted to help! Well, you're not doing it! If you insist on taking everything as an insult, you are no help! And *you*—" He spun to Slyt. "You keep your damned sharp mouth shut! It wouldn't bother me one damned paltry, petty bit to leave you up here on this mountain! Preferably with a broken leg!"

The three of them glared at each other. A short, dark shape swinging a big axe materialized from between two boulders.

"Wut's trouble?"

"Nothing, Balak." Keven scowled at the sword he was still holding and then slid it away. "The little girls were playing."

Balak looked from one to the other and back to Keven.

"An' ya stop dem?" He sounded disappointed.

Keven peered around their shelter. "Where's Claybrook?"

"Bedamned if I know," Slyt growled. "He was right there by that rock when Albina slid in here like a phantasm, and then he vanished. And I wasn't asleep!"

"This lightning you saw," Bestian said to Albina. "It is probably the storm breaking early in the north."

"No." Her voice rang with firm assurance. "Even from here, I can feel its evil source. It reeks of fetid powers!"

"No arguing with fetid powers," Slyt muttered.

Keven threw her a hard glance. "Can we settle down now?" He glared around at the assembly. There were answering mutters.

Albina's voice rose again. "A thief is—"

"Don't!" Keven said. "Just don't!"

They stood staring at each other. Balak's axe swung in small arcs like a pendulum as he regarded the woman. The dog growled. Eugon rubbed one of his dice.

"So be it," Albina said. "I shall defer to thy leadership at this time."

"Thank you!" He felt very sleepy. "Perhaps we can still get some sleep tonight."

Apparently the others agreed. They all resumed their places within the nest of rocks.

* * * * *

Excerpt from *The Various Methods There Be to Harbor and Exercise a Variety of Spells*, a most secret volume of the Brotherhood of Wizards:

"The manner by which spells are retain'd and utiliz'd by the employment of spell dice is far superior to old'r, often more cumbersome methods. Most advantageous of spell dice is that the requir'd energy drain upon the conductor of the spell is much diminish'd, as less concentration is requir'd to call forth the spell.

"Through the use of the spell dice, there is no need to carry about a bulky, awkward, all-too-often obvious spellbook; there is not the irritating problem of searching for a correct page in hasty time of need; there is no problem of what to do with the large spellbook if needs arise in which one must travel in disguise, unbeknownst to others of one's true mage nature. No untoward public suspicions are raised by dice as by the presence of the spellbook.

"Most conveniently, six spells may be kept ready'd in a single die, easily call'd forth by thumbing the proper face and reciting a short, appropriate phrase to release the spell, much as a trigger unleashes a crossbow bolt. If rais'd pips are utiliz'd on the faces of the die, a recommend'd practice, the correct spell can readily be call'd forth in total darkness by touch alone.

"Endowing wands or staffs or other appropriately prepar'd objects with a particular spell is easily accomplish'd from the spell dice, provid'd a spell of transfer has been includ'd. The administrator acts as a conduit through which the spell then passes from die to object.

"Older mages, us'd to more traditional methods, may find the spell dice inappropriate for theirselves. New users of spell dice must become aware that a spell once employ'd must revitalize within the die before becoming again available, a time dependent, of course, upon the power of the spell. Of course, a certain, frequently used spell may be duplicat'd in the dice; however, caution must be employ'd to avoid similar energy augmentation and dissimilar energy resonance. (See Section 28: 'Dangerous Situations Wherein Lie the Possibility of Self-Injury.')"

Chapter Nine

They ate breakfast in full dark—little, savory-spiced sausages baked into small bread rolls, dried fruits, and a rich, tangy tea—again from Bestian's apparently bottomless pack. It seemed as if he had brought enough for everyone, and he certainly enjoyed preparing the meals. Only Claybrook and Albina preferred their own food. The elf had again appeared sometime during the night, now wearing an overtunic of green, leaflike scale armor under his cloak. The pieces were fitted and shaded in such a manner that it seemed the wearer would be able to walk two steps into the shrubbery and completely disappear. Albina barely acknowledged her introduction to Claybrook with a curt nod; Balak and the elf merely considered each other with a sort of wary reserve. Claybrook now came back from the river with a small leather pouch full of water. It was open at the top, with two sewn loops through which he inserted sticks. He carefully placed it close over the glowing coals, the sticks suspending by two stones.

"The leather will burn," Keven pointed out, "and the water will put out the fire."

The elf's large eyes regarded him with a hint of amusement. He then pulled a mock frown. "This is powerful elfen magic." He made a fluid gesture over the bag with one hand. "The bag will not burn."

Balak gave a loud snort. "Powf'l alf'n *kat!*"

Keven was startled; he knew *that* warfen word. It meant "dung." He glanced at Claybrook and the others. Only Bestian showed a reserved reaction; he, too, watched the elf from the corners of his eyes. Claybrook resumed his normal secret smile, with no show of having heard. From his cloak, he removed another pouch and measured out a handful of what appeared to be a dull gold powder. He poured it into the water.

"What's that?" Keven asked uneasily, wondering if magic was being put to work right before his eyes.

"You truly do not know?" The elf seemed to be laughing at him. Keven shook his head.

"Ah, humans . . ." Claybrook shook his head sadly. "They would starve in a garden if it were not for the cultivation and the paths to mark it as such. This is called *tallental* in Elfish, which means 'golden-head.' It has other names in other tongues. You have seen it often." He looked at Keven as if awaiting an answer. "No? I think in your tongue it is known as 'yellow cattail.' "

Keven gave a small reaction of surprise; of course he knew yellow cattail. They sometimes grew with the common cattail in marshes and along the banks of slow streams.

"And did you know that one can eat the cattail plant?"

"Well, of course I knew that!" Keven frowned. "The stems, the roots—it'll fill an empty gut, but it's hardly what I'd call satisfying food."

"True," Claybrook said, nodding. "But that all depends on the preparation. However, you must try the yellow sometime. Take the head just before it blooms and drop the seeds into cold water, then boil. You will be quite surprised. Elfen magic."

"Alf'n *kat!*" Balak grunted again.

"Whatever your pleasure, warf." The elf smiled at Balak, but it was a cold expression. The two stared at each other for a moment.

"So it's just something to eat," Keven said, more to break the tension between the two than anything else.

"You sound disappointed."

"What keeps the pouch from burning through?"

Bestian smiled and answered. "A bag of water over a fire won't burn. Didn't you know that?"

They were all looking at him, four smiles and two stares, and he could feel the embarrassment rising. "Well, I try!" he retorted. "But strain as I may, I just can't seem to know everything as some people do."

So, Rusker, he boiled inside. There was actually something the old flintshard didn't know! Survival in the wilderness indeed! He remembered all that time out there grubbing for raw roots and . . .

He had a brief memory of a companion at the Academy, grunting and snorting through the woods like a hog. When asked what he was doing, he answered, "If I'm going to have to live like a wild boar out here, I might as well sound like one."

* * * * *

Daylight, wan and grim under a murky sky, found them half a league into the forest, Claybrook leading them south on a dim trail directly away from the road.

"Ah, yar," Balak had remarked as they set out into the forest. "Ol' sicret alf'n trail o'er th' mount'n."

Claybrook had glanced at him sharply; Balak winked at Keven.

"Extra great alf'n sicret, dis trail. Narbody know it. B'damn rougher'n ol' warfen road up mount'n. Ya see."

He and the elf traded looks; Balak looked very pleased with himself. After a moment's frowning consideration, Keven suggested to Balak that he cover the rear.

"Yar," he said. "Mebbe alf'n sicrets snick up from back, hah?"

Keven sighed as they continued; another pair to be kept apart. What a wonderful venture, this!

The trail angled closer to the rushing Mad River until they were following close along the bank. It should be called the Raging River here, Keven thought. It crashed along the foot of the steep mountain wall in white-foamed rapids. A cold, clammy, pale gray mist swirled through the trees, thickening as they advanced, and the roar of the river increased until it seemed to fall from the sky. The mist whirled away, and they saw that it actually did fall from the sky.

A seething pool lay at the foot of a long, thundering chain of cataracts careening straight down the mountainside. A surging wind born of the hurtling water lashed shrouds of spray and mist from the long frothing length of the falls.

"The Spirit of the Mountain!" Claybrook shouted in Keven's ear and smiled into the chill, wet wind. Pointing up the left side of the falls, he led the way around the pool. They were soon soaked from the curling mist, except, Keven noticed, Claybrook and Bestian's cloaks didn't seem to get wet.

The steep climb beside the falling river wasn't as treacherous as it first appeared. Although the surrounding rocks were slimy with moss and spray, the trail's steps, carved into the stone, were not slippery. Keven noted how the steps were deeply worn, dished into the solid stone, and he imagined hundreds, perhaps thousands, of years of elfen feet on border patrol. The steps led ever upward through the lashing spray and shout of the cascade.

Smaller streams rushed into the main one from the sides,

each adding its turmoil to the roar below. As they climbed, the crashing river beside them diminished little by little to a more understandable beast, finally to hardly more than a swollen stream leaping down its rocky bed. The main body of thunder lay misted beneath them.

Their strenuous climb broke suddenly onto a broad bench of dark fir trees. Slyt threw herself to the soft forest duff and gasped for breath. Bestian dropped down beside her. "Are you that exhausted?" Bestian asked.

"No . . ." She shook her head, glanced back at the whirling mist of the waterfall, then shuddered. "Just scared witless. I've never had to climb straight up a vertical river before."

They rested in the relative quiet, the cascades but a distant dull rumble over the valley. Partially recessed into the next sheer cliff face, a wide pool lay deep green under the trees, as if it were resting, too, before making that long plunge. The stream fell to the pool like a musical silver curtain from a high ledge. It was a moment of peace after the tumult and the climb.

"This is called 'Dawnspring.' It was once a very special place," Claybrook said, indicating the calm pool. "But in a time of war and vile acts within the mountain, the stream here was so befouled and poisoned that the Mad River gained its name."

Keven noticed that Bestian and Balak gave slight nods. He turned to examine the pool again. "But that was a long time ago, wasn't it? The water is clean now."

"It is and it is not," Claybrook said softly. "Clean to drink and bathe, yes . . . but still, it flows from the mountain."

His eyes rose to the mountain above in an expression Keven couldn't read. "You mentioned last night that you had observed things about the mountain and about the bandits," Keven said. "Are these things we should know about before we attack?"

The elf seemed to be considering his answer carefully. "I can tell you this, Keven of Kingsend. There are many men in this bandit band. There are also creatures."

"How many men, and what kind of creatures?" Keven asked.

Again the elf paused. "I do not know the answers to those questions," he said, and he strolled away.

"Well, all that was certainly of little value," Keven muttered to Bestian.

"You probably didn't ask the right questions," the littler said. "Or perhaps they were not worded correctly."

"And how should they have been worded?"

Bestian shrugged. "I don't know. It's an elfen thing." Keven nodded in a disgusted manner. "I can become very tired of that answer, you know."

* * * * *

Keven was surprised at the rate of their recovery. Considering the climb, it seemed that hardly any time passed before he felt completely rested. Everyone was soon showing signs of impatience. Slyt and Bestian were exploring off to the sides.

"We must cross the stream here at the foot of the pool, where it drops over the edge," Claybrook said. He pointed to a high ledge half surrounding the pool on the far side.

"The water is shallow on the other side, along the face of the cliff. We enter behind the waterfall." He glanced at Balak with his sly smile as if to say, "I wager you didn't know that!" Balak yawned and examined the sky with a bored expression.

Claybrook led the way across the stream, running lightly on the slippery rocks to the other bank. The others followed. Eugon uttered a surprisingly expressive street oath when his foot slipped, his arms wheeled, and he sat down in the stream.

"Don't get carried over the edge, Eugon," Bestian warned. "Bedamned if I'm going after you."

Keven smiled to himself; that abrupt curse had been the first indication that Eugon might have some humanity after all. One by one they followed the elf into the pool next to the sheer ledge. They were concentrating on their footing in the chilling water when Bestian's cry echoed in the rocky amphitheater.

"Holy Yondalla!"

Albina, the big, white dog in her arms, was striding directly across the surface of the pool, leaving spreading ringlets behind her with every step. Balak made several hasty signs in the air and then fumbled for the pouch at his belt. Albina halted at the waterfall, standing calmly on the dark green water, moving backward slightly with the flow of foam and bubbles.

The others continued after a shocked moment, wading cautiously along the vertical rock wall. Keven stood knee-deep in the water, while Balak and Bestian were up to their waists. Albina drifted slowly with the current from the waterfall. She took a step to maintain her position, then another. Her cold eyes seemed challenging as she watched them. As Claybrook came to the waterfall, he gave her a slight, knowing nod.

"Very good, Bishopess," he said. "Is it the boots or one of your rings?"

"Baalab supports those of the true faith." Her voice clamored in the rock confines.

Bestian whispered to Keven, "How does she do that?"

"Don't ask me!" he replied with a frown. "I don't even want to know!"

Eugon's smile seemed a bit tight for his face, and there was a tiny frown etched in his forehead. Casually, still staring at her, he brushed his nose with one finger.

Albina and the dog both sneezed at once. Her strange

gaze bored into each of them in turn. Eugon was carefully examining his footing, probing with his staff. Keven glanced back at Balak. The dwarf was muttering darkly as he returned objects to his pouch. Keven saw an oddly figured iron and silver amulet, garlic, what appeared to be sprigs of some herb, a peculiarly shaped gemstone. Albina fixed her stare on him for a long time, then swung back to Eugon and the elf.

"Baalab is not amused," she said in a steely voice. Eugon ignored the words as he waded forward; his smile seemed to have regained its superior nature. Claybrook merely glanced at her as he led the way through the thin waterfall. Eugon halted, making a mock bow to Albina, ushering her before him. She put the dog down and gave him a blank look before stepping through the waterfall. He and Slyt followed.

"Her *narver* git b'hind me!" Balak snapped.

"You can always watch the rear, then," Keven said, ducking through the veil of water. Bestian flipped up the hood of his cloak and followed quickly. Balak cast a final frown behind him, then followed.

They climbed steep, mossy stairs through a winding, tunnel-like cave, their way lighted by strange lichen that glowed with a dim green luminescence. Water sheened the walls and beaded on the ceiling. After well over a hundred steps, they emerged under a low canopy of thick, tangled spruce. They had to crawl beneath it to get clear. Looking back, the tunnel was invisible. Again no one seemed tired from the arduous climb, and again, Keven noticed, Claybrook and Bestian's cloaks didn't seem to be wet. And something else caught his attention.

"How can you keep your bow strung through all that mist and water?" he asked Claybrook. "Why doesn't the string stretch and slacken?"

The elf gave him that twinkly smile. "Elfen secret," he said. Keven frowned; it wouldn't take very much of that to be entirely too much. Claybrook led on, ever upward.

The trail wound along narrow shelves of high ledges, through more dark tunnels, up worn stairs cut from steep outcrops with stunted treetops far below. Keven noted that handholds and footholds always seemed to fall right where one needed them. Twice they climbed rope ladders swaying from overhangs. There were places where the apparent trail bent around a sharp corner only to end abruptly in a sheer drop and a rush of the wind; the true path branched some paces away into an overgrown, disguised cleft. There were places where the trail seemed to dead-end in blank rock enclosures, yet pressing close to one side or the other revealed a hidden way. Keven couldn't be sure if it was a matter of angle and perspective, a trick of actual illusion, or a bit of illusional elfen magic that hid these spots. He preferred to believe the first, and there wasn't time to study the effect.

Frequently they crawled upward through narrow, twisting passages that caused Keven some concern that he couldn't squeeze through. But squeeze he did, often at the directions of the smiling elf: "Pass your shield and bow through first. . . . Now start with your left arm. . . . Take a step to the left. . . . Now your left leg. . . . Reach a little higher with your right hand . . . farther yet—you will find a grip. . . . Now pull . . . both hands. . . . Twist, and your chest will slide through. . . .

He often wondered how Balak was negotiating these tight passages, but every time he looked back, the stocky dwarf was worming his way close behind like a marmot.

"Nar t' worry 'bout me," he said, glaring at Keven. "Nar be left b'hint on a mount'n by b'damn dog!"

At one of their brief rest stops, Bestian told Balak, "If grunts were progress, you'd be at the top of the mountain by now."

The coughing sounds Balak made sounded suspiciously like a chuckle. "Nar built lak li'ler ferret," he told Bestian.

Struggling upward, sometimes up seemingly sheer reaches of rock, Keven began to suspect that something was wrong—or perhaps something was too right. No one seemed to be tiring as much as reason dictated. Was there some magical assistance at work here? And if so, he wondered about the source. Eugon . . . ?

They rested a short while. Keven considered these all-too-brief rest periods compared to the hard labor of their formidable climb. It was all out of balance; they shouldn't be able to be keeping such a relatively fast pace up this steep mountainside. He turned to Eugon.

"This climb is easier than it seems," he commented.

"Yes," the mage nodded and stared at Keven with a puzzled look, as if to ask, "Is there anything else?"

Keven regarded the assured elf. "No one seems to be tiring," he said. Claybrook also nodded and seemed to be laughing inside. There was little more he could say. They ate. There was little talk. They climbed. Above them, the towering bulk of the mountain loomed into sullen clouds. To the east, the Vales lay colorless under the dull blanket of sky. And they climbed some more.

Although a breeze that could barely be felt on the face often brushed them, there was a distant, deep thrumming of winds high on the shrouded mountain above. The eerie sound of high places, Keven thought. The mountains talk among themselves; or it was indeed the wind prowling across the wide sky, murmuring in a voice too low for human understanding; or it was the hush mumbling of gods seated among the cold stone upper peaks. It was a soul-stirring sound that made a person feel very small on a mountain.

There was no way of accounting for time by the leaden sky—there was no indication of sun—but it felt as if it were well past midday when they were in position to examine the sharp shoulder above them called the East Bastion. It jutted from the bleak ramparts of the mountain like the prow of some enormous stone ship. They had rested but, as before, their recovery was exceptionally fast.

"No one seems as winded or as tired as they should be from that climb," Keven commented again to Claybrook, who made no response beyond his faint smile.

Keven frowned. "Any magic help at work here?"

The elf shrugged. "Possibly."

Keven nodded. "And that's all I'm going to learn about it, right?"

"Possibly."

Keven considered the others; they were studying the rock formation above them, tightening belts, adjusting equipment; they appeared as fresh and as ready as they had at dawn.

"That is the backside of the Waystation," Claybrook said softly, pointing up at the looming cliff face. "But we can still be seen. There are windows cut into the natural clefts all around. You can see some of them."

Keven nodded; the dark slits were there in the crevices if one looked for them. From this angle, the impression of a proud castle bastion topped by a watchtower was strong.

"Can we work around the base of that cliff to gain the road?" Keven asked.

"Yes," Claybrook said. "There is no trail from here, but it is an easy climb to the walls, and with care, we can remain hidden. Once at the walls, we cannot be seen unless someone actually leans forth from an opening above. It is possible that may happen."

"I think we should work our way around to the front and take it by assault," Keven said. "There will surely be someone there."

Claybrook nodded. "It is never left unmanned, true, but I can gain entrance from this side."

"How?" Keven frowned at the sheer face of the cliff.

"It's nearly twenty spans up to those first openings!"

"There is a way." Again there was the sly elfen smile. "I and another of stealth . . . such as that one." He arched an eyebrow at Slyt. "We can gain the interior from this side. It is large and complex in there, but we can lie in wait for your assault from the front and thereby trap them between us."

Keven pursed his lips. "Sounds reasonable. Slyt? Will you go with Claybrook?"

Slyt gave them a thin smile. "What alternatives are there? Do I lie here at my ease, waiting for the summer sun to appear? Do I return to the warm arms of the sheriff? Do I charge with you through the front door, pretending to be some mythic warrior?"

"Nice of you to volunteer," Keven growled. "Let's make our approach."

Claybrook led them through passages among the tumbled rocks, behind upthrust slabs and through one place where they crawled a tortuous channel under huge boulders. At its end, they could lay hands on the towering cold face of the East Bastion.

"There is evil herein!" Albina's voice rang too loud in the silence, echoing back to them from a nearby ridge like a ghostly warning.

"Quiet!" Keven hissed. They all froze in position.

Claybrook was scanning the sheer granite wall above them, one ear cupped forward, the other swiveling to one side. He moved, and almost instantly had an arrow nocked to his bow—a stunning arrow with a maple burl, about the size of a small fist, for a head. He aimed straight up the face of the cliff at one of the dark slits. They pressed in against the wall, watching above. A bucket of slop spewed forth from the opening and sprayed down on them.

"*Kat!*" Balak snorted, also too loud. Claybrook made a curious, sharp whimpering sound, like that of an animal in pain. A man's head appeared from the window slit, frowning down at them. The arrow streaked with hardly a fluff of sound; there was a solid *tunk*, like that of a rock hitting a tree, as the arrow met the forehead. The man's head snapped back, then forward, as he sprawled across the sill, eyes open and glazed. To Keven's ears, it had been a sound assuring, if not death, then severe damage to the brain. The arrow fell back, flipping over in the air; the elf took one step and caught it. He gave Keven a wink.

"We are well into the course of things now," Claybrook said softly. "Pray that fellow was alone and will stay that way for another four hundred breaths of time. Make your stalk around to the road. The most hazardous spot will be when you corner the cliff and see the building. If you keep very low, you will notice that a certain boulder screens you from the one window on that end. A shallow ravine beyond will take you to the front wall of the building. The door is in the other end. Burst in when you are ready. We shall be in position. Good venturing."

"And to you," Keven whispered, nodding. He strung his bow, selected an arrow, and led the way to the right as Slyt and the elf disappeared in the other direction. They crept past the abrupt prow of rock to where a worn channel showed how centuries of rain had carved a drainage from the natural courtyard in front of the Waystation. Sounds of raucous singing, interrupted by raw laughter, drifted to them from the two-story building backed up against the face of the vertical rock. They stacked their packs out of sight. Keven inspected the building, the cliff above it, the courtyard in front. The Waystation lay at the elbow of a switchback curve in the road. There was no one in sight.

"Balak and I first," he said softly. "Then Bestian and Albina. Eugon, where do you need to be to do whatever it is you do?"

Eugon was fondling three differently colored dice in the palm of one hand. He was wearing a faint, unaccustomed frown. "I can execute my talents from anyplace. There is no need to—"

"Are you planning to gamble with these people? What're the dice all about?"

"The dice are . . . never mind. I will accomplish whatever is required of me."

"Fine. Accomplish it from the rear, then. Now, I don't think they'll hear us with all that singing, but be as quiet as possible. Albina, keep your observations about evil to yourself. Will that dog behave?"

She fixed him with those hard, lifeless eyes but kept her trumpet voice low. "He knows. He is bound to Baalab and the defeat of evil, as am I."

"I should have known," he said, but immediately regretted the tone; he was beginning to sound like Slyt. "Balak?"

The dwarf nodded, his axe at ready and shield in place, his powerful crossbow slung across his back. Bestian quietly levered his smaller crossbow, selected a bolt, and loosened his shortsword in its scabbard. Albina shifted her shining mace to her shield hand and readied a sling. The dog crouched beside her, eyes as cold as ice. Keven tightened the elbow strap of his shield and loosened his sword over his shoulder. He held his bow at ready in his shield hand. The singing from inside continued its merry measure.

The shallow gully followed close along the front of the half-timbered wall to the far corner of the building. Keven moved slowly in a low crouch, his shield to the building, arrow aimed at the overlooking windows. They slipped along below the level of the windows, exposed to anyone outside. Keven scanned the mountainside around them and the roads up and down as far as he could see. He noticed that Bestian and Balak were doing the same; they both shook their heads at him. He reached the corner of the building and peered around it. The large, double doors were closed. There were no windows at this end of the structure, but two large, dark, square openings yawned in the high rock face beyond.

"Nothing to do but to do it," he breathed, stepping around the corner in full view of the windows carved in the rock. He centered his bow between them, waiting for any indication of motion in the dark interior of the cliff. Balak followed him around the corner, then Bestian, who immediately leveled his crossbow at the two openings. The others followed. Keven relaxed his bow and leaned it beside the doors. He unslung his quiver and lowered it to the ground, then drew his sword. Balak hefted his axe. Albina, with her ready sling, and Bestian, with his crossbow, never took their eyes or aim from the two openings in the rock. Eugon had a red die clamped between thumb and forefinger in his left hand; in the right hand, he held three darts in such a manner that they could all be thrown at once or one at a time. He wasn't smiling.

As before, Keven was again struck by the thought that the others were taking proper actions without direction; perhaps these people were not as diverse as he first thought.

He and Balak nodded to each other. Albina started her sling in slow circles around her head, the fingertips of her other hand just touching the dog's neck. The dog stood crouched like a white statue, watching the doors. Keven reached for the latch. It was free, and the door opened smoothly. He eased it back and entered, stepping quickly to the right; Balak slipped in immediately and moved to the other side.

It was one long room, low-beamed, with a wall of stone on their right where the building backed against the cliff. A wide, dark archway was cut in that rock wall next to a fireplace. The room was cluttered with a disorderly array of tables, chairs, and benches—apparently it had been a commonroom at one time. Kegs lined a heavy bench along the rock wall. At the far end of the room, six grinning men were lounged in a wide circle around a large table on which two naked women laughed, danced, and postured to a bawdy song. Two men on the far side of the circle saw them. One gaped foolishly; the other, propped teetering on the rear legs of his chair, cried, "*Whut*—" and crashed over backward in a windmill of arms. The others laughed. One applauded. The gaping one raised a hand and pointed. One of the women screamed. They all turned.

"*E-vil!*" Albina's cry rang out like a trumpet. "*Whores of sin!*"

Her sling hummed, and a stone dropped one of the women with a sickening crack to the head. The men leaped away from the table, scrambling for weapons. A huge man on the right lunged to his feet, grasping a great sheathed sword by its hilt. With a wide backswing, he flung the scabbard clear of the blade and lurched forward. His left leg was lame. His eyes were fixed on Keven with a mad glint.

"That one's mine!" Keven shouted, pointing with his sword. "The one whose mother ran with street dogs!"

He was aware of Balak and Albina charging through tables and chairs toward the others. The *tung* of a crossbow sounded behind him, and one of the men buckled with a choked cry, a bolt fixed in his breastbone.

"Come on, cripple!" Keven called to the big man. "You still have one good leg to hop on!"

The hulking man's face, now that he saw it unhelmed, looked like an oversized visage roughed from stone by an unskilled apprentice. The eyes were narrowed to slits, the heavy lips peeled back from yellow teeth. He snatched a shield from the floor and swung it in an easy motion.

"How's your arse work with another crack in it?" Keven taunted. "And how's your jaw? Met any rock-throwing dwarfs lately?"

The big man surged forward, crashing through the impediments of furniture with guttural grunts of rage.

"I changed my mind," Keven said with a smile. "By those sounds, I judge your mother lay with a pig."

An arrow streaked between them from the dark archway, and he glimpsed another man falling.

"Stand clear of the archway!" Claybrook called from the rock interior. "We're here."

Keven caught glances of Balak calmly slashing an armed man nearly in two, Albina hammering another into a wall with her silver mace, and a flash of white as the dog leapt at another.

The charging man hurled tables and chairs aside and came on with the same brutal attack as previously on the road, but he swung wide because of the low ceiling. Keven leaned into the assault, and his shield was driven back against him from the savage force. He thrust high at the face to raise the other's shield, then aimed a slice at that same left knee, but the arc of the blow was diverted by an intervening table and only nicked his thigh. With harsh grunts of effort on every swing, the big man drove against him. Steel clashed and rang. The vicious blows slammed against Keven's shield as if the man were chopping at a steel tree.

Keven dodged left, his sword low, leaving his right side open to tempt the other into making a backswing. It worked—but before the blow could fall, Keven lunged and gashed the low shoulder muscles at the armpit. The big sword chopped a piece from the floor as it whipped down. With a bellow of rage, the man struck with his shield. Driven backward, Keven tripped over a bench and went down. Sword in both hands, the enraged man braced for an overhand blow intended to cleave Keven from end to end, but in his fury, he forgot the low ceiling. His sword chunked into a beam. Keven tried to roll into the clear, but there was too much clutter of furniture. He stabbed a weak thrust at the man's feet to keep him off balance. As the big man wrenched his sword free, there was a small blur behind him. Bestian raced out from under a table and neatly backhanded a slice to the back of his right knee. The man squealed and slashed out behind him, but the littler was nowhere close. Keven scrambled to his feet in the moment's respite. With a banshee howl, the man threw himself at Keven, sword thrusting. Keven easily flicked it aside as the man twisted in a fall, his wounded right leg buckling under him. He crashed to the floor like a fallen tree and rolled onto his back. Keven put the point of his sword to his throat.

"Hold!"

But the lips were still peeled back in a snarl, and the eyes were wild. There was a guttural growl, and the big sword lashed at Keven's legs. Instantly he dropped his shield in its way and lunged. Twice. But the snarl stayed, even as the mad eyes glazed.

Keven spun to get his back to a wall, but there was an uncanny silence in the room. They were all watching him. This little skirmish was over.

"Well, *that* was easy," Bestian said, frowning as he scanned the room. "I don't like it."

Chapter Ten

The room was a rubble of overturned and smashed furniture, and the only figures standing were those who had entered. Balak was humming to himself, calmly cleaning his axe with piece of bloody shirt torn from one of his victims. Albina had her mad, unfocused eyes raised to the ceiling, muttering a monotonous chant in a strange language; the dog was poised beside her, licking blood from its muzzle. Bestian was recovering crossbow bolts, casually wiping them clean on the tunics of their targets. Eugon was motionless, staring thoughtfully at the body of one of the fallen. Claybrook and Slyt were standing in the large archway cut through the rock wall. The elf was relaxing his bow; Slyt was idly swinging a sling in her right hand.

"You people truly leave a mess behind you." The thief regarded the room with a crooked grin. "Do we find the gain now?"

Keven regained his breath and tried to govern his pounding blood. He was irritated at himself again for what he thought was a poor showing. "If there is any gain," he said.

"What a gloomsayer," Slyt laughed.

"Was it necessary to kill the women?" Eugon's voice was

devoid of its usual overbearing tone, and his face was empty of its smile.

"The eyes of Baalab espy evil wherever evil lies!" Albina declared. "His mighty wrath condemns not only the sin but the sinner as well, for all living things are both blessed and burdened with choice. The forward path is one of branch after branch, and all must decide which way to travel. 'Tis so written in the Book of Wrath, and so shalt it be through me, His faithful handmaiden!"

Slyt was staring at the cleric with widening eyes. She turned to face Keven with a slight shudder, and again crossed her eyes and stuck her tongue out the corner of her mouth. Keven frowned—but he had to agree.

There were injuries to attend. Blood was beginning to drip from Balak's left fingertips. He peeled back the sleeve of his leather jerkin to where it was sliced just below the coverage of his mail armor. He frowned curiously at the slash across his upper arm, as if it were some peculiar pathside flower he had never seen before.

"Huh!" he grunted. "Foxy barst'd gots in jist o'er me shiel'. B'damn." He grunted again at the mystery of it.

Keven pulled a handful of dried leaves from a small belt pouch. "Here. Woundwort."

"Nar!" Balak shook his shaggy head. "Woun'wort nar good! Got m' own." He pawed in a belt pouch, bringing out a dark, spongy mass. "Healmoss. Warfen. B'damn gooder'n woun'wort."

"Do it your own way!" Keven jammed the woundwort back into his pouch.

"B'damn true," Balak grunted.

Albina's tunic was showing blood, startlingly bright against the white. She tended herself with a salve while murmuring what sounded like a complex spell.

Eugon produced a small jar from his cloak and offered it to Balak. "This will promote healing."

Balak glared at it suspiciously. "Magic?"

Eugon hesitated only slightly before the smile curled his mouth again. "Healing herbs in a gentle oil, with but the merest touch of magic, my good warf. It would certainly do you no harm."

Balak packed his wound with his moss, refusing to look at Eugon or the jar. "Got m' own!"

Keven's left arm ached bone deep from the violent blows he had shielded, and he tenderly fingered some painful ribs where his shield had been slammed into him.

"Drink this." Eugon held out a small vial. Keven took it, realizing he was frowning at it much as Balak had reacted to the jar.

"Trust me," Eugon said, smiling. "One swallow will suffice."

Keven took the vial and swallowed, grimacing as an involuntary shudder followed the dose down. "Gods alive!" he rasped, handing it back. "That would gag a maggot, Eugon! I'd rather hurt than pitch my vittles all over the place!"

But the effect was instant and astonishing. A hot glow flared from his stomach outward. It flooded throughout his body, pushing pain before it and leaving a warm well-being behind. It washed the length of his arm and left it strong and limber. He touched his ribs and found no lancing pain. He probed deeper—there wasn't even soreness. He blinked at Eugon.

"It is indeed magic, isn't it?"

"It focuses your inner strengths and natural healing abilities," Eugon said, returning to his condescending manner. "In a magical way, of course. You actually healed yourself. You will feel somewhat tired until rest restores the spent strength."

Keven moved to where Balak was swinging his arm as if testing its action. "Are you all right?"

"Good. Take more than li'l bitch-son t' hurt warf." He picked up his axe and examined its edge. "A true dif'r'nt battle cry ya got, fighter. Wut it mean ya say, 'Hah! Hah!' like that?"

Keven busied himself with cleaning his sword. "Well . . . it's not exactly a battle cry. It's—" he shrugged—"just a sound."

"Ah, yar . . ." The warf considered him strangely from the corners of his eyes. "So 'tis jist a noise ya makes. Ya swings ya sard an' ya says, 'Hah!' "

Keven nodded. Balak raised a bushy eyebrow, the blue eyes twinkling. Keven wheeled away. Damn know-it-all dwarf! There was that surge of anger again, seemingly poised to leap, searching for a target. He nearly bumped into Slyt.

"Tell me something, Keven." The sly smile twinkled at him. "I heard you went to King's Arms."

Keven considered the statement for a moment; it seemed innocent. "That's right."

"M-m . . ." The laughing eyes glanced away, then returned with a slightly puzzled look. "What did you do there—deliver cabbages or something? That demonstration of swordplay a moment ago wasn't exactly the most dazzling thing I've ever seen. Do you finish all your fights on your backside?" The heat inside Keven flashed into fire.

"You want another demonstration right now?" His sword was still in his hand, and it started up. Slyt backed off, her hands raised as if to rub it all away.

"My apologies. I didn't know you were suffering some inner wound."

"Meaning what?"

"Nothing, for Seelas's sake! Nothing! Calm yourself. Gods!" She spun away, frowning. "It was a joke. Just a something to slacken the tension in this mayhem."

"And I supposed you'd piss in a fountain to help thaw the ice," Bestian said, frowning. "There are times, Slyt, when you need your mouth nailed shut. It flaps like a loose shutter in a high wind."

Keven stood for a moment, staring at Slyt but not really seeing her, pondering instead the sudden red rage that surged through him and wondering if that quiet voice he heard with it was correct.

The academy. Santon:

"*If one is to have control over one's life, Keven, it is a matter of gaining control over oneself. While I realize that is something simply said, it is nonetheless true. The mind is an unruly, half-hidden beast, and not easily tamed. The most devastating enemy you will ever face will come from within yourself—and you may not even recognize him when he appears. One must defeat his own demons before successfully facing others.*"

The thought occured to him that one of his demons was that he couldn't endure people laughing at him. He saw ridicule as a weapon and those who used it as aggressors.

"*You are much too serious,*" Santon had once told him. "*You must learn to laugh at yourself, Keven.*"

He became aware of everyone staring at him. He took a deep breath, then another, and the fires cooled, the tension shuddered away. He lowered his sword. His voice sounded to him as if some stranger was using it.

"There may be more of these so-called bandits around here!"

"There's a couple back there in the rock." Slyt said quietly, indicating the stone archway with a hook of her thumb. "But they're peaceful. And they'll stay that way for a long time, too."

"There may be some in hiding," Keven said. "Be wary."

He indicated a worn stairway beside the front door leading to the second floor. Weapons in hand, he and Balak climbed them and then stalked the length of the creaking hallway, searching each room. These had once been fine lodgings with true beds and nicely carved furniture, but the current tenants had cared little for that; the rooms were now more like the lairs of wild animals. Balak snorted with disgust. They found nothing lurking nor anything of value.

"Nothing worth a copper here," Slyt told them as they returned to the commonroom. She cast aside a tin mug. "Even the wine is swill!" She knelt to search one of the bodies.

"Later," Keven said. He pointed to the dark archway leading into the interior of the mountain spur. "What's back there?"

"A warren of rooms and corridors," Claybrook said. "They extend throughout this East Bastion rock."

"We should explore it all. Who wishes to stand guard out here?"

"Guard against what?" Eugon asked, surveying the room with an exaggerated expression of surprise. "I honestly do not think these corpses are going to rise and attack from the rear. You seem alert to challenge shadows, ranger."

Keven wasn't sure whether there was a sarcastic twist on that last word or not, but he felt the familiar heat flushing up his neck.

"I can tell you one thing, 'Apprentice'!" That word wiped Eugon's smile away. "When in any place with the potential of danger, it is best to expect it! There are a lot of dead fools who chose to laugh at someone rather than look over their shoulder!"

They glared at each other.

"We seem to have eliminated the threat," Eugon said, hands in a wide gesture. "So what is the—"

"We!" Slyt exclaimed. "What did you do? Hit someone with your dice?"

"I cast my darts." He drew himself to his full height.

"And they're stuck in the end wall there, if you want them," Bestian said, motioning. He picked up his crossbow and cocked it. "I'll stand watch."

Keven nodded. "There's a good spot at the head of those stairs—windows covering the courtyard and the roads both up and down. Claybrook, do you know the interior of this rock?"

"Most of it," the elf said with a smile.

"Then let's go."

The stone archway led directly into a huge hall, its high ceiling lost in the gloom. It was dimly lighted by two large openings onto the courtyard. In some distant time, it may have been a large cave, but now was a masterful hall of dressed stone. Timber structures had been erected around three walls, making semicircular second-and third-story balconies. The rear wall, rising sheer to the dark, vaulted ceiling, had a huge, centered fireplace inset within a tall, pointed arch, all carved in the stone; five men could have stood comfortably within the vault of that fireplace. Two wide, timber stairways flanked the fireplace, curving up to the balconies above. The stone floor was smooth and level. Though it was dirty now and cluttered with trash, one could see traces of its once high polish. The rock walls were carved into the appearance of decorated bas-relief columns. Old tapestries hung between them, so dusty as to seem almost part of the wall itself. Dark openings of corridors marked the walls.

"Those corridors, all interconnected, lead off to rooms carved in the rock," Claybrook explained. "Up there"—he motioned aloft—"there are rooms all around the balconies, corridors back into the rock leading to more rooms. Although I have never explored it, it is said the rock spire atop this spur contains a stairway to a watch station."

"We need some light to explore this place," Keven said. "Torches. I saw some lamps and lanterns in the other room, too. One person stay on watch here in the hall; the rest spread out into these lower corridors and rooms. Be wary.

I'd like to get some idea of how many people have been staying here."

They found nothing but dust and silence, trash and old rooms tunneled throughout the cold stone. Prowling the dingy, somber corridors, Slyt once dodged and hurled a slingstone at what proved to be Eugon's wavering shadow. Eugon, startled by the too-close, sharp crash of stone on stone, unleashed a choking spell in reaction. Neither of them were amused.

"Well, it *looked* sinister!" Slyt gasped, recovering with Eugon's aid. "I can't help it if you've got a weird shadow!"

"It's because of the light, you witless dullard!" Eugon shook his staff, the tip of which he had endowed with a ghostly glow.

"How am I supposed to know, if you go sneaking about with some supernatural, eerie light? If you look like a monstrosity, expect attack!"

"*Sneaking!*" Eugon's voice rose well out of its normal patronizing range. "*Monstrosity!*"

"Quiet!" Keven called, coming upon them with sword drawn. "You two could awaken dead spirits in the next kingdom!"

"He—" Slyt began.

"She—" Eugon started.

"Put it aside!" Keven shouted. "Now!"

They glared at each other and then muttered off in opposite directions.

Keven considered the ceiling and shook his head.

They compared explorations later in the dusky hall.

"A waystation?" Keven said incredulously. "This place is large enough to house hundreds!"

"It's thought to have been a garrison in an ancient time," Eugon noted. "There are large kitchen and storage facilities off that end corridor there, by the fireplace wall. Water still flows to the old cistern."

"And how many current residents would you say are here?"

Slyt shrugged. "Eighty. Mayhaps a hundred. Hard to tell. They live in nests like rats. And no sign of gain! It has to be hidden somewhere!"

"Then we search. You and Claybrook—"

At that moment, Bestian burst through the archway from the commonroom. "Men coming down the upper road!"

* * * * *

They watched from the two large windows in the rock wall that overlooked the courtyard, standing well back in the dim interior of the huge hall. Twenty or so armed men had come into view where the road curved around a sharp ledge. Two were limping badly, three wore bloody, filthy bandages—and in their midst shambled a massive, hulking, hairy, dark-skinned creature clothed in a short tunic of hides. It was fully half again the size of a man. A great, knotted club swung loosely in one huge hand.

"Merciful gods of my fathers!" breathed Slyt, easing farther back into the darkness of the hall. "It's an ogre!"

Keven frowned at the enormous figure. "How do you know it's an ogre?"

"Ogre! Troll! Goblin! Bogar! Bedamned altogether to all hells if I care! If *anything* is an ogre, it's *that!*"

Keven scowled thoughtfully and swung his sword in short arcs beside his leg, as if hefting its weight. He couldn't remember the identification of that particular creature from the drawings in the *Bestiary* at the academy. It seemed familiar, but he couldn't place it.

"Balak?" he asked.

"Uh," came the guttural reply, and there was the sound of the heavy crossbow being cocked. "Be a big'un."

"What is it?"

A shrug of the square shoulders. "Og'r mebbe. Somedin' lak og'r." He shrugged again. "Nar make a dif'r'nt. Be a big'un."

"There's enough wood in that club to keep a family of four warm all winter," Bestian mused.

Keven motioned toward the commonroom. "We need cover from that second story!"

But the stocky warf was already running through the archway to the commonroom, Bestian right behind him. Keven could hear the two of them mounting the stairs. He turned to where Eugon was standing back in the dim interior.

"You have anything you can use against that—that thing out there?"

The mage was rolling his dice in his hand, frowning. "I can try, but don't expect a marvel."

"Well, try to make it something better than a rain of toads! And don't bother with your damned darts this time. You might hit one of us!"

He swung back. Magicians! It seemed they were about as helpful as a pebble in a boot.

Claybrook stood well back from the farther window, his longbow drawn to the arrowhead; the arrow was stone steady. His voice was soft and calm. "If it were closer and not yet enraged, I could speak to it," he said. "It would probably obey me."

Keven sheathed his sword and unslung his bow. "We can wish for the best way, but let's prepare for the worst. All bow weapons at once at that . . . whatever it is," he said.

Claybrook nodded. "On your signal, then, if we must shoot."

"They've certainly been in a fight," Slyt said. "Look at the bandages. If they're the survivors of the fight on North Pass, it looks like they got their arses thrashed. But how did they get back here so fast?"

"Makes no difference how they did it. They're here," Keven grunted, nudging his quiver into position for an easy reach. "And they're the ones we want. I know the tall one. That's Sander, the leader. Go up and tell Balak and Best to wait for my shot, and then everyone target that . . . ogre, or whatever from the hells it is."

Slyt slipped away like a shadow. Albina stood behind Keven, murmuring something in a dull monotone. The dog growled softly, rumbling deep in its chest.

"Can you keep him quiet until we get a good range?"

"He knows evil when—"

"Fine! I'm glad he knows evil! Good dog! Just keep him quiet until we strike that thing down." He selected an arrow and drew aim at the V of the throat high on the creature's chest. About fifty paces away, the tall man in leathers called out, "Ho, the watch!"

As the echoes bounced away without reply, he slowed, then stopped. The others stopped, too, staring at the Waystation. The creature lurched onward another two or three steps before coming to a halt. It swung partially to face the men, head tilted in confusion. The leader frowned and turned to speak to the others. As the brute raised an arm to scratch its head, Keven released. Claybrook's arrow was in flight instantly, followed by two bolts from the second story. They all hit within two handspans, high in the rib cage on the left side.

The creature screamed, twisting to claw at the arrows. The men broke for cover in the rocks beside the road, the leader pausing to shout and point toward the Waystation. He dove for shelter just as another of Claybrook's arrows sliced the air behind him. Still roaring, the enormous thing focused on the Waystation, then broke into a lurching run toward the building. Keven released another arrow and hit it again, high in the chest. He heard Bestian's crossbow make its peculiar *tung* and saw another bolt strike home.

"Keep those other men away!" he said. He dropped his bow, shrugged off the quiver, drew his sword, and sprinted for the commonroom, nearly overrunning Slyt in the stone archway.

"Ah, gods an' demons!" she breathed. "It's coming!"

"Slyt! Take my bow! Help keep those others away! Balak!"

But the warf was already pounding down the stairs, his war axe in both hands. They nodded to each other and took positions on each side of the closed double doors. They heard the thundering approach but were unprepared for the entry; the creature never even paused as it crashed into the room, club swinging wildly. The doors smashed back as it charged through in a low crouch. Balak disappeared with a loud thump behind his door as it slammed back against him; Keven was flung into the wall by door and club. Off balance, he narrowly ducked under another powerful backhand swing from that massive club, then struck out with a weak thrust to the creature's ribs that barely touched. As he braced to counter the next attack, he saw Balak dart into the open, face twisted with rage. The creature was bent almost double under the low ceiling, facing Keven. Balak dashed behind it and axed the most available target, the bare buttocks.

The creature howled and spun surprisingly fast, aiming a terrible blow at the warf, but it slammed the beamed ceiling instead. Dust fell like a lowering fog. Balak scampered out of reach of the clawed hand that snatched at him.

"Keep him between us!" Keven yelled. He sidestepped and swung at a brawny shoulder, but the club arced around, blocked the blow, and nearly tore the sword from his hand. Balak dashed in again, watchful and poised. Again the hand reached for him, and he met it this time with his blade. The beast howled. In that instant, Keven was able to get in a savage slash across the massive upper muscles of its club arm. The creature scuttled away from them, farther into the room,

crashing through tables and chairs as if they were underbrush. It turned in a snarling crouch and watched them warily from tiny, glittering eyes. It licked the wound on its left
hand from Balak's axe, panting with great rumbling breaths.
Blood trickled from broken arrow shafts and flowed from the
open gash in its right arm.

Keven was aware of shouts from outside and the sounds
of longbows and Bestian's crossbow. Eugon was standing in
the stone archway, a hand upraised, chanting. The creature
shook its head and seemed to stagger but was instantly alert
again. It turned to scowl at Eugon with a savage glint in its
eyes. Keven and Balak approached from opposite sides. It
shifted its attention back to them, from one to the other,
heavy lips curling back from yellow fangs in a vicious snarl.
The deadly club swung in wide arcs. They made careful attacks to distract it from each other. Once it rushed suddenly
at Balak, roaring and battering with club and fist, and
Keven was certain the warf was down, but he emerged from
the wreckage behind the beast while it hammered furniture
into pieces, and slashed it again in the rear. Then he
dodged away, muttering.

"Miss backbone! B'damnt!"

They circled, wary of the range of the club and the force
of its blow; what could smash a heavy oak table to splinters
would leave a person little more than pulp.

Keven studied the beast. It had taken six arrows, deep
and well struck, and it still seemed as deadly as when they
first saw it. The only apparent effect of its injuries was that
it held its left limb clamped against its side.

He and Balak exchanged glances, nodded. Balak
shouted and hurled a chair at its head. Keven leaped,
swinging hard at a bent knee, connecting with a solid *chuck*
and rolling sideways to get clear. As the beast wheeled to
follow him, Balak aimed a mighty double-handed swing
that only nicked its rib cage. The momentum turned the

warf half about, and he stumbled over a broken table, but the stumble saved his head from being crushed. A backhand from the knotted club missed him by a finger and destroyed another table. The crippled leg gave way then and the creature went to one knee. As it turned to glance at Keven, Balak raised his axe over his head in both hands and threw it. It flipped once and lodged deep in midchest. The creature looked down at it with a puzzled expression as if wondering how it got there. Keven chopped a double-handed blow to the back of its neck. The head did not come off. Instead, it bent over, as if to kiss the axe head, and the huge body slowly toppled forward to the floor.

It seemed too quiet as they turned away.

There was a man sprawled facedown in the courtyard just outside the wrecked doors. Eugon was still standing in the archway, frowning at his dice. Keven tried to still his heavy breathing and listen. All he heard was Balak grunting.

"Stink'n' b'damn bist!" He was trying to roll the lifeless hulk off his axe. Keven helped him. Balak spat.

"Dark bist! Barst'd t'ing!" He yanked the gory axe free and regarded it with disgust. A sharp whistle echoed from the rock hall. Keven turned to see a flash of white dash past the doors and leap into the hall through one of the openings in the cliff. Slyt's voice sounded joyfully.

"Ho-o! Damn good dog!"

She came through the archway grinning, Keven's bow in hand. "Indeed the b'damnedest funny you ever saw! They wormed up closer while you two were sporting with that thing, and then they made a rush. We dropped three of them—no, four—Albina got that one by the door with a slingstone, and it looked like they'd have made it in when she set the dog on them. You never saw such a dance in your life! All those grown men trying to get away from one dog! And I'll tell you, it can't be done! Not that dog! Did you ever see a man jump a full half-span into the air and try to keep from coming down? They're out there in the rocks across the road now, bleeding in a lot of new places and probably wondering what it was from hell that hit them." She indicated the fallen ogre. "Is that thing dead?"

Keven nodded.

"You want to give it a couple of good, deep stabs just to make sure?" she asked, frowning.

"I'm not going next to the damned thing anymore," Keven muttered. "It stinks like a—"

"Like an ogre." She nodded. "I can smell it from here." Keven cleaned off his sword and caught his breath. He was a little more pleased with himself in this fight; he had certainly never faced such a thing, and he couldn't think of a tale wherein anyone had. It made him feel even better when Balak turned from washing his axe at one of the ale kegs and said, "Gud fight, Kiven. Nar many men do dat."

Claybrook was regarding the wreckage of the room from the stone archway.

"From what hell is this beast?" Keven demanded. "And what do you know about it?"

"It is a so-called dark-side beast," the elf said, "a poor, simple-minded thing. They are easily led into evil ways."

"And what is it doing here?"

"It was being used as an attacking weapon—also to gather food from the valley."

Keven frowned at the body of the creature. "And are there—"

At that moment, a voice called from across the road. "Halloo inside! Who from the hells are you?"

"Don't answer," Keven said. "Let them wonder. A mystery is as good as a threat any time."

"What is it you seek?" the voice called again. "You have raided our quarters and attacked us."

"You should know all about that sort of thing, you bandit barstid!" Slyt shouted cheerfully, then shrugged at

Keven's frown. "Sorry. I couldn't help that. It was too much of a temptation."

After a moment, the call came again. "Then I warrant you'll be paid for your effort in the same coin, one you'll dread t' see spent!"

"Threaten not with evil, thou putrid beast whose mother wallowed in the filth of the sty!" Albina's clarion voice echoed from rock to rock. "Thine evil most foul shalt be thy perishment, and Baalab shalt feast upon thy souls!"

Slyt peered from one of the front windows. "Well, that will probably cast a shadow on further discussions."

"Ranger!" It was Bestian, at the head of the stairs. "One of them took off down the road like a rabbit, but it didn't look like he was running scared."

"There's probably a watch force somewhere down below on the road," Keven said.

"There was," Claybrook agreed.

Keven scowled out at the darkening courtyard for a moment. "We can wait for their reinforcements to come up, or we can go out after them in the rocks and hope to ambush the others when they arrive."

"Charging armed men in hiding isn't my idea of an evening's pleasantry," Slyt said, frowning.

"Wait," Balak grunted. "Night come soon. Warfen good at dark."

Claybrook agreed. "There will be a certain advantage in waiting for dark," he said, smiling softly.

They waited. It began to rain a cold, drizzling, gray rain.

* * * * *

Balak, Bestian, and Claybrook were at the second-story windows overlooking the courtyard and the road. A group of perhaps fifteen or more men—it was difficult to tell in the rainy twilight—had trooped up the road and dispersed into the tumble of mountainside boulders across the wide courtyard. The sounds of bow and crossbows from the second floor had marked four who would be of no further bother—they had peered too eagerly from behind their cover. Keven wondered again how Claybrook's bowstring, and now Bestian's and Balak's, too, could hold tension in this dampness. His own bow, an arrow nocked and ready, was beginning to lose force as the bowstring stretched. Those outside in the gathering night and the rain would be nearly useless by now. A few arrows had arced into the room earlier. They carried little power but could still injure. He stood back from the broken doors, where he could watch a large part of the courtyard and the upper road. Slyt and Albina crouched at the front windows of the commonroom; Eugon sat at one of the few remaining tables studying his dice with a remote gaze.

"Anything you can do about this situation?" Keven asked Eugon. "There's well over thirty-some men out there."

"I threw a spell on that beast. It didn't work." He sounded peevish.

"Mayhaps you didn't throw it hard enough." Keven frowned at himself; he didn't have to say that. Sarcasm wasn't going to aid matters here.

"Magic isn't infallible, you know," Eugon replied. "Like an arrow, it sometimes misses."

There was the heavy *tump* of Balak's crossbow and a sharp cry in the rainy dark.

"Nodder dod," came Balak's cheerful rumble.

Slyt turned from her window. "Nodder-dod?"

"I think it's 'another dead,' " Keven said. Bestian's shout and the sound of his crossbow brought them fully alert.

"They come!" Albina cried and whirled her sling. The dog snarled at the window and braced itself. Keven saw dark figures dash across the courtyard. He tracked and shot.

His arrow had little force, but one man stumbled, turned, and lurched back to the cover of the rocks. Keven stepped back to better cover the doors, but no one appeared there. And it was suddenly quiet again. Claybrook slipped down the stairs, as silent as a shadow.

"They are close at the front wall," he said softly. "Perhaps four."

"Two made it to that large opening over there in the rock." Keven pointed along the face of the cliff to where it angled to follow the road up the pass. There was a black square there about forty paces away. "What is it—a cave?"

"Old stables," Claybrook answered. "There is no connection to the interior I know of, but from there they can shoot directly into here if they have dry bowstrings with them." He reached inside his cloak and handed Keven a coiled bowstring. "Here. Elfen. It will not stretch. You may need it."

Claybrook stared into the night, green eyes almost gleaming, it seemed. "There is something wrong in the night that I cannot perceive, but I shall take care of those two over there in the stables."

The elf drew his cloak about him and ran through the stone archway to the interior of the rock. A moment later, Keven thought he saw a flicker of movement at one of the stone openings to the courtyard, but he couldn't be certain. He slipped the string Claybrook had given him onto his bow, adjusted it, and tested the pull of the bow. He smiled to himself. He may not have an elfen bow, but he had the string; this venture was already one to be well remembered. All he had to do was survive. And if not? . . .

In an instant, he recalled an academy student ritual. It wasn't a rite endorsed by the academy.

On some midnight, in the dark of the moon of their final year, the graduating students would slip into the main courtyard, nick the base of their left thumb with a knife, and, while a few drops of blood fell to the flagstones, they would whisper, "While my blood will no doubt spill in some far place, a part of me will forever be in this place near to me."

He rubbed the small scar at the base of his left thumb and smiled.

The hum of Albina's sling brought him back. He turned to where she was poised beside a front window. She was spinning the sling vertically, and she slammed her hand down through the window opening. A solid *tunk* sounded instantly from close outside, and there was a choked grunt. Balak's crossbow released from the second story.

"Nodder dod," he called, then, "Somet'in'. . . *Wolfs!*"

Albina shouted a warning and stepped back from her window. Her silver mace swung just as a darker shape leaped through. It crumpled with a crushed skull. Slyt ducked at the other window as another lean shape soared over her head. The dog sprang to meet it. Keven dropped his bow and drew his sword. There was a flash of movement as another wolf dashed through the open door. And another. He spitted the first as it leapt at him and tried to shield against the other. Off balance from the leading animal, the impact of the second threw him backward.

Again he stumbled in a tangle of broken furniture. He couldn't withdraw his sword from the first animal, and even impaled, it twisted to snap at his throat. He fell, attempting to shield his face and throat from the rending teeth of both wolves. In the struggle, the snarl and slather, he felt a sudden increase in weight, and then the weight was gone. He managed to roll free. The first wolf was dying. Slyt was astride the other, one hand hooked in a collar, the other wielding a dagger to the shaggy beast's ribs and throat. There was a flash of gray behind her as a third wolf leapt through the doors. Keven lunged with his shield, drawing the old cutlass at the same time. He pitched the

animal off balance and then nearly beheaded it with the
cutlass. He whirled to face the door, but nothing more
moved in the dusk. It was quiet in the room but for a low,
droning monotone from Albina and Slyt's soft cursing as
she tried to wipe the blood from her hand and dagger. Albina was chanting over the motionless body of the white
dog. Its white fur was marred with blotches of blood. Two
wolves lay nearby, their throats torn out.

"I got one." Eugon pointed to another carcass. He
sounded pleased with himself. He started to say more, but
Slyt raised a hand and pointed to the dog.

It stirred, then lifted its head. Albina touched it once
again with her medallion. The dog rose slowly to its feet
and shook itself. Slyt threw Keven a wide-eyed look and
shuddered as she turned back to guard her window.

Eugon went from carcass to carcass, examining each.
"They all have collars," he pointed out. "And on each,
there's a small charm. They were controlled."

Keven nodded as he recovered his sword and bow. "And
there may be other—"

"Fire arrow!" Slyt raced for the stairs. "Went into the
second floor!"

"How could they have a fire—" Keven began, then saw a
man break from the dark rocks across the courtyard with
something flaming in his hand. Keven's bow and Bestian's
sounded together. The figure folded in midstride, buckling
to the ground. There was a sudden burst of bright orange
flame around him as the container he was carrying broke.

"Oil!" Bestian shouted down the stairs. "Watch out below!"

For a frozen moment, Keven watched the blazing oil
dance around the writhing figure, a well-remembered picture flickering in his mind of another body in a bath of
fire—his mother on the night of the murderous thieves.
The man screamed. Keven nocked an arrow, aimed care-

fully, and released. The screaming choked off.

"Eugon!" he yelled. "Watch the windows!"

The mage frowned up from his dice as if rudely interrupted in his own home study.

"For what?"

"For pots of burning oil, you ass!"

A track of flame lofted through a window, trailing an arc of smoke. Eugon made a surprisingly fast, fluid motion and caught it. He looked in amazement at the small earthen container with the lighted wick jammed in its neck.

"Oh," he said.

"That was tossed from just outside," Keven said.

"*If fire thou use, then fire thou shalt have!*"

Albina sprinted across the room and snatched the container from Eugon's hand. She pocketed it in her sling. Smoke looped around her head as she sprinted for the door. She dashed into the open and stood poised, sling whirling, the center of circles of guttering fire. Arrows rattled around her; crossbows answered from above.

"Nodder dod!" Balak called. Albina made her cast and stood to watch its flight. There was a splash of flame in the rocks. Dark figures scrambled away; Balak and Bestian made good use of their lighted targets. Albina stalked back through the doors. There was an arrow lodged in the links of her mail tunic.

"You make an excellent white target out there," Keven said, frowning. She cast the arrow aside contemptuously, her face without expression.

"More oil," she said. "Pots of it, and I shalt light their way for Baalab's fury."

"In the first room of the second corridor." Eugon said. "I'll show you."

The two of them ran through the arch to the interior. Another burning bottle arced through a window. It bounced from a slanted tabletop and rolled unbroken across the

floor. Keven picked it up and set it upright. The scene of
the burning man in the courtyard flashed before him again,
blending with that other, older scene in his memory.

"Beast bastards!" he growled softly and dropped his
bow. His sword whispered free of its scabbard, and he went
through the doors in a fast crouch. Around the corner of the
building, close against the front wall, a spark of flint and
steel showed him two huddled targets. They never saw him
coming. There was only the sound of the sword as they
crumpled. A furtive movement farther along the front of
the building caught his attention. He took a step and
swung again. There was hard contact and a moan. An arrow
chunked into the wall beside him, and another. He slashed
another dark mass huddled on the ground. Balak's crossbow sounded overhead.

"Nodder dod! An' ya, too, ranger, lest ya get back. Be
but four der by th' wall."

Keven ducked back around the corner to the doors. An
arrow glanced off his backplate. Slyt was coming down the
stairs.

"Slick work, Keven! They couldn't be hit from up there
because of the second floor overhang. I put the fire out."
She showed her burned cloak. "Can I get a new cloak out of
all this?"

With Eugon preparing the missiles and lighting the
wicks, Albina started fires all over the rocks, dashing from
the doors with arrows searching her out, hurling burning oil
containers high into the night, lighting targets for the crossbows. Balak's "Nodder dod" was a steady comment. He
would track the arc of fire to its burst and then shoot the
first shadow that moved; Bestian would drop the second.
There had been no answering arrows for some time.

"How many left over there?" Keven called up the stairs.
"Can't be more than ten," Bestian answered.
Claybrook slipped in through the door, smiling, "The

stable is clear."

Keven and Claybrook joined Balak and Bestian on the second floor, and their four bows covered the rocks across the courtyard.

"Thar'll be 'nother time, thiefs!" a call sounded from the night.

"Thieves indeed!" Slyt muttered from the commonroom, then raised her voice. "You give thieves a bad name, bandit! Come again when you have more time! Or more men or more courage, whatever is required for you to stand and fight. Enjoyed your company!"

Keven noticed that Balak and Claybrook had shielded their eyes from the dying flickers of flame across the courtyard and were both staring to the left, up the road to the pass.

Balak grunted and pointed. "Dey go."

"Not all that easily," Claybrook murmured, and was gone down the stairs. He slipped out the doors and disappeared into the night. Balak followed him as fast as possible.

"Well," Bestian said, relieving the tension on his crossbow, "it's just as well. I'm hungry, and I've had all the fun I can enjoy for a while."

But he still peered out into the night, a slight frown marring his face.

"You get something to eat," Keven said. "Everyone can relax for a while. I'll stand watch from up here."

"You think it's over?"

"When we're back in town, having an ale, then it's over."

* * * * *

Watching alone from the second floor, Keven almost missed the motion in the night. It was as if a shadow shifted within a shadow. He looked to one side of the spot, using the night vision trick of not gazing directly at an object. And there it was again, the merest suggestion of a motion on the edge of the road. He smiled; how dull did Sander think they were? He called softly down the stairs to the others, quoting an old childrens' rhyme.

"Something there is in the corner of the night. Something wrong that is not right."

He searched for the blur again. He was still smiling when there was a burst of motion in the dark, the pound of feet, and something huge was rushing for the doors.

"Get back from the doors!" he shouted. There was a scramble from below. He started down the stairs, sword in hand, when an immense dark shape crashed into the room. They had been eating by the soft glow cast from the tip of Eugon's staff. Eugon waved a hand, and the staff brightened instantly until it hurt their eyes. The great creature slid to a halt, a hairy limb thrown up to shade its tiny eyes.

"Demons damned!" Slyt yelled. "Another ogre thing!"

"And bigger," Bestian agreed.

Keven was aware that Slyt and Bestian seemed to drop into the rubble and vanish. Albina, standing by the rock wall, was muttering and holding her medallion, her mad eyes fixed on the beast. Eugon was fumbling with his dice. In the frozen moment when the thing was halted, trying to scan the room, Keven crept down the remaining stairs behind it. He was about to swing a blow at its neck when it gave a chilling roar, flung wreckage aside, and dashed to the side of the dead ogre. It dipped its hand in the blood, smelled it, and then faced them with lips peeled back from glistening fangs. It unleashed a deafening bellow.

"Eugon . . ." Keven said without glancing away. "You'd better do some magic."

The creature swung to glare at Albina. For an instant, it swayed and it eyes began to close, but as she leaped to swing her mace at its head, it snarled and backhanded her. She was flung back against the stone wall and crumpled to the floor, unmoving. The dog sprang and was cuffed aside as if it were nothing more than an unruly puppy. The creature turned then to face Keven and Eugon.

"Eugon?" Keven said again. The mage was scowling at his dice. The thing rumbled deep in its throat as it advanced. There was the sharp sound of a crossbow, and a shaft hit it in the back. It wheeled and growled, then turned back to Keven and Eugon again.

"Distract it," Eugon said, edging away from Keven. "You're the one with the apparent weapon. It will go after you."

Keven gave a snort of disgust. "Distract it while you find a way out?"

"I must prepare!"

"I hope you're fast at it!"

Another crossbow bolt hit beside the first.

"Higher, Bestian!" Keven called. "In the neck, if you can!"

It approached, snarling. Its clawed hands seemed as large as baskets. Keven took a double-handed grip on his sword and braced himself.

The creature lunged, arms wide to trap him. He ducked and dodged to one side, sword slashing hard across the tendons just behind the knee. There was a savage squeal. The beast swung a mighty backhand and sent him careening into the wreckage of the room. He lay gasping, his breath slammed out of him. The damaged leg buckled as the beast attempted to turn, and it crashed to the floor. But it began to crawl toward him, claws digging into the planks, mouth slathering. Keven poised his sword for a thrust at its face. It came on. He stabbed at the eyes, and again, hitting it twice. It screamed, but still it came on. Keven tried to wiggle farther into the rubble of furniture.

"Look away, ranger!" Eugon shouted. "Fireball! I have it now!"

There was an incredible glare and a tremendous blast of heat. The creature shrieked. Through blurred vision from the flash, Keven could make out what seemed to be a gigantic mass of flame plunging from one side of the room to the other. Someone grabbed his feet and dragged him away.

"I'm fine," he growled, rising to his knees. He shook his head; the aftermath of the flash blurred his vision.

"Get up!" Slyt shouted in his ear. "The damned place is ablaze like a broken lamp!"

The beast had collapsed, writhing in the doorway. Flames blocked the exit and were already feeding on the walls and timbers. The rest of the room was blazing where the beast had rolled. Eugon was beckoning anxiously from the stone arch into the cliff.

"This way!"

"Albina!" Keven shouted, pointing to where they had last seen her. He crashed through the debris.

Bestian appeared ahead of him, flinging a table aside. "Here!"

Keven picked up the limp body of the woman. "Get her mace and shield," he called.

Bestian nodded and shouted to Slyt. "Come get this dog!"

"You're not serious," she called over the roar of the flames.

"He's serious!" Keven yelled. "Do it! Eugon, get my bow and quiver! At the head of the stairs!"

"Can't!"

The stairway was fully ablaze. The whole building was beginning to groan. Smoke leaked from cracks and crevices in walls and ceiling, then licks of searching flame. Within the hungry, rising rumble came the growl of beams breaking, the cry of old dry timbers giving way.

Smoke was churning through the room as they stumbled through the stone arch and into the cool interior of the mountain. By the orange glare of the fire, they could make out five armed figures standing in the great hall.

"So . . ." one of the figures said. Keven knew the voice. "The survivors. I wanted to see what you folk looked like."

"Hello, Sander." Keven lowered Albina to the stone floor. He still couldn't see clearly. It seemed he was looking through a glimmering curtain. "Where's all your brave band? And your pets? We're serving roast ogre tonight—are you hungry?"

"You be as amusin' as before, fighter. D' you think the two o' you have the upper hand now?"

Keven peered around. Bestian and Slyt were nowhere to be seen. They had preceded him through the arch, he knew; then he saw that Albina's equipment and the body of the white dog were there. Keven laughed, thinking of Slyt's and Bestian's skill at seemingly disappearing at will.

"Perhaps you didn't notice, Sander, but this fine mage just burned up your father in there."

Eugon was wearing his arrogant smile and fondling a die. His staff still glowed with an eerie light, but it seemed to be dimming. One of the men with Sander licked his lips and glanced at one of the openings into the courtyard; it was almost a pleading look.

"I know a bit o' magic, too," Sander said with a smile. "And I know the young mage be some exhausted right now. That sort o' power weakens you. I don' imagine he could stagger a mouse right now."

Keven glanced at Eugon; the contemptuous expression was still there, but it seemed a little tight.

Sander hefted his sword. "You seem to have lost yer odd-lookin' shield, fighter, but one as able as you should nar have any trouble."

He advanced, and his men followed in the hellish glow of the fire flickering from the stone arch.

Keven stood at middle guard, eyes fixed just to one side of Sander to avoid the still lingering flare in his vision. Eugon backed away, threatening with staff and die, but with no apparent power.

Sander motioned to his men. "Just stand for a while," he said. "If the fighter manages t' hurt me, then I wants you t' butcher him out. Slowly. Don' worry 'bout that mage. He be harmless."

The men with Sander began to grin, then the one nearest the courtyard openings toppled, a long elfen shaft through his neck. The one on the opposite end of the line gave an abrupt gasp and folded to the floor. Slyt's laugh echoed in the dark. A crossbow sounded from somewhere behind Keven, and the man on Sander's left buckled. A stocky figure appeared at one of the openings, silhouetted against the glare from outside. It motioned with its axe.

"Behint ya, bandits. Be troublem here. An' thar be nar o' ya left outside either. Ya be all 'lone now."

The remaining man looked behind him, then looked at Sander, then backed away from Sander and dropped his sword. Almost instantly there was a shadow at his side and a glint of steel at his throat. Slyt spoke softly.

"Be very careful with your moves, my good man, I truly hate to take prisoners."

Sander continued advancing on Keven. They touched blades. "You be a too bothersome enemy, fighter," Sander said with a smile. "So no matter the outcome, I be enjoyin' this."

He attacked. Keven parried and backed when he had to, studying his opponent's strength and style. The great rock hall rang and echoed with the clash of steel. In the first few flurries of blows, Keven didn't attack, nor did Sander touch him.

The man was adequate, Keven had to admit it, with good speed and a few fine tricks, but he lacked in strength and he was predictable. Sander was also tiring rapidly; Keven could feel it through his blade.

Keven made some standard attacks, which were barely deflected, and he knew the conclusion. He backed away.

"You can't overcome me, Sander. Will you hold?"

Sander gave him a crooked grin. "An' face the ridicule o' the capture, an' the stones an' the stranglin'? Nar thank you, fighter. I be too far down my path. Kill me or I kill you."

"I can wound you and take you."

"Then do your damnedest."

In the roar and the flare of the flames from the stone arch, they slashed and parried. And Sander fell, unable to fend off a sudden thrust. It seemed he actually lunged into it. He laughed, coughing blood.

"See you in hell," he breathed, and died.

Slyt and Bestian appeared from the shadows.

"Is this thing over?" Slyt asked, glancing warily at the two stone openings to the courtyard, lighted by the blazing building.

"Narbody 'live left out der," Balak grunted, motioning to the road. There was a swift flicker of motion at one of the openings, and Claybrook slipped into the hall. He recovered his arrow and, before anyone could say anything, stripped a ring from Sander's hand and a small medallion from around his neck.

"These are elfen," he said. "They are the objects by which he could control animals and influence weather." He nodded then to each in turn, even Balak, and was quickly gone through one of the openings into the night.

They moved deeper into the large, stone hall, away from the heat of the fire. Albina recovered and once more revived the dog. After performing a strange ritual for the dead men, she insisted they be thrown into the fire.

"It doesn't matter to them," Bestian said, shrugging. "And I'm too tired to disagree."

They dragged the bodies to the archway, where Keven and Balak slung them into the fire. The dog was set to watch the man who had surrendered.

"How'd ya kill Willy?" the prisoner asked.

There was a moment when no one answered.

"Which one's Willy?" came Slyt's tired voice.

"Th'ogeree."

"The ogre?"

"Yar. The first one."

Bestian chuckled. "Dog killed him."

There was no further word from their prisoner, who seldom took his eyes from the dog.

The rainy night passed in uneasy silence as they tried to rest.

* * * * *

The Waystation was nothing more than charred timbers and steaming ashes in the morning. Keven stood at the edge of the courtyard where it fell away to the mountainside, gazing out over the valley. The sunrise brought a view from the mountain that he could hardly believe. The rain had blown away in the night, the sky was a clear, hard blue, and it seemed he could see all the way east to the academy. The Vales lay below like a mottled green tapestry on an uneven floor. He could see the sparkle of the two rivers, but Midvale was only a tiny smudge of morning smoke. For all the people living down there, all their scratching at the land, all their roads and buildings, there wasn't a mark to be seen from this loft. If it weren't for the wisp from chimneys and Keven's knowing where to look, even the town would have blended into the vast roll of the land. Pulling in his attention, he surveyed himself.

He was bruised in a few spots he hadn't been fully aware of until this morning and sore in a few more, but that was on the outside. Actually he felt good. Healthy. He took a deep breath and explored inside himself, deliberately calling on all the old, sinister scenes, probing for the pain.

It was there, but dulled. At least he could face those memories instead of flinching away, and he realized another thing that had been an affliction: He had behaved like a coward, frightened of these things, trying to flee from himself. But he was stronger now than those inner injuries. He could begin their healing. He had won here on the mountain . . . with help—no doubt about that—from good people who worked together regardless of their disparities.

"Hey, Santon," he called softly to the east. "I understand."

And then he added, silently, to himself: It's a beginning. He drew another deep, free breath and smiled. The demon on his shoulder was gone.

He was aware of Balak standing beside him. "T'ief fin' th' gain."

"Good." He was reluctant to break away from the view. The broken bulk of the Iron Mountains rose dark across the wide valley. He indicated the mountains opposite. "Your home?"

Balak nodded, gazed for a moment across the valley, then regarded Keven with the hint of a smile. "Face red lak burn."

"It burns like a burn, too. Eugon didn't give me much warning."

"No eyebrows."

Keven gave a wry laugh. "No eyebrows, no ogre."

The warf chuckled. "Good trade."

Keven turned to face Balak directly. "Tell me something,

Balak. How did they travel between here and North Pass so fast?" Balak didn't answer directly. His normal scowl fell into place as he stared again out over the valley.

"It be warfen t'ing," he grunted at last.

"No." Keven shook his head. "That's not good enough. If I have to fight this sort of mountain thing again, I have to know more about what I may face."

"Um-m." Balak seemed to be considering his answer a long time. "Der be . . . ways," he said. "Warfenhalls haf—how to say?—fast road." The scowl came again. "Dis be more than ya need t' unnerstan'."

Keven nodded, smiling at Balak's reluctance to reveal anything warfen. "There's a road through the mountains by way of the old warfenhalls, a road by which one travels faster than normal?"

Balak nodded, his gaze fixed on the valley.

"Dat much more than ya need t' unnerstan'. We pack up now 'fore t'ief steal gain."

*　*　*　*　*

Slyt was gleeful. She and Bestian were in one of the interior rooms, sitting cross-legged by a square opening in the stone floor. They greeted Keven with wide grins.

"It wasn't too slyly hidden for a sly one like me," Slyt said, lightly brushing her fingertips together.

She and Bestian had pulled a bed aside in the best of the occupied rooms within the rock bastion—probably Sander's room. There had been a stone slab fitted neatly into the floor beneath it.

"The dust just didn't look right," Slyt said, grinning.

"And Slyt knows all about dust," Bestian laughed, nodding toward the slim thief.

They were counting coins. Eugon stood in the corner, watching them with his superior smile. A bulky sack lay on the floor beside his feet.

"This is the jewelry and other items," he told Keven, nudging the sack with a toe.

"Is the dagger that the big fighter had in there?" Keven asked. "It had a gem in the hilt."

"Yes," Eugon replied. "Everything of consequence is in the sack but the coin."

"Good," Keven said and nodded. "I want that dagger if it clears Acclain and Lord Damon."

"A memento?" Eugon smiled. The sarcasm was back, too.

"Yes, Eugon, a memento," Keven said flatly. "Is that all right with you?"

Eugon looked away. Bestian made another mark on a stick with his knife and compared sticks with Slyt. They muttered together for a moment.

"Seven thousand, nine hundred and thirty goldworth!" Bestian announced. "That's eleven hundred and thirty-two goldworth and some coppers apiece! Not bad for two days' work!" He laughed. "I'm on my way to being a land-owner!"

"It doesn't seem to be much for a bandit cache," Keven said. He indicated the sack. "How much do you think is in there?"

Eugon shrugged. "We won't know until the final tally."

They divided the coin into seven piles.

"What about Claybrook?" Keven looked at Eugon.

The mage nodded. "I'll take his share to Acclain. It will find its way to the elf."

"Are you certain of that?" Slyt grinned.

Eugon stiffened. "*I* am not the thief here!"

Slyt made a wave of dismissal. "Everyone is so damned humorless."

They bundled away their individual gain, joking about its ponderous weight—about five stone, Keven guessed his share to weigh. Slyt told Bestian it didn't seem right for him to be carrying nearly his own weight in gain, that it should have been divided according to the weight of the person. Balak indicated agreement with his chuckling sound.

"Don't worry about me, Slyt," Bestian countered with a chuckle. "Believe me, I'll manage."

Eugon rigged shoulder straps on a sack and gave Claybrook's share to the captive to carry.

"Whatever clever ideas you may have about escape," Eugon said, "I suggest you dismiss them from mind. You may not believe it, but that dog knows what people are thinking."

The little man's eyes slid to the dog and quickly away. "Ah, I be total through with th' bad life, I be. M' true heart on it!"

"Excellent choice," Eugon said.

He and Keven divided the sack of jewelry and other recovered items between them to achieve a manageable load. Then Keven gathered what was left of his belongings. Suddenly he froze. Claybrook's bow lay propped against Keven's bedroll. He picked it up and examined it. There were delicate inscriptions carved in the wood. Some of them appeared fresh. He called Bestian over to him.

"Can you read these glyphs?"

Bestian released a low breath. "Gods above and loving," he whispered. "An elfen bow!" He peered at the writing.

"I can read but little of it. Some of it is in ancient Elvish, but this part here, this newest part, it says something about '. . . a weapon lost in . . . good calling . . . is a weapon . . . well replaced.' " He flashed Keven a wide grin.

"Your bow! You lost it in the fire! Claybrook has given you his!"

Keven shook his head. "I don't understand."

"You're not supposed to understand," Bestian laughed.

"It's an elfen thing."

Keven handled the bow as if it would break apart in his hands. He knew it wouldn't, probably *couldn't*, but still, this was something he would have to live with for a while to become used to.

When they were ready to leave the Waystation, they left by one of the openings to the courtyard.

"Where's Balak?" Keven asked the others. They all turned. The warf was nowhere to be seen.

"He was just here," Bestian said, glancing around and looking puzzled.

They scanned the rocks scarred with last night's fires. Ravens and mountain jays argued over the spoils.

"Well . . ." Keven adjusted his load. "For myself, I'll not worry about him. He's certainly capable."

He smiled to himself as he started down the road; capable wasn't even close. Balak was a first-rate warrior. And what about Slyt?

Capable . . . and pretty. But still a thief. That was a shame, but at least he could look at her now without the old surge of anger.

Bestian fell in beside him, a small frown marking his usually calm face.

"Balak was bothered about something," he said.

"Do you have any idea what it was?"

The littler shook his head. "It may be that he felt there wasn't enough gain to make it all worthwhile. I heard him muttering something in Warfish to himself. It's a saying: 'A thing around the edge of my eye.' It means there's something wrong you can't quite see."

Keven laughed. "I know that experience. I used to feel the same way. It's not a comfortable feeling. But what he's probably upset about is that he told me a 'warfen t'ing.' "

"Really?" Bestian looked truly impressed. "What was it?"

"I can't tell you," Keven said, grinning. "It's a ranger thing now."

Bestian laughed as they set off down the road.

"Keven!" Slyt called. "Slow down! I'll buy you a barrel of wine when we get into town."

He stopped to wait for her. With her share, maybe she wouldn't have to be a thief for a while. That was a pleasant thought.

"No thanks," he said. "One cup will be fine for me."

"Have it your way, ranger," she said, smiling.

"I intend to . . . Slyt."

And they came down from the mountain to the town.

FORGOTTEN REALMS
FANTASY ADVENTURE

THE MAZTICA TRILOGY
Douglas Niles

IRONHELM

A slave girl learns of a great destiny laid upon her by the gods themselves. And across the sea, a legion of skilled mercenaries sails west to discover a land of primitive savagery mixed with high culture. Under the banner of their vigilant god the legion claims these lands for itself. And only as Erix sees her land invaded is her destiny revealed. Available in April.

VIPERHAND

The God of War feasts upon chaos while the desperate lovers, Erix and Halloran, strive to escape the waves of catastrophe sweeping Maztica. Each is forced into a choice of historical proportion and deeply personal emotion. The destruction of the fabulously wealthy continent of Maztica looms on the horizon. Available in October.

COMING IN EARLY 1991!
FEATHERED DRAGON
The conclusion!

PRELUDES II

Paul B. Thompson & Tonya R. Carter | Mary Kirchoff & Douglas Niles

RIVERWIND, THE PLAINSMAN
PAUL B. THOMPSON AND TONYA R. CARTER

TO PROVE HIMSELF WORTHY OF GOLDMOON, RIVERWIND IS SENT ON AN IMPOSSIBLE QUEST: FIND EVIDENCE OF THE TRUE GODS. WITH AN ECCENTRIC SOOTHSAYER, RIVERWIND FALLS DOWN A MAGICAL SHAFT—AND ALIGHTS IN A WORLD OF SLAVERY AND REBELLION. ON SALE NOW.

FLINT, THE KING
MARY KIRCHOFF AND DOUGLAS NILES

FLINT RETURNS TO HIS BOYHOOD VILLAGE AND FINDS IT A BOOM TOWN. HE LEARNS THAT THE PROSPERITY COMES FROM A FALSE ALLIANCE AND IS PUSHED TO HIS DEATH. SAVED BY GULLY DWARVES AND MADE THEIR RELUCTANT MONARCH, FLINT UNITES THEM AS HIS ONLY CHANCE TO STOP THE AGENTS OF THE DARK QUEEN. AVAILABLE IN JULY 1990.

TANIS, THE SHADOW YEARS
BARBARA SIEGEL AND SCOTT SIEGEL

TANIS HALF-ELVEN ONCE DISAPPEARED IN THE MOUNTAINS NEAR SOLACE. HE RETURNED CHANGED, ENNOBLED—AND WITH A SECRET. TANIS BECOMES A TRAVELER IN A DYING MAGE'S MEMORY, JOURNEYING INTO THE PAST TO FIGHT A BATTLE AGAINST TIME ITSELF. AVAILABLE IN NOVEMBER 1990.

FORGOTTEN REALMS

FANTASY ADVENTURE

The **Dark Elf** Trilogy

HOMELAND
R.A. Salvatore

Strange and exotic Menzoberranzan is the vast city of the drow. Imagine the world of the dark elves, where families battle families and fantastic monsters rise up from the lightless depths. Possessing a sense of honor beyond the scope offered him by his unprincipled kinsmen, young Drizzt finds himself with a dilemma: Can he live in a honorless society? Available in September 1990.

EXILE
R.A. Salvatore

Exiled from Menzoberranzan, the city of the drow, Drizzt must find acceptance among races normally at war with his kind. And all the while, the hero must look back over his shoulder for signs of deadly pursuit—the dark elves are not a forgiving race. Available in December 1990.

SOJOURN
R.A. Salvatore

Drizzt makes his way to the surface world, finding even more trouble than he imagined. Available in May 1991.

TSR™ BOOKS

Outbanker
Timothy A. Madden

Ian MacKenzie's job as a space policeman is a lonely vigil, until the powerful dreadnaughts of the Corporate Hegemony threaten the home colonies. On sale in August.

The Alien Dark
Diana G. Gallagher

It is one hundred million years in the future. When the ahsin bey, a race of cat-like beings, are faced with a slowly dying home planet, they launch six vessels deep into space to search for an uninhabited world suitable for colonization. On sale in December.

NEW  BOOKS

DARK HORSE
Mary Herbert

After her clan is massacred, a young woman assumes her brother's identity and becomes a warrior--all to exact revenge upon the chieftain who ordered her family slain. With an intelligent, magical horse, the young warrior goes against law and tradition to learn sorcery to thwart Medb's plans of conquest. Available February 1990.

WARSPRITE
Jefferson Swycaffer

On a quiet night, two robots from the future crash to Earth. One is a vicious killer, the other is unarmed, with an ability her warrior brother does not have: She can think. But she is programmed to face the murderous robot in a final confrontation in a radioactive chamber. Available April 1990.

NIGHT WATCH
Robin Wayne Bailey

All the Seers of Greyhawk have been killed, each by his own instrument of divination. And the only unusual sign is the ominous number of black birds in the skies. The mystery is dumped on the commander of the City Watch's night shift, who discovers that a web of evil has been tightly drawn around the great city. Available June 1990.

DragonLance Saga

HEROES II TRILOGY

KAZ, THE MINOTAUR
Richard A. Knaak

Sequel to *The Legend of Huma*. Stalked by enemies after Huma's death, Kaz hears rumors of evil incidents. When he warns the Knights of Solamnia, he is plunged into a nightmare of magic, danger, and *deja vu*. Available June 1990.

THE GATES OF THORBARDIN
Dan Parkinson

Beneath Skullcap is a path to the gates of Thorbardin, and the magical helm of Grallen. The finder of Grallen's helm will be rewarded by a united Thorbardin, but he will also open the realm to new horror. Available September 1990.

GALEN BEKNIGHTED
Michael Williams

Sequel to *Weasel's Luck*. Galen Pathwarden is still out to save his own skin. But when his brother vanishes, Galen foresakes his better judgment and embarks on a quest that leads into a conspiracy of darkness, and to the end of his courage. Available December 1990.